CH00544698

Freeman Wills Crofts w
died in 1957. He worked
company as an engineer, w
he moved to England and turned to writing detective fiction
full-time.

His plots reveal his mathematical training and he
specialised in the seemingly unbreakable alibi and the
intricacies of railway timetables. He also loved ships and
trains and they feature in many of his stories.

Crofts' best-known character is Inspector Joseph French,
a detective who achieves his results through dogged
persistence.

Raymond Chandler praised Crofts' plots, calling him 'the
soundest builder of them all'.

THE 12.30 FROM CROYDON
THE AFFAIR AT LITTLE WOKEHAM
ANTIDOTE TO VENOM
ANYTHING TO DECLARE?
THE BOX OFFICE MURDERS
THE CASK
CRIME AT GUILDFORD
DEATH OF A TRAIN
DEATH ON THE WAY
THE END OF ANDREW HARRISON
FATAL VENTURE
FEAR COMES TO CHALFONT
FOUND FLOATING
FRENCH STRIKES OIL
GOLDEN ASHES
THE GROOTE PARK MURDER
THE HOG'S BACK MYSTERY
INSPECTOR FRENCH AND THE CHEYNE MYSTERY
INSPECTOR FRENCH AND THE STARVEL TRAGEDY
INSPECTOR FRENCH'S GREATEST CASE
JAMES TARRANT, ADVENTURER
A LOSING GAME
THE LOSS OF THE JANE VOSPER
MAN OVERBOARD!
MANY A SLIP
MURDERERS MAKE MISTAKES
MYSTERY IN THE CHANNEL
MYSTERY OF THE SLEEPING CAR EXPRESS
MYSTERY ON SOUTHAMPTON WATER
THE PIT-PROP SYNDICATE
THE PONSON CASE
THE SEA MYSTERY
SILENCE FOR THE MURDERER
SIR JOHN MAGILL'S LAST JOURNEY
SUDDEN DEATH

FREEMAN WILLS CROFTS

Enemy Unseen

HOUSE OF
STRATUS

This edition published in 2001 by House of Stratus, an imprint of
House of Stratus Ltd, Thirsk Industrial Park, York Road, Thirsk,
North Yorkshire, YO7 3BX, UK.

www.houseofstratus.com
Typeset by House of Stratus.
Printed and bound in Great Britain by
Antony Rowe Ltd, Chippenham, Wiltshire
A catalogue record for this book is available from the British Library
and the Library of Congress.

ISBN 1-84232-388-1

CONTENTS

1	ARTHUR WEDGEWOOD	1
2	MAUDE WEDGEWOOD	14
3	MAUDE WEDGEWOOD	29
4	ARTHUR WEDGEWOOD	44
5	ANNE MEREDITH	65
6	CAPTAIN ARTHUR ROLLO	80
7	CAPTAIN ARTHUR ROLLO	98
8	CHIEF INSPECTOR FRENCH	115
9	CHIEF INSPECTOR FRENCH	132
10	CHIEF INSPECTOR FRENCH	150
11	ARTHUR WEDGEWOOD	166
12	CHIEF INSPECTOR FRENCH	179
13	CHIEF INSPECTOR FRENCH	196
14	MAUDE WEDGEWOOD	212
15	ANNE MEREDITH	230
16	CHIEF INSPECTOR FRENCH	249
17	CHIEF INSPECTOR FRENCH	267
18	CHIEF INSPECTOR FRENCH	283
19	CHIEF INSPECTOR FRENCH	299
20	CHIEF INSPECTOR FRENCH	313

ARTHUR WEDGEWOOD

At eight o'clock on the evening of Friday, the 14th May, 1943, Arthur Wedgewood stood on the summit of a low hill near St Pols in Cornwall looking out towards the sea, which lay due south and some half-mile distant. He had stood there looking at that view on more occasions than he could remember, yet he was not tired of it. This was scarcely surprising, for in a mild way it was as pleasant a prospect as anyone could wish to see.

The water before him was St Pols Bay, and here at low tide was exposed a mile-long stretch of yellow sand with a surface like that of the proverbial billiard-table. Running up from the beach was an area of heather and bracken with clumps of gorse and stunted shrubs, more like a Surrey heath than a bit of the coast of Cornwall. Farther inland were isolated trees, windswept and showing a tendency to lean inland, but increasing in numbers with their distance from the shore, till at Wedgewood's hill they formed a straggling wood. To the left lay the little town of St Pols, an artist's dream with its steep streets and huddled collection of ancient houses. In the opposite direction the sandy stretch of shore rose into West Head, a low bluff on which lived the élite of the neighbourhood.

Though Arthur Wedgewood loved the country, he was not on Ruin Hill on this delightful spring evening to admire the view. He was in fact on duty. As officer in command of the St Pols Company of the Home Guard, he was waiting to see his subordinate commanders place their men for the evening's practice. The third anniversary of the formation of the Guard was at hand, and in common with others, the St Pols Company was to give to the world a demonstration of its super excellence.

St Pols was doing itself proud in military spectacles. During the previous week the regular forces in the neighbouring camp had joined in large-scale manoeuvres along the shore. Troops from adjoining centres, assisted by flotillas from the Navy, had attempted a landing, and the home defenders had repulsed them. "Fighting" had lasted for the whole of a night and the following day, much to the annoyance or edification of the inhabitants, as befitted their respective mentalities.

At first the Home Guard were to join with the regulars, then for various reasons it was decided that they should have their own demonstration. Wedgewood had worked out what he thought should prove an illuminating and spectacular exercise, and had been untiring in his efforts to instruct his officers in the details. Tonight was to be the final rehearsal, and he believed the result would do the entire area credit.

The chief item was simple but effective. The spectators were to assemble on the top of the hill where he was now standing – Ruin Hill, so called from the disintegrating remains of an old church on its summit. The men of one of the three platoons, simulating enemy paratroops, were to seize the south side of the hill. On the discovery of their presence the second platoon was to advance from the right and engage them in a frontal attack. This would be strong enough to hold them, though it would not be pressed home. Meanwhile the third platoon, creeping like Red – or Khaki – Indians round the hill from the left, would take them in the rear. The enemy was to observe all proper precautions, and his scouts would give him warning directly they saw the approaching force. Wedgewood hoped the latter would be successful, though he felt no conviction on the point. His doubts he considered a testimony, not to the defects, but to the excellence of the scheme.

The *soi-disant* paratroops had marched off inland, from where they would double round to the position they were to occupy, and Wedgewood had seen the necessary scouts going out. All, he believed, was now ready, so that when the alarm was received instant action could be taken. He turned back over the crest of the hill to have a last word with his remaining platoon officers, but just as he did so his second in command appeared and signed to him to stop.

Dick Little was a connection of Wedgewood's by marriage, their wives being first cousins. He was over age for the regular army, but was a keen member of the Home Guard, acting as quartermaster for the St Pols Company. Though the relations between the families were entirely amicable and both the Wedgewoods thought Jessica Little a dear, neither cared much for Dick. He was abrupt in manner and Wedgewood thought his eye was too firmly fixed on the main chance.

Owing to this family connection their Home Guard relations when alone were considerably less formal than those between the ordinary OC and his subordinate officers. Thus it was that Little did not hesitate to approach Wedgewood about a matter which normally would have been held over at least till after the exercise. Glancing round to make sure they were unobserved, he spoke in a low tone.

"I've made a rather unpleasant discovery, Arthur. I went to the munitions store with Gibson to change a jammed rifle for another, and when I put my key into the padlock the hasp fell open. It had been deliberately smashed and pushed back into place."

"Good Lord! Anything gone?"

"Not as far as I could see from a casual inspection, but of course I haven't checked over the stock. I propose to do it after the exercise."

"You put a guard on the store?"

"Yes, I left Gibson in charge."

Wedgewood nodded. Having seen his platoon officers, he walked back across the hill to the pre-selected position from which he would watch the encounter. He was slightly disturbed at Little's news, for if, as seemed likely, it meant that a theft had been committed, it would be the second within ten days. When one evening in the previous week they had tried to use their field telephone they had been unable to get through, and an investigation showed that over five hundred yards of the line was missing. The police had been called in, but without result. Wedgewood also had read of various recent prosecutions for thefts of explosives from HG stores, and he did not want trouble of that kind in his command.

Presently a sharp fusillade of rifle-fire rang out, switching Wedgewood's thoughts back from the theft to the exercise. Evidently the paratroops had come within range of their frontal attackers. This first burst of firing quickly died down and the exchange of shots became more desultory, both sides apparently manoeuvring for position. So far the operation was proceeding exactly to plan, and as Wedgewood watched, he grew more and more pleased. While certain of the men of the home troops were firing steadily to keep the enemy down, others were making little rushes forward, immediately dropping to cover behind whatever obstacles or inequalities in the ground they could find. These then held the paratroops with their fire while their comrades followed up. It was highly realistic. In fact it was what might actually be done should Jerry pay a call. More than this, it was a good spectacle and would certainly delight the civilian onlookers.

When this bluffing action had gone on just long enough to approach the point of palling, there was a diversion from the left. One of the paratroops placed to guard the rear fired his rifle, only to fall, obviously mortally wounded. Immediately, before his companions could more than look round, three warriors from the third platoon rushed forward, their helmets tastefully wreathed in greenery. Three hand-grenades, coloured a symbolic red and smoking realistically, hurtled forward and fell in the enemy's position. One was a direct hit and knocked out two men who were sheltering in a small hollow. The others fell a little short, but their advent evidently shook the paratroops, and by the time they had rallied, the attackers were upon them. Bitter hand-to-hand fighting ensued, until with a final display of immensely strenuous – though imaginary – bayonet practice, the position was captured. The men then drew up in a circle round Wedgewood – the killed and injured having miraculously recovered – and he gave them a short congratulatory address. This terminated the proceedings and the men left in little groups for their homes or the nearest pub.

For a few moments Wedgewood's pleasure at the success of the exercise drove everything else out of his mind. If things went as well on Sunday, and there was no reason why they should not, the St Pols Company need not fear comparison with any of its neighbours. After all the work he had put into the thing, the result was highly gratifying.

Then he remembered Little's story of the broken padlock. If this really meant another theft, the matter might be unpleasant enough. Frowning slightly, he walked through the wood to the munitions store. Little and Private Gibson were standing by the door, the former having apparently just arrived.

Situated near the base of the hill, the store was thickly screened by the trees from both air and land. It was a hut of the Niessen type, built on a slab of concrete, with sides and top of curved sections of corrugated galvanized iron. The ends were of brick set in cement, and in one of them was the door. The bricks and iron had originally been painted green, but this had gradually disappeared from the latter, which was now a rich shade of rust brown. Wedgewood and Little had often talked of getting the sheets repainted, but the building was so well hidden that the work had always been deferred.

The door was fastened by a stout running bolt, pushed fully home and with its slotted lug turned down over a staple. Through the staple was the padlock, hanging open. A moment's examination showed that the locking slot at the end of the hasp was broken off.

"No doubt of its being deliberate, I'm afraid," said Wedgewood. "I can see the marks of the tool."

"Yes, they're quite clear," Little answered. "I was proposing to check over the stock with Gibson."

"Right," Wedgewood returned. "Go ahead."

There was not much vacant space in the store, every available inch being occupied. On the opposite wall hung spare clothing, tin hats, great-coats, belts and such-like, with a row of boots below. Along one side were stacked arms of various kinds, rifles and Lewis and Sten guns with a Spigot mortar, while opposite were boxes of ammunition, haversacks, water-bottles and a variety of small articles. Wedgewood watched while Little took some papers from a rough desk in the corner.

"I'll read out, Gibson, and you count," Little directed. "Steel helmets?"

"Four."

"Overcoats?"

The check was systematic and thorough, and Little's stock-sheets came out of it with flying colours. Quickly they worked through the clothing, arms and etceteras, without finding a single discrepancy. At last only the ammunition was left.

"This'll take a bit longer," Little remarked. "The stuff in these opened boxes will have to be counted."

"Never mind. It has to be done and you may as well make a job of it."

The stock-sheets kept up their reputation till suddenly Little gave an exclamation.

"I'm afraid I spoke too soon, Arthur. Some grenades are missing. One unopened box of twelve."

Wedgewood whistled. "That's pretty bad. I suppose you're quite sure?"

For the first time Little smiled. "A tactful remark from the OC to his quartermaster! Strange as it may appear, I am. I checked the stock with Forbes a week or two ago and there has been little in or out since."

"A bit of a triumph I should say, knowing our heroic defenders," Wedgewood returned with somewhat tardy tact. "Very well, better go through the rest of the stuff. It'll make sure the box is nowhere else in the store as well as checking if anything else is gone."

The work was soon completed. One box containing twelve hand-grenades with their corresponding detonators had disappeared. The rest of the stock was intact.

"Job for the police," Wedgewood asserted. "Better let Gibson run into St Pols and ask Cundy to come out. He can take my bicycle."

"I have my own here, sir," Gibson put in.

"Right," Wedgewood returned. "Don't mention this to anyone else, Gibson."

Gibson saluted and vanished. Wedgewood turned to Little.

"I don't like this, Dick," he declared. "The second theft inside ten days! And grenades are a deal worse than wire."

"Very nasty. Besides, it's getting too common. I've seen a number of prosecutions for stealing explosives from HG stores recently."

"Yes, and there's another thing. Though we've taken every precaution and are not to blame, it will be a slur on the company, besides reflecting on ourselves."

They began pacing slowly up and down, chatting desultorily. Though he told himself he need not be so, Wedgewood felt worried by the theft. The handing over of these dangerous weapons to the Home Guard took the form of a trust: there was a very definite obligation to keep them safely. In this case the Home Guard had failed to do so, and as head of the company he felt a personal responsibility. That he was not the only company commander to be in such a position was but little comfort.

Quarter of an hour later Gibson reappeared.

"Sergeant Cundy'll be here in a few minutes, sir," he reported. "Inspector Vanson from Truro was with him and he's coming too."

"Right. Then we needn't keep you, Gibson. You may get off home."

"A bit of luck about Vanson," Little remarked when Gibson had gone. "He's as sharp as they're made."

"I suppose so," Wedgewood returned gloomily. "An inspector should have more experience, though Cundy's a good chap too."

As he spoke a car appeared, lurching along the rough track which led from the road. From it descended two men, one a sergeant of police in uniform, the other an officer in plain clothes. Wedgewood greeted them.

" 'Evening, inspector. 'Evening, Cundy. I'm afraid there's a spot of trouble here."

"Good evening, sir. Gibson tells me a dozen grenades are missing." Inspector Vanson was a tall, rather thin man of about forty, with grizzled hair and a shrewd but kindly face.

Wedgewood agreed and the newcomers moved to the hut, Vanson with his eyes on the ground.

"On this rough grassy approach we need scarcely look for footprints," he observed. "What about inside the store? I presume you went in, since you know what is gone?"

"We had to," Little returned. "When we looked in everything appeared normal, so we had to check over the stuff."

"Naturally, sir. I don't think it matters; no prints would show on that concrete floor. Now about fingerprints. Did you handle the bolt?"

"I took the padlock in my hand to insert the key," answered Little, "but when I saw the hasp was broken I thought of fingerprints and I didn't touch the bolt. I pushed it back with the blade of my knife."

"That was good, sir. But since you've handled the padlock I'd like to take your prints, so as to discount them wherever I find them."

"Certainly, inspector: no objection whatever."

Vanson nodded. "Who is in charge of the store?" he went on.

"I am," Little replied. "I act as quartermaster."

"Before this evening, when were you last in it?"

"Last night about half past ten. We had an exercise and after it was over I put back a Browning gun we had been using."

"Were you alone, sir?"

"No, Hastings was carrying the gun. He came in and put it in its place. Then I locked up and we left together."

"The padlock was then in order?"

"Perfectly."

"I follow. Could you say if the grenades were there last night?"

Little hesitated. "Well, no. I didn't count the boxes. But there was no appearance of anything having been disturbed."

"Surely," broke in Wedgewood, "we may take it the grenades disappeared at the time the lock was broken?"

"Yes, sir. I was only wondering if there was direct evidence." He turned again to Little. "Can you say how long it is since the boxes were counted?"

"Not since last stock-taking, but as it happens, that was just under a fortnight ago."

Vanson made an entry in his notebook.

"The question of keys scarcely arises," he said dubiously, "except that anyone who could get hold of them might not have broken open the door. All the same, for completeness' sake I think I ought to know about them."

"I can tell you in a word," said Wedgewood. "There are two keys, of which Mr Little has one and I have the other. You carry yours on your bunch, don't you, Dick?"

"Yes, I have it here."

"I do the same with mine."

Vanson asked if anyone could have got hold of either of the keys, and both men declared that this was quite impossible. He paused for a moment in thought.

"I think there's only one more question, gentlemen, and that is: Who knew the grenades were there?"

"All the members of the Home Guard," Wedgewood answered. "But I should think most people could have guessed we had them."

"They could have done more than guessed," declared Little. "Anyone can buy books about the Home Guard, and in several hand-grenades are mentioned. One I have in mind called *The Home Guard Training Manual* has a complete chapter about grenades, with a cross-sectional diagram showing their internal arrangement. There are also elaborate instructions for throwing them. That at least would be a pretty broad hint."

Vanson turned this over in his mind. "What you say would be an indication that grenades are likely to be found in all Home Guard munition stores," he presently admitted, "but could any outsider have known that there actually were some here?"

Little looked at his chief. "Could anyone, Arthur? I don't think so, inspector, not definitely."

"No one could have known from his own observation, I'm sure," Wedgewood agreed, "but we can't be sure that none of our men mentioned the fact. I didn't myself, but I can't answer for the company."

This, it appeared, was also Little's position.

"Two thefts inside ten days," Wedgewood went on. "It's certainly a bit disturbing. Do you think there can be any connection?"

"At first sight it's not easy to see how insulated wire and hand-grenades could be wanted by the same party. But of course we've no evidence as yet." Vanson closed his notebook. "Well, thank you, gentlemen, that will be all at present if Mr Little will allow me to take his prints. We'll look into the affair and let you know the result. Might I inquire what you're doing about locking up tonight?"

"I've been thinking about that," answered Wedgewood. "I have a good padlock on a barn at home. I'm not using it at the moment and I'll run over for it. Back in ten minutes."

"If you have two keys," Vanson put in, "I'd like to borrow one in case I want to pay another visit here."

"I'll bring them."

Wedgewood was in a considerably happier frame of mind as he wheeled his bicycle out to the road. His first reaction had been that some criminal activity was in contemplation, but now he was beginning to think otherwise. Explosives were used for all sorts of legitimate purposes; the theft was probably merely due to the present difficulty of getting them. A farmer who wanted to rid himself of a tree stump or to break up a boulder across the line of a new drain, a builder who wished to level a rock foundation, such men and many others like them might well help themselves to what they could not buy. Whether grenades as such would do these jobs Wedgewood was doubtful, but at least the explosive could be removed and used for a variety of purposes. He felt he had been worrying unduly.

All the same he had been right to call in the police. It was now their job and he might leave it to them.

Before the end of the ten minutes he had obtained his padlock and keys and returned to the store. He found that Vanson had taken Little's fingerprints and dusted the bolt and door with powder. Now he was photographing by flashlight the resultant prints, working slowly but methodically and with great care. As Wedgewood watched him he felt that his achievements, if not brilliant, would be utterly sound.

"Well, Dick," he said presently, "what about our making tracks? If you don't want us any more, Vanson, we'll say good night."

Little also had his bicycle, and their ways lying together, the two men rode off. Wedgewood put up his idea that they must not take the affair too seriously, and was relieved to find that this was also Little's view.

"At the first go off I thought it was going to mean trouble," went on the latter, "but on thinking it over I saw that there might be all sorts of innocent explanations. I agree: I don't think we need worry."

It was on this note of subdued optimism that the men presently parted.

2

MAUDE WEDGEWOOD

About ten next day Maude Wedgewood, Arthur's wife, set off from their home to walk to the little town of St Pols. A busy morning lay in front of her. She had to do some shopping – and even in St Pols there were queues – preside at a committee meeting of the local Red Cross, and spend an hour or two helping at a hospital supply depot.

As she walked, her thoughts were occupied with her husband. She was not very happy about him. He was looking increasingly tired and old. The reason, of course, was not far to seek. He was overworking. His own business was enough for any ordinary person, and then on the top of it was all this Home Guard stuff. Long hours and worry and little sleep! It was all for the war effort, of course, and was therefore given ungrudgingly. All the same she wished he could sometimes take things a little easier.

Wedgewood was a large farmer. Before the war, during farming's difficult delays, it had taken all his energy to carry on successfully. Now though the position had altered, it had not become simpler. The problem of how to sell his produce had certainly been eliminated, but a new one had taken its place; how to obtain a vastly increased output with reduced operating facilities. Wedgewood worked early and late. All the time that was not required for his Home Guard duties went into the farm.

He was a tall, lanky man in his fifties. He had served in the last war, but even had he not now been in a reserved occupation, his age and health would have prevented his returning to the army.

He and his wife were great pals. Maude Wedgewood was a real helpmate to him. Shortly after their marriage the farm had come on to the market, and it was with her as an active partner in the venture that Arthur had bought. She was not strong enough to assist out of doors, but she taught herself typing and elementary bookkeeping and took over the whole of the clerical work. And admirably she did it. She learned how to cost and plot curves, and delighted in putting before "The Board" – her husband and herself – graphical representations of all sorts of statistics and trends. Indeed it was largely due to her investigations and analyses that the "firm" had been as successful as it had.

Wedgewood kept little from his wife. Invariably he discussed his difficulties with her, and invariably he found her sympathy and her cold common sense helpful. Indeed, in spite of his instructions to Gibson and his own habit in connection with Home Guard matters, he had told her of the thefts. He had treated them lightly, but she could see that he was deeply worried.

The morning was fresh and clear as she reached the gate at the end of their drive. She had a choice of two routes to the village. One was to go inland to the main road, which ran east and west behind Ruin Hill and the munitions hut, the other to take a rough cart-track to the shore and walk along the sand. There was little difference in the length, over a mile each way.

She chose the shore, partly because she loved the sea, and partly because of the ease of walking over the smooth yellow sand. This, of course, was only possible below high-water mark, but now the tide, though flowing, was still half-way out.

She walked eastwards along the low cliffs of West Head, where lived the more opulent citizens of St Pols, soon reaching the winding path which led down to the sea.

The view as she reached the edge of the cliff, while not spectacular, was very pleasing. The coastline stretched irregularly to the east, with the town – it was little more than a village – of St Pols some mile off and the line of cliffs dying away into the distance beyond. Between where she stood and the town was St Pols Bay. It was a flattish sweep with a small projection in the centre, dividing it into two roughly equal halves. At some time erosion had taken place at this tiny point and the remains of a groyne stretched down from it across the sand. Inland the heather and bracken changed quickly to shrubs and then to trees, with the ruined church on its small sugar-loaf hill standing out over the coastal plain. Some mile out from the little point was Ram Island, a mere rock with grassy pockets and a favourite place for summer picnics.

Along the entire stretch of sand there was visible only one figure, that of a man. He was ambling along towards the town. Maude recognized him as her Uncle Joshua. He had a highly characteristic silhouette and an unmistakable walk. She had half expected to see him. About this time on most fine mornings he went to the village reading-room to glance over the papers and exchange the day's gossip with his cronies. He also preferred going by the shore.

Though he was some distance ahead she could see how slowly he was walking, feebly indeed, she thought. Of course he was an old man, sixty-nine last birthday. Latterly he had begun to show his age. She was fond of him, as indeed were all who knew him, and though she expected his death would be to her advantage, she genuinely hoped that it was still far in the future.

Joshua Radlett lived a little farther along West Head. His wife had died many years earlier and he was looked after by an elderly couple named Wilton, a reliable pair who made him comfortable. Close by was the Littles' house, and Jessica was always in and out. Radlett was a mildly wealthy old man. No one knew the exact amount of his fortune, but it was understood to be in the neighbourhood of £30,000. He had, however, disclosed the general terms of his will. There were to be small legacies to servants and charities and a larger one to Maude Wedgewood, but the bulk of his money was to go to his daughter Jessica.

How he had made it was a profound secret, though there was no obvious reason why it should have been except his own strongly expressed desire. He had indeed threatened that should the source become known, he would alter his will, leaving everything to charity. This threat was effective because only Jessica and Maude and their respective husbands had the information, and as Radlett had not failed to point out, a leakage could therefore only come from one of them. Needless to say, all four were careful to respect his wishes.

At the same time none of them could understand his insistence, for there appeared to be nothing of importance in the secret. It was simply that as a young man Radlett had joined the rush to Klondyke and had there struck it lucky. What was there in this, they asked themselves, which all the world might not know? Radlett, however, did not enlighten them on the point, and their curiosity stopped short of asking him.

Maude was now approaching Groyne Point, the little half-way projection where the erosion had taken place. As she did so a woman appeared from behind the low shrubs which fringed the shore on the little point. Maude recognized her as Mrs Crane, a member of her Red Cross committee. She stopped and waited for her.

"Good morning, Elmina," she called. "Coming to the meeting?"

"That and half a hundred other things," smiled the newcomer as they fell into step. "A gorgeous morning."

Elmina Crane was the wife of Wickham Crane, and they lived quite close to the shore behind the little point. Wickham Crane's name was well known in certain rather narrow circles, for he was a writer of thrillers. As he himself would have been the first to admit, they were poor stuff, designed like most films for the less intelligent sections of the community. He threw them off in great quantities and at an immense speed, and if the royalties on each were small, their sum total was considerable. Or rather it had been until the war. Now difficulties of printing and binding and a shortage of paper were making sad havoc with his receipts.

His wife was a pleasant though somewhat colourless woman, tolerated rather than actively liked or disliked by her acquaintances. She never came to the front in anything, always took the commonplace view, and where action was in question, voted for the traditional and the unenter-prising.

Maude at once began to discuss the coming meeting, for she wanted Mrs Crane's support on a matter which was coming up relative to the storage of medical supplies. By the time a satisfactory agreement had been reached they were close to the town. As they turned up a track to one of its streets a man appeared walking towards them.

He was short and stout and elderly. He had a red face and was dressed in a sports coat, pullover and plus-fours. There was a suggestion of a strut about his walk and his whole outline registered self-satisfaction.

"Oh," said Mrs Crane, "here's Mr Savory. I do dislike meeting him."

"I'm not fond of him myself," admitted Maude, "but all the same aren't you exaggerating? He doesn't actually bite."

"Doesn't he? He would if he could. But I'm not peculiar, as you know. No one could be more universally detested."

"I'm afraid that's true. Poor man! Sometimes I'm quite sorry for him!"

"I can tell you sorrow is not the feeling I have," and Mrs Crane grimaced to show how strong this feeling was.

Charles Savory, in spite of his unpopularity, was something of a power in St Pols. He lived in a large house near Radlett and the Littles on West Head, and had acquired the rights as lord of the manor. He was generous to local charities and strongly supported the government. As a result he had been made a magistrate and elected local member of the Rural District Council. In addition he was the Civil Commissioner on the triumvirate of the Village Invasion Committee. He not infrequently took advantage of his position to interfere in other people's affairs – invariably to their disadvantage – and his judgments on the bench were always severe and sometimes savage. Many people indeed wished he had been allowed to remain in his original obscurity.

He had had disputes with both Wedgewood and Crane. Wedgewood's was now ancient history: a matter of a right of way, but Crane's, a charge of libel in one of his books, was then in full swing. Both the wives had strongly backed their husband's point of view, and feeling had run, and ran, high. It was this fact which had given rise to Mrs Crane's outburst.

Savory apparently felt no embarrassment at the meeting. When he was close to them he stopped, made a casual movement suggestive of raising his hat, and glared at Maude.

"Hey!" he said in a loud, hectoring tone. "What's all this I hear about the Home Guard?"

"The Home Guard?" Maude repeated, taken aback.

"I said the Home Guard. Thefts of high explosive from their hut and what not."

Maude recovered herself. "I really don't know what you've heard," she returned coldly, "and I'm afraid I'm not particularly interested."

"Meaning that you don't know all about it, eh? That cat won't jump. I know your husband too well for that."

"If the matter's your business you've only to ask my hus – "

"My business!" Savory broke in aggressively. "Of course it's my business! The Home Guard's got a lot of dangerous stuff there, and if they can't look after it we're all in danger. My business indeed! The thing's everybody's business."

Maude turned on her heel. "Well, you're wrong there: it's not mine. But as I was going to say when you interrupted me, if you want information you'd better ask my husband."

He snorted. "Not I. I'll go a good deal higher up than that. I'll go to the Zone Commander. He'll see that efficient people are put in charge."

Maude, two red spots showing angrily in her cheeks, was walking on. Mrs Crane, aghast at the interchange, hung back at first and then followed. Savory, muttering, made as if he would follow them, then thinking better of it, he turned and went on along the sand.

Mrs Crane was quite white. "Well, really!" she exclaimed. "That's beyond everything! Did you ever hear such rudeness?"

"No, and I'll be careful never to hear it again," Maude returned angrily. "The *impertinence!* How dared he blame Arthur for the thefts?"

"Oh, then there were thefts?" Mrs Crane said interestedly.

"*If* there were," Maude amended belatedly. "How could Arthur be to blame no matter what there were?"

"Of course he couldn't," agreed Mrs Crane with an air of disappointment.

"Next time I meet Mr Savory I simply shall not see him," Maude went on, "neighbour or no neighbour. I hate feuds and all that, but really one must draw the line somewhere."

Mrs Crane agreed that this would be the proper and the dignified course, but doubtfully, and Maude felt that if a stand were to be made, she would make it alone.

"Oh, look!" Mrs Crane said suddenly in a lower tone. "Be careful of what you say. There's Mrs Savory."

The rather striking-looking, middle-aged woman she indicated turned at that moment, and seeing them, came forward with a smile. She was tall and well built, and as she walked her carriage was superb. Her face was plain, yet pleasant to look at. It was dependable and its expression showed kindliness and goodwill as well as care and some strain. She was as popular as her husband was the reverse. People liked her for her own sake, and even if they had not, they would have been nice to her because it was felt that hers was no bed of roses.

"What a lovely morning," she greeted the others. "Have you just come in?"

"Just arriving. The committee meeting's at half past ten, you know."

"Of course, I'm not forgetting it. Did you happen to meet my husband?"

"Yes, just at the end of the town. He was going down on the shore."

Mrs Savory made a gesture of mock annoyance. "How like a man!" she smiled. "I wanted him to take home the fish, and now he's gone off without it. But I suppose I can't blame him, as he didn't know anything about it."

"I think that might be accepted as an extenuating circumstance," Maude pronounced judicially.

The three women walked on chatting, and then after a pause Mrs Savory turned to a new subject. "Did you hear that Anne had found a job?" she asked, glancing from one to the other.

"Oh," said Maude, obviously interested. "I hadn't heard. What is it?" Mrs Crane bent forward too, as if eager to hear the reply.

"Not very good, I'm afraid," Mrs Savory answered. "It's here in St Pols; a clerkship at the gas works. I didn't want her to take it, because she could have done far better elsewhere. But you know" – she smiled again and her face grew kindlier than ever – "there's a local attraction."

The affairs of Anne Meredith had recently caused a good deal of surreptitious talk in the neighbourhood. She was Charles Savory's niece and had for a couple of years been acting as his secretary.

But quite recently and without any apparent reason he had given her notice to leave. His chauffeur had been called up and he had found a middle-aged woman who would act not only as chauffeuse, but secretary. That there was more in the affair than met the eye was universally believed, but if so, none of the parties concerned was giving anything away.

"When does she leave you, Mrs Savory?" Maude asked.

"At the end of the month, in just a fortnight. I wanted her to live on with us, but she thought it would be rather far from her work and she's moving in here. I'm glad she's at least staying in the neighbourhood."

Maude shrewdly suspected that distance was the least factor in her decision, but Mrs Savory was always loyal to her husband, and Maude naturally accepted the suggestion.

When they reached the committee room they found it buzzing with rumours about the Home Guard theft, and as the CO's wife, Maude was the immediate target for a battery of questions.

"But Arthur never tells me about Home Guard affairs," she countered loyally. "He did mention that there had been a theft, but he didn't seem to think anything of it."

"Oh, but it's dreadfully serious," she was told with bated breath. "Enough high explosives have been stolen to blow up half the town. The police thought so seriously of it that Sergeant Cundy wouldn't handle it himself. He sent for the inspector from Truro."

Maude laughed it off, though she felt uneasy. She was sure that Arthur had been much more worried than he had admitted. She decided to tell him what was being said, so that if he thought it advisable he could contradict the rumours.

He had gone that morning to Truro and was not back to lunch, but at tea-time he appeared. The break for tea, when he could achieve it, was a welcome interlude in Wedgewood's afternoon. Today he gave a sigh of satisfaction as he lowered his long body into an easy chair in the cool sitting-room and glanced at the dainty meal which Maude was placing on the table between them.

"Clayton's going up to London tomorrow," he said, referring to the business which had taken him to Truro. "He won't be able to start on the wretched thing till he comes back."

Maude sympathized with him, and it was not till tea was over and cigarettes had been lit that she referred to her morning at St Pols.

"That theft business has got out," she remarked. "They were all making the most of it. You never heard such tales. Mrs Rowse told me that enough H E had been stolen to blow up half the town."

"She would," Wedgewood retorted, "and I'm sure the old cat hopes it's true. What did you say?"

"That though you didn't talk of Home Guard affairs, you had mentioned there had been a theft, but that you didn't seem to think anything of it."

"Good. Let them talk. It's all they can do."

From all this Maude saw that he was really worried. She bent forward and lowered her voice.

"You're upset about it, Arthur," she said quietly. "Is it really serious?"

For a moment he paused. "I don't think so," he said at last. "It's probably been taken for some perfectly legitimate purpose, and if so, no great harm is done. Of course, and this is between ourselves, old girl, there's just the chance it's for some fifth column work. Then it would be."

Maude nodded. "But even if it were, you're not responsible? No one could blame you?"

"As OC it was in my charge."

"Oh, yes, in theory. But not actually."

"If it comes to that, Dick was actually in charge, but that wouldn't save me. We'd both be for it, at least as far as prestige and all that goes."

"The reason I ask," Maude said slowly, "is that I'm afraid Mr Savory's out for trouble."

"Savory? Good Lord, what business is it of his?"

"That's what I asked him – in other words. He said it was everybody's business, because if the stuff was in the wrong hands, everyone was in danger."

"Infernal impertinence! Just like him! Tell me about it."

"I was walking in to the village with Elmina Crane and we met him on the shore. Oh, Arthur, he was so *rude*."

"You bet he was. He can't speak in any other way. What did he say?"

"Well, nothing much in words. It was his manner. I said that if he wanted information, he should ask you."

"He knew how much he'd get from me."

"He said he wouldn't ask you; that he'd go higher up; to the Zone Commander, in fact."

"Blast him! Who does he think he is?"

"He was probably only throwing his weight about, but I thought I'd better tell you."

"Quite right. Damn the man, if he rings old Blossom up, he'll get in first with his information. I should have reported the thing this morning, but I had only just time to get the bus. I'll do it now. But that's only part of it. If the insufferable swine was rude to you he's going to apologize, and pretty humbly."

"No, no, never mind that. It's over and done with. Besides, he got as good as he gave."

"No one's going to be offensive to my wife and get away with it," Wedgewood declared firmly. "I'll let him know just – "

The information to be given to Savory remained un-revealed. "May we come in?" a woman's voice interrupted, and Jessica and Dick Little entered the room.

"Oh, good!" exclaimed Maude, springing up. "You're just in time. Come and sit down and I'll have some fresh tea before you could wink."

The cousins were a complete contrast in appearance. Maude was tall and dark, with a square bony face and a chin which might have been chiselled out of marble. Jessica was more of the fluffy type, small and fair and with all her features curved and rounded. Jessica was technically the better looking of the two, though Maude gave a stronger impression of character and competence. Jessica held up her hand.

"No, no, Maude, thanks; don't get tea. We've had it, just finished. We came across to have a word with Arthur, or at least Dick did."

"It's about that blessed theft," said Little. "It's all leaked out."

"We were just talking about it," Wedgewood returned. "Where will you sit, Jessica?" He pulled a chair round while Maude carried away the tea things.

Jessica gestured with her hand. "No, thanks, Arthur. I'll go and help Maude to wash up." She also disappeared, leaving the men alone.

"How did you hear?" Little asked. "I thought you were to be in Truro all morning?"

"So I was; I'm only just home. I didn't hear anything myself, but Maude went to the Red Cross meeting, and she said the place was buzzing with it. The usual exaggerations of course."

"So Jessica heard. I thought of ringing up Vanson to ask how he was getting on, then I thought perhaps you had done so and we needn't worry him twice."

"I hadn't, but I'll do it now. Maude says that swine Savory's out for trouble."

"About this? What's it to him?"

Wedgewood told him.

"Meddling old devil! What can he do about it anyway?"

"Said he was going to complain to old Blossom."

"Good Lord, the Zone Commander! Have you reported it, Arthur?"

"No, that's just the devil of it. I thought it wasn't necessary last night. It was latish when I got home and this morning I left early for Truro, and, as I say, I'm just home. I was going to do it as you came in."

"I should, if I were you. Better not let that devil get in first."

"I appreciate that," Wedgewood answered. "I'll ring up Vanson now and then get through to Battalion."

Inspector Vanson was out, but Sergeant Cundy answered. So far as he knew, the inspector's inquiries had not as yet had much result, but he was still prosecuting them and he hoped before long to reach a conclusion. Wedgewood then telephoned to Battalion Headquarters, briefly giving the circumstances and saying that a full report was following.

"Apparently they've heard nothing about it," he told Little, "so that's all to the good."

Little nodded. "I'm sorry the thing happened," he said. "I'll not come out of it in too good a light."

"Neither of us will for the matter of that, but we can't help it and there's no use worrying."

"The fastenings on that door," Little persisted, "were a standard pattern. I mean, there are scores of munition huts locked up in the same way."

"I know there are, and we took the same precautions that other companies took. No one can blame either of us, Dick, though, of course, the thing's a slur."

"That's right, but Savory'll make out as bad a case as he can."

"He can't alter the facts. I wish he'd try, then we could get him for lying."

"What a swine the man is! Is there anyone in the neighbourhood he hasn't got across?"

"If he's not careful someone will do him in one of these days."

"I'm surprised that no one has."

"Well, keep up your heart, perhaps someone will."

With these charitable sentiments the men parted, Wedgewood to write his report, and Little to find his wife and return home.

3

MAUDE WEDGEWOOD

Some ten days after the raping of the Home Guard store Maude received a letter from one of her earliest playmates. His family had lived beside hers when they were children and he was now an engineer serving with the Forces. He wrote saying that he was shortly due a week's leave which he would like to spend in Cornwall, and asking her to engage a room for him somewhere in the neighbourhood.

She felt that this old friend of the family's should not be allowed to go to an hotel, but it happened that her own guest-rooms would be occupied at the time of his visit. She therefore decided that before replying she would ask whether her Uncle Joshua or the Littles would care to put him up.

As has been mentioned, it was Mr Radlett's habit on fine mornings to walk into the village to meet his friends at the reading-room. He generally left somewhere about ten, and to catch him Maude set off to his house a little before that hour.

Since the evening of the theft, life at St Pols had moved with its accustomed tranquillity. The only event at all out of the common had been the Home Guard Demonstration. This had taken place on the Sunday following that eventful Friday evening, and it had been a huge success. Crowds had poured out to Ruin Hill and had followed the various evolutions with gratifying attention. The approach and subsequent annihilation of the paratroops had been carried out even more realistically than at the practice and had proved a fitting finale to a really first-class show. Wedgewood's satisfaction was also Maude's. She was glad that his anxiety over the matter was past. He had received congratulations on all hands and she knew he was pleased.

She felt that his uneasiness about the theft was also passing away. It looked as if the affair would fizzle out. Certainly no explosions or other untoward events had broken into the village's calm. It was true that, so far as she knew, Inspector Vanson had made no progress towards finding the thief, but about this she was sure her husband was pleased rather than otherwise. He had admitted that he would regret a prosecution. It would cost him time and trouble, besides advertising the apparent slackness of his command. Also, should it prove that he knew the thief, the proceedings might become embarrassing in the extreme.

The affair with Savory had also come to nothing. Maude had not seen him since the meeting on the strand, and she believed Arthur had not either. Arthur seemed to have forgotten his annoyance, and she was sure that there would be no further trouble in that direction.

As these thoughts passed through her mind, Savory himself turned out of the drive from his home a little distance ahead, and walked to meet her.

For once he was reasonably polite. He pulled off his hat and actually smiled.

" 'Morning, Mrs Wedgewood, you're early abroad. Nice day."

At this proffering of the olive branch Maude reversed her decision to ignore him. What was the good of perpetuating bad feeling? She agreed pleasantly that the day was all that could be desired.

A hundred yards farther on was the lane leading to Joshua Radlett's house, and there an almost identical incident took place. Just as she reached it Radlett himself appeared, coming in her direction.

"Good morning, uncle," she greeted him. "You're before time this morning, aren't you? I was just coming to talk to you."

"Delighted to see you, my dear. Let's go back."

"No, you're off to the village. I'll walk part of the way with you."

They fell into step and she put her question about accommodating her old friend. Radlett was sorry not to be able to oblige her, but he must refuse. Mrs Wilton, his housekeeper, was going on a week's holiday just at the time, and while Wilton could manage for himself alone, he could not cope with a visitor.

"Then perhaps Jessica can do it," Maude answered. "I'll call and ask her on my way home."

They chatted of this and that and then Radlett glanced at Savory, walking on some couple of hundred yards before them.

"Like myself," he commented, "he's growing old. I don't think he's going a scrap quicker than we are. I thought I was the slowest walker in St Pols."

"Nonsense," declared Maude. "You get along as well as anyone."

"Very nice of you, my dear, but I'm not ashamed of taking it easy. Can't help it with my heart."

"It's been pretty well lately, hasn't it?"

"Yes, I've had a good spell. Well, I turn off here. Sorry about Mulholland."

He waved his hand and followed Savory down the winding path to the shore, while Maude turned inland. A few steps brought her to the Littles' house, which stood in a commanding position on the headland.

"Anyone at home?" she called, passing in through the open door.

There were shouts from her left. "Come in, Maude. We're in the study. Dick's being troublesome about his wretched words."

"An opportune call, Maude," came Little's voice. "I just wanted a second opinion. Come and tell me what you think of these."

Dick Little carried on an unusual but interesting job. He composed crossword puzzles for one of the big London dailies. It had begun as a hobby and then he had sent some of his efforts to the editor. They were approved and he was commissioned to do some more. These also had given satisfaction and he had obtained a semi-permanent engagement. The work was difficult but reasonably profitable, and satisfactorily augmented his rather meagre income from a few investments. The sums he made from his bees, to which he devoted all his spare time, were too precarious to count for much.

The study was a small, not very well furnished room with a large bow window and a magnificent view. It looked down on St Pols Bay from the west side, and on to the sandy beach, which stretched from just beneath the house where the little path debouched, right to the village and the headlands beyond. The ebbing tide had left a strip of smooth, brilliantly yellow sand. On it could be seen the two slowly retreating figures, first Savory and then Radlett a couple of hundred yards nearer. Apart from them the entire stretch was deserted.

In the window was a flat-topped knee-hole desk at which Little was seated. He had swung his revolving chair round and was facing Jessica, who sat on the end of a table.

"Try the armchair and take a cigarette," Jessica went on before her husband could speak. "What's the best news with you?"

Maude explained.

"Jimmy Mulholland? Why, yes, of course we can put him up. I'd like to see old Jimmy again. It's donkeys years since we met."

"Yes, rather," Little added. "Good fellow, Mullholland. Glad to have him."

They discussed their old friend and then Little turned round again to his desk. On it were several crossword diagrams with sheaves of notes. Beside them a dictionary and a book of quotations lay open, and an encyclopaedia and several other books of reference stood in a small rotating bookcase at his right hand. Little seemed a trifle nervy and Maude supposed he had one of his periodical headaches.

"Can't get on with this confounded thing today," he remarked. "I expect because the sea looks so good. I want to go and bathe, but if I do, the job won't be done. Tell me, you two, what do you think of this for a clue? 'But this is not for preventing a gale from being heard. Query.' In ten letters."

"He's dreadful when he gets like this," Jessica protested. "He goes on and on till one feels one's sanity breaking down."

"Bless my soul, girl, it's your bread and butter as well as mine. Now can you guess that? I'll read it again."

Both women registered expressions of anxious thought and both presently shook their heads.

"Ah," said Little, "that's what I wanted to know: too difficult. Now what about this. 'But this ship is not for preventing a gale from being heard. Query.' That easier?"

Again the others appeared to concentrate and again they shook their heads.

"For shame!" he exclaimed. "Windjammer. *Windjammer!*"

The women stared. Little jerked about impatiently.

"You jam wireless to prevent programmes from being heard, don't you," he explained irritably, "so why shouldn't you jam wind to do the same with gales? Jolly good, I call it."

Jessica shook her head. "Too far-fetched," she declared. "No one would ever guess it."

He seemed disappointed and turned to Maude.

"A little difficult, I think," she pronounced more diplomatically.

"I don't think so when you put in the word 'ship'," he returned seriously. "I'd follow it with an easy one such as this." He turned over his papers. " 'What you want is in Adrian swerved from the danger,' in six letters. Even you, Maude, should get that."

"I see it," said Jessica: "answer."

"Of course. See it, Maude?"

Maude saw that the last part of Adrian and the first of swerved made the word, but she thought the whole thing silly. However, she must not feel superior. These problems amused a lot of people, not to speak of the grist they brought in to Dick's mill.

"Now here," Little went on as she nodded her comprehension, "is a really good one. In fact, one of the best I've ever done. I don't think it's too difficult. 'In this life is bounded by infinity,' in three words, one, seven, three."

Maude did her best, but she could not attack the clue as did Jessica, who was a crossword fan. Unprofitably she puzzled over life and infinity and the boundaries of the former, and then, giving it up, her eyes strayed to the view. The two figures were still the only ones to be seen on the beach, but now they were reduced in size. Savory had just passed Groyne Point and Radlett was approaching it, still two or three hundred yards behind. Idly she watched them creeping forward.

"Don't say you give it up," Little protested, swinging round to his desk, and fumbling among his papers. "I think that's disgraceful. You should both get it quite easily."

"I can't see it," declared Jessica, "and I'm sure Maude can't either. Tell us."

"A newlaid egg!"

"A newlaid egg?" Maude repeated. For a moment she could not see any possible connection.

"You're both hopeless!" Little declared with exasperation. "Look here. There's life in an egg, isn't there? And a fly could crawl on the shell forever without getting to the end of it: that's infinity, isn't it? So that life is bounded by – "

He stopped suddenly and grew rigid, staring fixedly out of the window. Maude had turned to exchange smiles with Jessica, but now, warned by a sudden tenseness in the atmosphere, she swung back and looked down at the shore.

Just below the groyne at the little point some disturbance was taking place. Sand seemed to be flying in all directions and her uncle staggered suddenly and dropped to the ground as if flung violently backwards. Immediately there came the sharp crack of an explosion.

Maude felt herself gripped as in a vice as she watched a faint wisp of smoke rise into the air and begin to drift

35

slowly seawards. Then as she realized what must have happened, her blood ran cold with horror.

"Dick!" she gasped, while Jessica gave a low moan.

For a split second Little remained staring out rigidly, then with a muttered "Good God!" he leaped to his feet and ran to the telephone in the hall. As he dialled he shouted to Jessica to get their first-aid outfit. Maude heard him reporting first to the doctor and then to the police. He slammed down the receiver and seized the outfit.

"You're good at first aid, Maude," he exclaimed. "Better come along with me. We may get there before the doctor. Jessica, will you go over and tell Wilton to fix up a bed downstairs in case we take him home."

This was obviously good advice and both women hastened to carry it out. Maude went as fast as she could, but she was quickly left behind by Little, who was running like a boy. Through the confused welter of her ideas she could not help pondering on the extraordinary fitness the Home Guard training could produce in an elderly man.

As she hastened down the winding path to the beach she could see that Savory had turned and was running back to the scene of the explosion. Then reaching the sand, she lost her perspective and could no longer judge relative distances. But the sequence of events was clear enough. Savory obviously reached the body, for she could see him stop and stand motionless, looking down. That meant, she told herself grimly, that no first aid was required.

Presently another running figure appeared from among the shrubs growing near the head of the groyne. She recognized Wickham Crane, the novelist. His house was close to the little point, indeed she knew that from some of the rooms the groyne, and therefore presumably the point of the explosion, could be seen. Crane, probably writing in his study, could not have failed to hear the detonation, and a glance would show him the rising smoke. He might even have seen that ghastly, falling figure.

He hurried down along the groyne, and then she saw Savory moving to meet him and holding up his hands. They stopped and began to talk, Savory gesturing and pointing behind him. At this moment a car which she had noticed on the sand in the far distance reached the groyne. From it descended Dr Petherick, Sergeant Cundy and a couple of policemen. Savory repeated his warning movements as he and Crane walked over to meet them. For a few moments they all stood talking, then Savory happened to notice Dick Little coming up. He halted him as he had done the others, motioning him to approach in a wide circle round the scene of the tragedy.

Maude could now see that not far from the groyne there was a crater in the sand. She had seen many craters where Jerry had dropped his eggs, and as craters went, this was a tiny one. It was only a few inches deep, though all round it were radial markings where the sand had been blown back. And there beside it lay the motionless, distorted figure of Joshua Radlett. The head was twisted at a hideous angle to the body, and her shrinking glance told her that the neck must be broken and that no medical aid would be of any use.

"Terrible business!" Savory was saying. "Poor old Radlett. You can't do anything, doctor. He's dead."

The sergeant turned deferentially to Savory. "What happened, sir, can you tell us?"

"How the hell can I tell you what happened? I know no more than you do. I was walking to the village and heard the explosion behind me and turned back. I found what you see."

37

The sergeant clearly found his position difficult. "Better have a look at him all the same, doctor. We'll want your evidence at the inquest," he added diplomatically.

"Just a moment," went on Savory. "I've stopped everyone from going near, so as not to obscure footprints. I don't know whether you want them preserved, sergeant, but it's up to you now. You can take over."

"Thank you, sir, I'm grateful for that. Perhaps, doctor, you wouldn't mind approaching the body from the outside of the circle? Meantime" – he drew his notebook from his pocket – "I'd like a short statement from you gentlemen and from you, Mrs Wedgewood."

The statements were simple and clear. Savory had been walking towards the village, and when he had passed the groyne but a couple of hundred yards he had heard the explosion. He had swung round and seen the body falling. He had gone back immediately. It was not till he had come close that he had recognized Radlett, and satisfied himself that he was beyond help. While he was considering the best thing to be done, Mr Crane had come up. He had asked him to go and telephone for the police while he kept watch, but at that moment the doctor and police had arrived.

Crane stated that at the moment of the explosion he was in his study. He was, in fact, using the telephone. He had been idly looking towards the shore as he stood at the receiver and had actually seen the explosion. He had recognized Radlett walking along, and just before the man had reached the groyne the ground had gone up all round him. Crane had seen the deceased fall, and of course had heard the detonation. He had at once broken off his telephone conversation and hurried down. Mr Savory was there when he arrived, and he had stopped him from approaching the body. Maude and Little then told their stories.

By this time Dr Petherick had completed his preliminary examination.

"Yes, poor fellow," he said; "he's dead. You had better take the remains to the mortuary, sergeant, till I make a more detailed examination." He turned to Maude. "I'm sorry this is necessary, Mrs Wedgewood, but we can then have him taken to his house, if you and Mr Little so desire."

"We can talk about that later, doctor," Little answered. "I think you'd better come home, Maude. You can trust the sergeant to do everything necessary with reverence."

The sergeant saluted at the compliment. "Yes, sir, I'll see to it," he answered. "When the doctor's finished I'll communicate with you to learn your wishes."

"Thank you. Then I think we'll be off. Come along, Maude." He took her arm and drew her gently away.

During the first shock the horror of the actual tragedy had filled Maude's mind to the exclusion of everything else. Her uncle, the man whom she had been almost as fond of as if he had been her father, that good, kind, unselfish man to whom she had been speaking only a very few minutes before, was *dead*! It was a shock to her and she could see it was a shock to Dick Little, but to Jessica it would be a greater shock still. Jessica had been very fond of her father, and in these recent months since his health began to deteriorate, had seen a lot of him. Of course the explosion had warned her of what she might expect, but even so, his death could not fail to affect her deeply.

These were Maude's first reactions, but now as she walked slowly back with Little, she began to consider another side of the affair. Radlett's death would affect them all profoundly. Why, they would now come in for their money! It would revolutionize the lives of Jessica and Dick. Instead of struggling to make ends meet, they would be wealthy! She herself would receive her vastly smaller, but still substantial legacy. What a help that would be to Arthur, who so sorely needed capital for the farm! Not for a moment did it enter Maude's head that she might keep the money for her own use. Her husband's purse and her own were one. She would be only thankful if its use were to ease the burden of anxiety he was carrying.

She glanced at Little. He was certainly looking very much upset. His expression surprised her. He had not been particularly fond of the dead man, indeed he had never pretended to be. He could not therefore be really distressed at his death. Moreover, he had suddenly become wealthy. Knowing him, Maude did not believe that he had failed to grasp this factor in the situation. Why then the anxiety?

Suddenly she understood. The theft from the Home Guard! Could the explosives stolen from the hut have had anything to do with the tragedy? She grasped his arm.

"Oh, Dick! The theft of the grenades!"

He looked down at her. "I know," he muttered. "That's what keeps coming into my mind. But it couldn't have anything to do with this. It's simply not possible."

"You're sure of that?"

"Well, how could it? Just think. The thief would have had to have dropped them on the sand or into the sea. Why should anyone do that? If they were worth stealing, they were too valuable to lose like that."

"If they had been dropped, the sea would have covered them with sand."

"*If* they had been dropped, yes. And Uncle might have kicked out a pin, though it's not very likely. But I can't see why they should have been dropped."

Suddenly an idea shot into Maude's mind. "I believe I've got it," she exclaimed. "A German mine! Washed in and covered with sand!"

"I thought of that at once," he answered, "but it's not very easy to see how it could have been. A mine's a big thing. If it had gone off there it would have made a hole fifty feet across. Besides it could never have been washed so far inland and buried in the sand without hitting some of its horns and going up."

"There's been no gale to wash a big thing in."

"No; there you are."

"Are there no small mines that might float in?"

He shrugged. "There may be. I've never heard of any, though, of course, I don't know all Jerry's tricks. But the same thing would apply. Contact with the shore ought to have detonated it."

"Something dropped from a plane?"

"Perhaps; but there again one would have expected it to go off when it hit the ground."

"Then what do you think it was?"

He shrugged. "Beyond me." There was a silence and he went on: "One other thing has occurred to me, though I can't see that it could have been that either. The manoeuvres. It was on this beach that the landing took place and mines may have been laid."

Maude nodded emphatically. "You've got it, Dick! That's it, I'm sure! Of course! It was just there that the worst of the fighting was supposed to take place."

Dick shook his head. "It's not so simple as that, I can assure you. If that was a military land-mine, it was a live one: fully charged. Now they just don't use those on manoeuvres: they have harmless ones. Besides, I'm pretty sure they check what's sent out and how it's used. So the theory's by no means plain sailing."

She thought this over. "It's the most likely so far," she declared presently. Then with a change of manner. "But, Dick, have you thought of another thing? It seems heartless to speak of it with poor Uncle lying there on the sand, but he would know we were not that. Have you realized that Jessica will now come into her money?"

He smiled grimly. "Oh, yes, that had occurred to me. It's really that which makes the Home Guard possibilities so worrying. I mean – the grenades were in my charge – "

She made an emphatic gesture. "Dick! Don't even *think* of such nonsense! In the first place there was no carelessness; you did everything that other Home Guard quartermasters did. Besides, even if you had made a mistake, you couldn't be responsible for what the thieves did with the stuff. Do be sensible."

He seemed somewhat reassured. "You're a good friend, Maude, but that's not the way the thing would be looked at."

"Arthur'll feel exactly the same, I know," she went on. "He's not responsible for it, but he thinks he is."

"Technically he is of course."

"It's horribly unfair."

"It's not so bad as it looks. If the company does well, he technically gets the credit. Admittedly it doesn't usually work out like that, but that's the idea."

"Well, don't let's think about it. I'm afraid, Dick, this will hit Jessica pretty hard. She's been so much with Uncle Joshua lately."

"She saw the explosion and she'll scarcely be surprised. All the same, I'll go and tell her. I dare say you'd like to tell Arthur? Or shall we go to them together?"

"No, no. We needn't waste all that time. You go to Jessica and I'll see Arthur."

They separated at the path up the cliff and Maude, perturbed and puzzled, hurried home to find her husband.

– 4 –

ARTHUR WEDGEWOOD

On that morning of the tragedy Arthur Wedgewood had followed his usual programme for a day on his farm. Out shortly after half past six, he had begun with a number of inspections, including visits to every point at which work was in progress. Then in for breakfast at eight, and after it out again to discuss current farm affairs with his mechanic and general factotum, Angus Macdougal. Today at eleven he had a meeting with a representative from the Ministry of Agriculture relative to his allocation of ground for future crops. Lunch would follow and after it a short rest, and then at last he would have a chance to carry on with a stock job which had been on his hands for some time, long overdue repairs to his chicken coops. Being a fair carpenter, he did such work himself.

Breakfast was now over, and as he walked to the yard to see Macdougal, his mind was full of the coming interview with the Ministry's representative. He considered that the crop rotation he had worked out was extremely good and he was afraid of his plans being upset. No doubt the heads of these Ministries were reasonable men who understood when to interfere with technicians and when to let them alone. But their underlings were often of a very different kidney. They did not know their job well enough to be sure of themselves, and when a farmer raised objections to their impracticable proposals, they thought they were being tricked and insisted on their demands more rigidly than ever. However, Crawford, the man who was coming, was a decent fellow and would be as accommodating as his instructions allowed.

Presently Wedgewood pushed open the door of the mechanic's shop, nodded to the man working at the rough bench, and sitting down on an empty crate, began slowly to fill his pipe.

Angus Macdougal was an Argyllshire man of about forty, short and thickset, with grizzled red hair, a slight cast in his left eye and an aggressive jaw. He was short-tempered, and when roused his language, as Wedgewood put it, would blister the paint off the walls, but he was the soul of loyalty, utterly dependable and as straight as a die, and highly competent at his job. He had been with Wedgewood for many years. They had got to know each other in France during the last war, where Macdougal was Wedgewood's batman. In the Salient they had learnt each other's ways, and a mutual respect, growing gradually into a real friendship, had developed between them. After the war they had drifted apart, but when Wedgewood had embarked on the venture of the farm and was looking about for a man to take charge of his machines, he remembered his former servant. Macdougal was in a job in Girvan, but was dissatisfied with it, and at Wedgewood's invitation he moved south. By his own choice his salary was small, but a generous allowance of bonuses gave him a reasonably good income as well as an interest in the business. In the present war his work was considered essential and he was not called upon to change it. He had therefore enlisted in the Home Guard, where he was one of Wedgewood's most valuable followers. He was married and had two children, a boy and a girl, at the present time aged seven and nine respectively.

"What's the matter with that?" Wedgewood asked, glancing at the carburettor of his tractor, of which the dismembered components littered the bench.

"Not so much, I'm thinking," answered Macdougal, scratching his head with an oily hand. "She gave up half an hour since, and I found she wasna getting the gas. So I brought in the carburettor to have a squint at the jets."

"Awkward if she's out of action long. I hoped we'd get that ten-acre field finished today."

"So you will too. That is, if it's the jets."

They discussed the tractor and a number of other technical matters, and then Wedgewood stood up to go. Macdougal eyed him speculatively.

"I was wanting an hour or two this afternoon if you've no objection," he suggested. "It's to see Pengelly about the cottage."

A wave of exasperation swept into Wedgewood's mind at the reminder. Here was Savory making trouble again! For years Macdougal had lived in one of Savory's cottages, and now quite recently he had been given notice to quit. The alleged reason was that Savory wanted the house for his chauffeur, but both Macdougal and Wedgewood knew that this was the flimsiest of excuses; the motive was spite and spite only. Macdougal had had what he called "worrds" with Savory about an alleged trespass of his children on the other's ground, and the notice was the result. Pengelly was one of St Pols' many lawyers, and Macdougal had asked him whether any way of ignoring the notice could be found.

"Right," Wedgewood returned, "and I wish you the very best of luck."

Macdougal contented himself with a short nod, but he grinned appreciatively. He usually avoided speaking about Savory in Wedgewood's hearing, as Wedgewood pretended to object to his language. But Macdougal knew well his employer's feelings, and was satisfied that he had his sympathy.

Wedgewood glanced at his watch. It was just quarter past nine. He would not have to leave for his interview till nearly eleven. He might therefore put in a bit of time on his coops.

The chicken run was in the corner of a field at the back of the big barn. The tools were there where he had left them last time he did a spell, and he walked across and set to work. The place was very secluded. The barn, a really large building, cut off his view of both yard and house, and the outdoor work in progress was at the other end of the farm.

Wedgewood was fond of carpentry and he sawed and hammered away contentedly. Repairing coops was not in itself an interesting job, but it was a pleasant relief from his usual mental work: constant planning, watching of costs, and devising ways to overcome all sorts of irritating little difficulties. What he really enjoyed was making something of his own design, particularly something that he had invented to meet some special need. There were separate and mutually intensified pleasures in making the plans, in seeing the apparatus grow, in trying it out and in modifying it to get better results. In such activities Macdougal was a tower of strength. He entered whole-heartedly into them, helped with the construction, and often put forward a suggestion which turned an incipient failure into a success. Obviously he enjoyed it all as much as his employer.

Wedgewood had been working for nearly an hour when he heard the boom of the explosion. He thought it was a gun or bomb. At St Pols such booms were frequent, occasionally from Jerry dropping eggs in the distance, but more usually from practices in the camp a mile or so inland. This noise sounded nearer; it was more a sharp crack than a boom. For a moment Wedgewood listened, but the sound was not repeated and he presently resumed work.

Some minutes later he put away his tools and set off to the house, where the Ministry's representative was to call. As he reached the farmyard he saw Maude hastening towards him. She looked pale and distressed and he thought a little frightened. At her expression foreboding gripped him.

"Good Lord, Maude, what's the matter?" he cried sharply.

"Oh, Arthur" – she wrung her hands – "something dreadful has happened; absolutely ghastly! Did you hear an explosion?"

"Yes, a few minutes ago. What about it?"

"I saw it – from Dick's window. It was on the shore. Oh, I can hardly speak of it, but Uncle Joshua – was there and – "

"Go on, for heaven's sake!"

Maude made a gesture of horror. "He – was blown up!"

"Good God! Not – "

"Yes! Dead! Killed instantaneously!"

Wedgewood was deeply moved by the story. He rang up the representative of the Ministry at his hotel and postponed his interview. Then with Maude he walked over to the Littles'. Dick seemed much upset and Jessica was sobbing gently.

"Oh, Maude," she cried, "isn't it *awful*! *Poor* daddy! I just can't realize it!"

Maude tried to comfort her while the men talked in low tones.

"There's just one alleviation," Wedgewood said presently, "and that is that if it had to be, it couldn't have been easier – for him. It was sudden: so sudden that he would know nothing and suffer nothing."

They agreed and the discussion dragged on till Wedgewood touched on a new point.

"But what gets me is the cause of it," he said wonderingly. "I suppose a mine was washed in and he stepped on a horn."

Little shook his head. "Maude and I were talking about that. She suggested it, but I thought it unlikely," and he repeated his reasons.

"That sounds convincing enough," Wedgewood admitted.

"I think," Maude put in, "Dick hit on it on the way home. The manoeuvres. Tell him, Dick."

"Well, I did mention it," Little admitted, "but I don't put it up as a theory. I wondered if a live contact mine could have been buried there by the military?"

Wedgewood made a gesture of satisfaction. "The very thing! It hadn't occurred to me. Why aren't you satisfied? What's the snag?"

Little said that live mines were not used on manoeuvres.

"Nothing in that, I think," Wedgewood returned. "Quite easy for a live mine to get mixed up with the others. I believe you're on it."

They discussed this for some moments, and then Dick, with a gesture as if throwing discretion to the winds, declared: "We're not mentioning what's in all our minds, and it would be better if we did. The theft!"

"I've not forgotten the theft," Wedgewood returned, "but I can't for the life of me see how that could have had anything to do with it. What exactly do you suggest?"

"I don't suggest anything. I can't think what happened. But what I can't forget is that first we have a theft of explosives, and then ten days later we have an explosion. I don't say there's any connection, but – there it is."

"Surely that's only a coincidence?" put in Jessica. "Far stranger things than that are always happening."

"Yes, I agree with Jessica," Maude declared. "It's nothing like coincidences which have happened in our experience."

"I wonder if Cundy has any ideas," said Little. "Would you think of ringing him up, Arthur?"

"I think I'll go in and see him," Wedgewood decided. "Care to come?"

Little hesitated. "I don't think so. I've seen him today already. Besides, I haven't your excuse. Any outsider can't go questioning the police."

"One point we must settle," put in Maude gently. "Sergeant Cundy wants to know what we should like done with the – er – body. I think that's for you to say, Jessica. Will you have it brought back to his home or would you prefer to have the funeral from the mortuary?"

For some time they discussed the matter, finally deciding to have the remains brought back so that the funeral might be from the home.

A little later Wedgewood took his bicycle and rode into St Pols. At the police-station he asked for Cundy, but it was Inspector Vanson who came out and called him into his room.

"Good morning, sir. I'm glad to see you. May I say first how very distressed I am at what has happened?"

"Thank you, Vanson. It's a sad affair."

"Very, sir; particularly in the case of a gentleman so well respected as Mr Radlett. I hope you've come to give me some information?"

"I'm afraid not," Wedgewood smiled crookedly; "I was hoping to get some from you. I'm interested from two points of view, as you know; first, owing to my wife's relationship with the deceased, and second, because of my position in the Home Guard. To be quite candid, I'm worried lest there should be a connection between the tragedy and the recent theft."

He thought that Vanson looked at him a trifle curiously. "I thought of that myself," he admitted, "but there's no evidence for it that I can see."

"What then do you think took place?"

Vanson shook his head. "I wish I knew," he declared. "So far I don't, but we're going into it and I hope we may be able to clear it up."

This was all that Wedgewood could get out of him, probably, he thought, because the man was speaking the exact truth. He gave the message about the disposal of the remains and was turning away, but Vanson held up his hand.

"I wonder, sir, now you're here, if you'd be so good as to view the remains and give formal evidence of identification at the inquest? Mr Savory has no doubt of the identity, but when possible we prefer someone connected with the family."

"Yes, of course, but Mr Little has seen him and he's more closely related to him than I."

"I understand Mr Little didn't really see him at close quarters. Mr Savory kept everyone away so as to avoid spoiling the footprints."

"Oh, well, I'll do it."

Dr Petherick was just finishing with the remains and Wedgewood was presently taken to the room at the back of the police-station which did duty as a morgue. The sheet which was over the dead man's face was raised. Except for the dreadful angle of the neck and a bruise on the temple, the head was not disfigured. A glance was sufficient and Wedgewood undertook to give the necessary evidence.

"When is the inquest?" he inquired as they returned to the office.

"Three o'clock tomorrow at the Wellesley Hall has been suggested, but it hasn't been absolutely decided. I'll let you know in good time. Mrs Wedgewood and Mr Little will be required also."

"I'll tell them."

"Thank you, sir."

Vanson was as good as his word. That evening he sent confirmation of the hour together with formal notifications to the three witnesses to be present.

The Wellesley was the one large hall in St Pols, and it was in a side room, the Minor Hall, that the inquest was to take place. There shortly before three a crowd of the interested and the curious assembled. When Wedgewood and Maude and the Littles arrived, they found the place already packed. Places had been kept for the witnesses, and an adjoining seat was quickly found for Jessica.

The proceedings began in the time-honoured manner. The coroner was a Mr Trevelyan, a solicitor from a neighbouring town. He had the reputation of being a shrewd lawyer and a hard fighter, though always by strictly fair methods. He was quiet and unassuming in manner, yet his remarks carried weight and were always listened to with attention.

When the preliminaries were over he made a short speech to the jury. "You are here," he told them, "for two main purposes, first, to say, if you can, whose body this is which you have just seen, and second, to record, again if

52

you can, how the deceased came by his death. Further, if you are satisfied from the evidence that any person or persons were to blame for the tragedy, you may state that also.

"I should perhaps say at this point that it is possible that we may not be able to complete the inquiry today. I propose to take such evidence as is available, but if this proves insufficient to enable you to reach a conclusion and if it should seem that more might become available later, I shall adjourn the proceedings to a later date."

With deep disappointment, but without much surprise, Wedgewood heard this announcement. It meant that the authorities were not satisfied as to what had taken place and were making a serious investigation. This was more than unfortunate. The theft would be remembered, and whether there was any connection between it and the tragedy or not, attention would be focused upon it.

His reverie was sharply broken by a call from the coroner. He was the first witness. He gave evidence of identity and then answered several routine questions as to the deceased's life, health and circumstances. All were purely formal, and when he presently gave place to Savory, no mention of grenades or Home Guard thefts had been made.

Savory was quieter than usual, less flamboyant, less aggressive. He did not try to hector the coroner – perhaps because he knew he could not – but answered his questions not only courteously, but fully and yet with brevity. Indeed as Wedgewood listened to him, he had to admit he was a model witness.

Savory repeated very much what he had told Cundy at the time of the tragedy. He had not known that Radlett was behind him; the sound of the explosion attracted his attention and he had looked round and seen the body falling; he had gone back to find out what had happened, and then had identified Radlett. He had realized that his neck was broken and that he was beyond medical aid. In a few minutes Mr Crane, Dr Petherick and the police, Mr Little and Mrs Wedgewood had arrived, in that order. He had kept everyone away from the place so as to leave footprints intact, and had then handed over to Sergeant Cundy.

Crane, Little and Maude were then called and told their stories. The four accounts dovetailed so exactly into one another, that no doubt could exist in the minds of those present as to what really took place.

Dr Petherick followed. He stated that he had examined the remains and that death was due to a broken neck – though he did not call it by so simple a name. Both legs were broken and they and the lower portion of the trunk were burnt and mutilated. There was a heavy bruise on the right side of the head and shoulder. It was clear that death had only just taken place when he first saw the body.

"In your opinion, Dr Petherick, might death have been caused by an explosion such as we have heard about?"

In the doctor's opinion it might, and he further agreed that the injuries were consistent with the theory that such an explosion took place in the sand beneath the deceased's feet and threw him forcibly down on his head, breaking his neck.

Sergeant Cundy was the next witness. At ten-ten a.m. on the previous day he had been rung up by Mr Little, who informed him that an explosion had taken place on the shore at Groyne Point and that he feared Mr Radlett was injured. The police car happened to be at the door and he had instantly gone round to Dr Petherick, whom he found had also heard from Mr Little, and who was preparing to start for the place. As the doctor preferred not to take his car on the sand, he had joined the police. They had reached the scene of the tragedy in six minutes, at ten-sixteen, to find that Mr Savory and Mr Crane had already arrived. A couple of minutes later Mr Little turned up. Cundy corroborated the previous witnesses as to the proceedings on the shore. He had had the remains removed to the mortuary and had noted the traces remaining on the sand, which, thanks to Mr Savory, had not been obscured.

"What did these traces consist of?" the coroner asked.

"There was first the crater," answered Cundy, and he described what Maude had seen. "Then there were footprints. Two lines of prints came from the direction of West Head and led straight to the crater. One went on past it towards the village for a couple of hundred yards, where it turned back and approached the remains. This was Mr Savory's and it accurately confirmed his statement; not, of course, sir," the sergeant added hastily, "that any confirmation was needed."

"You're not concerned with that, sergeant," the coroner remarked gently. "We understand that you must report what you found. And the other line of prints?"

"The second line did not appear at the other side of the crater. They were the deceased's."

"Quite. Any more?"

"Not near the crater, sir. At a little distance from it the prints of Mr Crane, Mr Little and Mrs Wedgewood could be plainly followed, and showed that these witnesses had acted exactly as they said."

The coroner nodded. "It's satisfactory to have no difference of opinion as to the facts. Now, you've said that the footprints of both Mr Savory and the deceased appeared to go straight over the centre of the crater. That means, I take it, that they were on top of one another?"

"Practically, sir. The actual footsteps did not coincide, but the lines of walking almost did."

"How was the tide at the time?"

"It had been ebbing for about an hour. There was perhaps a dozen yards of hard sand uncovered."

"That is to say that these gentlemen had a width of a dozen yards to walk on, yet they chose the same strip. How do you account for that?"

"Quite easily, sir. They both passed round the end of the groyne."

"Their shortest way?"

"Yes, sir. The groyne's at a projecting point, so they don't go farther down the beach than is necessary to get round it. It's easier to go round the end than to climb over it."

"That's very clear. Did the explosion then take place at the end of the groyne?"

"No, sir, not exactly. The centre of the crater was about twenty feet to the west of the groyne, but it was just below the end."

"Oh." The coroner looked interested. "Close to the groyne and just below its end? Did you see any significance in that?"

"You mean a suggestion that it was deliberately planted?" returned Cundy bluntly. "Well, no, sir, we didn't think that followed."

"That sounds as if you knew what happened. As a matter of fact, have you discovered the cause of the explosion?"

Cundy looked embarrassed. "No, sir, I'm afraid not. Nothing's left to show that."

"You can make no suggestion?"

"No, sir; there's no evidence."

The coroner hesitated. He seemed about to continue the interrogation, then apparently thought better of it. Before dismissing Cundy he followed his practice with the previous witnesses and asked whether any juror wished to put a question.

Immediately the foreman stood up. "I should like to know, sir, whether the sergeant thinks it might have been a mine washed in from the sea?"

Nodding of heads on the part of several jurors showed that this was in their minds also.

Again the coroner hesitated. "The sergeant has declared definitely that there's no evidence as to the cause of the explosion," he said slowly, "and the value of theories in an inquiry of this kind is negligible – or perhaps I should say nil. However, I don't wish to prevent any discussion which may throw light on the tragedy, and I will therefore allow the question. Will you please answer it, sergeant?"

"The inspector and I talked that over, sir," Cundy replied a trifle unwillingly. "We thought it might have been a mine, and if so, we thought it might have been buried by the waves at that place. There have been a lot of mines found on the shore, both German and our own."

"Not here?"

"Not, here, sir, but at several other places along the coast."

"Very well. But tell me, would contact with the shore not have detonated a mine?"

"We thought not necessarily, sir. It has not done so in other cases."

"Did I understand you to indicate that there might be a reason why a mine might sink at the point of the explosion?"

"Because of the tide and the groyne, sir. The tide flows from the west, as you know, and we thought that if a mine got on to the west beach, it might be driven eastward till it was stopped by the groyne. There'd be a backwash from the groyne which might hold it and the end of the groyne would make eddies. As you know again, a heavy object halted on sand will settle where there is broken water."

The coroner followed this attentively. "That's an ingenious theory and I think we all" – he glanced at the jury – "know of our own knowledge that your assumptions about the tide and about objects sinking in the sand are correct. But would a mine not have made a larger crater than this one?"

"The ordinary large mine would, sir, of course, but we didn't know whether there might not be smaller varieties."

"Suppose you are correct and that it was a small mine, can you account for its going off when the deceased passed, but not when Mr Savory walked over the place a few moments earlier?"

"We thought that the deceased might have kicked one of its horns and that Mr Savory might have passed without doing so."

"You've certainly a suggestion for everything, sergeant. Have you inquired from the military and naval authorities whether such small mines exist?"

Sergeant Cundy's face fell. "I'm afraid not directly, sir; at least I think not. I didn't do it and I didn't hear of its being done. But the inspector's here, if you wish to ask him."

"I shall do so." Mr Trevelyan glanced at the foreman. "Anything else you'd like to ask this witness?"

"No, sir; that's all, thank you."

The coroner then called Vanson, but without learning anything fresh. He stated that he agreed with the theory put forward by Cundy, but emphasized that it was purely theory, unsupported by any actual evidence, and that the police did not offer it officially, but only in response to the coroner's request.

Before Vanson left the witness chair the coroner inquired as usual whether any juror wished to ask a question. Up to the present only the foreman had taken advantage of the offer, but now a tall man with a spiky nose began shuffling on his seat, eventually rising.

"As you know, Mr Coroner," he said after these preliminaries, "there have been large-scale military exercises in the neighbourhood, including this very stretch of shore. I should like to ask if the witness has made any inquiries as to whether this disaster could be due to any explosives having been dropped at that time?"

"Seeing that we have considered floating mines," the coroner answered, "I cannot object to this question. What do you say to it, inspector?"

"Yes, sir, I made the inquiries indicated. I called on the military authorities. They assured me that no explosives of a kind that could have produced such a crater were used in the manoeuvres."

"Is that satisfactory to you?" the coroner asked, glancing at the spiky juror.

The man still seemed uneasy. "What was in my mind, sir, was that land-mines are one of the principal means for protecting a beach against invasion, and it is difficult to believe that none were used on this occasion."

"They don't use live mines, sir," Vanson put in.

"I realize that," returned the juror. "What I suggest is that a live mine might have got mixed up with their practice ones."

"They assured me that could not have occurred."

"I don't question their bona fides," the spiky man persisted. "I suggest an error."

"The military authorities have given their assurance," the coroner intervened a trifle testily. "Is not that satisfactory to you?"

"It's not first-hand evidence, sir. Personally I think we should have had a military witness before us."

The coroner frowned. "I think," he declared, "that if any suspicion had been aroused that the explosive came from military sources, such would have been desirable. As it is, I question its necessity. But I'm anxious to meet the wishes of the jury, and if you would like such a witness I'll adjourn till suitable arrangements can be made."

Confronted with the prospect of another day's attendance, and having become a focal point for the wrathful glares of his colleagues, the man subsided.

"I certainly do not wish to press it, sir," he conceded. "If you are satisfied, I'm sure I am."

"Quite. Any other question?"

At this the local veterinary surgeon, a heavy-browed, red-faced man, cleared his throat impressively.

"I'd like to ask the witness whether it's true that a quantity of explosives were stolen from the Home Guard hut some ten days ago, and if so, whether he considers that the theft may have a connection with this affair?"

It was evident that this question also found a response in the minds of other jurors, as several again nodded and all looked interested. A cessation of movement in the body of the hall showed that others who were present appreciated its dramatic possibilities.

Wedgewood had been beginning to congratulate himself that from his point of view the affair was well over, but at this he felt his hopes dashed. He listened more anxiously to what was coming.

"I accept that question for the same reason as the last. Will you please answer it, Mr Vanson?"

"I thought of that, of course, sir," Vanson answered, "and it's quite true that a box containing twelve hand-grenades was stolen from the Home Guard hut at the time stated. But I could find no evidence to suggest any connection between the two affairs. I could form no theory as to how the grenades could have got to the point of the explosion, nor how, if they had, a passing footstep could have set them off. Such evidence as there is seemed to be against the idea. As you know, the pulling out of a pin releases a lever which explodes the grenades, and I don't see how it would have been kicked out."

"Suppose," said the coroner, apparently interested in spite of his reservation, "that by wave action knocking it against the sand, the pin was partially displaced, might a kick have then knocked it out altogether?"

"That's possible, of course, but even in this case the evidence is against it. With these grenades there's a time lag of four seconds between the pulling out of the pin and the explosion: that, of course, is to give time for the throw. Now at the speed the deceased was walking he would go about eighteen feet in four seconds. Therefore if he had kicked out the pin he should have been well away from the crater before the explosion. But the evidence shows he was just in its centre. I argued therefore that it couldn't have been a grenade."

The coroner looked across at the veterinary surgeon. "Does that answer your question?"

The veterinary surgeon made a half bow. "Yes, sir, it satisfies me."

"It satisfies me also," returned the coroner, "and I think, inspector, we may congratulate you on the thought you've given to the affair. That's the last witness, unless anyone has any further information to give?"

He looked round, and as no one moved, bent forward to arrange his notes. Then straightening up again, he addressed the jury.

He repeated what he had already said about their threefold duty; first, to state the identity of the deceased, second, to specify the cause of death, and third, if they could do so, to say whether blame attached to any person or persons.

"With regard to the first of these," he went on, "I feel sure you will have no difficulty. Formal evidence has been given to you, which there is no reason to question. I have no doubt that you will find that the deceased was Joshua Mordaunt Radlett.

"The second matter seems equally obvious. There is direct evidence that the deceased met his death as the result of an explosion while walking along the St Pols Bay strand. Here again I do not think you will have any difficulty in reaching a decision.

"But the third question is by no means so clear, and I should like to direct your attention to it for a few moments. In the case of a death such as this, three possibilities have to be considered: accident, suicide and murder. To enable you to decide between these three you will, in my opinion, require to know how the explosive came to be where it was. If it came there by chance or oversight, the affair was an accident. If it were brought to the place by the deceased and deliberately exploded by him in order to cause his own death, it was suicide, whereas if it were planted by some person or persons and exploded by them when the deceased was at the danger-point, it was murder.

"Now I particularly want to remind you that according to the evidence we have received, the cause of the explosion is unknown. When this evidence was given directly by the police witnesses, my feeling was to pursue the point no further. However, when you, gentlemen, wished to consider possible causes, I did not desire to stand in your way. We have therefore discussed theories, such as that a British or German mine may have been washed ashore, that some explosive used in the recent Army manoeuvres may have become buried on the shore, and that the grenades stolen from the Home Guard hut may have found their way there. But, let me repeat, all these suggestions are purely theories; there is no evidence whatever for any of them. On the contrary, such evidence as exists appears to rule out at least the last two. I wish to impress on you therefore that you must neglect all of them in considering your verdict.

"From all this it would appear to me that it is not possible to say with absolute certainty whether the affair was an accident, suicide or murder. But here you must use your own common sense and knowledge of life. How an accident might have happened has not been suggested. You may believe that the probability of suicide in the circumstances is extremely remote, and consequently reject it. You will certainly remember that not one scintilla of evidence suggesting murder has been offered, and this may affect your decision. The matter, of course, is one for you alone, and if you are satisfied as to what happened, you will say so. On the other hand, if you have not a clear conviction in your mind as to the exact course of events, you will return a verdict that on this third point the evidence is insufficient to enable you to reach a conclusion. Now if there is no further matter upon which I can help you, I shall ask you please to retire and consider your verdict."

For half an hour the jury deliberated, then they returned and the foreman read out importantly: "We find that on Tuesday the 26th of May, 1943, Joshua Mordaunt Radlett was killed on the shore of St Pols Bay, Cornwall, by an explosion, the cause of which there is insufficient evidence to determine."

With a deep sigh of relief Wedgewood stood up to join the others as they filed out of the room.

– 5 –

ANNE MEREDITH

Anne Meredith sat before her typewriter, staring with slightly wrinkled brow at the hieroglyph in her notebook which represented a crucial word in her uncle's most recent dictation. It looked like monogamist, but as the letter was to his coal merchant and concerned the latter's failure to supply a promised ton of anthracite, this did not seem a very hopeful interpretation. Having no particular wish to hear Savory's comments on the value of illegible shorthand, she decided she would not ask him what he had said, but would redraft the sentence avoiding anything suggestive of marriage practices.

Anne at this time was a tall, rather delicate-looking young woman of some five and twenty, and would have been pretty had she been a little more robust. At the beginning of the war she had been living with her mother, who was Charles Savory's only sister and the widow of an air force officer. Though able to get along sufficiently comfortably, their means were straightened, consisting only of a small annuity and the air force pension. With a view to helping the family budget, Anne had learnt shorthand, typing and bookkeeping. She had made a start in two or three jobs, but owing to her delicate health she had been unable to hold any of them down.

Then during the blitz Mrs Meredith was killed. It had been a terrible experience for Anne. Caught in a raid while out shopping, she had been knocked down and cut on the hands and arms by flying glass. When she had received first aid and had made her way home through the devastated streets, it was to find that their house had completely vanished. It was not till the next day that her mother's body was recovered.

Weak from her injuries and the shock, and penniless owing to the ceasing of both her sources of income, Anne found herself up against it. It was then that her uncle, Charles Savory, offered her a home, an offer which she gratefully accepted.

This was a kind action, but it was not Charles Savory's habit to do good turns without a *quid pro quo*. She soon found that she was to pay her way. In return for board and lodging and pocket-money, he asked her services as his secretary. To her this was no grievance. On the contrary she was thankful. She disliked her uncle and would have resented being under a compliment to him. As his secretary she could accept his hospitality and keep her self-respect.

At first Anne had been only thankful for a place where she could rest, for her experiences had left her with a feeling of deadly lassitude, and her secretarial work occupied only a small portion of her time. Then as she had gradually recovered from her shock she had begun to react more normally to her surroundings. The household consisted only of the two Savorys, a maid, a chauffeur and a gardener. She would have been lonely had it not been for Mrs Savory, of whom she soon grew fond. As it was, the elderly atmosphere with its war-time limitations made it dull for the girl, and she presently began to look round for some other way of earning her living.

At the same time it was not the monotony of the life with which she was chiefly dissatisfied. The war occupied her mind. She felt that in working for her uncle she was not pulling her weight in the war effort, and she wanted to do something of more value. What she would have liked was to enter one of the services, preferably the WAAF. But though her health had improved at Kelwyn House, it still precluded anything so strenuous. When hesitatingly she had suggested the idea, her Aunt Doris, as she had come to call Mrs Savory, had had her examined by their own doctor, who promptly vetoed the plan. Munitions, her second choice, was equally out of the question. She could not even be sure of carrying on a clerical job to release a man. Regretfully she resigned herself to remaining where she was.

Then a new factor had entered into her life. When an enemy landing on the shores of England seemed inevitable, St Pols followed the example of its betters and set up its Invasion Committee. As a leading resident who was over age for other war work, her uncle was chosen as Civil Representative. He took a great interest in the scheme and did really excellent work, or rather directed it, for the actual labour devolved upon her and the secretary, a young man named Vane. Vane came to Kelwyn House after his normal working hours, in the evenings and sometimes on Sundays, and for several weeks Anne was busy typing innumerable letters, lists of addresses, statements about emergency water-supplies, labour squads and the burial of the dead.

Here was real war work at last, and she did it with eagerness. But she presently found there was more than war work in it. She began to take an increasing interest in Vane, and it was soon evident that her interest was more than returned.

Reggie Vane's life-story was somewhat similar to her own, and this early made a bond of sympathy between them. He was employed in the St Pols Labour Exchange, and when hostilities had broken out he also had wished for a more definitely war job. He had applied for the Air Force, the Navy, the Army and the Home Guard, and had been turned down by all on the same grounds, a delicate chest. He also was glad to get the Invasion Committee work, for if not the real thing, he could at least feel that he was working for the country.

Vane had been intended for a better career than that of a clerk in a Labour Exchange. His father was a naval commander, who after retirement had become Harbour Master at St Pols, a small and poorly paid job which the commander had treated as a hobby. Vane had been educated at a good school and had gone to college. He had hoped to take his Arts degree, and after a period of journalism, to settle down to the work he longed for, the writing of novels.

But before he graduated his father had died and his mother's circumstances had become too straightened for him to continue at the university. He had to find an immediate job, and as his father had bought the house they were living in, he wanted it at St Pols. It happened that just then there occurred a vacancy for a junior clerk at the local Labour Exchange. He obtained it, made good, and when at the beginning of the war some of the staff joined up, he was promoted to second in command.

At first the course of true love had run so slowly as to be practically imperceptible, and it was not for many weeks that its first tentative signs began to appear. One Sunday afternoon Vane met Anne walking to St Pols along the shore. He took his courage in both hands and turned and walked back with her. She was paying a call in the village, and he begged permission to wait and see her home. During this second walk he became what seemed to him afterwards absolutely foolhardy. Daringly he asked her to have tea and go to the pictures with him on his next free afternoon. When she agreed he was overwhelmed.

After that they met at fairly regular intervals. Anne by then knew she was in love with him, and she believed he returned her feeling. But as no word of love passed his lips, she began to think she was mistaken. It was not till afterwards that she learnt that never for a moment had he imagined that a girl in her position could contemplate marrying a man in his.

Matters were in this state when an event of a totally different kind occurred, which filled Anne with a distressful excitement, and for a time occupied her mind to the exclusion of all else. To understand this we must go back a little in our narrative.

She had not been long at St Pols before she realized that all was not well in the household. There was a feeling of strain in the atmosphere, normally hidden; but which revealed itself on special occasions. Soon she discovered that it lay in the relations between her uncle and aunt.

Before moving to Kelwyn House Anne had had few contacts with Charles Savory, though the little she had seen of him she had not liked. Now she began to learn how objectionable he really was. Selfish and overbearing, his manners could be, and often were, atrocious. He was exacting and irascible, quick to take offence, and quicker to give it. But worse than all these, there was in his nature a strain of pure malice. He seemed to enjoy wounding others, and it particularly pleased him if he could twist their actions to their own undoing.

At home his chief butt was his wife. For some time after Anne's arrival he had evidently put a check on himself and veiled his remarks, and it was only on thinking them over afterwards that she saw their true hurtfulness. But as he got accustomed to her presence he grew less careful, and often she blushed at the way he spoke. Her Aunt Doris handled him well. She never showed injury or resentment, but answered in a cool and often joking way, not seldom giving as good as she got.

At first Anne imagined that her aunt did not really mind these encounters, but as she grew to know her better, she found she was wrong. Gradually she saw that beneath the surface Doris Savory was miserably unhappy. In fact, she loathed her husband, and her marriage was a hateful bond. But she was always loyal to him, a matter, Anne supposed, of her own pride.

So things stood when the event took place which so much distressed and excited Anne. It was in the late summer, an afternoon of heavy and somnolent heat. There was a haze in the air which suggested a coming storm. Anne's head had ached wearily all day, and after lunch, her work finished, she decided to go out with a book to the garden. She carried her deckchair to a sheltered place in the orchard which she had discovered and which she alone frequented, sat down, and opened her book.

But she was too lazy to read. She lay back in the chair, enjoying the shade and the relaxation. Presently the expected happened and she fell asleep. Then suddenly she was awake with all her senses alert.

The chair was close to the hedge dividing the orchard from a small spinney included in the property, a bit of heathland which the various Kelwyn House owners had had the good sense to leave in its primitive wildness. There was a small gate connecting the two, but it was farther down the hedge. Coming from the spinney were voices, low, but urgent and passionate and perfectly distinct.

"My dear," she heard a man's baritone, "we can't go on like this. Let me speak to Savory. That'll bring the thing to a head."

Anne felt embarrassed, listening to something she was not intended to hear. She glanced about her anxiously. To reveal her presence or to continue to listen seemed equally out of the question. Yet she dared not try to creep from the place lest a cracking twig should give her away. She was just about to cough discreetly when a woman replied, and instantly she felt frozen with horror. It was her aunt.

"Bertram, dear, there's no use. He'd never agree. A divorce would make me happy; therefore he wouldn't have one."

"Then, dear, don't let's ask for one. Come away with me as you are. We'll go abroad and start life afresh."

The voices were moving slowly along the hedge. Anne breathed more freely. In a moment they would be out of earshot.

"It would be no good," came her aunt's voice again. "You know that yourself, dear. We'd be happy for a time, but in those circumstances it wouldn't last."

"I know it's not what I'd like to offer you, but it would be better than this. Come now, Doris, let's try for a divorce. If you get it, then everything's all right: if you don't, then let's go abroad without it."

Though Anne heard the murmur of her aunt's reply, she could no longer distinguish the words. The man's voice rumbled again and there was silence. After a judicious interval Anne tiptoed softly away.

It was not till she was in the shelter of her own room that she allowed herself to think. Her Aunt Doris! That quiet, kindly, matter-of-fact woman who had been so good to her and of whom she had become so fond! The last person she would have expected to have such a secret in her life! What depths of hope and fear and misery people hid beneath unruffled exteriors!

The man's voice had sounded familiar, though at first Anne had been unable to place him. But now she remembered who he was: a Mr Bertram Forrester, St Pols' leading solicitor. He acted for her uncle and she had frequently written to him, though only once had she actually met him. She had then taken a fancy to him. Tall, long-faced and thoughtful looking, he had been unassuming, polite and quietly kind. What a really nice pair he and her aunt were, and what a happy marriage they might make, if only her disagreeable uncle were out of the way!

She could not see the solution of their difficulty, but as to her own course she had no doubt. She must simply forget what she had learnt. No unguarded word or look must ever betray that she knew their secret.

Another event which was profoundly to modify Anne's life, followed hard on this distressing experience. It began with the receipt by Charles Savory of a politely worded note marked "Confidential". It was on Labour Exchange paper and was signed "R Vane", and in it the young man said that he was writing privately to give Mr Savory advanced information that owing to an adjustment of the age limit his chauffeur, Kellow, was now liable for National Service and would shortly be called up. An official intimation would be sent in due course, but he hoped this earlier advice might minimize Mr Savory's inconvenience.

When Anne saw the letter, she thought how nice and kind of Vane! But her uncle looked at it in a different light. He took the note as a twofold personal insult: first, that his chauffeur should not be considered as doing sufficiently important national service where he was, and secondly, that Vane should take it upon himself to write about it. As he thought of his wrongs and Vane's iniquities he grew absolutely livid with rage.

"Wanting to do the big fellow over me!" he stormed. "Thinking I'll be inconvenienced and gloating over it! Conceited young puppy! Got swollen head because he was noticed over that blessed committee! I'll get him taught his place! He'll find St Pols too hot to hold him before he's a week older!"

Anne had never seen her uncle in such a fury. She grew seriously alarmed lest he should burst a blood vessel. He went out storming, and though Vane would never say what happened, she believed he had gone to the Labour Exchange and made a scene.

Whatever action he took, if any, had no effect. In due course the official intimation came that Kellow was to go, and Savory had to accept the inevitable.

All the same Savory scored, though unexpectedly. Shortly before the date of leaving, Kellow developed a weakness in a lung, and though he remained able to drive Savory, the doctor held back his call for several months.

The respite did nothing to dispel Savory's grudge against Vane. It was this hatred indeed which caused Anne's first definite unpleasantness with her uncle. Somehow he had learnt that she was meeting the young man and he tackled her about it.

"Look here," he shouted, "what's this I hear about you running after that young rip? You let him alone! If you must play the fool, keep to people in your own walk of life!"

It was not only the rudeness of this speech which hurt Anne. Its complete injustice infuriated her much more: not only the false insinuation as to her own conduct, but also the reference to Vane. It was true that Vane was in a subordinate position and badly off according to her uncle's standards, but he was highly educated, had excellent manners and was truly upright and good-hearted. Anne believed him easily the equal of anyone at Kelwyn House.

"I'll be friends with him if I want to," she retorted, quite sharply for her. "He has at least one advantage; he's a gentleman."

Her uncle had snorted and dropped the subject. She thought her shot had gone home, for he was more polite when they met at dinner.

Their next disagreement was more serious. Vane lived with his mother on the outskirts of St Pols, and early in their acquaintance he asked Anne to go home with him and meet the old lady. Anne agreed to go to tea on the next Saturday afternoon.

She did not exactly mean to keep the matter a secret, though she did not speak of it. Somehow her uncle got wind of her plan. Just as she was getting ready to go, he called her and handed her a bundle of pencilled notes.

"Look here," he said, "I want these put into shape and typed out. When can I have them?"

"You don't want them today, I suppose?" she asked.

"Yes, I do," he retorted aggressively. "I want them now. At least before six."

Anne felt that she had reached a turning point in her life. She knew all about the notes and that he did not really require them for several days, and she also knew that if she failed to assert herself, her future life at Kelwyn House would be a long drawn-out misery. She summoned all her resolution.

"I'm sorry, uncle. I've promised to go out to tea. If I had known about this I shouldn't have done it, but it's too late to break my appointment now."

He seemed amazed at her temerity.

"You mean," he went on threateningly, "that when you want to go gadding about, my work must take second place?"

"Of course not, uncle. I mean that when I make an appointment with other people on my free afternoon, I can't let them down unless there's a real emergency."

"Suggesting this is not one?"

She knew she was on shaky ground, but she felt he was bluffing and determined to call his bluff.

"You know the notes aren't really wanted till Mr Spender comes on Wednesday," she hazarded. "But if you wish to look over them, I'll do them when I come back. You can have them about nine."

He grunted vindictively, but she saw that her stand had shaken him and he made no further attempt to prevent her going. On her return she typed the notes, but though she left them for him before the nine o'clock news, she knew for a fact that he didn't look at them that night.

Some months later Kellow's lung had so much improved that the doctor certified him fit and he received a second notice to leave. Once again Savory indulged in a paroxysm of fury, and this time there was something so sinister and threatening in his manner that Anne felt actually frightened. Presently she found her intuition had not misled her.

Two days later he put his head into the room where she was typing.

"You can pack up and go at the end of the month," he told her brutally. "I've got a new secretary."

For a moment she couldn't believe her ears, but with evident enjoyment her uncle proceeded to give corroborative details.

"I'm losing my chauffeur as you may have heard," he said with an evil smile, "and what with the labour shortage and this and that, I can't get another man. So I've had to get a woman, curse it! But she's a trained secretary also, so she'll do your work as well as Kellow's. She'll come when Kellow's called up, so you can go then."

Anne at once realized that this was his way of getting his own back on Vane, whom he still believed to be the cause of his annoyance. She longed to be able to thank him for nothing and tell him she would go that day, but she just couldn't afford to. Her pocket-money had been so small that she had been unable to save more than a very few pounds, and she had nowhere to go and no other means of supporting herself. She simply must stay where she was while she looked round for other work.

She did her best to keep her end up, answering shortly that that would suit her all right, as she was tired of the place and for some time had been considering giving him notice. But when with a somewhat puzzled look he withdrew, her strength evaporated and she burst into a flood of tears.

She was touched and heartened by her aunt's distress. Doris Savory had grown really fond of Anne and more and more had made a companion of her. Both for her own sake and the girl's she looked forward with dismay to the parting.

"Whatever will you do, my dear?" she said as they talked it over. "Have you any plans?"

"I might try for some of the services again," Anne replied. "Also I thought I'd ask Reggie Vane if he knew of anything. I'm a lot stronger than I was, you know."

"Well, whatever happens, you'll be all right for money. Don't let that fear weigh on your mind. I haven't much, but I've enough to share with you, and when you make your fortune you can repay me."

Upon this they kissed each other and wept a little, and Anne felt much comforted.

She rang up Vane and that evening they took a walk along the shore while she told him her news and asked his help. Two minutes later she was listening to an impassioned proposal of marriage.

"If it hadn't been for this," he went on, "I don't believe I'd have squeezed up enough courage to ask you. There's first your position: so much better than mine. Then there's – "

"So much better," she mocked with a tender smile. "Merely penniless and out of work."

"That's only passing," he went on seriously, "and anyhow I shouldn't take advantage of it. But there's something even more serious: I couldn't give you what you're accustomed to."

"My dear," she interrupted, but he went on: "You see, my mother has a little money, but not enough to live on, and I have to help her. That would leave enough, to get on with, but things would be very tight. Could you face it, Anne?"

To Anne it seemed a glimpse into heaven. Guiltily she told herself that to encumber him with a wife at this stage in his career would only drag him down, then she was swept off her feet. She found herself sobbing in his arms.

They presently went to his home and told Mrs Vane, and her reception of the news almost made Anne weep again.

"I'm absolutely delighted," she declared, kissing Anne warmly. "It's what I knew he wanted, but I scarcely dared to hope that it would come about."

On the following evening they met again at his house and went into a committee of ways and means. Reggie was anxious for the marriage to take place at once, and for Anne to come and live at his mother's. But Anne would not agree and Mrs Vane backed her up.

"More marriages have been wrecked by that than by anything else," she declared, though Anne wondered how she knew. "Anne's quite right, she must have a home of her own. But I'll tell you what we'll do: I've thought it all out since last night. I'll go and join up with Maisie Wynn, you know she's looking for someone to share that flat she's got. Then you two can have this house."

Though both the young people cried out at this, Mrs Vane insisted, and as it really did seem a solution satisfactory to all parties, the proposal was carried *nem. con.* But when next day Mrs Vane called to make inquiries, a hitch developed. Miss Wynn had just let her rooms for three months. She was full of regrets, declaring that at the end of the time nothing would please her more than to have her old friend.

"It seems to me that's all right as far as you two are concerned," Mrs Vane went on. "You'd do better for at least a three months' engagement, and you needn't be married till the house is ready. The only question is what Anne's to do in the meantime."

It was then that Vane remembered that the local gas manager was looking for a secretary to replace a girl who had been called up. Anne went to see him, was appointed, and with Mrs Vane's help found a comfortable room in the town. Contrary to the usual experience, her salary proved better than she had expected and the room more reasonable, and she calculated that by the end of three months she would have saved quite a useful sum.

It was while matters were in this state, shortly before Anne was due to leave her uncle's, that Joshua Radlett's death occurred. It upset Anne, for she had known and liked the old man and was good friends with the Wedgewoods and Littles. But her mind was too full of her own affairs to let it make the deep impression on her it otherwise might.

6

CAPTAIN ARTHUR ROLLO

Major-General Sir John Weston KCB, KCMG, DSO, turned to the good-looking young woman in the ATS uniform who was driving him.

"In there," he pointed.

She deftly swung the car into a gateway which bore on its pillars the name Kelwyn House. Passing up the narrow, curving drive, she came gently to a stop before the porch to which it led.

General Weston was about to sacrifice himself on the altar of social convention. This was the residence of Charles Savory, and Weston had been asked to lunch. He had known Savory for many years and detested him through all of them, but as commander of the troops in the neighbourhood he felt it would be impolitic to refuse the invitation of one of its most influential residents.

Normally the visit might have been paid and the general might have returned to his headquarters without anything of the slightest importance to any other person resulting. But it happened that during lunch Savory made a remark which unwittingly crystallized a train of thought which had already been passing through his guest's mind. This in its turn produced action, and that action profoundly affected the lives of a number of people in St Pols, the Wedgewoods, the Littles and Anne Meredith among the number.

After greetings and some desultory conversation the talk turned on the recent army manoeuvres, and when this had been adequately discussed, not without acid criticism from Savory, it passed on to the inquest on Joshua Radlett. Savory, his guest soon learnt, felt strongly about the tragedy. To his amazement the general also learnt that he himself was not considered free from blame in the matter.

"We may thank your fellows for it," Savory declared with heat. "Damned carelessness. I might have been killed."

Weston, in the face of this unexpected attack, fought a delaying action while regrouping his forces. "My dear fellow! he expostulated. "Do think of what you're saying! That's too serious a matter to joke about."

"Joke be damned," returned Savoury rudely. "You wouldn't think it funny if it had happened to you."

"But," essayed the general, attempting a reconnaissance in force, "it didn't happen to you."

"No thanks to your lot. It might just as well have been me as old Radlett."

Weston threw in some heavier support. "Bless my soul, I believe you're serious! How can you be? What do you suggest actually happened?"

Savory grunted. "Pretty clear what happened, isn't it? I could have laughed yesterday at the inquest when I heard that ass Vanson reporting about it." He mimicked the inspector. " 'The military authorities assured me that they had used no explosives which would have produced such a crater.' Bah! What did the fool think you people would say?"

"But look here, Savory" – Weston essayed a counter-attack – "joking apart, what do you mean? You're not seriously suggesting that the troops left explosives on the beach?"

"Then what happened? Where else could the mine or whatever it was have come from?"

The general pressed his advantage. "Where do most mines that are found on the shore come from?"

"Ah," said Savory, stabbing in the air with his finger, "that cat won't jump. That was dealt with at the inquest too. The mines you're speaking of are large. If it had been one of them, there'd have been a hole the size of a house and half the windows in the place would be out. This was something quite small. No, Weston, you can't get out of it. It must have been one of your land-mines."

Savory seemed to have recovered his temper, and Weston, who had found the exchange embarrassing in the presence of Mrs Savory and Miss Meredith, felt relieved.

"I can't have such carelessness planted on the army," he said good-humouredly. "Must stand up for my own men, you know." He smiled at the ladies.

"Had you no mines at the exercises?" Savory persisted.

This question put Weston's back up more than all that had gone before it. The infernal impertinence of the man! It was a suggestion that his personal word was insufficient. It took a considerable effort, but he succeeded in answering pleasantly enough: "Only practice ones, unfortunately for your theories."

"Practice ones, eh? There was one feller in that jury that was no fool. He argued you'd got 'em mixed. Bet you ten to one in guineas it's what happened."

Weston made a determined effort to close the subject. "I'm not taking you, Savory," he said firmly, "for two reasons. First, I couldn't prove they weren't, and second, you couldn't prove they were, so we'd be unlikely to reach a conclusion. How charming your tulips are, Mrs Savory."

Though Weston felt that these insinuations were merely the product of Savory's spiteful mind, he was worried by them. He had hoped that the rejection of such a possibility at the inquest might have meant that it could be ignored. Now he feared that this would be impossible. What Savory suggested was by no means as absurd as he had pretended. The troops had been using practice mines, buried in the sand. These went off with noise and smoke, but harmlessly. Was it impossible that by some mistake a live one had been issued with the others? Was it out of the question that one such had been left there by the recovery party?

Weston indeed was so worried that when he returned to headquarters he called his adjutant and quartermaster.

"I've just been lunching with Charles Savory," he told them. "I don't know if you've met him?"

Both, it appeared, had done so.

"Then you'll know who he is and what he's like. He blames us for that accident on the shore, insists that we got our mines mixed up and left a live one buried beside that groyne. He was quite hot about it, said he might easily have stepped on it instead of old Radlett. Indicated that that would have been a much more serious matter for the nation."

His subordinates laughed. "Entirely characteristic, I should say, sir," answered the adjutant, Raikes. "He's delighted when he finds a really offensive remark."

"I agree with Raikes, sir," added Hamilton, the quartermaster. "If you had been head of the Home Guard he would have told you it was caused by the grenades you failed to look after."

Weston nodded. "I fancy you're both correct, but quite apart from anything Savory says or thinks, I'm not too happy about the affair. I wish I were more certain that what he suggests could not be the truth. We all know how easy it is to make a mistake, and we all know" – he smiled crookedly – "that if a mistake was made, the person responsible isn't going to broadcast it."

"The stock of mines came out right, sir," said Hamilton. "It was checked over after the exercise."

"But not by you personally?"

"No, sir, but Milman, who did it, is a very reliable man."

General Weston hesitated. "I think for my own satisfaction I should like the matter to be gone into. Savory will certainly repeat the story. Probably other people will also. There will be talk and the army will get the credit. Questions may be asked in the House. Not, of course, that any of that matters, but I should like to be in a position to give the tale an authoritative denial."

"I quite understand, sir," Hamilton answered. "You wish me to check up everything personally? I'll get on with it at once."

"I'm afraid I want a little more than merely checking the stock. I want that of course, but I also want discreet inquiries made among the men. Who laid mines and where? Were any placed near this groyne? Did any live ones go up? All sorts of questions. I doubt if you could do it, Hamilton. I think it would be a whole-time job for someone."

"Might I suggest Rollo, sir?" put in Raikes.

"As a matter of fact, it was Rollo I had in mind. You might send him in and I'll have a word with him and then turn him over to you two."

Captain Arthur Rollo was a recent recruit to the army. In civil life he was a specimen of the new police. A graduate of Hendon College, he had served for some time as a constable at Scotland Yard. Sir Mortimer Ellison, the Assistant Commissioner, thinking he seemed a likely lad, had given him his chance. He had sent him out as assistant to Chief Inspector French on a murder case: that which became known as the Elton Case, at Chalfont, near Dorkford, Surrey. Having made good, French reported favourably upon him, and his temporary rank of sergeant was confirmed.

Just after this case ended the War Office applied to Scotland Yard for a number of young officers to undertake certain secret service work of a military character. Among those sent was Sergeant Rollo. Before he could be of use it was necessary that he could learn the rudiments of army life. For this purpose he was given the temporary rank of captain and drafted from company to company, so as to get in touch with as many branches of the services as possible. He had recently been sent to the St Pols camp as assistant to the adjutant, so that without going abroad he should see the war machine in action, in as far as the invasion manoeuvres illustrated it.

A moment later Rollo entered the room, and saluting smartly, stood to attention before the general's desk.

He was a personable young fellow enough. While not in the least handsome, he looked straight and eager and clean in body and mind. A steadiness in his eye and a certain massiveness of his chin suggested character. His record since joining up had been admirable.

Weston leant back in his chair. "I want to talk to you, Rollo. How are you liking your work here?"

"Very much indeed, thank you, sir. It's most interesting."

"You can find your way about in the army?"

"I think so, sir. I've learnt a lot since I came."

"Well, I hope you have, for I want you to do a special job for me; the kind of work that you're supposed to be training for."

The young man's face glowed. "Yes, sir," he said smartly.

"I suppose you heard of the explosion on the beach at St Pols Bay two days ago when an old gentleman named Radlett was killed?"

"Yes, sir. I heard of it, but not in detail."

"I want you to find out just what happened. It's being said that it was caused by a mine which we buried and failed to recover, and I should like to know what position to take up about it. Follow?"

"I quite understand, sir."

"You'll continue, of course, to work under Major Raikes. Report to him now what I've told you. One word more. Keep your inquiries as quiet as you can. I don't want it to be thought that I have taken these rumours seriously."

The general nodded to show that the interview was over, and Rollo, again saluting, left the presence.

His feelings were mixed as he went to find Raikes. About his new job he was wholly delighted. He had rather resented being drafted into the army as a non-combatant. If he had to leave the Yard at all, he would have preferred the Air Force. The life of a fighter pilot appealed strongly to him. But the powers that be were decided that a man with his training would be lost in any line but his own. He had therefore to put up with months of learning army organization and routine, ten per cent of which he found interesting and the remainder deadly dull.

This job would once again test his powers and give him scope for initiative and resource. That was the part of the general's directions which delighted him, but their sting was in the tail. If he had to work under Raikes' orders, he would get nowhere. Raikes was a good fellow. He had been extraordinarily kind and helpful, and personally Rollo liked him immensely, but he knew nothing about detection. His interference would mean Rollo's failure.

But Rollo soon found he had underestimated the major's insight.

"In this job," Raikes told him, "I'm afraid you won't get much help from me: it's outside my line. You'll have to do everything for yourself, so you'll have a completely free hand. All I want is to know where you are."

"I understand, sir."

"You may find it hard to get the information you want from other units, and if so, come to me and I'll give you a chit. That clear?"

"Yes, sir; thank you very much."

"Right. Oh, one other point, though I don't fancy you need to be reminded of it. Avoid raising bad feeling. Inquiries like this could easily stir up a hornets' nest. See that that doesn't happen."

When Rollo left the room his tempered pleasure had given place to undiluted satisfaction. Here was his chance in the army! If he did well now he would probably be transferred at once to that military secret service work for which he had been called up, and this tedious period of preparation would be over. While he hoped to succeed for his own sake and that of his future career, this was by no means his only desire. He felt himself the standard-bearer of the Yard in the midst of an alien service, and he wished to uphold it with honour. Nor did he want to let Chief Inspector French down. He had a profound respect and admiration for French, who had not only recommended him for his present job, but whose goodness during that Chalfont case he could not easily forget.

His thoughts turned eagerly to the job itself. At least there could be no doubt as to how he must start. The first thing must be to find out what was already known of the affair. Reporting his movements to Major Raikes, he went into St Pols and bought copies of the local papers. Then over a cup of tea in a restaurant he proceeded to study all that had been reported of the case. Feeling that he had got the general hang of things, he went to the police-station and asked for Sergeant Cundy.

His uniform and rank assured him of immediate and respectful attention, and when Cundy understood that he wished to discuss the Radlett tragedy he said that Inspector Vanson, who had been handling the case, was at the station, and ushered him into a small office at the back of the building.

"Good afternoon, sir," said Vanson, standing up. "If you will tell me what you want to know, I shall be glad to give you any information in my power."

Rollo took the indicated chair.

"Thank you, Mr Vanson. But I'm afraid you mustn't call me sir. In fact, that's the way I should address you. Will you please keep a secret?" He grinned broadly and handed over his official police card. Vanson's shrewd face expressed surprise.

"I wanted to go into the Air Force," Rollo explained, "but they wouldn't have me at any price. I'm now learning about how they run the army, and they tell me I'm to do military secret service, whatever that is. But in the meantime I've been ordered to look into this affair from the army point of view. I'd like to tell you in confidence all I know. It seems that the army has got the blame for planting the mine that went up, and General Weston wants to know if he can deny it."

"I'll be glad to help you as best I can," Vanson repeated, tactfully omitting any form of address. "What would you like first?" He picked up a file and turned over the pages. "Here are Sergeant Cundy's notes of what he found and the statements he took at the time, and here are some photographs we got before the tide rose. Here" – he turned again – "are the depositions taken at the inquest, and here are our conclusions and reports. There are also some bits of the mine which Cundy picked up."

"Terribly good of you," returned Rollo, also avoiding a form of address. "I'd like to read these over, if I shouldn't be in your way."

"Not in the least," said Vanson. "You can sit here, and anything you want you've only to ask for. Cundy, clear that table for Captain Rollo and set out your exhibits on the corner of it."

Rollo soon made himself familiar with the contents of the file. Then he turned to the exhibits. These consisted of four small objects. There was the rusty nut of a three-eighths inch bolt, a small brass pillar some inch or more long by about three-sixteenths diameter with a hole and a broken screw at one end, a curved bit of thin bakelite like part of the shell of a nut, and a torn bit of tin some six inches square tacked on to a piece of board. For some moments Rollo pondered over the collection, then he turned to Vanson.

"I should like to ask a question. I see from the photographs that the sand driven out from the crater fell on the beach all round it, of course as was to be expected. Was this fallen sand dug over to see if it contained any other objects?"

Vanson shook his head and Cundy looked annoyed. "I'm afraid not," said the former. "You think it worth it?"

Rollo saw he was on treacherous ground. He summoned all his tact. "I was just wondering, Mr Vanson. What do you think?"

Vanson considered. "I'm not sure that it mightn't be," he presently admitted. "When we went into it the question of blame hadn't arisen. Now the conditions are altered. Perhaps we shouldn't neglect the chance."

He was obviously saving his face, but Rollo was wise enough not to see this. He pretended a naïve pleasure that his idea was considered valuable, and asked would Vanson do the work or should he get men from the camp.

"We'll do it," Vanson answered, evidently not wishing discoveries to be made by another investigator. "Let's see, it's low water about six in the morning. We'll go out when it gets light and we'll have finished before anyone's about."

"Splendid! Any objection to my joining you?"

"Of course not. Delighted to see you."

Shortly before five next morning Rollo left the camp and walked down to St Pols Bay. The sun had just risen, though the sky was overcast. The day promised to be fine, but rain had fallen earlier and the breeze blowing in from the sea was raw and cold.

Rollo reached Groyne Point as Vanson approached from the opposite direction, followed by two constables armed with shovels and a rake. Vanson began by explaining that the Chief Constable would like a word with Rollo and that he would be at the station all the afternoon, if Rollo would call. The four men then walked down the shore to the end of the groyne. The sand stretched away smooth and unbroken in every direction.

"Here's about where the centre of the crater was," Vanson pointed. "Not much trace of it left now."

"My word, no!" Rollo answered despondently. "Looks as if we're late. Everything must have been washed away by now."

"You can't tell," Vanson returned. "If there was anything heavy it would sink in the sand."

"Let's dig round a bit in any case."

They began at the groyne and worked back over where the crater had been. It was not long before one of the men gave a shout and held up a small object. It was of iron or steel, recently deposited for the coating of rust was fresh. It consisted of a spindle about three inches long by quarter inch diameter, swelling out into a disk near its centre. This disk was about an inch and a half in diameter by an eighth of an inch thick. The whole thing was like a piston whose rod passed through it and out at both ends of the cylinder. Vanson laid it aside for later examination.

Three more bits of tin-covered wood were quickly found. One of these was a corner, and showed that the tin was on the outside. It looked to Rollo as if a wooden box had been covered with tin which had been soldered air tight.

For some time they made no more discoveries, then just as they were about to give up the shovel was caught by a long, thin black line. At first Rollo thought it was a stalk of seaweed, then he saw it was a rubber-covered electric flex.

"Good Lord, it's been worth it after all!" he exclaimed. "Can we have it dug out, Mr Vanson, so as not to tear off anything it may be fastened to?"

Vanson, who for some time had been looking bored and slightly resentful, once again took energetic charge. He superintended the removal of the sand till the entire flex was uncovered.

It was of considerable length, nearly thirty feet, and it stretched away towards the south-west. The end next to the crater was torn as if from the explosion, but the other end was fastened to what looked like the broken remains of an electric light plug. One brass pillar and a bit of the bakelite casing remained, and Rollo saw at once that the pillar and scrap of bakelite found originally by Cundy might well have belonged to this plug.

The find stimulated their interest, and for some time they continued digging, but except for two more nuts, they uncovered nothing further.

"That flex surely should be some help to us," Rollo said when at last Vanson called off his men. "If you agree, Mr Vanson, I'd like to show it to some of our technical people. They might recognize it at once."

"Good idea," Vanson approved, "and if you'd like the other exhibits and a set of photographs, you're welcome to them."

For his purpose Rollo thought a Major Humphries would be the best man, and after breakfast he rang him up asking for a confidential interview. A little later he took the exhibits over to his office.

"I've been ordered, sir, to go into this matter and report," and he explained the circumstances. "The police inspector and I wondered if from these finds you could tell us what sort of explosive went up?"

Major Humphries examined the flex. "It's a new one on me," he said, "if this flex had anything to do with it. I know of no mine nor shell in which anything like it is used. What's more, I don't see what it could be for. And the same applies to this spindle." He turned to the nuts. "These might be used in a mine, but it doesn't seem to me very likely. If they belonged to one, where are the bolts? I mean, the detonation would tear the bolts in two; it wouldn't unscrew the nuts."

"I follow you, sir," Rollo said hesitatingly. "It's certainly a bit of a puzzle."

"It may not be such a puzzle as you suggest," Humphries returned. "You're assuming those came out of whatever went up. But did they? From what you tell me, it doesn't seem to follow."

"But, sir, where else could they have come from?"

"Well, I don't know: that's not my pigeon. But couldn't the old man have been carrying them? Taking a lamp or some electrical gadget to the village for repairs?"

This was a new idea to Rollo. It was certainly a possibility, and yet it seemed strange that if Radlett had had something of the kind, no one had mentioned it. Then again he thought that there was no reason why anyone should.

At all events this was the first thing to find out, and after leaving Major Humphries he went to see the Wiltons and Maude Wedgewood. Here the information was conclusive. Wilton had seen his employer start, and he had certainly taken no electrical gadget of any kind with him, and Mrs Wedgewood was equally certain that when she met him he was carrying nothing but a stick.

Rollo felt somewhat mystified. He was convinced that the flex was connected with the explosion; but how? The interview with Major Humphries had been a bitter disappointment. He had expected help which he had not received. Humphries was supposed to be a pretty know-ledgeable person, but he had made no suggestions. All the same Rollo must get his information. Was there anyone else he could ask?

He felt his isolation keenly. At the Yard when one was up against a technical difficulty one did not hesitate, one went to an expert. There was a file of specialists covering every conceivable department of knowledge. But here, since Humphries had failed him, there was no one.

It did not take him long to reach a decision. Ringing up the Yard, he fixed up an appointment with the required specialist for the following morning. In the afternoon he called on the Chief Constable, who, he discovered, did not really want to see him at all. Lastly he took the evening train for Paddington.

Colonel Crosby, to whom he was sent at the War Office, was a big man with a heavy, inscrutable face and eyes alive with intelligence. He studied Rollo for a moment and then said: "Good morning. Are you Captain or Sergeant Rollo?"

Rollo smiled. "Sergeant, sir, at Scotland Yard. Temporary captain in the Southshires. I'm here from the Yard as sergeant."

"Very well, sergeant; sit down there and tell me what I can do for you."

"Thank you, sir. It's to show you some articles which were found after an explosion, and to ask if you could tell what sort of appliance, mine or shell or otherwise, they came from. I should like to tell you the circumstances, if you could spare the time?"

"Go ahead."

As concisely as he could Rollo related what had happened, and then produced his photographs and exhibits. Colonel Crosby seemed interested. He heard the story with attention and examined the exhibits carefully. Then for some time he sat in thought.

"I at least agree with your Major Humphries on one point," he said at last. "These exhibits are not from any form of explosive known to me."

Rollo, half thrilled and half disappointed, wondered if this was all he was going to learn. "No, sir?" he said rather inanely.

Colonel Crosby did not seem to notice his inadequacy. "What do the local people think about it? The coroner and the police?"

"They can't account for it, sir, but at the inquest three possibilities were discussed: a mine washed in from the sea, the land-mines that I'm interested in, and some of the grenades stolen from the Home Guard."

"As a matter of fact, were mines buried in the sand for the manoeuvres?"

"Yes, sir, though not at this point. But I'm assured that no live mines went out of stock and that all the practice ones were accounted for."

"Have you gone into this yourself?"

"Not yet, sir. It would give a lot of trouble to all concerned, and I thought that if I could get proof it was due to something else, it might not be needed."

"Let me have the trouble instead of you, eh?" A twinkle in the keen eyes made this innocuous.

He turned again to the exhibits. "Well, let's see if these give us anything. Suppose we take them in turn. This spindle with the disk. Might have been used for a variety of purposes, perhaps some kind of trip. Impossible to say without further information." He put it down and turned to the nuts. "I agree again with Major Humphries about the nuts. It's quite true that nuts are used in certain mines, but never without bolts. But nuts without bolts, Sergeant Rollo: that's something for you to think over."

"Yes, sir," Rollo answered, trying to keep the eagerness out of his voice.

"And those pieces of tin," Crosby went on slowly, "came from no Government arsenal."

Positive excitement was rising in Rollo's mind. He strove hard to appear normal.

"A German shop, sir?"

"Most unlikely. The Germans do as good work as we do."

"I meant through shortage of materials?"

Colonel Crosby shook his head. "We've no reason to suppose they're as short as that. Well, never mind. Come on to the flex." He fingered it absently. "Several types of mine are, of course, detonated electrically by means of connecting wires, but I know of none with fittings of this kind. You say you're positive the dead man was not carrying the flex?"

"The evidence is extremely strong. It convinced me."

"Quite. And I presume the presence of the flex apart from the explosion could not be assumed?"

Rollo hesitated. "Of course, sir, we only have the probabilities. But it would be a pretty extreme coincidence if it were brought to that place at that time in connection with anything else."

Crosby cocked an eye at him. "So I should think," he said dryly, "and if so, we seem forced to the conclusion it was used for the purpose of bringing about the explosion."

Rollo did not quite know how to take this, but his excitement grew still stronger.

"You mean, sir, that Mr Radlett, let us say, caught his foot in the flex and so put the thing up?"

"No," returned Crosby, "I didn't mean that. I mean that someone was at the other end of the flex and sent a current through it at the critical moment. In other words, Sergeant Rollo" – he spoke more crisply – "I think you're investigating a murder."

At last it had been put into words! Rollo no longer tried to hide his feelings. This was what had been in his mind from the first, but he simply had not dared to hope that anything so splendid would come his way. A murder case! And his own, for seeing that he had begun so well, they would surely let him finish it! Well, there was something to be said for joining the army after all! He would never have had such luck at the Yard.

Colonel Crosby was looking at him curiously. "Not a new idea to you?" he asked.

Rollo pulled himself together. "I had wondered if it might be that, sir," he answered a little sheepishly.

"And not so displeased either? Oh, well, I suppose one man's meat will always be another man's poison. You think you'll be put in charge?"

Rollo grinned. "I am in charge, sir, and I shall require a good deal more information before being in a position to report."

Crosby's heavy face took on the semblance of a smile. "Then good luck," he grunted unexpectedly, "and if you want anything more, don't hesitate to come back to me."

With a feeling of warm pleasure Rollo found his way out of the great building and returned to the Yard.

7

CAPTAIN ARTHUR ROLLO

Though another officer had dealt with his request for technical advice, Rollo felt that he could not be at the Yard and not see his old chief, Joseph French. French had been engaged when he had called on arrival that morning, but now when Rollo rang him up, he was told to come right along upstairs.

French was seated at his desk examining with a lens some photographs of the print of a man's shoe. He glanced up.

"Hullo, my doughty warrior! I thought you'd have mopped up the Germans by this time. Like to see a good print?"

He pointed to a chair and pushed over the photographs. "Nice bit of boarding, that," he went on. "Bet you can't tell me what it is?"

The print was that of a rubber sole on a floor of narrow boards with fine joints. Everything was extraordinarily clear, though the wood under the lens showed countless tiny scrapes in every direction. Rollo shook his head.

"That's the bridge of His Majesty's ship *Blanche*, formerly the Earl of Sorroway's private yacht. An unusual case. She was lying two nights ago in a certain harbour on the east coast – that's the way we talk in war-time, you understand – with all watches and sentries set or posted or whatever they do. Nothing was seen during the night, but in the morning the skipper was found knifed in his bed and a rather useful codebook had vanished from his safe."

"My word, sir! You've got a job there all right."

"Nothing to the Admiralty's," French returned with his old twinkle showing in his eye. "They're all het up about their watches and their sentries. You see, owing to the washing of the decks no footprint was found, and now they're dancing to know how this piece of it was missed. But there," French pushed the photographs aside, "enough of other people's troubles. Let me hear yours. How did you find old Crosby?"

"Very helpful and decent."

"You did, did you? Then you've got on the right side of him. It's not always the tale I hear. Well, go ahead. What's your worry?"

Sure of a sympathetic hearing, Rollo plunged into his story with eagerness. French seemed interested.

"You certainly seem to be on to something there," he commented. "Any reason why anybody should want old Radlett out of the way?"

"He was a well-to-do bloke and I suppose he had an heir. But I haven't gone into that yet. Until now I couldn't assume it was murder."

"Well, that'll be your next line, or one of them. In fact, you've a good many lines to work on. Let's see now, have you formed a theory?"

Rollo looked somewhat dashed. "I'm afraid, sir, not a very satisfactory one. I thought that somebody, wishing to kill Radlett, had stolen the grenades from the Home Guard. I assumed he had taken the grenades to pieces and made a bomb or mine out of a wooden box, covered it with tin to keep it dry, and put in a lot of nuts to act as shrapnel. That seemed easy enough, but I couldn't get any further. There are two main difficulties and I can't see the way out of either. First, how was the mine put up? And second, how was it timed to get Radlett?"

"If what Crosby says is true, someone sent a current down that flex at the proper moment."

"But that's just it: no one did. There was no one near the place at that time."

French considered this. "Perhaps that other fellow – What was his name again?"

"Savory."

"Perhaps Savory went back earlier than he said, perhaps by way of meeting Radlett and walking with him. Perhaps he had his battery or magneto somewhere about the groyne and touched it off at the right moment?"

"No, sir, it wasn't that. That other man Little and his friends were looking out of his room. They saw the whole thing. Savory was a couple of hundred yards away at the time."

"Someone may have been hiding about the groyne. It seems to stick up a good way?"

"About three feet."

"Well, couldn't someone have done that? The flex would have reached to the groyne?"

"Yes, the flex was long enough. But here's the funny thing about that. It didn't lie in the direction of the groyne. It stretched away in the opposite direction. The end with the broken plug was in the middle of a perfectly clear space of sand where no one could have hid."

"H'm, there's a difficulty there."

"That's the smallest difficulty, sir. No one could have hid beside or behind the groyne without leaving footprints, and there weren't any. And no one could have got along the top of the groyne without being seen. So I don't see how any other person could have been there."

French laughed. "That's where Sergeant Rollo of the CID comes in. Quite a problem for you."

"But is it so difficult? Must we take what Colonel Crosby said as gospel? Why not stick to what everybody has thought up to the present: that it was a contact mine of some kind and that Radlett set it off himself?"

"Why not indeed? I never suggested that should be given up. But what then arises is: What was the flex for?"

"Could it not have been a trip wire, sticking up out of the sand, and Radlett caught his foot in it?"

"Savory apparently didn't see anything."

"But surely he might have missed it? As a matter of fact, when I saw it first, I thought it was one of those roots of seaweed. He might have thought the same and it therefore made no impression on him."

"But it wasn't on the surface when you saw it?"

"No, sir, one of the men dug it up. But it might have been uncovered at the time of the explosion."

"You may be right," French admitted. "But this is an untidy discussion. You should be systematic: make a list of the ways a mine can be put up and consider them in turn. Put them down in your book and we'll discuss each."

Rollo eagerly agreed. Here was a piece of luck he had never expected. He was getting French's brains and experience, and without losing the credit for whatever he did. He recognized French's kindness trying to help him. Gratefully he wrote down the word *Weight*.

"First, weight, sir. I understand the ordinary land-mine goes up when a weight comes on it. Radlett's foot should be enough."

"How then did Savory fail to put it off?"

"Chance, I suppose: his foot missed it."

"Then your argument about Radlett's money and heirs goes west."

Rollo was disappointed and must have looked it, for French went on: "Never mind, you're only trying to get facts. I don't mean that you should rule out weight, only that you should weigh that difficulty. Rather neat that, I think? Well, what's your second way?"

"What we've already spoken of: a trip of some kind, perhaps a loop of flex."

"Quite. Well, we've seen the difficulty that neither Savory nor Radlett saw it and that – "

"Excuse me, but how do we know that about Radlett?"

"Would he have put his foot into it if he had? Do use your grey cells occasionally."

Rollo grinned. "Sorry, sir."

"The same difficulty crops up as with the weight theory: how Savory came to miss it."

Rollo had grown serious again. "I've noted that. The third possibility we've also dealt with: Colonel Crosby's charge of current along the flex."

"Quite. The flex ended in a clear stretch of sand and there was no one there to send it. Carry on."

"I'm afraid that's all I can think of."

French shook his head. "I'm ashamed of you! You've left out at least three methods. Two I grant you are unlikely, but the third might be possible. I don't know enough about it to say. What? Can't you think of any more?"

" 'Fraid not, sir."

"We'll take the two unlikely ones first. What about a magnetic mine?"

"But Radlett was carrying no metal."

"I said it was unlikely, didn't I? The other was detonation by sound."

Rollo smiled happily. "Savory would have made as much noise as Radlett."

"I said this was unlikely too. But what about wireless?"

Rollo was quite still for a moment. Then he made a quick gesture.

"You've got it, sir! As sure as we're alive, you've got it! Exploded by a radio beam from the shore! That's the ticket!"

French shook his head. "Don't be too cocksure. As I said, I'm not an expert, but I seem to remember that it's a complicated business. When do you go back to Cornwall?"

"One-forty from Paddington."

"Then take my advice and see Rutherford. You know him?"

" 'Fraid not, sir."

"One of our wireless engineers. I'll ring him up. He'll tell you all about it, then when you get down there you'll know what to look for."

"Thank you; that would be fine."

"Then what else? I said you had plenty of lines to work on. Let's hear what you propose?"

Rollo began a new list.

"First, motive. Go into Radlett's affairs and find out who'd benefit by his death."

French nodded.

"Next, who could have known the old boy was going to walk there at that time?"

French held up a warning finger. "Right, but be careful there. It's not who knew that he was going to, but who believed he might? It may not have been the first day someone watched."

"That may include a lot of people. It came out at the inquest that he often did go to the village on fine mornings."

"There you are. Next."

"The theft from the Home Guard: whether anyone interested in Radlett's death could have taken the stuff. I'd want to look into his wireless set and to know where he was at the time of the explosion."

"Right. That's something to be going on with. What about the local police? That chap Vanson. Is he any good?"

"First-rate, I think, and very pleasant to work with."

French nodded approvingly. "That's the stuff. Work with him and not against him. Remember he's the man in charge and you're an outsider. Now you haven't too much time. I'll ring up Rutherford before he goes to lunch. And just one thing more." French's look was almost paternal. "If you're up against it give me a ring – to my house, if you like. Now be off with you."

Rollo was really grateful as he went up to the radio engineer's office. It was just like French. He had been more than good at that Chalfont case and it would be a tremendous stiffener to know he was behind this one.

Rollo began well with the engineer. "I'm terribly sorry, Mr Rutherford, for coming about lunch-time, but I have to catch the one-forty at Paddington and what I want will only take a minute."

Rutherford leant back in a leisurely way. "That's all right. No hurry. Go ahead."

Producing a rough sketch of the locality, Rollo put his question. Once again he succeeded in interesting his host.

"Quite a nice little problem," Rutherford approved. "I'll have to think a bit over it. Let's see now. How far away is your sending station?"

"I'm afraid that's what I don't know. But if the operator was watching Radlett, as he must have been to know when he came to the right place, he couldn't have been very far. Less than half a mile, I should think."

"Half a mile: that's not so bad. And I suppose the person whom you so politely call the operator wouldn't want to build a new aerial: he'd want to use his own?"

Rollo grinned. "I think that goes without saying."

"Very well. Now the first thing is that an aerial would be wanted at the mine, and if the mine was buried in the sand I doubt whether an internal aerial would do. In fact, I'm pretty sure one sticking up in the air would be needed. But quite a short one would be enough, a couple of feet high or even a few inches. Was one found?"

"No, sir."

"Perhaps it wasn't looked for. A wire behind one of the uprights of the groyne would have done."

Rollo stared, then smacked his leg. "That would account for the flex, wouldn't it: to plug in at the bottom of an aerial on the groyne? It was just long enough."

"If you find the aerial, yes," Rutherford returned dryly.

"If it's there I'll find it."

"Unless the operator's been and gone and removed it," Rutherford smiled. "Now here's something else. You'd also want a source of electric power in the mine."

Rollo's face fell. "That wouldn't be so easy. A battery? Would a battery last out?"

"Depends on when it was put in."

"It would have to be before the previous tide: there were no marks on the sand."

"How long altogether?"

"High water was about nine that morning and this place would have been uncovered about eight. But the work would surely have been done before daylight. I should say five or six hours must have elapsed before the explosion."

"H'm. Not very promising. By the way, did your hypothetical murderer know the victim was going to take this walk at this time?"

Rollo smiled. "That's one of the things I'm trying to find out," and he explained the circumstances.

"Then the trap might have been baited for several mornings in the hope of getting the old fellow sometime?"

"It's what Mr French suggested, but we don't know."

"If anyone did that, he'd have to dig it up and change the batteries each night, and with the tide coming in at different hours, that doesn't seem a very hopeful proposition either. However, it's your pigeon, not mine. All I have to tell you is that some source of current would have been needed."

"I follow that."

"You can amuse yourself thinking out schemes to get over the difficulty. Did the old chap go at the same time each morning?"

Rollo said he went on most fine mornings.

"Old people tend to get into habits, so it's what one would expect. I was wondering whether a couple of alarm clocks could have been used, one to switch on the current before he was due, the other to switch it off again some minutes later. I don't know. It's only an idea for you to think about."

"You mean that the batteries would then last? That's ingenious, Mr Rutherford. But then – the clocks would have to be wound, and wouldn't that be as bad?"

"Well, you'd get over the difficulty of the tide. You could wind any time in the twenty-four hours. But I don't put that forward seriously. I don't think it's likely. Besides, you'd have been pretty sure to find part of the clocks."

"It means that the receiving part is just possible. What about the sending end?"

"Not so promising. He'd want special valves and I don't think he'd get them. Not now. They're only to be had under licence and there's a pretty stringent inquiry before a licence is granted. Then there are all sorts of checks on the dealer who supplies the valves, to make sure they don't get into the wrong hands. If you can find a suspect in the trade or in a Government wireless department he might be your man, but I don't think you need consider an ordinary member of the public."

"Not very hopeful, as you say."

"No. If I were in your place I shouldn't spend time on it unless everything else had failed."

As a little later Rollo sat squeezed in the corner of an overfilled compartment of the 1.40 from Paddington, his enthusiasm for his new case had slightly waned. Not that he admitted to himself the possibility of failure. He would certainly pull it off. But it wasn't going to be easy and it wasn't going to be quick. What he had learnt in town made the thing more puzzling instead of less. Everything was negative. The mine or whatever it was was not of any known kind. Apparently it was not detonated in any known way, either by contact, sound, magnetism, electric charge or wireless waves. In fact, what he had been told went to prove that there was no mine, and if there was, it had not been exploded! Not particularly helpful so far.

In spite of all its difficulties he thought the radio theory the most likely. It would at least be the easiest to test. It involved an aerial and that could surely be found. If it existed, it could only be at the groyne, because at any other place it would have been seen. The first thing must be to search for it.

But if there was an aerial at the groyne, it must have been connected to the mine by the flex. Then a little wave of excitement shot into Rollo's mind. Of course! There was the explanation of the plug! The flex could not be fastened to the aerial, as if so the explosion might have torn it in two, leaving an end to lead investigators to the aerial. Hence the plug, which the least pull on the flex would draw out.

Rollo's mood changed to optimism. This was better! Here was a factor which worked in with something else, the first he had found. Could he go a step farther? That puzzling point about the position of the flex? If it had been plugged in to the groyne, why was it stretching away in the opposite direction?

Suddenly he saw. The explosion would pull out the plug. But it wouldn't do it gently. It would give it such a pluck that it would fly off exactly as it had, carried on by its own momentum. And that would account too for the plug end being farthest from the centre. Yes, certainly this was working in all right!

Then another idea occurred to him. All this business of the flex might have quite a different explanation. Suppose it had been plugged in, not to an aerial, but to an insulated wire running up the groyne, along which an electrical charge could have been sent? Suppose someone with a magneto machine were hidden up in the bushes, watching old Radlett pass? Wasn't this more likely?

Rollo felt sure that it was. As a boy he had been shown over a large stone quarry, and he remembered how in blasting, the big shots were exploded by a magneto and connecting wire. Yes, he believed he was on to it at last.

Though the next day was Sunday he managed to see Vanson and arrange for another daybreak meeting at the groyne.

"Any of your chaps able to use carpenters' tools?" he went on. "We might have to cut away a plank or two from the groyne."

Vanson was not sure that they had a right to interfere with the groyne, but when Rollo urged that it was in a good cause and that they could repair any damage they did, he agreed to bring along Constable Umpelty, who he said was a right handy chap.

After he was in bed an objection to his theory occurred to Rollo. The flex between the mine and the groyne must have been buried beneath the sand, as otherwise it would have been seen. But if so, it must have left a track where it was jerked out. Why had Vanson not noticed this?

He got up and with his torch re-examined the photographs of the crater. Then smiling with satisfaction, he returned to bed.

In the morning he took the photographs down to the beach. He was there just as it grew light and Vanson and Umpelty soon joined him.

"Look at this photo, Mr Vanson." He pointed to a shadow stretching from the crater to the last set of piles in the groyne. "What about that being where the flex was buried?"

Vanson was obviously impressed. "I saw that at the time," he declared. "It was a sort of little scrape in the sand and I thought a bit of the mine flying out had made it. There were lots of marks radiating out all round that looked just the same. But if you're right, it'll show us where to look."

"That's what I hoped."

Opposite the cut was a space between two of the piles. They had originally been close together, but decay and the action of the sea had worn them down till they were nearly three inches apart. Rollo knelt down and stared in. There was no sign of a plug or wire.

"Can you get your hand in?"

"Only on edge."

"You can feel nothing?"

"I'm trying to."

Then Rollo's disappointment once again changed to satisfaction. In the angle at the back of one of the piles he felt a wire. It came out of the sand and went up for a couple of feet, when it seemed to disappear.

"Try and follow it down," Vanson advised unnecessarily.

It was not easy working in the confined space, but slowly Rollo scraped away the sand. Then his efforts were rewarded. About two inches below the surface he came on the plug, fixed opposite the opening as he had foretold.

"How on earth was it put there?" he queried as he stood up.

Vanson shook his head. "Beats me," he said with some bitterness. "But the main thing is that it's there. That fixes the accident theory."

"Looks like it."

"And the police agreed with the coroner! Well, we can't help it. Better late than never, I suppose."

Umpelty stepped forward at what might have become an embarrassing moment.

"Let me clear it a bit further, sir."

"Go ahead."

Umpelty knelt down in his turn and pushed his hand into the space. For some minutes he worked, then he gave a grunt.

"Got it; I think."

As he spoke he brought out a piece of wood about five inches by two, with the plug and wire fixed to its centre. He held it up and demonstrated.

"You see, gentlemen, they've scraped out the sand and pushed this in upright, then turned it across the opening like so. It keyed in behind the rounded corners of the piles on either side. Quite a firm job and easy to do."

"That's ingenious. Good man, Umpelty!" Vanson had forgotten his annoyance. "Quite a help, that is. Now we've got to follow that wire up."

It disappeared between the timbers near the head of the pile. Rollo stared thoughtfully at the woodwork, noting its construction. There were the main twelve by six piles in pairs at intervals, with behind them a wall of sheet piling. At the top and near ground level were horizontal walings, keeping all in place. About six feet behind the front wall was a back wall of similar construction, the space between being filled with stones. No doubt the walls were tied together, but in what way was not apparent.

If the wire ran up the groyne, he thought it must be somewhere about the upper waling. A few moments' search revealed it. It was pushed down into the space between the slightly rounded edge of the waling and the tops of the sheet piles. Staples at intervals kept it in place. Except by close scrutiny, it was quite invisible.

"Look at that, Mr Vanson! We're getting on!" Rollo called in high good-humour.

"Follow it up," answered Vanson, "we must see where it goes. And look here, Captain Rollo" – Rollo noted the Captain with amusement – "above this let's keep on the groyne. All these prints we've made will be washed out when the tide rises and there's no need to leave any to call attention to our search."

"Good idea, sir," returned Rollo, determined not to be outdone in politeness.

A short exclamation showed that the wire ran right up to the head of the groyne and there ended. Just where the timberwork disappeared into the grassy bank it was cut, a fresh cut, to judge by the brightness of the metal.

"It has been led in among these shrubs somewhere and the murderer has hidden there and watched Radlett pass, just as you suggested," Vanson commented. "We'd better search round for signs of where he lay. He might have dropped something. Get down to it, Umpelty. Look for grass beaten down, twigs broken, bits of cloth on thorns, anything."

They spent some time searching, but without result. Admittedly traces of occupation some days earlier were scarcely to be expected. The ground was too rough for prints and the grass and shrubs were coarse and sturdy. The fact that signs were not to be seen did not therefore mean that no one had been there.

"At least we haven't been observed," Vanson remarked as they ceased work. "I think no one should know we're on to this. Forget all you've seen, Umpelty."

"You don't mean, Mr Vanson, that you'd rather I didn't report to General Weston?" asked Rollo.

"No, no, of course not. But tell him we want it kept quiet. He'll see the need for it."

"One other thing I'd like to do before we go, sir: measure the length of the wire."

They quickly did so. It was almost exactly fifty yards.

"What do you want the length for?" Vanson asked.

"Well, just this: there may be nothing in it. I think you said that over five hundred yards of wire was stolen from the Home Guard. Can you say if this is the same sort of wire?"

"Oh, yes; I noticed that at once. It's identical."

"Fifty yards from five hundred leaves four hundred and fifty. May I see the map?"

Vanson unrolled the ordnance sheet when they reached the station.

"I wondered if it would give us anything if we took the head of the groyne as centre and four hundred and fifty yards as radius and described a circle?"

Vanson looked annoyed for a moment, then agreed. "I hadn't thought of that, but it's an idea," he admitted handsomely.

Unfortunately the experiment came to nothing. The curve swept through the heathland, remote from all houses and points of vantage. They had made progress, but had not solved their problem.

Later that day Rollo asked for an interview with the general.

"I think I've got the answer to your question, sir," he began. "There was no oversight or carelessness about the affair, so I don't think the army comes into it. We've been able to prove it was a well-planned murder."

General Weston stared. "Murder?" he repeated. "Tell me."

Rollo quickly outlined his discoveries. The general listened in silence and seemed impressed.

"I think you've done well," he said. "What happens now? Do the local police take over?"

Rollo's face fell pitifully. "I had hoped, sir – " he stammered.

Weston also looked grave. "Your mind was set on carrying on? I'm sorry, Rollo, but you're in the army now and that's not army work. I gave you a job and you've carried it out, I may say, to my complete satisfaction. But you'll be more use to your country doing the military secret service work you joined up for."

Rollo could scarcely speak, so bitter was the disappointment, but he managed to murmur, "I understand, sir, and thank you for what you've said."

"I appreciate your feelings, and as I say, I'm sorry about it," Weston went on kindly. "Now I'll tell you what I'll do. I'll recommend you for transfer to that work at once. You'll find it more in your own line."

"Thank you very much, sir," Rollo said again.

"Then I think you should see this inspector and tell him how you're situated and that he'll have to take over the case. You carry on as before till you get your marching orders."

Though there were to be compensations, Rollo's disappointment remained very deep. But he was somewhat cheered by the way in which Vanson took the news.

"I'm sorry to hear it, Captain Rollo. I was thinking that we were getting on very well together, and I should have been glad to work with you to the finish. If you care to drop in at any time, I'll keep you advised as to what happens."

It was nice of Vanson and Rollo appreciated his generosity.

8

CHIEF INSPECTOR FRENCH

Rollo's story had considerably interested French, and for two reasons. The first was for the young man's own sake. When the Assistant Commissioner, Sir Mortimer Ellison, had told him to take Rollo with him as his assistant on the Chalfont case he had at first felt deeply aggrieved. He had had a prejudice against him because he was a product of the Police College. He had expected a swelled head and veiled insolence, coupled with slackness, inefficiency and a continuous grouse. He had found none of these things. Rollo's manners were good, he was out to do his best, and he had no more self-conceit than was proper. He was hard working and resourceful, and tactful enough to work with other people without putting up their backs. Altogether French was agreeably surprised.

Since the young fellow had joined up he had done equally well. French had seen a confidential report on him, and it was highly satisfactory. French was pleased also with his eagerness about this St Pols case. He sympathized with his desire to be allowed to carry it through, though he expected that neither the military authorities nor the Yard would consider this for a moment.

The story had also interested French for its own sake. He had often wondered why war conditions had not been more widely taken advantage of by criminals. What more easy than to blow up an enemy during a blitz or to knock him on the head and set fire to his house? With the roads stiff with military traffic during the blackout, how unsuspicious the discovery of an injured body? When every second man was carrying lethal weapons, how easy to drug his drink and obtain them? Killers were certainly missing their opportunities!

But this St Pols affair looked like an exception. At first sight French imagined Rollo was right in supposing that the explosive which killed Radlett was that stolen from the Home Guard. If so, the murderer had by no means missed his opportunity! When the authorities had thoughtfully placed instruments of death all over the country in insecurely fastened huts, why should not any taxpayer with murderous designs take advantage of their complaisance?

French knew that in due course he would learn the result of Rollo's search for the wall-plug, but he did not anticipate how quickly the information would come, nor its source. On Tuesday Sir Mortimer Ellison rang for him.

"Did you see Rollo when he was here on Saturday?"

"Yes, sir. He told me what he was up about."

"Oh, then you know all about it. Did you hear they'd found a wire running up the groyne?"

"No, sir. I take it that puts things beyond doubt."

"You means that it's murder? Yes, I agree. But except for this, they're not much further on. The wire was cut off at the head of the groyne and there's no hint of who used it."

Remembering the sweat and tears which had gone to the solving of his own problems, French felt irritated.

"They can't expect everything at once."

"How true! Rollo took that view and wanted to go ahead with the investigation, but the army people won't have that at any price. They say it's not military work."

"I should think not!" The idea that anything military could rank with his own job caused contempt to creep into French's voice.

"Oh, you agree, do you? Well, Rollo's a sick and a sorry young man at the moment – all to his credit of course. In any case he was too young for the job."

"He should have known better than to expect it, sir."

"I expect he did really. But that's not what I wanted to discuss with you. I should have been glad if the matter had stopped there, but, alas! it hasn't. Their Chief Constable has just been on the 'phone and his miserable officers want help. Can you forecast the course of my further remarks?"

"I should like to think so, sir."

"Isn't that fortunate. Well, I'm glad you want to go, for you're for it. You're about through with that Dorchester case, aren't you?"

"Yes, sir, just squaring up the papers for the Public Prosecutor."

"Then can you finish them this evening and go to Cornwall by the night train?"

"Yes, sir, I'll see to it."

"Right; I'll ring the CC."

Having taken the precaution to see Rutherford and learn all he could about wireless discharge of mines, French with Sergeant Carter caught the 1.35 a.m. from Paddington. It brought them to St Pols about half past eight in the morning. Vanson was waiting on the platform. He singled them out at a glance.

"Mr French, isn't it? Good morning, sir. Good morning, sergeant. Sorry you had to come by the night train."

"Not at all, inspector. I slept well, and as Carter sleeps at all times, we were quite all right."

Carter grinned. "I remembered nothing till I looked out and saw we were crossing the Saltash Bridge, which I think's not too bad."

Vanson seemed slightly surprised at the exchange. However, he tactfully replied in the same vein, going on: "I've booked rooms for you at the Lizard Arms and I dare say you're ready for a bit of breakfast. The Chief Constable wants to meet you, and he's coming in for a conference at eleven. He thought you might like to see the place and go over the papers first?"

"So I should."

"Then I'll call for you with the car in about an hour."

After a tub and breakfast French felt ready for anything. They drove out along the shore and inspected the site of the occurrence and the wire along the groyne. Then returning to the police-station, French saw the exhibits and read through the file. By the time he had finished the Chief Constable made his appearance.

Major Tredinnick was a tall, dark man with a sleepy manner belied by a very alert eye. He spoke in a leisurely way with a pleasant drawl, yet French felt that in moments of crisis he would be anything but easygoing. He greeted his visitors casually, made one or two perfunctory remarks by way of introduction, and then got down to business.

As French noted with quiet amusement, his first care was to explain in minute detail why he had applied for help to the Yard. French knew all the opening gambits. Usually it was a wave of crime which had swamped the local men, often that the key man of their CID was sick, occasionally that the case had ramifications in London, or at least outside the local area. The one reason which never weighed was that the job was beyond the local men or that they wanted technical help. In the present instance it seemed that Vanson was engaged on another murder case and that they had no one left for this one.

This point being satisfactorily dealt with, the Chief Constable touched on Rollo.

"Not a bad young man that," he declared. "Told me he had worked under you?"

French mentioned the Chalfont affair.

"Quite. Well, in my opinion he does you credit. I confess I was sorry for him: he seemed so cut up at not being allowed to carry on."

"He shouldn't have been, sir. He ought to have known he was too young."

"True, of course, but he wouldn't think so. I thought of asking him here this morning, then I felt I'd better not interfere with the army."

"Very considerate of you, sir, if I may say so. I'll ask him round to the hotel tonight and let him get it off his chest."

"Good. Now for the case itself. I think it's a rather important one, and so does Vanson. I'll tell you why. There's an immense amount of weapons and ammunition and explosives stored all over the country in these Home Guard huts. They're secure in a way, but in my opinion not secure enough: I mean, any resolute fellow with a tommy-bar could break into them. And, of course, they're not guarded. Now I think it's important that no one who does break in should get away with it. This case mustn't be an encouragement to others to do the same. See what I mean?"

French was interested to find his own opinions being put to him.

"Very clearly, sir," he agreed. "I was thinking coming down that it was surprising that sort of thing hadn't been done oftener."

"I suppose it is really. Of course in saying all this I've been assuming that the theft and the murder were connected, which obviously may not be the case."

"It's likely on the face of it."

"I think it is, particularly as the stolen wire seems to have been used. However, I presume that's one of the points you'll consider. Now, there's another thing that Vanson and I were discussing. It seems to us that if this connection does exist, I mean between the thefts and the murder, there'll be three fairly clear pointers to the murderer. I'm not trying to do your thinking for you, chief inspector; just giving you another point to consider."

"I'll be very grateful for any help, sir."

"It won't be much help because you'd be on to it yourself immediately. First, if the murderer used the Home Guard stuff he must have had the knowledge and the opportunity to steal it, second, if he killed Radlett he must have had a motive, and third, he must be enough of a mechanic and electrician to have made and exploded the mine."

"That's good, sir."

"You can see it all for yourself as well as we can, but being a stranger you mightn't know that there are two men who fairly well fit the bill. If I mention their names you'll realize that it's not to make an accusation: probably both are innocent."

"I quite understand the position."

"Their names are Little and Wedgewood, and we are informed that both benefit under the deceased's will, Little to a considerable extent and Wedgewood slightly. That you'll have to verify. Wedgewood is local commander of the Home Guard and Little acts as quartermaster, so he actually has charge of the munitions. Wedgewood is supposed to be fairly handy with tools; I am told he does a lot of repairs on his farm. Little I don't know anything about in this way. I've never heard that he was a mechanic."

"I can find out."

"Yes, it would probably be worth it. Then with regard to character, Wedgewood is a highly respected man and one would say offhand that he'd be unlikely to murder for gain. About Little I again don't know enough to say. I know nothing against him, but his general reputation is not so high."

"That's all most helpful, sir. Is there anyone else who fulfils the conditions?"

"We couldn't think of anyone. You haven't thought of anyone since, Vanson?"

"No, sir; only those two."

"Well, there you are, chief inspector; that's all I have to say to you. You act on that or not as you think right. Now about help for you. Vanson unfortunately won't be available after today, so if you want anything apply to the superintendent at Truro. He'll do everything he can. I'm sorry he couldn't be here today, but he's carrying on for Vanson in that other case. Anything else you'd like now?"

"Only to know what Mr Vanson did about the thefts?"

"Oh, yes, Vanson, tell him about that. You had no luck?"

"No, sir, unfortunately. I took all the usual steps. Anyone, of course, could have taken the wire. Then about the grenades; I found out that everyone in the district knew or could have known that they were stored in the hut. All the Home Guard knew it, and though all said they hadn't talked, that's a statement one could scarcely take at its face value. Further, anyone could have broken the padlock and removed the stuff. On the negative side we found no one with a tommy-bar or other suitable tool, and there were no clear prints, either finger or foot. During the critical time no one was seen in the locality, and no strangers were observed arriving in or leaving the district. Lastly, no one is known to have visited or worked at the groyne."

French shrugged. "You seem to have covered that pretty well, inspector. I don't see that you've left me much to do."

"Glad to hear it, sir," Vanson smiled.

The Chief Constable nodded. "Now, Mr French, you'll want a room and a car. Will you fix that up, Vanson? For the room, I dare say that Cundy could move his things out of this one, but that's a matter for you both."

As soon as Major Tredinnick was satisfied that French would receive all necessary facilities, he wished him good day and good luck and took his leave. French could see that Vanson was also anxious to be off, so after some further discussion he said he would like to think over what he had heard and would not therefore trespass any more on his time.

As a matter of fact French did not want to think over anything. His course was plain. The facts could scarcely bear any interpretation other than that this was a deliberately planned murder, and if so, his duty was to check up on everyone who could have benefited by the death. So far Wedgewood and Little were the only suspects, and he must settle about them before going further.

After lunch he took the car and drove out with Carter to Redryn Farm. Maude opened the door and directed him to the field behind the yard, where he found Wedgewood working at his chicken coops. French introduced himself, handing over his official card.

He was impressed with Wedgewood's appearance and manner. He certainly looked a man of the highest type, with his open face, shrewd but honest eyes, and kindly expression. His high forehead and delicate features suggested the thinker rather than the man of action, and as they talked he revealed an outlook both wise and charitable.

"I'm sorry to trouble you, Mr Wedgewood," French began, "but this matter of the death of Mr Radlett has turned out more serious than was at first suspected. I want you please to keep it to yourself, but we've found that he was murdered."

Wedgewood seemed more troubled than surprised.

"I'm terribly sorry to hear it, Mr French, but, you know, I half suspected it. The theory of an accident seemed to me altogether too far-fetched. Is it permissible to ask how you know?"

"From an examination of the site. We find that the mine was exploded from the shore by a wire running down the groyne."

Wedgewood now did show surprise. "Bless my soul, planned as deliberately as that! Well, I imagine that settles it. Any clue to the perpetrator? Or perhaps I shouldn't ask that? I know you people are not fond of giving away information."

"I don't mind answering it," French returned. "So far there's no clue, but, of course, we're only just beginning work. In fact, you're the first person I've called on."

"Then how can I help you?"

"You're the commander of the local Home Guard?"

"I am, yes."

"You had some wire and explosives stolen recently?"

"Ah, that's what you think, is it? I don't mind confessing the thefts have worried me a lot, also my cousin by marriage, Dick Little. He's quartermaster and was technically responsible for the loss; as, of course, I was myself."

"I want to know all you can tell me about the theft. You can see how important it has become."

Wedgewood said he fully appreciated this, but unhappily he was unable to give any information. He had thought over the matter almost day and night since it happened, and he could think of nothing in any way helpful.

When French had sufficiently pursued this line he turned to another.

"Now I come on to rather delicate ground, and these questions you are not bound to answer unless you like. As you probably know, in a crime of this kind we have to ask everyone interested where he or she was at the time it took place. Now I understand Mrs Wedgewood, and therefore yourself indirectly, benefits through the will. I am making no accusation when I ask you to account for yourself at the time."

"I know you ask that, and you've put it so tactfully that I can have no objection to answering. I was here, working at these coops. It's a stock job that I do when not otherwise engaged. I heard the explosion, but one hears so many noises of the kind that I thought nothing of it. It was only when my wife came hurrying up that I learnt what had happened."

"Can anyone beside yourself vouch for that?"

Wedgewood shook his head. "I don't think so. No one came here at all events, and you can see that this place is pretty secluded."

"Were you hammering?"

"At intervals, yes."

"Could anyone have heard you?"

Wedgewood shrugged. "I don't know of anyone who was near enough. Macdougal might have – that's my mechanic – but I don't think it's likely. Firstly, he was busy himself on a tractor motor, and second, hammering, even if he heard it, is not unusual enough to attract his attention."

"I'll have to see him in any case, so I may as well do it now. Tell me about him, please."

When a little later French left Wedgewood, he had to admit that his own estimate of his character was the same as Major Tredinnick's. French just could not imagine a man of this type committing a deliberate and premeditated murder for gain. On the other hand, he knew from bitter experience that such ideas could be wrong. Wedgewood's story, further, was just the kind of tale he would tell were he guilty. Here already the exasperating but familiar feature of detective work was appearing; the amassing of indecisive facts. French always felt that he would grudge no labour if only it led to certainty. What was so irritating was to slave away endlessly, and at the end find oneself in the same state of doubt in which one began.

However, that was the peculiarity of his job and grousing would not alter it. Perhaps this Macdougal might be able to help him.

The mechanic was welding a new prong on to a broken fork. He seemed bored with it and quite willing to knock off to talk to French. But he had nothing to tell. On the day in question he had been engrossed with his work on the carburettor and did not even hear the explosion, much less Wedgewood's hammering. But that, he pointed out, did not mean that there was no hammering. He was accustomed to hearing hammering and probably would not notice it.

"What's yon?" he went on, cocking his head and holding up a hand for silence.

It was hammering, obviously Wedgewood back at his work. It was audible but faint. French realized that no help was to be looked for here.

Having learnt disappointingly little from his visit, he went on to see Little. He found him in his study, busy on a crossword.

It was clear that Little was no more surprised to see him than Wedgewood had been.

"Between you and me and the wall," he said, "I didn't find the mine theory, either land or sea, very easy to swallow. I couldn't see how Mr Savory could have escaped. But, of course, that was only my opinion and I'm not an expert."

Little was obviously upset about the theft of the grenades, and admitted readily that he had wondered if it were a preliminary of the tragedy. But he could offer no suggestions as to a possible thief. He thought that only members of the Home Guard could have known the grenades were there, though others might have guessed it, but there wasn't a man whom he could possibly suspect.

Like Wedgewood he unhesitatingly admitted his wife's legacy from Radlett, saying he thought that this would amount to about £20,000 free of legacy duty. Mrs Wedgewood's amount was far less, only some £5,000. There were no other important legatees. He had no objection whatever to stating where he was at the time of the tragedy. He explained about his crossword job and told how he and his wife and Mrs Wedgewood were together in his study discussing clues.

To French this seemed a much more conclusive interview than that he had had with Wedgewood. Admittedly his opinion of Little coincided with Major Tredinnick's – that he had not the character of his relative – but here again he knew that this meant absolutely nothing. On the other hand, Little did seem to have a genuine alibi. If he were really in his room with the two women when the mine went up, he could not have been in the spinney setting it off. That his statement was true French could scarcely doubt, for the whole subsequent development of the situation depended on it and corroborated it: the telephoning to the doctor and the police, the running down along the shore, the discussion with Savory. And these details had been amply established by Vanson.

French spent his afternoon interviewing Jessica Little – from whom he learnt that her father had made his money at Klondyke – Maude Wedgewood, Savory and Crane, more to form his own opinion of their personalities than to check their statements, which he did not doubt. Then he saw Messrs Munce and Carveth, Radlett's solicitors, about the legacy. Mr Carveth was not at first willing to give any information, but when French recited the provisions of the will, he reluctantly admitted they were correct. Finally French returned to the Lizard Arms to meet Rollo, to whom earlier in the day he had telephoned an invitation to dinner.

During the meal French would not allow any reference to the case, discussing instead Rollo's experiences in the army, but afterwards they adjourned to French's bedroom and had a conference. This was an act of pure kindliness on French's part. He did not expect to learn anything from Rollo, but wanted the young fellow to feel that his work was appreciated and that he was not completely shelved.

But as often happens in such circumstances, virtue proved more than its own reward. A chance remark of Rollo's gave French a hint which altered the whole direction of the inquiry.

French had recounted his activities during the day and they were discussing the deadlock in the case which these had produced. As far as could be learnt, two persons, and two only, stood to gain by Radlett's death. Neither of these appeared to be guilty. Where was the flaw?

"There must be some facts which we've yet to learn," French declared. "Either Radlett had a secret in his life and a mortal enemy, or someone else we don't know of benefited by his death, or the whole four of those people are in it, Wedgewood, Little and the two wives. But there's no evidence for any of these theories."

"There's a good deal against all of them, isn't there?" Rollo returned.

"I think there is, but let's hear you spouting on them."

"Reminds me of Chalfont, sir," Rollo grinned. Then he went on more seriously: "All the information I could get showed Radlett as a quiet, kindly, harmless old man, not exactly popular – he was too retiring for that – but disliked by no one. He was liked most by those who knew him best, which I take as a good sign. I got that not only from Vanson's notes, but from talking to all sorts of people. It's most unlikely that he should have an enemy bitter enough to murder him."

This sounded reasonable to French. "I agree with that and it's supported by another consideration. If he had an enemy there must have been something to bring things to a head just now. The enmity must have been caused by something which happened in the past, because the old man was doing nothing latterly which could have aroused it. What then touched it off? I mean, if it was murder, why was it delayed till the present?"

"That's fine, sir; a great point. We certainly know of no recent change in the old man's way of living which could have hurt anyone."

"No, I think therefore we may eliminate the mortal enemy."

"I agree, sir, and I think we may also eliminate the unknown who benefited by the death. You've seen the solicitor and there was no one."

French nodded. "Just my view. I didn't take to Carveth, but I've no reason to doubt that he's a perfectly honest man, and anyhow, I don't think he'd lie in a murder case to a man from the Yard."

"The other suggestion that all four who will benefit are in it," Rollo went on, "or even Little and the ladies only, seems to me equally out of the question. Those people wouldn't do such a thing, at least I don't believe it. Is that nonsense, sir?"

"I don't know," French returned, "but it's my idea also. Those women in particular seem thoroughly straight and decent, and besides, their manner is perfectly normal. I don't believe they could look and speak as they do if they had murder on their conscience."

"They have just that reputation in the place: thoroughly straight and decent. I tell you, sir, the thing's a puzzle and no mistake. What will you do now?"

French laughed. "That's just it." He was going on to ask what Rollo would do in his place, but checked himself in time. In the circumstances such a question would be hurtful. But Rollo answered it for him.

"I know what I should have done: I was planning it before I was – withdrawn," he smiled crookedly. "Two things indeed: first, I was going to try and find out whether Wedgewood or Little could have made the mine and gone down to the groyne at night – several nights, for I'm sure all that work couldn't have been done in one."

French approved with qualifications. He did not say that the idea had already occurred to himself and was noted under "Possible Lines" in his book.

"We think those two are innocent," he pointed out, "and if we're right that test would add nothing to our knowledge."

"I see that, sir" – Rollo again smiled wryly – "but I hadn't your corroborating views at that time. The second thing I was going to do we've also rather poured cold water on, and that was to go into Radlett's history. I wasn't hopeful because of his character, but I thought there was just the chance of finding something."

"That's a better point. I may have to do it myself if things don't clear up soon."

It was then that Rollo made his momentous remark. "It's certainly a pretty tough puzzle," he repeated, then added: "If it had been that man Savory instead of Radlett one could have understood it. Half the people in the place are his mortal enemies."

French sat up as if a pail of cold water had landed on him. Here was an idea! Was this the explanation? Had the trap been intended for Savory and through some mischance had Radlett sprung it?

With a growing excitement French followed up this line of thought. Could the wire up the groyne have been not to explode the mine, but to *set* it for explosion on the application of weight or some other contact? Could the murderer, waiting in the shrubs at the head of the groyne, have seen Savory coming, set the affair, and rushed off to establish an alibi? Could Savory then have failed to explode it, and Radlett, following on his heels, have operated the mechanism?

French gave a deep breath. The idea was like a beam of light in a dark cellar. If this were possible the affair would become intelligible at once. From Rollo's remarks and

Vanson's notes a lot of people would be glad to see Savory dead. The problem of motive would be solved. *Was* it possible?

French decided that his next move must be a further consultation with Rutherford.

9

CHIEF INSPECTOR FRENCH

Late that evening French rang Rutherford up at his home. The engineer laughed when he heard his question.

"You've certainly got originality in your problems," he returned. "Electrically switching in a contact device on a land-mine? I never heard of it."

"But is it possible?" persisted French.

"Now, now, chief inspector, have a heart! You don't seem to realize how embarrassing it is to have these conundrums hurled at one's head without a moment's preparation. I'd have to think about that before I could give an opinion."

French laughingly apologized. Would Mr Rutherford consider it and let him know the result at the earliest possible moment?

"I'll do so, of course, but at first sight and subject to later correction, I should think it is possible. There are all sorts of electric gadgets for making one moving piece of an apparatus pick up or release another, mostly by an electro-magnet throwing a trip lever into or out of gear."

"That sounds promising."

"I can give you an example. Do you happen to know anything about railway tablet instruments?"

"Not very much, I'm afraid."

"Well, they're a safety device for single line working. They're boxes containing tablets or metal tickets which when handed to a driver authorize him to proceed through a section. It's essential, of course, that a tablet should only be withdrawable when the section is clear of trains. Now tablets are carried in a sort of drawer and are obtained by pulling out the drawer. Am I making myself clear?"

"Quite, so far."

"Well, here's the point. The drawer can be pulled out at all times, but unless the signalman in the box at the other end of the section is sending a current, it comes out empty. It's only when the current is passing that it brings out a tablet. In other words the far-away signalman controls the issue of a tablet. So you see, here's an example of a current giving a result to an action which without the current it wouldn't have had."

"But that's just what I want! Could that be applied to a mine?"

"I think so. Suppose your contact-mine is constructed with a pillar reaching from the contact portion to the detonating mechanism. When the weight comes on it pushes down the pillar and releases the mechanism."

"I follow that."

"Now suppose the pillar to be divided into two parts, leaving a space in the centre. You could then depress the contact without setting the affair off, because the upper part would simply come down through the space without touching the lower part. Still clear?"

"Perfectly."

"Very well; it would be quite easy by exciting an electro-magnet to insert a block into the space, so that any movement of the upper part would be transmitted through the block to the lower part."

"Splendid! That would surely do the trick?"

"I think so. Of course the upper part of the pillar would require a spring to raise it again. But you may take it the thing's possible, but the apparatus would require careful construction by a skilled man. Not only that, he'd have to be an ingenious bloke, a bit of an inventor and so on."

French was delighted. His theory was possible and it covered all the known facts. Further, it should be easy to test its truth.

Next morning he began by rereading the references to Savory in the file and finding out all that Sergeant Cundy could tell about him. Then he drove out to Kelwyn House and sent in his card. Savory was at home and saw him at once.

"What are you back again for?" he called out rudely before the door had closed.

"Because," French answered politely, "I wish to take you more fully into my confidence than I did yesterday. In brief, sir, I want to put up a rather startling theory."

As he spoke French was amazed to recognize well-known symptoms developing in his host's manner. Savory was obviously apprehensive, and as obviously trying to hide it. Why a man of his reputed character should exhibit such signs was an intriguing problem. For a moment French recalled his own suggestion to Rollo that Savory might be guilty, then he remembered that this had been shown to be impossible.

"Well, what is it?" Savory growled. "Have you found who wanted to do Radlett in?"

"That's just the point. It has been suggested that no one did."

Savory's face grew red. "What the devil do you mean? If you think you can come here and try to be funny with me you'll find you're pretty wide of the mark. Even a chief inspector is not God Almighty!"

"Sorry, sir, nothing was farther from my intention. I have to tell you that we think this murder miscarried, that Mr Radlett was killed by mistake. Someone else was intended."

Savory stared. "You mean?"

"You yourself, sir."

"Me!" Savory bulged with indignation, then something seemed to strike him and he sat quite still thinking it over. "But damn it all, man, that's completely absurd! What put such an idea into your head?"

"Two considerations. First, no one who could have committed the murder had any motive for killing Mr Radlett. Second, I am informed that you have enemies in the neighbourhood."

"If that's all your proof, I don't think much of it."

"Then let us take these points in turn. Can you suggest anyone who had a motive for killing Mr Radlett?"

"Me? It's not my business to do the police dirty work. All the same you wouldn't have to look very far to find someone."

"You mean Mr Little and Mr Wedgewood and their wives?"

"I'm making no accusations."

"Of course not, sir, but I may tell you they're innocent. Can you suggest anyone else?"

"I can't suggest anybody, and incidentally it's a lie to say I suggested them."

"I didn't say so," French returned mildly. "Now the second point: do you deny that you are on bad terms with a number of your neighbours?"

"Why should I? There are a lot of swine about this one-horse place that no one could be on good terms with."

"Quite so, sir; that's the point. We think that one of them tried to murder you."

For some moments Savory did not reply. Then he shrugged. "If you're right, what are you going to do about it?"

"Test the suggestion and try to find the truth. For that I want to ask you one or two questions."

"I'll bet you do! I know something about police. Questions without end and without rhyme or reason also. Well, if you must, you must. Go ahead and get done as soon as you can."

"Thank you, sir." French smiled amiably and received a scowl in return. "Then first can you tell me who knew that you were going to walk along the sand on the day and at the hour in question?"

Again Savory paused in thought. "A number of people knew I was going into the village about that time on that day, but no one knew I was going to walk along the sand."

"Might not that have been deduced?"

"It might. In these days of petrol shortage I naturally don't take out the car for a short trip, and when the weather's fine and the tide's out I always go by the shore. No one could have been sure, but anyone could have made a sporting guess."

"Quite so. Then about the people who did know you were going to the village. Who were they, sir?"

"Well, there was my wife for one. Going to charge her with the murder?"

"I don't think that was called for, sir," French returned good-humouredly. "Mrs Savory might have mentioned it to someone else. Who else, please?"

Savory snorted. "I suppose nothing but the whole story will satisfy you," he said ungraciously. "Then if you must know, the thing was this: some time ago I rented one of my cottages to a man named Macdougal: he's one of Wedgewood's employees. Latterly I found I required the cottage for a new chauffeur. I discovered there was some difficulty about getting Macdougal out. It was to discuss the matter with Forrester, my solicitor, that I was going in."

"I follow, sir. Then Mr Forrester knew?"

"Of course Forrester knew. And probably his clerk and half a dozen others in his office. Then my niece Miss Meredith knew, for she acts as my secretary and wrote to Forrester making the arrangement. Here again I suppose you'll scarcely accuse her. My wife knew, as I said, for I mentioned to her that I was going to see Forrester and what it was about. Ellen, the maid, may have overheard: we have only one maid now. There was no secret about the affair."

French nodded. "Thank you very much, sir; that covers the ground. With your permission I'll have a word with these persons to see if they passed on the information."

As he brought the interview to an end French was once again surprised by Savory's manner. The apprehension obviously passed from his mind and relief as obviously took its place. That the man knew more than he had stated, French felt convinced.

From Mrs Savory, Anne Meredith and Ellen, French learnt nothing. All had known Savory was going into St Pols that morning, and Anne Meredith had known the time of his appointments but all denied having mentioned it to any other person.

But though French learnt nothing definite from these further interviews, his interest was deeply aroused by the first two. It was not the personality of either of his witnesses which attracted his attention. He could not picture either Mrs Savory or Anne Meredith as party to a serious crime.

All the same both were undoubtedly frightened. Their relief, further, when he thanked them and took his departure was equally marked.

It was obvious that in this household there was some unhappy secret. Whether it was connected with the tragedy French could not say, but he made a mental note to go into it if his other lines failed.

As he left Kelwyn House he felt that so far as he had gone, his new theory might well be the truth. Apart from the persons who had known that Savory was going to St Pols, it must have been common property that weather and tide being suitable, he frequently took the walk. If the groyne wire had been used to switch in or out a contact device on the mine, the murderer would only have had to watch his chance, knowing that it would not be long till his victim came past.

Unhappily all this was nebulous. It might have happened, but there was not a scintilla of evidence that it had. How could certainty be achieved?

After some further thought French decided that a wider knowledge of the local politics would be necessary before any conclusion could be reached. He must make a list of Savory's enemies and estimate the strength of their various grievances.

He began with the matter of Macdougal's cottage. He had given little thought to Macdougal when he had seen him on the previous day, but now he remembered that the man had seemed one who might take a strong line if crossed. He decided to interview him again.

"Sorry for troubling you so soon, Mr Macdougal," he greeted him, "but we're going into Mr Savory's movements at the time of Mr Radlett's death, and he tells me he was going to St Pols to see Mr Forrester about your cottage. I don't know whether you'd care to explain about that?"

Macdougal looked at him with obvious surprise. "I've no objection," he answered slowly, "but I was thinking it was the death of Mr Radlett you were inquiring into?"

French laughed. "A valid objection and tactfully put. But you don't know Scotland Yard. When we're on a job like this we get every bit of information we can about the place and people, whether relevant or not. But if you don't care to speak of the affair it's all right. I can't compel you to."

Macdougal put down the shovel he had been reshafting.

"I said I hadna any objection to telling you and neither I have, and your reasons for asking about it dinna concern me. It began with me being Mr Wedgewood's batman in the last war. That early enough for a start?"

"It'll do fine, Mr Macdougal," French smiled.

A gleam appeared in the mechanic's eye and French suddenly realized that he liked him.

"Well, when Mr Wedgewood was starting this farm he wrote and offered me a job, and I came with my wife and the two wee bairns. I couldna get a house, and then I found yon cottage of Savory's. It had been lying empty for years and was in a rotten condeetion, but I couldna do any better. Savory agreed to let me have it, but only at a terrible rent. More than that, he wouldna spend a penny piece cleaning it up. I had to pay what should'a' bought it before we could move in. I put it in better condeetion than it had been for many a long day, but Savory wouldna allow me as much as a farthing for it."

French was interested. Here was a grievance emerging, an old and evidently deep-seated grievance. There was animus in Macdougal's manner.

"Hard luck," he said sympathetically. "Some people are like that."

"No such a lot, thank the guid Lord." The man was warming to the story. "Well, we made the best of a rotten house and got along fine. My wife's guid at that."

French murmured inconclusively.

"Then there came this present trouble. There's a wee bit copse over there" – he pointed vaguely to distant trees – "not far from the cottage. It's Savory's ground all right, but it's a wild, heathy place, no good for cultivating. By now you'll understand the bairns have grown a bit. Barbara's nine and Angus is seven. Well, they sometimes went into the copse to play. Of course in a way they were wrong: it wasna my ground. But they wouldna have done a penn'orth of harm, not in ten years.

"It happened that one morning about three or four weeks ago Savory took a walk there, a place I'd never seen him before. As luck would have it, he found them there and he ordered them out – as if they'd been lepers. Barbara was crying when she came home, and Angus wasna much better. Then Savory came over and shouted at me. 'Keep your brats off my property,' he called, just like that. I spoke to him civilly, though I was pretty hot. I said I was sorry they had gone, but that they were very young and had done no harm. 'I dinna care what age they are,' he shouted, and I'll say his tone was offensive, 'I'm not going to have any Tom, Dick or Harry's children on my ground!'

"Would you be blaming me if I saw red? I told him he was a dirty piece of work, and to gang away to hell out of my sight. He said nothing, but his face was the colour of beetroot.

"Three days later I got a letter from him noticing me out of the house on the ground that he wanted it for his chauffeur. The dirty liar! Gratifying his spite like that! I'd sometimes thought Mr Wedgewood was a bit hard on him, but now I saw he'd known him better than I."

"How had he got across Mr Wedgewood?"

"Well, it's a long story. About a right of way. He'll tell you himself if you're interested."

"If it throws light on Mr Savory's movements, I may ask him," French said mendaciously. "Go on with your own story, please."

"That's about all there is. I went to my solicitor, Mr Pengelly in St Pols, to see if Savory could put me out. Pengelly's going into it. From what you tell me, Savory can't be too sure about it either, if he was going to Forrester."

"I suppose not," said French. "War legislation has complicated these matters. Can you remember what you happened to be doing yourself that morning of the tragedy?"

Macdougal stared, but he made no comment on the question.

"I mind it well enough," he answered. "That was the day the tractor gave up. The driver called me about eight. She'd stopped on him and he couldna start her again. I thought it was the carburettor, so I took it off and brought it in here and opened it up. The shot went off when I was working at it: not that I noticed it, but I heard about it afterwards."

"Thank you. That seems to be all I want."

French chatted on for a few moments, then took his leave. He was very much dissatisfied with the interview. Here again was the usual indeterminate evidence. Suggesting Macdougal's guilt were the facts that he had sufficient ability and knowledge to have made the mine, that he was a member of the Home Guard and could have stolen the grenades, that through Pengelly he might have known of Savory's appointment with Forrester, and that he could probably have left his workshop long enough to operate the trip. Against this French doubted that his motive was sufficient, nor did he believe that were he guilty he could have told his damning story in the way he had.

On the whole French did not think Macdougal was his man, though he realized that his name must be kept on the list of suspects.

But what about Wedgewood? Macdougal had dropped an interesting phrase about a right of way. Hopeful or otherwise, the matter must be looked into.

French glanced at his watch. It was ten past twelve. He would have time to see Wedgewood before lunch. Going over to the farm, he ran him to earth in the little office in his house.

As was his custom in such cases, French began by apologizing for his rapid reappearance. Wedgewood cut him short.

"Please don't hesitate to come to me if I can do anything to help," he said earnestly. "I look upon you as an ally. Because of my connection with the deceased and the theft from the Home Guard, I want this affair cleared up. And if you can't do it, I don't know who can."

"It's about a rather different matter, sir," French answered. "I've begun my routine work of learning about everybody who in any way figured in the case, and at the moment I'm concentrating on Mr Savory. I want you confidentially to tell me about your relations with him."

Wedgewood frowned. "Do they really come into it, Mr French? I confess I don't see a connection myself."

"At present I can't tell what comes into it and what doesn't. I ask you the question, Mr Wedgewood, but of course you're not bound to answer it if you don't wish to."

"I've no objection to answering it if it's really necessary. But it's rather a painful subject to me, and I don't want to talk about it unless I need."

"I would still like to know, sir."

Wedgewood shrugged. "Oh, all right. My relations with him, then, have been consistently bad. Personally I hate squabbling, and I would like to be friends with everyone, but one has to draw the line somewhere, and I draw it at Mr Savory."

"Then there has been some special cause of disagreement?"

"Yes, special and continuous. If I were given to a poetical turn of phrase I should call it a running sore. It began when I came to the district and wanted to buy the farm. I found that every possible difficulty was being put in my way, and a lot of obstruction I traced to his influence. However, that passed. What I find it so hard to forget happened two years later."

"And that was, sir?"

"It's a little complicated, but I'll be as clear as I can. This property, Redryn Farm, has two approaches. One is a bridle path following the boundary between the cultivated ground and the heath. The purchase of the farm carried the legal right to pass over this path with any kind of vehicle. It is a long and difficult route with heavy gradients, and as I said, is at present unfit for wheeled traffic. It would cost a large sum – much more than I could afford – to make it passable for vehicles, though I have the legal right to do this at any time I choose."

French nodded.

"This approach was so impossible that I should not have bought the farm if there had been no other. But there was another, short, direct and level, and connecting with a main road. The only snag was that for about three hundred yards it ran across the heath, which is here common land. I had no special right to use this track, only the ordinary right of everyone to pass over common land. I went into the matter with my solicitor before completing the purchase, and he assured me that the occupants of the farm had used it for years. He said that without a special Act of Parliament it could not be closed, nor could my right to use it be curtailed."

"Was this right mentioned in your lease?"

"No. In the lease the long unmade bridle path was shown as the only legal approach."

"I follow."

"Well, I was advised that it was good enough, and I bought and we moved in. At first everything went all right and we used the short track. It was not a properly made road. It just had a gravelled surface and was a bit sandy in dry weather. But it was good enough for our purposes.

"After a couple of years the farm began to produce, and to get the stuff to the station I bought a lorry. Then my troubles began. The gravel road across the heath didn't stand up to its weight. I therefore began to repair it. Immediately Savory noticed me to stop."

"How did he come into it, Mr Wedgewood?"

"Oh, I thought you understood that. He was the lord of the manor. It's not a thing I know much about, but I believe you can buy the rights, and he had done so. Apparently he was not exceeding his powers; he could stop me if he wanted to.

"As you can see, this put me in a very awkward position. I hadn't the capital to make the bridle path into a road, I couldn't get my lorry in or out except over the heath, and I couldn't make my farm pay without the lorry. I saw Savory and explained the position, saying that what I proposed –

just a bit of hardening with water-bound macadam and a roller – would not do any harm to the heath or affect the amenities in any way whatever. But nothing would move him. He was in a position to down me and perhaps get me out of the country, and he was going to take advantage of it. I don't know if you'll believe me, Mr French, but his gloating manner and obvious pleasure in being able to do me an injury incensed me almost more than the injury itself."

"I can well understand it."

"Of course I went to my solicitor, who should have foreseen and warned me against such a thing. We discussed the question of my going on and making the repairs and letting Savory take me into court. But before we came to a decision Savory made me an offer. He said if I paid him a hundred a year he'd withdraw his objection. He wouldn't allow tarmac, but I might use broken stones and a steam roller. A pretty complete give-away of his motives!"

Upon this French expressed no opinion. "What did you do, sir?"

"What could I do? I was advised that he had the power to stop the repairs if he wanted to. I paid. I've paid ever since. Often I've despised myself for doing it, but I was afraid that if he took me to court he might get an injunction against me, and then I'd be finished. I couldn't carry on the farm."

"A very awkward situation."

"You see there was no reason behind it; no question of damaging the amenities or anything of that sort. It was simply spite and ill-will and perhaps greed. No wonder I couldn't stand the sight of the man. For years we didn't speak."

Here was another problem for French. Wedgewood had been injured by Savory, and in a particularly needless and exasperating way. Moreover, it was a continuous injury, annually renewed. Obviously Wedgewood felt bitter about it, as well he might. But to feel bitter and exasperated was one thing, and to commit murder quite another. Was there here any real motive for killing Savory?

Once again French did not think so, though again he could not be sure. The grievance was long seated. For years Wedgewood had been paying his blackmail, for that was what it came to. Why should his feelings now suddenly overcome him? If Wedgewood had been driven to murder, there must surely have been some recent cause. But Wedgewood had not indicated any such, and his manner was such that French felt convinced that he was telling the truth.

Here also obtained the argument he had noticed in Macdougal's case, the readiness with which his suspect had related the damning tale. But of course here also Wedgewood understood that French was investigating Radlett's death, not an attempt on Savory. As in the case of Macdougal, French felt that he had not reached his goal. He would keep Wedgewood on his list of possibles, and before coming to a conclusion he would carry on his inquiries in other directions.

Feeling he had been wasting his time, French left the farm and drove back to St Pols. There were two lines of inquiry with which he wished to deal as soon as possible. One concerned Crane, the novelist. Crane had been the first after Savory to arrive at the scene of the tragedy, and as a matter of routine French must obtain his statement. But there was more than that in it. During Mrs Wedgewood's examination she had revealed that love between Crane and Savory was a minus quantity, and it would be necessary to find out to what this really amounted. The other investigation was into the cause of the uneasiness which all the members of the Savory household had shown during his visit.

Neither of these could be dealt with *immediately* after lunch – it was now just on to one o'clock. In both houses the meal would probably drag on for some time. He thought therefore that before tackling either he might work off one other item of the inquiry. Though this occupied a prominent place in his notebook, it was not logically connected with his present series of interviews, and he proposed to take it now merely as a matter of convenience.

On reaching the police-station he rang up a Mr Sands whose name had been given him by Vanson – to know if he could spare him a few minutes about two. Sands agreeing, he went off with Carter for lunch.

Sands was the proprietor of a small shop selling electric and wireless fittings, but it was in his capacity as member of the Home Guard in charge of telephones that French wished to see him. He proved a wizened little man with sharp, ferret-like features. He was elderly but energetic, and evidently keen on whatever he took up.

"As you've probably guessed, Mr Sands," French began, "I've called about the theft of the wire. Can you give me any particulars?"

"Certainly, Mr French, I'll tell you anything I can. Just what do you want to know?"

"Perhaps you could give me a general idea of the Home Guard telephones first, then details of the theft?"

The question seemed to please Sands. He was evidently proud of his work and eagerly embarked on a detailed account.

It appeared that there were two types of telephones in the Home Guard: permanent lines which had early been put up, the position of which had been fixed by the layout of the ground, and temporary lines run for special purposes, which were removed when they were no longer needed. Of the former there were two main lines. The first ran along the shore, varying from a few feet to two or three hundred yards from the beach. This stretch, Sands explained, was part of a general line which ran round the entire coast of England, and it was used not only by his own company, but was connected to the companies on either side of them, east and west. The second line ran inland through the centre of the local company's area and finally connected with the adjoining company to the north. Both these passed through a tower on a low hill beside St Pols, which the Home Guard used as a headquarters and lookout. In addition there were three permanent dead-end branches which between them served the remainder of the St Pols company's area. It was from one of these that the wire had been stolen.

"When you speak of a dead-end branch, just what do you mean?" French asked.

"Why, one that stops when it has gone far enough to cover the required area. I mean, that has no through connection."

"Then how is it used? Is there a box with a telephone at the end?"

"Oh, no, you haven't got the idea." Sands was more in his element than ever. "With these lines anyone can speak from anywhere. Whoever's doing the 'phoning carries a small portable instrument – it's only about eight inches by two and a half by an inch. It has two wires, one ending in a small sharp pin, the other in a skewer about a foot long. If he wants to speak he pushes the pin through the insulation of the line so that it touches the metal inside, and he sticks the skewer into the ground. That gives him a connection from line to earth through his instrument and he can speak to headquarters, which for us is the look-out on Tower Hill."

"Very ingenious," French commented. "Then is all the wire insulated?"

"Yes, all the circuits are single insulated wires with earth returns."

"You've seen the wire we found on the groyne and you're satisfied it's the same as was stolen?"

"Perfectly satisfied."

"Just one other question, I think. What are the chances of such a theft of wire being discovered?"

"You mean with regard to time? Quite unlikely during the day. Except under special circumstances the Home Guard is not on duty. At night the two main lines connecting to the areas north, east and west are in fairly frequent use and a theft would probably be quickly found. On the three dead-end branches I couldn't form an opinion. They might or might not be used on any given night."

"Then since the thief chose a line which was less likely to be used it would seem that he was someone who knew the layout intimately?"

Sands thought this was scarcely a matter for him, but as he evidently agreed, French felt justified in noting the point as a clue.

With thanks and mutual compliments the two men parted.

– 10 –

CHIEF INSPECTOR FRENCH

It was now getting on to three o'clock and French decided to go back to the line he had been working before he interviewed Sands. The time now seemed propitious for a call on Crane.

Gorse Cottage was situated under two hundred yards from the shore just opposite Groyne Point. It was a small, irregular stone building with a high-pitched roof, a porch covered with climbing roses, and bow windows in every wall. It stood in the middle of a tiny garden, charmingly laid out, though a trifle windswept and in need of the gardener's hand. On the St Pols side was a thickish plantation of shrubs and birches, probably planted as a shelter from north and east winds, but to the south and west the ground was open to the sea. It gave a fine view of the western half of St Pols Bay and West Head. Mrs Crane was working in the garden as French and Carter approached.

"Good afternoon, madam. Could we see Mr Crane if he's not engaged?"

Crane, it appeared, was writing. He did not like to be disturbed when at work, but as Mrs Crane supposed Mr French's business was urgent, she would interrupt him. In a moment she returned and invited French in.

The study was a surprisingly large room for so small a house. It was a later addition, built out from the south wall of the building, with a flat window looking out west and a bow facing south. In the bow was a huge flat-topped desk piled with untidy sheets of manuscript, books of reference, pins, rubbers, clips and the other paraphernalia of writing. Two deep saddle-bag chairs stood near the empty fireplace, which was in the east wall. Tables bore a tantalus and cigarettes, besides more papers and loose leaf covers. Most of the wall space was covered with bookshelves, and most of the books in them bore Crane's name and had lurid jackets. On another table to the left of the fireplace was a telephone.

The master of these amenities was seated at his desk, but stood up as French and Carter entered. He was a small, thick-set man of fifty or more with a red, apoplectic face, a heavy jowl, bushy eyebrows and dark, angry eyes. He looked as if normally he might be peppery, but now he seemed worried and anxious, not to say alarmed. French, to whom that appearance was well known, felt his interest quickening.

Crane's manner, however, was easy, or fairly easy.

"Come in, chief inspector," he said, glancing at French's card. "I heard you had come down about this unhappy business. Won't you sit down?" He indicated the armchairs, and having swung his revolving chair, lowered himself carefully into it. "Cigarette?"

"No, thank you, sir. We don't smoke on duty. I'm sorry to trouble you after you've already made your statement to the local police, but you were one of the first to be on the scene after the explosion, and I must hear about it at first hand."

"That's all right, Mr French. I shall be only too glad if I can help you. I hear" – he bent forward with a serious expression – "you don't think the affair was accidental?"

"No, sir, we've found the mine was detonated electrically by a wire running up the groyne."

"So I was told. Poor old Radlett! He was a harmless, kindly old man and I can't imagine anyone having a down on him."

French nodded. "That difficulty is fully appreciated, I can assure you."

"I suppose so. Then what can I do for you?"

"Answer a few questions, please. First, about the actual explosion. Where were you when it took place?"

"Here. I mean in this room. Actually I was telephoning. I saw the thing go up. If you step over to the instrument you'll see what a view there is."

French did so. From the table beside the fireplace there was certainly a splendid outlook. Through the bow window was visible the entire beach and sea from Groyne Point on the left to the residential ground on the right. The end of the groyne could be seen emerging from behind trees. The point of the explosion was in full view, with immediately behind it Ram Island, the little place of rocks and green patches much frequented by picnic parties.

"You've certainly got a magnificent situation here," French remarked. "When you saw the mine go up what did you do?"

"For a moment nothing, I'm afraid. I was so absolutely staggered that I simply couldn't believe my eyes. Then I saw poor Radlett's body falling and I realized that whatever the cause, he was hurt. I dropped the telephone and ran down, but before I reached the place Mr Savory had arrived. I suppose you know what followed?"

"Yes, thank you, sir. But just before we leave this may I have the name of your caller?"

Crane raised his eyebrows. "Why, yes, if you want it. I mean, there's no secret about it. But why do you ask?"

"Corroboration, sir. I have to check everything and it doesn't in the least mean that I doubt your statement."

"Oh, well, if that's your duty, I suppose you must do it. It was my call to Holly and Greaves of Suffolk Street, WC2. They're my literary agents."

"Thank you. You were asking me if I knew what followed the tragedy? Yes, to the extent of having read the depositions at the inquest. What did you think had happened?"

"At first I thought of nothing except to try to help Radlett. Then afterwards when the first shock was past I began to wonder. I supposed it was a mine. After the evidence at the inquest I didn't know what to think."

"It certainly is a problem," French agreed. "You didn't know it was Mr Radlett at the time, I presume?"

"Oh, yes, I did. I saw him walking up just before the thing went off."

"Did you see Mr Savory?"

"No, I didn't notice him."

"I think you said you knew the deceased personally?"

"Yes, but not intimately. I have been in his house a couple of times and he was once here. We had nothing particular in common, and though we were friendly enough when we met, there was no reason why we should look each other up."

"Quite. Your own work is about my business?" French smiled discreetly.

Crane seemed to be growing more at ease. He took a cigarette from a box.

"Sure you won't change your mind?" he invited.

"No, thank you, sir."

"Then I'll have one."

With interest French watched him swing round to his desk and hold down an electric switch at the bottom of a little box which stood there. Presently a tiny coil of wire in a recess at the top of the box began to glow. At this Crane lit the cigarette. When he removed his finger the switch sprang up and the wire blackened.

"A handy little apparatus you have there, Mr Crane," French commented. "I've never seen anything like that before."

"I don't suppose you have. It's my own gadget and I got the idea from my car. I couldn't get aviation petrol for my lighter and matches are hard to come by, so I made it in my workshop. Had to put in a small transformer to get a safe voltage. It's quite all right only that you can't carry it about with you. But you were asking about my work?"

"Yes, sir. Your books. In my line, I imagine?"

"Yes and no," Crane answered. "I write thrillers. Detective stories are more about your kind of work, but I distinguish very clearly between the two, and I fancy detective-story writers do too."

"That interests me, Mr Crane. I'm afraid I hadn't properly appreciated the difference."

"A very serious error." Crane was now smiling almost genially. "The detective story is the story of the elucidation of a problem. The solution is reached by inference and deduction from the given facts. In any story worthy of the name all the facts are given to enable the reader to find out the truth for himself. If he fails and continues reading, he can watch the detective succeed by the reasoning he should have employed himself."

"He always does succeed! Unhappily that's where one departs from real life."

"Oh, yes, he must succeed or else the story has no ending."

"I wish we could say the same of our cases."

"I dare say. Well, the thriller is quite different. Here the object is thrills. Premise and deduction take a second place and conflict is in the forefront: the struggle of the criminal and the police, or of the evil gang and their righteous pursuers."

"Very interesting."

"Of course, both have their public. One man's meat, you know. And lucky for us writers that it is so."

"I can understand that. You spend a good deal of time at your work, I suppose?"

Crane looked surprised. "Well, it's my job, isn't it? I spend the same time at my books that other men spend in their offices, or very nearly. Must, you know. If one only worked when one wanted to, one would soon give up altogether."

"It's a nice sort of job, if I may say so. I mean, being able to work at home and keep your own hours and so on."

"It has its advantages, of course. But it's a lonely job. You miss working with other people. Of course it's not the job I want to be doing now."

"You mean, sir?"

"That I want to do war work. I can't do warden or fire fighting or go into the Home Guard because my heart's a bit dicky. But there's lots of clerical work I could do far better than the people who are doing it. But no one will have me. They say, 'Oh, your books are valuable to morale. Keep writing them.' "

"I expect that's true."

"I hope so."

French glanced at the clock on the chimney-piece. Time was getting on.

"I'm afraid, sir, I'm indulging in the pleasure of a chat instead of attending to business. I have a question to ask you which I hope you will understand is purely routine. The idea has been put up, for what it's worth, that Mr Radlett's death was an accident: that the murderer was really out for Mr Savory – and missed him."

Crane stared. "Good heavens, chief inspector, that's a suggestion!" He thought over it, then added: "It might be true enough. He wasn't popular, you know."

"So I've heard. As a result we're asking everyone who had special dealings with Mr Savory to give us the particulars. I understand, sir, you were having a dispute with him, and while I can't demand the information, I should like to hear about it."

French expected Crane's look of anxiety to increase as a result of this question, but it did not do so. On the contrary, the man seemed relieved. But his tone remained serious.

"I cannot fail, chief inspector, to see the implications of that remark. You think I may have tried to murder Mr Savory? Well, I didn't, but – "

"Please don't read into my question more than it contains, Mr Crane," French interrupted. "I may tell you that I've already put it to Mr Wedgewood and Mr Macdougal, and I expect to put it to a lot of others before I've finished."

"Oh, very well. I can't help what you may or may not think, but I'll answer your question. I was, and am, having a dispute with Mr Savory, a very simple matter but troublesome. In my last book I described an objectionable character, an Englishman who had retired from sheep farming in Australia. Mr Savory thinks I intended to portray him and is threatening an action for malicious libel."

"Was your fictitious character really like Mr Savory?"

Crane smiled rather grimly. "My character, Murgatroyd, was crooked, foul-mouthed, without manners, delighting in taking advantage of others and in doing them down, and out to make all the mischief he could without actually breaking the law."

French could not resist smiling in his turn. "If Mr Savory recognized himself from that he certainly has no illusions. But surely there were special circumstances suggesting a parallel?"

"Unhappily there were. Murgatroyd in my book did a man down over a right of way much as Savory did Wedgewood. If you've seen Wedgewood you'll know about that."

"Yes, he told me. It almost looks as if Mr Savory was the model for your Murgatroyd?"

"You can hardly expect me to admit that, Mr French."

"No, sir, I don't, and in any case it isn't my business. If Mr Savory goes on with his action, what will it mean to you?"

Crane again looked worried. "Quite a lot, I'm afraid. These things are expensive. If you're to win you must have good counsel and that costs money. If you save on the counsel you probably lose and pay damages, which also costs money. Incidentally you may have an expensive counsel and also lose, which costs more money still."

"Have you taken any steps in the matter?"

"I've consulted my agents and my publishers, and we've agreed on the firm to defend the action if Savory goes on: Templeton, Gray and Templeton of Lincoln's Inn."

"Thank you," said French, "I think that covers all I want. Now about general confirmation of your statement: the usual routine. Your agents can prove you were on the telephone to them on the morning of the tragedy, but can anyone prove it was just at that time?"

"Well, my wife could, but I don't know whether her evidence would be admissible. Miss Avory also could, at least I think so."

"Miss Avory?"

"Yes, she's staying with us. She's a writer of children's books and was working on the veranda. You'd better see her. Oh, and now I come to think of it, old Treglown was here at the time; that's our jobbing gardener. He might be able to tell you something."

"Thank you. Could I see Miss Avory now?"

The authoress proved to be an elderly woman with a quiet, competent manner, steady eyes and a firm but kindly mouth. No fool, French felt the moment he began to talk to her. A careful observer, he was sure, and able to describe what she saw in terse and accurate language. He found her evidence convincing.

She had been staying with the Cranes for a week. Crane had offered to let her write in his study, but when she could she preferred working in the open air. For this reason and because of the view she had chosen the veranda. She had heard Crane typing on and off. He had not left the study since breakfast. Then he had gone to the telephone, and in the middle of his conversation the sound of the explosion had come. She had looked up and seen the debris flying. Crane had rung off: she could not say whether he had given any explanation to his hearer. He had run quickly out of the house and disappeared among the trees on his way down to the beach. Presently he had come back and told them what had occurred.

French thought this so conclusive that he felt tempted to drop the matter, but as the old man, Treglown, was working in the garden, he decided he might as well have his testimony also. It entirely corroborated what he had already heard. Treglown was doing a bit of weeding when he heard the explosion, and before he could find out what had happened Crane had run out of the house and hurried off in the direction of the beach.

In the face of this testimony French felt he could no longer retain Crane on his list of suspects. Gloomily he accepted the fact that he would have to try elsewhere.

It was scarcely five as the two police officers turned away from Gorse Cottage, too early to think of knocking off. French decided he might begin on the next item of his programme: the uneasiness shown by members of the Savory household. There would be time to interview Mrs Savory and perhaps Miss Meredith before dinner.

When he reached Kelwyn House and inquired for Mrs Savory he was told that she was out. He therefore asked for Miss Meredith and was shown into a small room fitted up as an office.

Anne Meredith was typing when he went in. Now that he saw her for the second time, French found her distinctly good to look at. From her appearance he tried to read her character. Her eyes showed intelligence, her mouth sensitive feeling, her chin determination, and her expression honesty and goodwill. But she was too thin and too pale for perfect health. French summed her up as an estimable young woman, reliable and straightforward and anxious to do what she thought right, but without the stamina to take strong or decisive action.

"I'm now working at the preliminary stage of my investigation, Miss Meredith," he began, "which involves finding out who everybody is and the relations between them all, and I'm hoping that you can help me."

With interest French noted the look of uneasiness flash into her eyes. Whether connected with the crime or not, she certainly knew something which embarrassed or alarmed her.

"I'm rather an outsider at St Pols," she answered, he thought unwillingly. "I really don't know anything of what one might call the politics of the place."

"Well, no, Miss Meredith, I scarcely expected that. But" – he smiled – "you can at least tell me about yourself?"

She did not look at all relieved at this. "Oh, yes, I can do that, of course. What do you want to know?"

"Just a very brief outline of your life as a background and how you came to be here and so on."

"There's not much mystery about that." He thought her manner a little bitter as she sketched her life history, the loss of her parents, her poor health, her offer of a job by Savory and her subsequent dismissal.

"When Mr Savory told you he no longer required your services, was there any – er – unpleasantness?"

"The whole thing wasn't exactly what I should call pleasant, but there was no particular row, if that's what you mean."

There was now not merely bitterness in her manner, there seemed positive hate. French was surprised. There was certainly more in the affair than had come out.

"I follow. And have you decided what you're going to do?"

"Yes, I've got a job at St Pols, as a clerk in the Gas Office."

French all but whistled. "Then you're stronger? You expect to be able to stand it?"

"Oh, yes, I'm much stronger. I'll stand it all right." For a moment she hesitated, then went on: "Perhaps since you're interested I ought to explain that I've recently become engaged – to a Mr Vane. He's secretary to the Invasion Committee: that's how we met. He's in the Ministry of Labour, in the Exchange in St Pols."

French wondered if there had been a blow up about this. An officer in the local Labour Exchange might not have appealed to Savory as a husband for his niece. Yet it was not this which seemed to cause her uneasiness: when speaking of it she had been more normal. French was sure there was some other cause and he began a series of random questions in the hope of finding it.

"I see. Thank you for telling me this. Now let us come to the day of the tragedy. Did you know Mr Savory was going to St Pols that morning?"

"Oh, yes, I made his appointment for him."

"He tells me it was about getting possession of one of his cottages?"

Her expressive face again changed. Indignation was now her strong feeling.

"Yes, I had done all the correspondence about it."

"I follow. Who else knew Mr Savory was going at that time?"

"He had spoken of it at breakfast. Aunt Doris knew. Ellen may have been in the room and heard, I don't remember. Ellen's the maid, I should explain."

"And, of course, there was the solicitor? Was it Mr Forrester?"

"Yes, Mr Forrester."

The conversation had given French a number of mild surprises. Here was another. Unless he was greatly mistaken Forrester was the source of anxiety, or connected with it. As they spoke of him Anne's manner changed again and she grew suspicious and reserved. French determined to pursue the subject.

"How was the appointment with Mr Forrester made?"

"By letter."

"Oh, you didn't use the telephone for that sort of thing?"

"Sometimes, but when possible Uncle Charles liked to have things in writing. He said there was less chance of a misunderstanding."

French was reminded of a game he had played as a boy called Hot and Cold. Someone searched for a hidden object and the onlookers said "Hot!" as he approached it and "Cold!" as he got farther away. Now he said to himself "Hot!" Anne's embarrassment was steadily growing.

"Tell me, did any of these people you have mentioned know that Mr Savory was going to walk to St Pols by the shore?"

"Oh, no, no one knew that."

"But could they not have guessed?"

"I don't think so. They couldn't have known that Uncle Charles wasn't going on somewhere else, in which case he would have taken the car."

French nodded. "That seems reasonable." He racked his brains for more questions about Forrester.

"Did Mr Forrester reply confirming the appointment?"

It was an inane question, yet it worked. Anne's embarrassment approached confusion.

"Yes," she said after a pause. "At least he didn't write. I happened to meet him and he said he had got my letter and would be ready for Uncle Charles."

"Same thing," French answered easily. "When," he went on, determined to keep on the same line at any cost, "was that?"

"The day before the tragedy," she answered miserably.

"I follow," French went on relentlessly. "And where?"

He felt that at last he had reached the root of the trouble. Anne glanced round her like a hunted deer, an almost desperate look in her eyes.

"Oh, what can that matter?" she cried. "I'm – I'm tired of all these questions. In any case, what has my meeting Mr Forrester to do with Mr Radlett's death?"

French moved deprecatingly. "I'm terribly sorry to distress you, Miss Meredith. I can well understand my questions bore you, but the mere fact that your meeting with Mr Forrester could have had nothing directly to do with the tragedy should make you willing to humour me. I'm afraid I must press the question."

"Must I really answer it?" she said with an air of desperation.

"No," French returned, "you are not bound to answer any of my questions, but you will see that if you refuse to do so you will make me suspect that you're trying to cover up something serious. If so, I'll naturally go to Mr Forrester and ask him, and if he refuses to answer I'll know there is something wrong. And believe me in that case it'll not be long till I've discovered what it is. We have ways of finding things out that you've no idea of."

"Oh, there's nothing illegal, I assure you. I suppose by 'wrong', you mean illegal?"

"I accept your word that there's nothing illegal in the affair, but there's certainly something that's worrying and distressing you. Now I must ask my question again, but I can assure you that nothing that's not directly connected with the case will pass my lips."

She made a despairing gesture. "It was coming out of the wood at the bottom of the garden."

"Oh, yes?" French felt at a loss. "The garden of this house?"

"Yes."

"About what time in the day was that?"

"About half past two."

French was puzzled. What could have brought a presumably busy solicitor to a wood near Kelwyn House at two-thirty on the afternoon of a working day?

"What was he doing there?" he asked abruptly, and once again he felt he was on the right track.

"Oh, how do I know! We didn't discuss it."

"Again I accept your word, but I put it to you that though you don't actually know, you're pretty well satisfied. Come, Miss Meredith, I've got to know this and I'm going to. You're only prolonging a painful interview. Tell me what's in your mind. Again I assure you that unless the law has been broken or it directly affects my case, no one will hear of it."

She was obviously on the verge of tears, looking desperately this way and that as if seeking some way of escape. Then at last, with a gesture, as of throwing everything to the winds, she went on.

"This is perfectly hateful, but I see you won't stop till I've told you. I didn't want to say anything, particularly since Aunt Doris has been so good to me, but I think he was meeting her."

French's pulse leaped. Here was news indeed. But he made light of it.

"You mean he and she were lovers?" he answered easily. "Oh, well, Miss Meredith, there's nothing to be so distressed about in that. I'm afraid it's not such an uncommon thing as you seem to suppose."

Surprise and relief showed on her face. "Then you won't have to repeat it?" she asked wonderingly.

"Not, as I said, unless it turns out to be connected with my case, and you can see for yourself how unlikely that is. But all the same, when you have gone so far I'm afraid you must go the whole way and tell me all you know."

She made no further difficulties. She explained that since she came to live with them she had known that her uncle's and aunt's married life was unhappy, and told how she had learnt of her aunt's relations with the solicitor through overhearing their conversation in the spinney. On that afternoon her aunt had afterwards been in an excited state, and a similar condition on other occasions had suggested to Anne further clandestine meetings. When on the afternoon of the day she met Forrester she found the same symptoms, she drew her own conclusions.

It was with a good deal more to think about that French presently thanked her and took his departure.

11

ARTHUR WEDGEWOOD

Like most small towns, St Pols had a flourishing unofficial intelligent service. Few secrets of the neighbourhood remained secrets for long. Rumours, started no one knew where or by whom, spread with incredible speed. That those who passed them on should be so unenterprising as to confine themselves to what they had heard was scarcely to be expected, and often the people of St Pols knew of facts which had never happened.

An hour after French's arrival the place was humming with the news and its following train of speculation. The knowledgeable explained that Scotland Yard never took up a case unless called in by the local authorities, and that the latter never appealed for help unless serious crime was suspected. Therefore serious crime had reared its ugly head at St Pols. What could this crime be? Not the theft of a few hand grenades from the Home Guard store. That would be small fry for a chief inspector! No, it was something more important than that, something more deadly. Elimination led to Radlett. Soon everyone was repeating the rumour that Radlett's death was not the accident which had been supposed.

Thus it came to pass that when French began his investigation there were few who did not know just what he had come to do, and an analysis of the questions he asked, kept the knowing *au fait* with his progress. Enthusiasts repeated the news hopefully to the members of the coroner's jury.

While the sensation delighted the outsiders, to those actually involved the affair became a very considerable anxiety. Among these latter was Arthur Wedgewood.

Shortly after French had paid his second visit Wedgewood knocked off work and walked wearily back to his house for tea. He was looking tired and worried, and when he and Maude were seated together in the lounge she remarked on it.

"It's this tragedy," he answered. "I don't like the turn things are taking. That chief inspector has just been with me again."

"The second time in two days! What did he want?"

"More questions. Very polite and all that, but abominably inquisitive and searching."

"Well, of course, isn't that his job? What was the special point this time?"

"Savory."

Maude stared.

"But how extraordinary! I've just been talking to Doris and she told me the very same thing!"

"You mean?"

"Mr French had been there this morning and had asked all sorts of questions about Mr Savory."

"What questions? Did she tell you?"

"Principally about his walk to the village. Who knew he was going and all that."

Wedgewood moved uneasily. "Why on earth should French want to know that?"

Maude shook her head helplessly. "She told me he had a long interview with Mr Savory himself. It must have worried Mr Savory, because he was like a bear with a sore head afterwards."

"Nothing unusual in that. All the same I'd like to know how he comes into it."

"What exactly did Mr French ask you?"

"About my relations with him. He'd evidently heard we'd had a dispute. I didn't want to speak of it, but he insisted on having the whole story: the difficulties about the purchase of the farm and the right of way affair all from A to Z."

"Extraordinary! Even suppose my poor uncle was – murdered – which I simply can't believe – what on earth could our right of way have to do with it?"

"I more or less put that question to French, but he wasn't giving anything away; said he couldn't tell what might or might not be relative, but he wanted all the information he could get. All camouflage, of course: I'm certain he's on to something."

"It certainly looks like it."

"He wasn't with me only. He'd seen Macdougal on the same point. He'd somehow heard about trouble over the cottage and he got the whole thing from him: children's trespassing and everything."

Helen gave a slight shiver. "One wouldn't mind it being puzzling, because after all it's no business of ours, but it all strikes one as – what shall I call it? – *malevolent*. Threatening! Don't you feel it?"

"I suppose it's inevitable. But French is polite and seems a decent fellow personally."

"That doesn't matter, it frightens me. I can't help feeling that something dreadful may be sprung on us."

Before Wedgewood could reply, the hall doorbell trilled, and as Maude had household help only in the mornings, she went to answer it. Wedgewood heard Crane's voice.

"Come in, Mr Crane," came the reply. "He's in the lounge. You're just in time to catch him before he goes out. Have you had tea?"

"Yes, thanks. Just finished." The voices approached and Wedgewood rose to his feet.

"Hullo, Crane. Glad to see you. Come in."

"Thought I'd like a word with you, Wedgewood, about this fellow French. Please don't go away, Mrs Wedgewood; it's nothing private."

Wedgewood pulled round an easy-chair. "Sit down and have a cigarette if you won't take tea."

"Thanks, I'll have my pipe if you don't object?" He looked at Maude, who reassured him.

For a moment they chatted about nothing in particular, then Crane reverted to the object of his call.

"About this fellow French," he repeated. "I understand he's been to see you?"

Wedgewood nodded. "Twice in two days. Yesterday and again this afternoon."

Crane cocked his head on one side and looked knowing. "Your row with Savory?"

"Yes. How did you know?"

"That's what he was on to with me. A bit unsettling, this idea he's got?"

"What is it? We were just wondering."

Crane looked surprised. "Do you mean to say he didn't tell you?"

"He explained nothing. His questions were a mystery to me."

"You don't say so! Then I've been putting the wrong procedure into my books. I thought they had to tell."

"Tell what?"

"What their questions meant. It's a bit disquieting, I'm afraid. He thinks the – er – wrong man was killed."

"What! You mean they intended to get Savory?"

Crane nodded. "I don't know what he founds the theory on, but that's certainly what he thinks."

Wedgewood made a gesture. "Good heavens! What an idea!"

Crane nodded. "But it would explain his line?" he suggested.

"Oh, yes, it would explain it all right. He can prove that I had reason to hate Savory, and that Macdougal had too."

"And I also," Crane added.

"Motives!" Wedgewood declared. "It's clear now what he's after. And he's getting on. Motives proved in the case of three suspects."

"Oh," Maude cried, "didn't I say there was something threatening about it! Something malevolent! This must mean that he – *suspects* you!"

Wedgewood shrugged. "Not necessarily. He's probably got a list of the people who had quarrelled with Savory and is going over them all."

"That's it," Crane nodded. "That's what I thought."

"And that explains the questions to Doris and Anne," Maude declared. She turned to Crane. "He got a list from them of all the people who knew Mr Savory was going to the village that morning."

"That's it," Crane repeated.

"Maude added that he'd had an interview with Savory himself," went on Arthur, "and that it evidently upset Savory, for afterwards he was like a bear with a sore head."

"Surely a description of the normal Savory," returned Crane. "But as a matter of fact one can't imagine him being very pleased at the news. If someone wanted to murder him and didn't bring it off, he'll probably try again. Something for Savory to look forward to."

"I think it's all horrible!" Maude declared.

Crane grew serious. "It is really: you're right, of course. I'm being selfish, I'm afraid. I'm not worried because I can personally prove my innocence. How are you fixed, Wedgewood? Have you an alibi?"

Wedgewood shook his head. "Unfortunately I haven't. I was mending my chicken-coops when the thing occurred, but I can't prove it. And Macdougal was working in his shop, but he can't prove that either."

"Proof won't be necessary," Maude asserted. "You've both got known characters, haven't you?"

"That's right, Mrs Wedgewood," Crane approved. "In your husband's case French's questions are only a matter of form."

"All the same, I wouldn't mind having something more convincing," said Wedgewood. "What's your alibi, Crane?"

"Just a bit of luck. As luck would have it I was actually telephoning when the shot went off."

"Oh, yes, you said so at the inquest. That's certainly lucky for you."

"Yes, and by another bit of luck Bertha Avory was just outside the window and can prove it."

Wedgewood's congratulations were interrupted by other voices and Dick and Jessica Little appeared at the door. Both were thrilled at the news of French's theory and both immediately accepted it as the probable truth.

They began to talk about alibis. When Crane and Little had swapped theirs, they turned to Wedgewood.

"You say neither you nor Macdougal have one," Crane remarked, "but are you sure? I think you've probably a pretty good one."

"I'd like to know what it is," Wedgewood answered pessimistically.

"Did either of you know that Savory was going to the village that morning?"

It was a point Wedgewood had not thought of. "Why, no," he answered with some eagerness, "I certainly didn't, and I'm sure Macdougal didn't either."

"Then," Crane declared, "you're all right."

Misgiving again swept over Wedgewood. "I can't prove I didn't," he objected.

"You wouldn't have to," Crane spoke with assurance. "If French were to accuse you, you'd simply deny it, and it would be up to him to prove your statement false."

"Which of course he couldn't do," put in Dick. "Yes, that's certainly a point."

"It's complete enough for anyone," Crane said dogmatically. "Don't you worry any more, Wedgewood."

This was pleasant hearing to Wedgewood, and the more he thought over it, the more satisfying it became. It was true he had not, and could not, possibly have known Savory's plans. And that was not all. To bring about the death of Radlett he had an obvious motive in the money which would come to Maude. This was a motive which remained continuously operative. But his motive for killing Savory necessarily grew weaker with the mere passage of time. If he had not committed murder when his feelings were heated, it was unlikely in the last degree that he would do so now when resentment had become dulled. On the whole Wedgewood felt considerably relieved.

It proved an afternoon of interruptions, for scarcely had Crane and the Littles left when Anne Meredith arrived. She came ostensibly to return some books Maude had lent her, but Wedgewood imagined her real motive was to unburden her feelings to some sympathetic listener. At all events she chattered away to Maude of her experiences.

"You know," Maude said presently, "we've discovered what was behind all those questions of the chief inspector's," and she went on to repeat Crane's news.

Wedgewood was amazed by its effect on Anne. For a moment at first she showed a normal interest, as anyone would at the solution of some puzzling problem. Then her face fell. A look of alarm flashed across it and she stumbled and almost broke off in the middle of a remark. A moment later her expression changed to one of absolute consternation, and so engrossed was she by her thoughts, that she left a question of Maude's completely unanswered.

"You've thought of something?" Wedgewood said kindly.

She looked at him uncomprehendingly and with horror in her eyes. Then she made an obvious effort to pull herself together.

"Oh, no, no," she stammered. "At least, I mean, Aunt Doris and I knew uncle was going to St Pols. I wondered – er – if the police might – er – suspect us?"

That this was not her real fear Wedgewood was convinced, but she so obviously did not wish to be questioned, that he pretended to be satisfied. As soon as politeness permitted she excused herself and went hurriedly off.

"*Well!*" said Maude when they were alone, "if that wasn't a surprise! What do you think it was all about?"

Wedgewood had considerable faith in his wife's perspicacity. If she didn't know, he felt he needn't be ashamed of his own ignorance.

"Why not what she said?" he suggested: "that she was afraid she and Doris – probably Doris – might be suspected?"

Maude was scornful. "My dear, do have some sense," she begged. "Quite obviously it's something much more serious than that."

"You're not suggesting that she's guilty, I suppose?"

"Do use your wits, Arthur! Anne couldn't hurt a fly. But she knows something: that's clear enough."

"She couldn't know who did it."

"So one would say. And yet, can you think of anything else which would upset her so much?"

Wedgewood shook his head. "Let's see," he remarked, "what was the exact point which did upset her?"

"The idea that her uncle was the intended victim."

"Yes, that was it. And she lives at Kelwyn House and knows all about the household and Savory's connections."

"What do you mean?"

"Only what you suggested yourself: that she might suddenly have guessed who was guilty. Perhaps we shouldn't be talking like this, but I suppose it couldn't be – Doris?"

"Doris! No! Doris is one of the best who ever walked!"

"That may be, dear, and far be it from me to suggest otherwise. All the same, fancy being married to Savory. How long would it be before you wanted to kill him yourself?"

"I suppose Doris dug a hole in the sand and planted a mine?"

"Not very likely, I admit. But look here, Maude, here's something a good deal more likely. That chap Vane!"

"Reggie Vane? Nonsense again! He's quite a good fellow."

"There was some story about Savory and he having had a row."

"If that's any criterion half St Pols would be guilty. But oh! isn't it horrible! Already there's an atmosphere of secrecy and suspicion in the place. I noticed it in the village this morning: people not looking straight at one another and stopping talking when others appear."

"An unsolved murder case usually involves that."

"Well, I felt it, but I thought we'd be able to keep clear of it ourselves. And now here we are, as bad as anyone!"

"You're right; we mustn't allow ourselves to be carried away." He levered himself slowly out of his chair. "But this discussion won't help to get those wretched lists completed. I must be off."

Meanwhile Anne was hurrying back to Kelwyn House, perplexity and fear gnawing at her heart.

The news that her uncle might have been the intended victim was a terrible blow, for she could not but see that if so, trouble might easily fall on the two people she most loved in all the world. Her Aunt Doris, of course, was personally beyond suspicion, but what about Mr Forrester? If he were arrested her aunt would suffer horribly. And it was *she*, Anne Meredith, who had told Mr French about their affair! Bitterly Anne regretted answering his questions, yet what else could she have done? He had jockeyed her into an impossible position, assuring her that if she didn't reply he would go to Forrester, and that if Forrester didn't reply he would know there was something wrong and probe till he got it.

175

But there was even worse than this in it. Reggie! Could Reggie possibly be suspected? Reggie had had that row with her uncle and hadn't been too wise in the things he had said. Moreover, her uncle had been rude to her, and indeed had treated her badly. Could Mr French think that there was motive enough here?

Pressing and troublesome also was the problem of what, if anything, she should do. To be forewarned is to be forearmed. Was it not her duty to tell these dear people of the danger which might be threatening them?

In the end it was a tiny matter which tipped the balance and made her decide that, at whatever cost to herself, she must give her warning. This was the fact that as she turned into the Kelwyn House drive she saw her aunt waving to her from a seat in the garden. She felt she dared not fail to take advantage of such an opportunity.

Doris Savory took one look at her face and cried out in alarm.

Anne sat down beside her. "Oh, Aunt Doris, I've just had a piece of bad news," she began, "or at least it may be bad. I saw the Wedgewoods and they told me. What do you think, Mr French believes that Mr Radlett was murdered by mistake; I mean, they got the wrong man! They intended to kill Uncle Charles!"

Doris stared at her without speaking, but her face slowly grew white and strained.

"How do you mean bad news, my dear?" she said presently in a low voice.

"Well," Anne found progress terribly difficult, "there are two things. One is Reggie. There was their dispute, and you know Reggie has spoken foolishly about uncle."

"And you're afraid Mr French may suspect him? Oh, nonsense! No one could do that."

"Mr French might, and if he did, Reggie mightn't find it so easy to prove his innocence."

"There's not the slightest fear of Mr French suspecting him. Why, Reggie's character is guarantee enough."

Anne smiled faintly. "Good of you to say that, but you never know. I'm frightened about it."

"You needn't be: not the least bit. But you said there were two things. What's the other?"

Anne moved uneasily. Her hands clasped and reclasped her bag. For a moment she did not answer.

"I just don't know how to say it," she murmured at last. "Oh, Aunt Doris, what will you think of me?"

"Say what? Come on; out with it!" Mrs Savory's voice had grown quite sharp.

"Oh, this is dreadful! But I must tell you. One day, it's a good while ago now, I had a headache and went to sit in the orchard near the spinney fence. I fell asleep and when I woke I – heard voices. I didn't know what on earth to do; it seemed equally bad to listen or to call out. Then while I was thinking it over, the voices faded away. But" – she looked bravely at her aunt – "I heard enough to know."

Doris Savory took her hand and squeezed it. "My dear, it was a dreadful position for you! However, all's well now."

Anne made a gesture of despair. "Oh, but that's just it, it isn't! There's worse to come. I – I – didn't mean to, but I – let it out to Mr French!"

Doris stared. "You told Mr French?" she repeated incredulously. "Anne, dear, I can hardly believe you'd have done that!"

Anne was almost crying. "He got it out of me! I can't tell how he did, but he trapped me into telling," and she went on to describe the interview. Presently Doris nodded.

"Oh, well, it wasn't your fault. I understand; you couldn't help yourself. But why have you told me now?"

This didn't seem any easier to Anne. "Well, don't you see? I was afraid for the same reason as about Reggie. I mean, might Mr French suspect Mr Forrester?"

"Oh, so it's occurred to you too?"

"I thought you might like to warn him, as I'm going to warn Reggie."

Again Doris squeezed her hand. "My dear, for a moment I misjudged you. I'm so sorry. I can't thank you enough for your courage and honesty."

"Oh, aunt, I'm so glad to have told you! I hated knowing, and keeping it to myself! Now I'll go and ring up Reggie and ask him to meet me after supper."

Anne did indeed feel that a weight had gone from her mind, and her interview with Vane still further reassured her. For Vane pooh-poohed her fears.

"Nonsense, old thing," he answered, "it's very sweet of you and all that, but I'm not afraid of being suspected. Why, your respected uncle has given me my wife! You may think I should have murdered him for that, but no one else will!"

His attempt to joke over it comforted Anne for the moment. But as she tossed sleeplessly that night she recalled the look of anxiety which had appeared in his eyes at a moment when he thought he was unobserved.

So fear and dread and mutual suspicion grew among the inhabitants at St Pols in an ever widening circle.

12

CHIEF INSPECTOR FRENCH

That night French sat in a corner of the hotel lounge writing up his notes and considering his next move. His results in the case so far were a warning against over optimism. He had already found three people, Wedgewood, Macdougal and Crane, each of whom had a motive for wishing Savory dead. But it had turned out that not one of these was guilty of the murder. Here were two more, Mrs Savory and Forrester, who had the necessary motive, and now he reminded himself that motive involved guilt no more in their cases than in the others.

While it was possible that Mrs Savory had tried to kill her husband, it was unlikely in the last degree, not only from the general circumstances, but from the report he had received of her character. Forrester, however, was a different proposition. If Forrester really loved Mrs Savory, and there was a difficulty about a divorce as was suggested by Anne Meredith's tale, he might well have been tempted to proceed to extremes. French felt that about Forrester he must know a good deal more.

Another line of investigation was suggested by Anne's statement. She had been given notice by Savory and was evidently feeling bitter about it. That she herself should therefore have tried to murder Savory was, of course, absurd, but if she were engaged and if her fiancé thought she had been badly treated, he might have done so. Not perhaps a very likely proposition, but here also French must be sure.

What a man Savory must be, French thought, to have made all these enemies! And from what Vanson had said, there might be many more. Surely he could not be normal? Such ill-will and malevolence could only be explained by some mental twist. The man was certainly qualifying for a lunatic asylum, if he was not already a fit subject.

French thought his next step must be to interrogate Mrs Savory. She would be easier to handle than Forrester, and primed with her knowledge he could deal more efficiently with the solicitor.

Next morning, therefore, he went out again with Carter to Kelwyn House. As they approached he was glad to see Savory going down the path to the shore. He did not think Savory would insist on being present at the interview with his wife, but it was all to the good that he should not have the chance.

French was but a few moments in Mrs Savory's presence when his opinion of the previous day was confirmed, that whatever she might have done, she was no party to a murder. She was obviously kind and good-hearted and hatred seemed entirely foreign to her nature. Her anxiety was clearer than ever, but now that French could guess the cause, this was no longer suspicious.

He began by asking for particulars about herself, which he had not previously obtained. He learnt, however, little of interest. Her maiden name had been Sinclair and she had met Savory in London, where he had lived before moving to Cornwall. He had had private means and was not engaged in any kind of work, though he was at that time considering taking up politics. Nothing, however, had come of this. They had one son, now in the Air Force.

Of Anne Meredith, to whom French then switched the interrogation, she had more to say. She was, French was sure, genuinely attached to Anne. The offer of work as Savory's secretary had been her idea, and she had welcomed the girl to Kelwyn House. Anne had more than repaid her in help and affection. The only thing Mrs Savory regretted was that the job was not financially a better one for Anne, but as her husband truly said, the work was a bagatelle and was certainly not worth more than the comfortable home and pocket money she was receiving.

About her leaving Mrs Savory was more reserved. She repeated the story of the new chauffeur who was going also to act as secretary, and said that while she was extremely sorry to lose the girl, it was obvious that if there wasn't enough work for one secretary, there wouldn't be enough for two.

French then asked about the fiancé in the Labour Exchange. At once he saw that Mrs Savory was disappointed about the engagement. The man, she said, was named Vane, a nice youth, estimable in character, and to whom there was no personal objection. But unfortunately he was only second in command, and his prospects were, from what ought to have been Anne's point of view, simply nil. Moreover, he was classed C3; too delicate to be called up to any position in the Forces. In fact, from a worldly point of view Anne was proposing to throw herself away.

It was then when French had, as he hoped, lulled his victim to sleep with innocuous questions, that he turned suddenly and without warning to his real business.

"One other question, Mrs Savory, and one that I'm really sorry to have to ask, but will you please tell me about your relations with Mr Forrester?"

To his amazement his little squib missed fire.

"I thought you would ask me that," Doris answered calmly; "Miss Meredith told me you had obtained the information from her. What exactly do you want to know?"

"Just the circumstances of the affair, please?"

"I've little to tell you that you don't know. It's true that my married life has not been happy. Mr Savory and I don't see eye to eye on a number of matters, and I suppose that was why I at last looked elsewhere. Mr Forrester and I love each other, and we're considering my trying for a divorce so that we may be married."

"Thank you, madam. Is there any difficulty about the divorce?"

She looked doubtful. "I really can't tell you. I haven't yet broached the subject to my husband."

"I'm afraid I must press the question. Why have you hesitated in the matter?"

"Well, I think you might understand that. It's a considerable step and I have to think of my son. There are pretty strong arguments against as well as for."

"Of course I understand that, Mrs Savory, but it was not that I meant. Have you any reason to fear that your efforts to get a divorce might not be successful?"

He could see from her manner that this was it. "I don't know," she said lamely.

While again he gained time by writing in his notebook, he racked his brains to think of the hitch. It could not be want of evidence. Forrester, a solicitor, would know how to provide that. What else could it be?

At once he saw. Given a mentality like Savory's, what more likely than that he would refuse the divorce merely to prevent the happiness of these two?

"You mean, I suppose, that Mr Savory might not agree?"

There was that in her manner which told French he had guessed right.

"Do you police know everything?" she said tremulously.

He smiled. "No, madam, but we know more than we're given credit for. And now I have again to express my regret for these questions and to repeat my assurance that unless, as I said, the law has been broken, not one word that you have said will ever become known."

The visit had indicated that there might well be a definite motive on Forrester's part. French saw that his next step must be to interview him.

While they drove back to St Pols he continued pondering over the affair. He thought it strange that under the circumstances Forrester had continued to act as Savory's solicitor. Then he saw that until a decision about the divorce had been taken, the man could scarcely have done otherwise. He could not have resigned without giving some explanation, and it would not have been easy to provide a false one which was still convincing.

The solicitor's office was in an old Georgian house in the St Pols square. He was engaged with a client when they arrived, but after some minutes they were shown up to a large front room on the first floor. Forrester proved to be a tall, distinguished looking man with a long, shrewd face and a firm jaw. He gave the impression of being both able and cultivated.

A few introductory remarks convinced French that only direct methods would have a chance of succeeding, and he therefore went straight to his point.

"As you probably know, sir, I was sent here to investigate the death of Mr Radlett, because it had been found that the affair was not the accident which had been supposed, but was a deliberate murder."

"So I heard," Forrester answered. "I confess I couldn't see how it could have been an accident. Did you learn how the explosion had been caused?"

"Yes, sir. The mine was detonated electrically from farther up the shore by means of a wire which passed down the groyne."

Forrester nodded slowly. "A deliberate affair with proof of prearrangement. Well, go ahead, Mr French."

"I began by looking into motives, and I found that four persons stood to benefit by Mr Radlett's death, and so far as I could ascertain, four only. These were Mr and Mrs Little and Mr and Mrs Wedgewood. I therefore concentrated on these and soon satisfied myself of their innocence."

"I'm not surprised to hear that. I couldn't imagine any one of them guilty."

"I dare say, sir, but I hadn't your knowledge. Then, as you can imagine, I found myself rather at a loss, until a new idea was suggested. This was that Mr Radlett had been killed in error, the attempt, which had miscarried, having really been on Mr Savory."

Forrester looked genuinely surprised. "That's very ingenious. I confess I hadn't thought of it. I wonder if you're right."

"I don't know," French returned, "but I found myself forced to examine the possibilities."

"Naturally."

"As you can understand, I had first to make a list, as complete as I could, of those who had grudges against Mr

Savory or who might have wished his death. And here, sir, we come to the object of my call. I much regret that I have had to include your name."

"My name! I don't understand you, chief inspector."

"Your name, sir. I have therefore come to see you and I propose to put all my cards on the table, in the hope that you will make a statement to clear up the matter."

Forrester looked a good deal worried. "I don't follow you there. I presume you're scarcely accusing me of attempting to murder Savory. However, I'm here to listen to what you have to say."

"I'm accusing you of nothing whatever. I only wish things cleared up. The point at issue concerns your relations with Mrs Savory."

Forrester stared without replying.

"Also," French went on, "your fear that Mr Savory will not collaborate in the divorce. It's therefore obvious that as long as he lives you may both be in a difficulty."

Forrester jerked about, evidently exasperated. "Damn it all, you are accusing me of attempted murder!" His voice grew harsh and vindictive. "You come to me with a tale about putting your cards on the table and it turns out to be a lot of guesswork; which no doubt you hope I'll confirm and so give you a case against me. Well, I'm not falling for it. I'm saying nothing."

"I'm afraid, sir, you're rather seriously mistaken. I'm quite sure of my ground; it's all been admitted by Mrs Savory in the presence of a witness. As I say, I'm making no accusation, but if you cared to make a statement mentioning where you were between nine-thirty and ten-thirty on the day of the tragedy, I'd be glad to hear it."

"No doubt you would," Forrester looked at him appraisingly, then repeated heavily, "No doubt you would." He paused, then added: "Let me think about this."

French nodded and had recourse to his notebook, in which he began writing. Five minutes passed in a silence broken only by the scratching of his pen. Carter had the faculty of motionless rumination, and unless directly addressed, seldom made a remark. At length Forrester moved sharply and spoke with his former crispness.

"I've thought over what you've said, chief inspector, and decided to tell you everything, though as far as I can make out, that will be little that you don't already know. I don't do it willingly, but I see that I can't help myself. How you learnt so much in the time beats me, but then, of course, I haven't had a Scotland Yard training."

"I'm glad, sir, that you're going to make the statement. I hope it will end the matter as far as you're concerned."

"Since that's your attitude, I'll do what I can to get the thing cleared up. In face of all you've said, I needn't deny that I want to marry Mrs Savory. We would both like it. You're right so far."

French nodded.

"But when you suggest there's a difficulty in getting a divorce which only Savory's death can overcome – for that is your suggestion – you're entirely wrong. We don't know what his reaction to the idea might be, for the simple reason that it hasn't yet been put to him."

"Mrs Savory seemed certain of it."

"She's wrong. I agree that we discussed the possibility, as we discussed all the other pros and cons. But we have no reason to believe, and I for one do not believe, that he wouldn't be glad of the divorce. What happiness could he hope for with his wife, if he compelled her to remain chained to him?"

"Very reasonable, sir."

"And I put another point to you, Mr French. What sort of a fool would I be if I had tried to murder Savory – again as you suggest – without first finding out his views? Why, the idea's absurd."

A convincing argument – if true! Did they not know Savory's views? It was hard to say, and yet one point seemed to support Forrester. If Savory knew about the affair, why the secret meetings in the wood? These surely could only be explained by the desire to keep them from him.

"Also a strong argument, sir," French admitted.

"Well, that seems to cover the thing. What else do you want to know?"

"Just one or two small points." French went through the form of consulting his notebook. "I gather that in spite of this affair you still acted professionally for Mr Savory?"

Forrester drew back as if annoyed. "I don't see what that has to do with your inquiry," he said, then as if a fresh idea struck him, he went on more eagerly. "But on second thoughts I'm glad you asked the question, for it has just occurred to me that the fact is proof of my statement. As you know, Mr Savory was coming in to see me on business when Mr Radlett met his death. He has stated that himself, and it can be proved beyond question by the letters fixing up the appointment. Now do you think he would have continued to consult me if he had known of the relations between myself and his wife? Use your own common sense, chief inspector, and you'll see that the idea is absurd."

French saw this very well, provided the consultation had been about getting Macdougal out of his cottage. But suppose it had been about the divorce?

The point, he decided, could be considered later, though it did occur to him that Savory would not call on the solicitor on such a subject; if he consented to see him at all he would let Forrester go out to Kelwyn House.

"It was about Mr Macdougal's cottage?" he asked.

Forrester grimaced. "Oh, you've heard about that, have you? Yes, that was it. As you know, I can't say anything against my client and I'm not going to, but I may tell you that had it not been for my friendship with Mrs Savory, I should have given up Mr Savory's work."

"You mean that you disapproved of the position he took up?"

"That's just what I do mean, not once, but many times, though I know I shouldn't admit it."

"What you say won't go any further, sir. I gathered that spite was really behind that matter of the cottage. Would you be willing to discuss it?"

"I don't think you can expect me to do that. Owing to the special circumstances I've already said more than I should."

"Very well. I appreciate your scruples. But just to complete your statement, will you tell me where you were between nine-thirty and ten-thirty on the day of the tragedy?"

Forrester looked a good deal more worried. "This, I'm afraid, chief inspector," he said with some hesitation, "is very unfortunate for me. The fact is, not foreseeing what would happen, I have no alibi."

"Never mind. Just tell me what you did."

"I thought before Savory called I'd go round and have a chat with Pengelly, that's Macdougal's solicitor. I wanted to make finally certain that we couldn't agree to some compromise. If there was any hope of it I'd have put it up to Savory. But Pengelly was positive no compromise was possible."

"I follow. What time did you leave your office?"

"Let's see. I'm not quite sure. About quarter to ten, I think. Miss Tregenza may remember. She rang up to see if Pengelly was there."

"And when did you get back here?"

"About twenty-five past ten. I know that because I was watching the time for my appointment at half past."

"Were you all that time with Mr Pengelly?"

"Well, no." Forrester's manner grew more hesitating and embarrassed. Then with a shrug he seemed to make up his mind. "I suppose I must tell you the whole thing. That morning I was feeling pretty bitter against Savory. It was not only for his treatment of Mrs Savory: the Macdougal business put my back up rather badly too. I admit this fully, though I know you can twist it against me if you want to."

"I try not to twist evidence, Mr Forrester."

"I didn't mean that literally, though in any case I shouldn't have said it. What I want to convey is that I felt hot and doubted if I would be able to talk to Savory civilly. I was there outside Pengelly's office. It was a fine morning and I had half an hour to spare. I decided on a stroll to walk myself into a cooler frame of mind. I did so. I went up to the top of Tower Hill, that's the hill at the back of the town which the Home Guard use as a lookout. When I got back to the office I had myself well in hand."

At this all French's suspicions flooded back. Was this a likely tale? Could Forrester have gone, not to the top of Tower Hill, but to Groyne Point?

It certainly seemed possible. The strip of heath land with its shrubs and birches stretched for the whole distance, and would have provided adequate cover. Forrester knew almost to the minute the hour at which Savory would probably pass the groyne, and would have been able to detonate the mine and reach his office by ten-thirty.

At this point an old difficulty cropped up once more. If Forrester had done all this, how did the wrong man come to be killed?

Then French thought again of the settling of the trip. Forrester could have seen Savory coming down the path to the shore, realized that he would be the first to pass the groyne, and set his apparatus. This would have ensured his return to his office in ample time to complete the alibi.

"Did anyone see you during your walk?"

"In the town I'm sure a number of people did, though I don't actually remember meeting anyone. Beyond the town I saw no one."

"There was no one on the hill?"

"Not that I saw."

French put away his notebook. "That's all I want in the meantime, sir. I'm grateful for what you've told me, but you understand, of course, that I must check your statement."

"I hope you'll be able to do it," Forrester returned gloomily. It was what French also hoped – and doubted. He turned to Carter as they left the house.

"We'll go over to this man Pengelly's office and have a look round. I'm afraid we're up against something pretty stiff."

"Did you believe Forrester's tale about going to the top of the hill?"

"I don't know. It wasn't very convincing, but of course it's possible."

"I thought he was lying."

"You did? And why?"

"Manner, sir. It changed when he said that."

French was slightly surprised. It was not often that Carter was so positive. He was inclined to agree with him, though he recognized that such impressions could be very misleading.

A passer-by directed them to Pengelly's office. French did not go in, but stood on the pavement looking about him.

"Let's see. This road leads north-west up into the country and joins the main east-west highway. It's one of the two approaches to the town. And that first crossroads is the turn for Tower Hill: right for the Hill and left for Groyne Point."

"That's right, sir. The left road goes to some cottages and then peters out on to the heath."

"Quite. And that's – I say, Carter, here's a bit of luck! See that building at the crossroads? What does that board say? 'Convalescent Home', isn't it?"

"Yes, 'Convalescent Home'."

"The very place! Those patients are bound to find the time drag. They probably sit looking out of the windows. Quite a chance that one of them saw Forrester. Come along and we'll try our luck."

The matron saw them after a short delay. She proved a rather severe-looking woman with a smile which transformed her face and made it radiate kindliness and goodwill. She raised her eyebrows on seeing French's card, but made no remark as she took the visitors to her room and invited them to sit down.

"I want to ask for your help, madam," French said when he had explained what had brought them to the town. "I needn't worry you with the details of my inquiry, but it's in connection with the timing of various events which took place on that morning. We want to settle Mr Savory's movements, as they will fix the time of the tragedy. He was meeting Mr Forrester, the solicitor, and therefore we want to establish Mr Forrester's movements also. About ten that morning Mr Forrester passed this Home. The exact time is important, but he can't himself fix it. I wondered if any of your patients happened to see him pass and noted it?"

The matron looked doubtful. "I should think it unlikely," she answered. "Even if anyone had seen him, why should they note the time?"

"I'm afraid it's a long shot," French agreed. "But I should like to make sure."

"Then what do you want me to do?"

"Either, madam, to make the inquiry yourself or to allow me to do so."

She hesitated. "I think if I could do it, it would be better. A little thing upsets some of our patients and I'd rather they didn't see strangers. You just want to know if anyone saw Mr Forrester, and if so, at what time?"

"Yes, please, and also where he was going. You see, he passed twice."

"I'll do what I can. I'm not busy at the moment, so you may as well wait."

French was well content to do so. He felt that if the information was obtainable, this quiet, competent woman would obtain it. His confidence was justified. In ten minutes she returned with a tall, good-looking girl, whose pale cheeks and bloodless lips showed she was there as a patient.

"This is Miss Pascoe. She happened to notice Mr Forrester, and I don't think it would do her any harm to tell you about it. But she's just recovering from an operation and must not be tired."

"I shall not tire her, madam," French returned, "and I'm most grateful to you both."

"Then I'll allow you five minutes."

The matron smiled and went out. French turned to the girl.

"I expect Matron explained what I want, Miss Pascoe," he said pleasantly. "It's just the fixing of times. You happened to see Mr Forrester that morning?"

"Yes, I saw him twice. I was sitting in the window looking out. I was supposed to be knitting, you know, but one gets tired."

"I can well understand that. Can you remember the times at which you saw him?"

"The first time, yes. He passed just as the clock was striking ten. I happened to notice it."

"Splendid! And the second time?"

"I'm afraid I can't tell that so accurately. He went back, I should say, in about twenty minutes."

"Good enough. Could you just add the direction he was taking each time?"

"Yes. The first time he came from the direction of his office and turned down towards the shore. Next time he went back in the opposite direction."

French repressed his interest. "Yes, that's what he said," he answered easily, "but I'd like to be sure I've got it correctly. You're sure it wasn't to the right towards Tower Hill that he went?"

"Oh, absolutely. I saw him quite plainly."

Then Forrester had lied, and lied on what was really a vital point! Not actual proof of guilt, of course, but suggestive. Further investigation was obviously required.

Two points on the man's itinerary were now known with accuracy. At ten he passed the Home going west, and at twenty-five past ten he arrived back in his office, for French felt he must accept a figure which could be so easily checked. Would Forrester have had time in that twenty-five minutes to commit the murder?

"Let's have a walk to Groyne Point," French suggested; "at an ordinary pace where we're overlooked and quickly where we're not."

The results were again highly suggestive. They went from the Home to the head of the groyne in nine minutes, and back to Forrester's office in twelve: twenty-one in all. This meant that Forrester could have done the walk and have had four minutes at the groyne to explode the charge.

But steady! Was it really so simple as all that?

French began whistling tunelessly under his breath as he considered times. Forrester could scarcely have reached the groyne before nine minutes past ten. But the explosion took place at ten minutes past. He would not therefore have had much time to get into position. Moreover, when the explosion occurred Savory had already passed the site by about two hundred yards. To walk that would take at least two minutes.

This was by no means clear. As always under such circumstances, French put it in railway timetable form.

10.08 a.m.   Savory passed point of explosion.
10.09   »   Forrester reaches groyne.
10.10   »   The explosion.

If these times were correct it was obvious that Forrester could not possibly have murdered Savory, though he could just have murdered Radlett. But then he had no motive for murdering Radlett, but only Savory.

French whistled more loudly. This was an unexpected snag. He had been doing so well on this line, and now he did not know what to think.

Of course, he presently reminded himself, when one is working to minutes, a very slight error will upset one's conclusions. Could he be absolutely certain of the times?

They certainly seemed well substantiated, and yet, he supposed a mistake might have crept in. How could he settle the matter?

After some thought he decided to concentrate on finding out whether or not Forrester had been to the groyne. This really was the vital question on which everything else depended. He would try to find someone who had seen the man during the crucial period, and if that failed, he would confront Forrester with his new discovery and see what he had to say.

13

CHIEF INSPECTOR FRENCH

Local knowledge seemed to French so essential in the further tracing of Forrester's movements, that he decided to ask Vanson to take over the job. Vanson, however, was out, and he saw Sergeant Cundy.

"What I thought was this," he explained. "That road towards the shore serves a lot of bungalows, as well as those cottages near where it dies out on to the heath. At ten in the morning there ought to be movement of some kind on it; the post or the newspapers or shop deliveries, or perhaps people coming into the town. You would know all that better than I. Question is, can we find someone who saw Forrester?"

Cundy rubbed his chin. "The milk and the post and the newspapers would have been delivered by that time," he said thoughtfully, "and it's too early for the shops. The baker might have been there if it suited his round, and residents might have been coming into the town. You'd like inquiries made, sir?"

"I should," French answered. "Could you take it on?"

"Certainly, sir, if you'd kindly fix it with Mr Vanson."

"I'll leave a note for him."

It was after lunch when French was called to the telephone. "I've got a man who saw Mr Forrester that morning," came Cundy's voice. "He's on duty, else I'd bring him to the station, but if you'd care to step down as far as Bridge Road you could see him."

"With you in ten minutes."

Bridge Road was a residential area on the north side of the town, and in less than the allotted time French and Carter reached it. Cundy was waiting for them.

"On thinking over what you said, sir, it occurred to me that I'd seen the Council dust-cart working on that road on Tuesday mornings. I rang up the office to find where it was, and I've just seen the men in charge. One of them noticed Mr Forrester. That's the cart and the man's with it."

"A bit of good work, sergeant. I'll see the man."

"Thank you, sir. He's the driver. Name of Wilkie." As Cundy spoke he waved in the direction of the cart and a man came slowly over.

"Good afternoon, Wilkie," said French. "The sergeant tells me you can give me a little information?"

"About people I sees in West Lane Tuesday week morning? Well, I don't see everyone. I don't be with the cart all the time, you know, sir. I stops the engine and helps my mate to clear the ashpits."

"You say you saw Mr Forrester?"

"Yes, sir."

"Where were you at the time?"

"Right by the end of the road. There be three cottages there, if you know them."

"I've seen them. And where was Mr Forrester?"

"He was going on to the heath."

"What time was that?"

Wilkie couldn't be sure, but thought it must be somewhere about ten.

More and more it seemed to French that Forrester must be his man. Certainly if the solicitor were innocent, the facts would require some explaining. Thinking it unlikely that he would learn any more from inquiries in the town, French decided to put the issue to the man himself. Ten minutes later he and Carter were again in his office.

"Since I left you, sir, I have obtained some information upon which I should like your views. The official caution which I gave you still applies."

Forrester looked his question.

"In short, sir, at ten o'clock on the morning of the tragedy you were seen going down the High Street and turning at the Convalescent Home, not towards Tower Hill, but towards Groyne Point. Would you care to make any further statement on the matter?"

Forrester was obviously taken aback. For some moments he did not reply, then slowly he nodded his head.

"I must, mustn't I? Else you'll think I'm guilty of murdering Radlett. I see I'll have to tell you everything. But it would be rather awkward for me if the facts became known. I hope you'll be able to keep them to yourself?"

"As a solicitor, sir, you know the answer to that. Nothing except what is required by the law will come out."

"Very guarded. Well, I'll have to trust you for I can't help myself. The fact is, your information's correct. I didn't go to Tower Hill that morning, but to a group of trees in a secluded spot to the west of the town. I had an appointment there for ten."

"With whom, sir?"

"A man called Vane, if you must know."

"Is that the Mr Vane to whom Miss Meredith is engaged?"

Forrester looked at him with rueful admiration. " 'Pon my word, you haven't wasted your time since you came down here. Yes, that's the man. He works in the local Labour Exchange."

French nodded. "I'm afraid, sir, I shall have to ask you what your business with him was."

"Yes, I suppose you must." Forrester seemed very unwilling to proceed, then shrugged and went on more quickly. "As a matter of fact Mrs Savory and I had reason to suspect – though we didn't actually know – that Savory wouldn't grant a divorce. I was trying to devise a plan to force him to do so."

"What was that, sir?"

"Well, it's an involved story. I'd better tell you. Part of Vane's job was to keep track of people who were due to be called up for national service. Savory's chauffeur, Kellow, was one of them. He'd been exempt for a time through a physical disability, but when that got better he'd become liable. Vane sent him his papers as he was bound to do, and then Savory went off the deep end, saying that his chauffeur was doing national service where he was, and wanting to hold him. When the call-up was insisted on – of course it was the law and no one had any option about it – Savory took the dirty kind of action he does take. As he couldn't get at Vane directly, he struck at him through his own niece. He engaged a chauffeuse who he said could also do his secretarial work and told Miss Meredith she could go. The immediate result was that she announced her engagement to Vane and took a job as clerk in the gasworks till they could be married."

French, of course, had heard this elsewhere, but he was interested to notice that Forrester's manner had completely altered, and all his instincts would in any case have told him that he was now hearing the truth.

"Rather plucky of Miss Meredith, if I may say so."

"She's a fine girl, is Anne Meredith. Well, to continue. These changes made a complication for Savory," and he went on to tell of the man's alleged need for the cottage, the trespass of Macdougal's children, and the notice to quit. "That," he continued, "was what our meeting on Tuesday was ostensibly to be about. But I shouldn't say ostensibly. It was to be about that, but it was also to be about something else, though Savory didn't know it."

Forrester paused and French could see the perspiration glistening on his forehead. It was evident that he found his revelations extremely irksome.

"I may as well admit, Mr French, that I intended that morning to tell Savory three things: first, that I would do no more legal work for him – though I don't suppose I should have had the chance in any case; second, about my feeling for Mrs Savory; and third, that unless he granted a divorce, I would expose all that he had done in the chauffeur–secretary–cottage case."

"But would he have objected to that, Mr Forrester?"

"Yes, he would. He was aping, you must remember, to be a man of great patriotism, a supporter of the war effort, a local leader, and all the rest of it. If it could be shown that he had fought for his own convenience at the expense of the war effort, it would be highly damaging to his prestige. He's not loved in the neighbourhood, and if his treatment of those three people, Miss Meredith, Vane and Macdougal, became known, his unpopularity might take a very embarrassing turn. I felt sure he would do a good deal to have it kept quiet."

"Wouldn't it have come out in any case through those three people?"

"I don't think so. Miss Meredith certainly wouldn't mention her part in it: her pride would prevent her. It's very unlikely that Vane would either, partly for her sake and partly because his service instincts would make him keep business matters secret. Macdougal would, and probably has, told all he knew, but he was ignorant of the facts which really mattered. In fact, the evidence of all three would be necessary to give the complete story."

"I see that. And you thought that the mere threat of exposure would force Mr Savory to agree to the divorce?"

"I was sure it would."

French glanced at him quizzically. "Was that quite in accordance with your professional traditions?"

Forrester made a gesture. "Do you think I don't know it? If it became known to my colleagues it would be the end of me as a solicitor, and if it went to court I should probably have to meet a charge of blackmail. I recognized all that, but I was prepared to take the risk. But I hope that has made another point clear to you?"

"Namely, sir?"

"My reason for trying to keep the matter from you."

"I'm only interested in the death of Mr Radlett. Anything not connected with that – " He shrugged as if to indicate the blotting out of all such extraneous matters, then rose.

"Thank you again, Mr Forrester, for telling me this, though if I may say so, you should have done it on my previous call."

"But you understand the reason of that?"

"It wasn't valid. You should have trusted me. However, it hasn't made much difference in the end. May I use your phone?"

"Of course."

French rang up the Labour Exchange and asked for Vane. "I'd be grateful, Mr Vane, if you could step across to the police station for a few moments. A question has arisen about which I think you could give us some help."

French stood up as he replaced the receiver. "I hope, Mr Forrester, that finishes our business with you, though if some fresh point arises, I may have to come back for more information."

"I'll help you if I can."

"Well, Carter," said French when they reached the street, "was he telling the truth that time?"

The sergeant's eye twinkled. "I believed it, sir," he answered demurely, adroitly evading the question.

"Oh, you did, did you? My feeling also, though unhappily that won't let us out of testing it."

"Cute way you prevented Forrester from getting at Vane," went on the sergeant. "Arranging the thing and telling him he needn't try all in one go."

"It seemed the simplest way. I hope to goodness Vane will be worthwhile. We haven't had much luck so far."

"Done a lot of work and precious little to show for it. We've had a good many cases of that sort, sir."

"You're defining life, Carter, though I don't suppose you know it. Incidentally you're also defining detective work, though I don't suppose the public would believe it. Well, here's the station: save you from more of my moralizing."

Vane had just arrived. "As I didn't know what you wanted me for, I didn't know what to bring," he observed when French had introduced himself. "If it's about our work, I'm afraid I can't tell you much without our records."

"I don't think you'll want your records to answer the few questions I wish to ask, Mr Vane. Sit down and smoke if you want to."

Vane seemed slightly surprised at this opening. He took a cigarette from his case, then as an apparent afterthought held out the case to French. French declined on his usual fallacious grounds of not smoking when on duty.

"I think you know why we came to St Pols," he went on when Vane's cigarette was alight. "It was suspected that the death of Mr Radlett was no accident, and I may tell you we've found he was murdered. Hence inquiries from all and sundry."

Vane nodded without speaking.

"Now," French went on, "I want to ask you some questions, but I have to warn you you needn't answer them unless you want to, and also that anything you say may be used in evidence." Misgiving was now obviously added to Vane's other emotions. "But isn't that what you say to people you're going to arrest?" he stammered.

"Yes, but we say it to a lot of others as well. When we begin a case like this we suspect everyone, and therefore have to protect ourselves against developments."

Vane's eyes grew rounder. "You mean you suspect me of murdering Mr Radlett? Oh, you surely couldn't!"

"As I said, we suspect everyone. But if, remembering my warning, you care to answer my questions, you may dispel that suspicion in your case."

The young man drew back as if sure of his own mind. "Oh, yes, I'll answer. I don't have to think about it. I've nothing to hide."

"So much the better. Then I'll begin. You're employed in the Labour Exchange?"

The formal questions showed that Vane was thirty-one, that he lived alone with his widowed mother, that he had volunteered for the Air Force, the Navy, the Army and the Home Guard, and been turned down on physical grounds by all. At the Labour Exchange he was now second in command, having been promoted to take the place of a man who had joined up. It was his chief who had suggested him as honorary secretary to the Local Invasion Committee when that body was set up, and he had done quite a lot of work in that connection, though it was now practically over.

"That's very clear," French commented. "Now I must ask some even more personal questions. I want to know about your relations with Miss Meredith."

Again Vane looked surprised, as well as slightly indignant. But he answered without hesitation. French accepted every word, as the statement agreed with all he had heard from other sources.

French then went on to the disagreement with Savory. This was as Forrester had stated. When the chauffeur, Kellow, had become liable for national service, Vane had notified him, and, of course, Savory. Savory had rung Vane up and told him peremptorily that he couldn't spare Kellow, and to have the call-up cancelled. On Kellow's becoming fit again after his illness this was repeated.

"What did you do?"

"What could I do, Mr French? I was only carrying out the law, and Kellow's services to Mr Savory did not constitute grounds for exemption. I was going to say so over the phone, but Mr Savory rang off when he had given his orders. I therefore consulted my chief and we wrote him to that effect. You can see the letter if you like, but I can tell you it was extra conciliatory and polite."

"I'm sure of that, Mr Vane. What happened then?"

"He called at the Exchange – Mr Savory, I mean. He forced his way into my room past the clerks and started blackguarding me. He went off the deep end properly; said I could do what he wanted if I liked, and that he'd report me to his friend, Sir Digby Armstrong – he's right up at the top in the Ministry. He made such a row that Mr Dawson, that's my chief, came in. Mr Dawson tried to quiet him and then Mr Savory started slanging him too. In the end we had quite a job to get Mr Savory out."

"Seems rather characteristic from all I've heard."

"Yes, but I think this was worse than usual. He told me among other things that if I didn't instantly cancel the call-up and he caught Miss Meredith speaking to me, he'd dismiss her on the spot. It was that that got my goat, Mr French. I told him to go to hell."

"If this wasn't an official interview I'd say congratulations, but I can't do that. What happened then?"

"He was delighted; said he'd got me now and that he'd see I was dismissed for swearing at clients in office hours. Well, I don't deny I was a bit scared, for of course I'd given him a technical case. But Mr Dawson saved me. He told me to make a technical apology, and I did. Then Mr Dawson went for Mr Savory. He told him that if he made the slightest move, he'd report the whole of the interview to headquarters, 'and I think, Mr Savory,' he ended up, 'it wouldn't be Mr Vane that would come out worst.' But Mr Savory tried it all the same."

"Oh, he did, did he?"

"Yes. We shortly got a letter from headquarters saying that a complaint had been received that I used insulting language while dealing with clients, and asking for a full report. Mr Dawson made one," Vane smiled, "a good one."

"Was the explanation accepted?"

"Must have been, for we never heard another word about it."

"That's all very clear. Now, Mr Vane, you've recently had some dealings with Mr Forrester?"

Again surprise showed on the young man's face, this time with some dismay. He was obviously amazed at the extent of French's knowledge. He hesitated, then said slowly, "Well, I've spoken to him recently."

"Rather more than that, I fancy. Perhaps I should tell you that Mr Forrester has already given me an account of your talk, and what I want is a check on his statement. Just let me know in your own words what took place between you."

Vane seemed embarrassed. He hemmed and hawed and made one or two false starts, as if he were afraid of giving Forrester away and were wondering what he had said. Then as French remained silent, he went on.

"I didn't want to mention this, Mr French, but I suppose I can't help myself. I hope you won't make more of it than you need. Mr Forrester wanted to know about Mr Savory and Kellow. I told him roughly what had happened, not in detail, you know. But of course I shouldn't have. We're not supposed to speak of what goes on in the office."

"I shouldn't think it was a very serious matter. Did Mr Forrester tell you what he wanted the information for?"

"Yes, he said Mr Savory had annoyed him too, and he wanted to get one back on him. He said my information would help him, and that he would keep my part in it secret."

"Did he tell you exactly what he was going to do?"

"No, and I didn't want to hear."

"I see. Now I think there's only one other point." French made a show of consulting his notebook. "Will you tell me where you were between nine-thirty and ten-thirty on Tuesday morning week?"

Vane was not slow to realize the implication of the question. Apprehension showed suddenly in his eyes. "You don't mean – ?" he gasped, and stopped.

"I mean just what I say, Mr Vane. Answer my question and let it go at that."

Vane nodded sadly. "All right. I've told you so much I may as well tell you that too. In any case I can't help myself. I was in the office up till just ten. About half past I was going to see Mr Osborne, the manager of the grist mill, about women to replace some of his men who had been called up."

"You *were* going?"

"Yes. But just before ten Mr Forrester rang up to say that he wanted to see me urgently. He asked me to meet him immediately at a certain big tree on the heathland near the village. I went there on my way to the mill."

"What did Mr Forrester want?"

"Just more complete details of the Savory business."

"And you gave them?"

"Yes."

"H'm. How long did your meeting take?"

"About ten or twelve minutes. He took notes of what I said."

French closed his notebook with a smack. "That's all I want," he said pleasantly, "and I'm sorry to have kept you so long. Unless some further point arises, I don't think I shall want you again."

When Vane had gone French sat on at Cundy's desk thinking over the interview. He had taken rather a fancy to Vane. From his appearance and manner he could scarcely believe him to be either a murderer or the accomplice of a murderer.

However, estimates of character were all very well in their way, but his job required something more positive. Obviously a pretty strong case could be made against either Vane or Forrester, or both together. Forrester's motive he had already gone into. What about Vane's?

At first it looked as if it could only be revenge. Savory had treated Vane badly. However, French did not believe anyone was sufficiently vindictive to murder for treatment such as Vane had himself suffered. But Savory had acted badly towards Anne Meredith. Here was a much more plausible cause. A man like Vane might go to any lengths if the girl he loved were injured.

It was a possibility, though perhaps not a very likely one. What, then, about Forrester?

French had already concluded that Forrester had an adequate motive, as well as the necessary personality and character for the deed. Moreover, his own statement was no proof of innocence. It was just the kind of story he would invent, were he guilty. So far as the evidence went, he might be guilty or he might not.

But did not Vane's statement supply him with an alibi? Vane had said that Forrester had been with him under the big tree for ten or twelve minutes, and those minutes must have been between ten and ten-fifteen on the morning of the murder. If Forrester had been there, it was absolutely certain that he could not have killed Radlett.

The fundamental question, then, was whether or not Vane's statement was true. Was there any way of finding this out?

French's thoughts turned to the second possibility. Could Vane have been Forrester's accomplice? What easier than for Vane to swear Forrester had been with him under the tree, while the solicitor was actually hurrying to Groyne Point to set his trip? All this evidence of Vane's might easily have been prearranged.

Once again the fundamental point was whether Vane's statement was true. For some time French continued pondering the matter, then finding himself unable to reach a conclusion, he regretfully decided that he must check as much of the story as he could.

The work proved tedious, but he amassed a good many facts. Forrester's secretary had heard her employer ringing up the Labour Exchange shortly before ten, and a clerk in the Exchange had noticed Vane taking a call at the same time. This clerk had also watched Vane collect his things on receipt of the call, and leave the office. That was just about ten. Miss Pascoe, the patient in the Convalescent Home, had seen Vane pass about a minute after Forrester. He had also turned down towards the heath.

French then estimated how long it would have taken Vane to ride his bicycle from the big tree to the mill – it came to at least fifteen minutes. Finally he went out to see Mr Osborne, the manager.

Here he obtained two pieces of information, both tending to support Vane's innocence. The first was that the young man had reached the mill at exactly half past ten. This was stated by several people. Moreover, Vane had done nothing to call attention to the hour. Vane must therefore have left the big tree at the time he said: between twelve and fifteen minutes past ten. As it would have been quite impossible for him to have reached Groyne Point *before* leaving for the mill – he could not have ridden his bicycle over the heath – this was definite proof of his own innocence. It did not follow that he was not Forrester's accomplice, but still at least represented one step further towards French's goal.

The second point was a statement by the mill manager that Vane had been perfectly normal in his manner during the call. The business they had discussed was complicated, and Vane had been cool and collected and had given his whole attention to the points at issue. The manager did not believe he could possibly have been so detached, had disturbing thoughts been in his mind.

This was strong evidence, and in addition there were four other facts, all pointing in the same direction. Vane's known character was not that of a man likely to commit murder. Anne Meredith's love for him was also to some extent a guarantee of character. His personal ignorance of Home Guard matters did not count for a great deal, still some knowledge would have been required to break into the hut and find the grenades. Lastly, as he was ignorant of electrical and mechanical subjects, had no tools or workshop, and was known to be unskilful with his hands, French did not believe he could have made the bomb. On the whole, then, it seemed impossible to doubt his innocence. And as French had already seen, Vane's innocence practically assured Forrester's.

The next day was Sunday and French spent it in arranging his notes and recapitulating the whole of his inquiry and conclusions.

The result was more than disheartening. He had now looked into the circumstances of everyone whose conduct or position suggested that he might be involved, in every case without result. Despondently he glanced down the list of names in his notebook. Wedgewood, Maude, Little, Jessica, Macdougal, Crane, Forrester and Vane – and Savory himself if Radlett's and not Savory's death had been intended. Not one of them seemed guilty. Though he could not be absolutely positive in all cases, he was at least certain that in no single instance could he put up a case for the prosecution which would have the slightest chance of success.

Tired and deeply worried, he pushed his papers aside and fumbled for his pipe.

– 14 –

MAUDE WEDGEWOOD

We must now go back to the previous day, the Saturday on which French was inquiring into the statement of Vane.

On Saturday forty-eight hours had passed since Maude Wedgewood and her husband had sat in their lounge discussing Anne Meredith's reaction to the suggestion that her uncle might have been the murderer's intended victim. Those forty-eight hours had brought no news and no lifting of the atmosphere of distrust and suspicion which Maude had so greatly deplored. French and his sergeant had been seen going about the little town, though no one knew what they were doing or where their blow might fall. Whether they were baffled or on a hot scent was an unfathomable mystery, but at least no arrest had yet been made.

Maude had begun to recognize a universal attempt to make the best of the situation, to carry on as if nothing had happened. So, like her neighbours, she went to the village to shop, to help with the Red Cross, to see the picture papers and to talk to her friends, trying to be natural in manner and to forget the grim possibilities lying beneath the surface of things.

Then a new series of events took place which gradually increased her anxieties till they became a veritable nightmare. The first of these was an encounter with Wickham Crane.

It happened that on that Saturday evening she had gone to St Pols to attend a committee meeting in connection with a National Savings Week which was shortly to be held in the neighbourhood. It had been called after supper to suit the convenience of the collectors, most of whom were working during the day. Dick Little was in the town on some other business, and as both expected to be done about the same time, they had arranged to walk home together.

Owing to some talkative members, Maude's meeting ran on a good deal longer than she had expected, and it was well after ten as she and Little left the hall. It was a fine evening, still daylight though beginning to get dusk. It had turned slightly chilly and they walked smartly to keep themselves warm. Since the tragedy Maude had hated the shore and particularly the neighbourhood of the groyne, but she knew this was a weakness which she must overcome, and when Little turned as a matter of course towards the sea, she followed without remark.

Normally she intensely loved the sea, and walking by it always thrilled her. Though it was now calm, there had been some wind earlier in the day and a ground swell was breaking in small rollers on the sand. They made a ceaseless roar, waxing and waning as each successive wave broke. She could see the sand stretching away as far as the groyne, after which it merged into the indeterminate shadows in the growing dusk. It lay smooth and flat as a pale and ghostly billiard table, with the dark cushions of copse and sea to right and left. Only at one point was its clear expanse broken. Straight ahead was the figure of a man. He was walking slowly and they quickly drew up on him, to find it was Wickham Crane.

They wished him good evening, and though he replied normally enough after a slight delay, Maude instantly noticed something unusual in his manner. He seemed to be walking and speaking with a conscious effort, as if both were difficult operations, requiring his full attention. He made no attempt to develop the conversation, but repeated his greetings for a second and then a third time.

Then a sudden waft of air told her what was wrong.

She was astonished. Crane she was aware took his glass like most other men, but never before had she known him to exceed in the slightest degree. But she now remembered having heard that earlier in life he had been subject to occasional bouts of drinking, though it was believed that this was a thing of the past.

Now he was quite definitely drunk. Not helplessly drunk, but drunk enough to walk with extreme care and dignity and to talk, when once he started, in a ceaseless and rather maudlin monotone. He was not, however, in the least offensive, and when they reached the groyne he bid them a laboured good night and turned up towards his house as if quite sure of his whereabouts.

"Crane!" Little ejaculated as they watched him stagger up through the soft sand above high-water mark, heavy going at all times. "Well, you never know! I shouldn't have believed it!"

Maude felt a little disgusted. "Do you think he's all right?" she asked. "That heather's not easy walking. Do you think you ought to follow him?"

Little hesitated. "Perhaps you're right," he agreed. "It'll only take a minute or two."

"I'll go with you."

"No, I'll see to him. You get along home."

Rather unwillingly Maude assented. She nodded abruptly and strode off. As she did so her disgust passed away. Perhaps she had been wronging Crane. He was normally a temperate man, and he had shown strength of character in overcoming those earlier lapses. It was evident that tonight something quite exceptional had taken place. In any case it was not her place to judge him.

It happened that next afternoon she met him, again on the shore. He stopped and in a shamefaced way made an apology. He admitted to an error of judgement in estimating the effect of certain drinks on an abstemious man like himself. Maude had never cared much for him, but as they parted she felt she liked him better than ever before.

This episode of Crane's drunkenness was the first of the series which Maude afterwards realized were heavy with fate. The second occurred on the next day, Monday.

It was in the morning and she was walking to the village, once again by the shore. Looking out over the beach on the way down, she had believed that the entire expanse of sand was untenanted, but when she got near the groyne she saw that a man was seated on a stone, half hidden by the timbers. As she approached he got up and pulled off his hat. It was Charles Savory.

"Morning, Mrs Wedgewood," he greeted her, quite politely for Savory. "Going to St Pols?"

"Yes," Maude smiled pleasantly. "A morning of queues and frustration! In other words, the weekly shopping."

"Walk with you if I may." He fell in beside her.

"Delighted," Maude lied, wondering what this might portend.

For a time it didn't seem to portend anything, then she thought from his manner they were approaching the point. With a show of indifference he switched the conversation on to the tragedy.

"I suppose you know what that nosy parker of an inspector has got into his cracked skull about the thing?" he grumbled. "Thinks the fellow was out for me."

"Yes, I heard that was Mr French's idea."

"Huh. Pretty serious thing, if he's right."

"I should have thought it even more serious that the wrong man should have been killed," Maude declared illogically, though with some indignation.

"Oh, yes, your uncle and all that. But don't you see the point? If he was out for me and missed me, he may try again!"

"Yes," Maude returned brightly. "I hadn't thought of that, but of course he may. And he may succeed the next time."

Savory gave her a sour look. "Well, if he thinks I'm going to sit back and wait his convenience, he's got another idea coming to him. These fools of police are no good. I'm going into the thing myself."

"That should clear the affair up quickly."

Again he glowered at her. "If I couldn't do better than they've done, I'd deserve anything I might get," he snorted. "I want you to answer me a question."

So here it was. He must think it important, for he had clearly come out to meet her.

"What is it?" she asked.

"You know that study of Little's? You were there when the thing happened, weren't you?"

Maude was frankly surprised. "Why, yes," she answered. "I said so in my evidence at the inquest. What about it?"

"Is there a wireless set in it?"

"A wireless set? What on earth do you want to know that for?"

He smiled in what was obviously intended to be an ingratiating manner.

"You might as well tell me. It's perfectly easy for me to make an excuse to call on Little and see for myself."

This was, of course, true. Maude decided to tell him in the hope of finding out what was in his mind. "Yes," she said, "there's a wireless set on the wall near the fireplace."

He nodded as if pleased. "I thought so. One other question and I've done. Was Little at the set when the explosion took place?"

"No. Not near it. He was at his desk with his crossword papers. You say that's all your questions: now it's my turn. Why did you want to know this?"

He looked at her calculatingly. "Well, I told you I was out to get the truth. If I can prove someone murdered Mr Radlett, I'll be free from the fear of another attack. See?"

Dimly his meaning began to dawn on her. "Do you mean to insinuate," she asked with a slowly mounting fury, "that my cousin's husband – is the murderer?"

"Insinuate nothing," he returned roughly, then became ingratiating again. "Look here, Mrs Wedgewood, I'm only out for the truth. What set that mine off? Answer me that."

"I've no idea."

"Well, I have. It wasn't a German mine nor a British one nor anything of that kind – that's all poppycock. It was planted there deliberately to kill someone, and if you go over all the ways of exploding it, you'll see there's only one it could have been. Method of elimination and all that."

"And what might the method be?"

"Radio. Wireless waves. Easy as kiss. You send out from your own aerial, and there's an aerial on a tree at the head of the groyne which picks up and operates the detonator."

"And you think my cousin's husband arranged it?" Maude's voice was icy, though internally she felt on fire.

Savory shrugged. "I don't say so. But who had a stronger motive?"

Maude stopped. "I'll wait till you go on, Mr Savory. I don't wish to have any further discussion with you – on any subject."

He shrugged again. "Oh, well, if you feel like that it's all the same to me. But remember that facts aren't altered by mentioning them."

He turned on his heel, touched the brim of his hat, and stumped back in the direction of his home. Maude continued on her way, fighting down her indignation. By the time she reached St Pols she was outwardly calm, but a new source of fear was gnawing at her heart. She told herself that Dick Little must be quickly warned of possible danger.

But it was not till the following day that she saw him, and before that the third of the series of fateful events had taken place.

It happened that that afternoon Wedgewood had to attend a Ministry of Agriculture conference in Plymouth, and to obtain some private discussion with the Ministry representative he decided to stay overnight. Maude was anxious to do some shopping and went with him. She did not go home from St Pols, but Wedgewood followed her in, and they went on by train, so as to reach Plymouth about midday.

The hotel was crowded, and at dinner the headwaiter begged them with apologies to let him place a third visitor at their table. They were presently joined by an elderly man, evidently an American. He proved friendly and talkative and they were soon on excellent terms.

He was, he said, a manufacturer of excavating machinery, and had been over in this country in connection with supplying the British Government with some of his products. Next morning he was sailing on his return journey to the States. He had lived, it appeared, a varied and adventurous life, but it was not till he mentioned Klondyke that his hearers grew interested.

"When were you there?" Wedgewood asked him, when for a moment he paused for breath.

"Well, right in the thick of things, as you might say," replied the American, who had given his name as Jefferson. "Ninety-nine, the year of the big rush."

Wedgewood turned to his wife. "Wasn't it in ninety-nine your uncle was there? Ever heard the name of Radlett in the district, Mr Jefferson?"

"Radlett? Let me see." Jefferson gave a study of a man thinking. "Not young Josh, I suppose?"

"Joshua Mordaunt Radlett's the name."

Jefferson made a gesture of amazement. "Josh M Radlett!" he exclaimed. "You don't say Josh M is related to you! Well, if that don't lick creation! Why, sir, I knew him like a brother!"

"My wife's uncle. I'm sorry to say he has just died."

"Say now, that's a pity. I'd like to have looked him up on my next trip over. Why, Josh M was well known in the Klondyke. Made history at the diggings. Yes, sir! A sort of romance."

"How was that, Mr Jefferson?"

"Well, it's a long story, but seeing you're related, you'll maybe stand for it. You see, Josh M wasn't quite cut out for the life. Too quiet. Too decent, if I may put it that way. In a place like the Klondyke in ninety-nine you'd got to fight your hand, and young Josh M just wasn't a fighter. He was straight himself, and he expected other people to be straight with him, but that don't always work, not in a place like that anyway."

"It applies to most places."

Jefferson nodded ponderously. "You've said it. Well, young Josh M was no fool. He recognized his limitations and did what many another has done in the same circumstances, joined up with a partner who'd more push and less brains. By brains I mean the sort of highbrow kind Josh M had, for the other fellow was cute enough, specially where a bit of profit was to be made. The boys were kind of interested to see what would happen, and there were sweeps on how long it would be before Savory would do Josh M down."

Both the Wedgewoods goggled, while Arthur burst out, "*Who* did you say?"

Jefferson looked at him shrewdly. "Savory was the name," he answered. "Does that intrigue you? You don't know him too, by any chance?"

"We know a Mr Savory," Wedgewood admitted, "but there's no reason to suppose it's the same man. Was the name Charles?"

Jefferson shook his head. "I just don't remember that, though I dare say you could find out from the claim records if you wanted to know."

"We don't really. But your story's interesting. Do carry on. How did those two become partners? I mean, why did they select each other?"

"Well, they were both English and about the same age and type. Been at the same college, they said. It was sort of natural they'd get together, for the boys there were a pretty mixed bunch."

"I can believe it."

"In due course they staked a claim and worked it good and hard. But they had no luck. They didn't get enough out of it to pay for the grease on their boots, and their stock of dough was believed to have run down pretty low. I remember Josh M wanted to pull out and make tracks for home while they could buy the transport, but Savory was for sticking it to the last dime. Savory was the strong man of the two and what he said went. Then Josh M got ill, ill with a queer stomach complaint."

"A nasty position."

"Savory brought him to a sort of hospital we had and then went back alone to their shack. As luck would have it, he'd scarcely got to work again when he struck it lucky. He got what most men would call a fortune out of it, and then what did the skunk do? Eh, I mean" – Mr Jefferson looked alarmed – "I'm assuming it's not the man you're acquainted with."

"It doesn't matter if it is," Wedgewood assured with a glance at Maude. "The Savory we know is no friend of ours. Say what you like."

Jefferson again nodded ponderously. "He wouldn't be if it's the same man," he declared cryptically, "unless he's got reformed since. Well, I was telling you what he did. Took the dough and cleared out."

"You mean he didn't share with his partner?"

"You've hit it. Cleared out with every cent. Left Josh M alone and sick and in debt and cleared out with a fortune. I never saw Josh M raised till then, but by heck he was stark staring mad when he heard the news. If Savory had been around he wouldn't have survived till evening."

"I should have thought the law would have protected Radlett?"

"Well, that's so, of course. But you can get round the law. You can get your dust changed into money on behalf of yourself and your partner with all the papers in order, and if you work it right you can vanish with both shares. And that's what Savory did."

"Dirty skunk, I'll agree."

"Yes, sir! The morals of a mining camp ain't any too bright and shining as you can figure for yourself, all the same Savory knew better than to stay around. He wouldn't have found it healthy."

"The illness turned out lucky for him at all events."

The American looked quizzically at Wedgewood. "So," he drawled. "It's what the boys thought too. I'm not making any charge, because I can't prove it, but we all believed that illness was more than lucky."

Wedgewood whistled. "You mean attempted murder?" he queried.

"Well, no, we didn't go so far as that. We thought Savory'd found the gold and had wanted Radlett out of the way while he was working it. The boys opined that Radlett had had a shot of arsenic. But we didn't know for sure."

"Good Lord! If that wasn't attempted murder, it was very close to it."

"It wouldn't have paid Savory to have Josh M die on his hands."

Wedgewood laughed shortly. "I appreciate your opinion of him," he declared dryly.

"But did my uncle take no steps?" put in Maude.

"Well, madam; it's not easy to know what he could have done. He couldn't prove the doping, and Savory had kept on the right side of the law about handling the gold. It was only the private matter of cheating his partner that Josh M could have got him for, and before Josh M was well enough for that, Savory was out of the country with a cold trail. But a strange thing chanced. Josh M's hate of Savory vanished when he got better."

"Not very usual that. How did it happen?"

"In a way you wouldn't quickly guess, and yet it was natural enough. When he was well enough he went back to his claim, and before he'd been there a week he struck it lucky in his turn."

Wedgewood and Maude exchanged glances.

"We knew that's where his money came from," remarked the former.

"Well," Jefferson agreed, "he certainly did pull out a pile. Ten times what Savory had got, ten times that and more. He was so tickled by what Savory had missed that it turned his hate to ridicule."

"A great story, Mr Jefferson. And what happened to our relative then?"

"Now you're asking me. I don't know. He had the wit to turn his stuff into cash and to quit. I left myself shortly after, and I never heard of him again till I met you and your good lady this evening."

It was at this critical juncture that Wedgewood's acquaintance in the Ministry arrived, and between one thing and another he and Maude had no time to discuss the story that night. Indeed it was not till they were at tea in their own home on the following afternoon that an opportunity arose. Before they had got well underway Dick and Jessica Little dropped in. Their greetings were characteristic.

"Hullo, Arthur," said Little. "What about your crop-rotation scheme?"

"Well, Maude," queried Jessica, "did you get the dress?"

Their curiosity was soon satisfied, and then the Wedgewoods went on to tell of Jefferson and his revelations. The tale was greeted with exclamations of incredulity and amazement.

"It's beyond belief," Little declared. "So intimate with us all those years and never a word about it! You had no suspicion, Jessica, had you?"

"Not the slightest!" Jessica assured them.

Little seemed annoyed. "Her own father! Why should he want to keep it such a dead secret?"

"It was only the Savory part, of course," Maude pointed out. "We knew he'd made his money at Klondyke."

"Yes, but we weren't to repeat even that, on pain of losing our inheritance," Jessica returned. "But the other! Why did he never hint that he knew Mr Savory?"

"We don't know it's the same Savory," Wedgewood put in.

"Rubbish, Arthur," Little retorted. "The same name and the same nature! And coming to live in the same place. Of course it's the same!"

"Might be a brother."

Little shrugged. "It *might* be the man in the moon. But it's darned unlikely. No, I bet any odds it's Savory himself."

"I think so too," said Maude.

"Oh, yes," Wedgewood agreed, "for the matter of that I think so myself. I'm only pointing out we don't know for certain."

"But if it was the same man there's a double mystery," Jessica declared. "It wasn't only that father said nothing about knowing Mr Savory, but also that Mr Savory said nothing about knowing father."

"That's true," Maude agreed. "And there's another strange thing. Though they weren't friends, they weren't enemies. I mean, they didn't visit, but they spoke quite normally when they met."

"I think that's not so difficult," Wedgewood suggested. "Suppose Savory's the man. After his conduct uncle wouldn't have wanted to have anything to do with him, and he could only avoid suspicion that he knew him previously by acting as he did."

"You mean that if he'd shown hatred it would have pointed to a cause?" Maude replied.

"Exactly. Then Savory naturally wouldn't want to say anything about their partnership."

"Do you know," remarked Little, who for some time had seemed abstracted, "I've just had a rather upsetting thought. Does this relationship between them, supposing it exists, suggest anything to you?"

They all looked at him in silence, and he went on: "Could it have had anything to do with what's happened?"

"You mean uncle's death?" Wedgewood answered. "But surely – " His voice trailed off and he also looked grave.

"You're not suggesting," Maude said slowly, "that Mr Savory murdered uncle?"

"Well," Little returned, "I've suddenly begun to wonder."

"Oh, Dick," Jessica cried, "I believe you've got it! That would explain everything!"

"It would explain a lot," agreed Little.

"But would it?" Wedgewood demurred. "It seems to me there are two pretty serious difficulties in the way."

"Very well," said Little. "Expound."

"They're both simple. The first is, how could he have done it, and the second is, why?"

"Go on," said Little again.

"Well, take the first point; how could he have done it? When the shot went off he was two hundred yards away and on the open beach, in sight of anyone who might be looking."

"Could he have fixed something for father's foot to catch in?" Jessica suggested.

"What about the wire up the groyne?" Wedgewood objected.

"Ah, yes," Little agreed, "that's a snag certainly. That wire wasn't put in for fun."

"Not for fun perhaps," put in Maude, "but for a blind to divert suspicion?"

"That's an idea," Wedgewood admitted. "It would be an extraordinarily effective blind at all events."

"By Jove, yes!" Little seemed quite excited. "Let's see if we can work up anything on that. Suppose Savory stole the grenades and buried them with some kind of cord or wire that would pull out the pins. Suppose he found out the old man was walking in that day and watched him so that he could get in front of him. Suppose that when he got to the place he pulled out the wire, got it into position, and went on. The – "

"You mean he set a trigger for anyone following him to operate?"

"Yes, something like that. If all went well, the next person to pass would then be for it. And if by chance the old man got past safely, Savory'd only have to go back and remove the wire."

"But surely," Wedgewood objected, "if Savory had done that, he'd have had to stoop and fumble at the place?"

"How do we know he didn't?" Little queried.

"Wouldn't Crane have seen him?"

"That's a point," Little admitted. "He might or he mightn't. I don't know."

"We might ask Mr Crane," suggested Jessica.

"We'd have to do it carefully," Little pointed out. "We daren't let him know what was in our mind. What was your second difficulty, Arthur?"

"Simply why should Savory have done it? The fraud was ancient history – nearly half a century old as a matter of fact – and those two have been living here amicably for years. Why should Savory suddenly run off the rails?"

Little shook his head. "Not knowing, can't say. But because we can't think of a reason is no proof that there wasn't one."

"That's true," Wedgewood admitted. "And it all leads to a very awkward and difficult question. If we have this information – I mean about the old man and *someone* called Savory – dare we keep it to ourselves?"

"You mean, tell the police inspector?" inquired Jessica.

"Yes."

"Would you include our suspicions?" Little put in.

"Good Lord, no! We don't know what happened."

"But it would be the same thing," Little persisted. "If you tell French what that American told you, he'll guess what's in your mind."

Wedgewood shook his head. "We'd have nothing to do with that. The other is information we've received."

"We don't know if it's true."

"We wouldn't say it was true. We'd only say how we heard it."

"We told Mr French that uncle made his money at Klondyke," Maude interposed. "Don't you think that's enough? After all, we don't really *know* any more. I mean we've given Mr French the hint. It's up to him to inquire at Klondyke, if he thinks that's a useful line."

"Bravo, Maude!" Little seemed pleased. "You're dead right. We were bound to tell what we knew, and we did it. We're not bound to repeat hearsay."

Little moved as if to bring the talk to an end, but Maude stopped him with a gesture.

"Look here, Dick," she said, "I've something to tell you. I should have done it at once when you came in, but to be candid, I found it hard to begin. I'm afraid Mr Savory's going to make trouble if he can."

Little looked at her. "You bet he is," he returned. "What's it about this time?"

"Well – " Maude hesitated.

"I wondered when you were going to get it off your chest, Maude," Wedgewood put in. "I'll help you. Dick, old man, I don't expect he'll be able to give any real trouble, but he suspects you."

Little looked completely taken aback. "Suspects me? Of – ?"

"Yes, the old man's murder. Tell him how, Maude." As Maude described her interview, Little's perturbation turned to fury. For some minutes he breathed out threatenings and slaughter, then he cooled down.

"I'll get him for malicious slander," he declared vindictively. "He'll not talk like that and get away with it!"

"You can't," Maude answered. "Even if it wasn't only my word to his, I'd have to admit he made no accusation."

"No, you can't do anything," Wedgewood remarked, "and even if you could, I don't think it would be wise. We agreed you should know, so as to be on your guard, but otherwise I'd let it go."

"What about challenging him to repeat the thing?"

"No good." Wedgewood was emphatic. "He could quite correctly repeat the suspicious points and you couldn't object."

Dick considered this. "Tell me," he said at last, "is what he suggests possible? Could one blow up a mine by wireless?"

Wedgewood shook his head. "I haven't the slightest idea, though I'm as interested as you. I mean, if Jessica stood to gain, so did Maude."

"If you can control aeroplanes and tanks and boats by wireless, you should be able to set off a mine," Maude pointed out.

"I think so too. I wonder who could tell us."

They knew no one who was a sufficient expert. But after further discussion they agreed it would be wiser to take no steps in the matter. The overriding factor was, as Jessica put it, that if they were innocent, French could not prove them guilty.

This sounded convincing enough, yet a little gnawing fear remained in Maude's heart, and she felt sure from the manner of the others that it was in theirs also.

15

ANNE MEREDITH

Shortly before six on the second evening after this conversation, Anne Meredith set off to walk back to Kelwyn House after a visit to St Pols. She had been arranging some of her few possessions in her new room, and as she stepped down on the beach she thought how soon she would be moving into it and how few and far between walks to Kelwyn House would then become.

Now that her departure was approaching, her uncle had been much more pleasant, almost as if he regretted his action and at least wanted to part friends. He had even somewhat gruffly congratulated her on her engagement, which was so complete a change of front that she had been scarcely able to reply. For this change she was profoundly thankful, as there was nothing she hated more than an atmosphere of constraint and ill feeling.

From her point of view everything had gone well during the last few days, with one exception. Vane had told her of his interview with French. She had been terrified. That Vane might be suspected had been a nightmare for some time, and now the horror had become a reality. Of course neither of them knew how strong the suspicion was. It might be, as French had hinted, just part of that doubt of everyone concerned which obtains in all serious criminal cases, or it might be that he had actually made up his mind and was only waiting for some confirmatory piece of evidence before acting. The uncertainty was hard to bear, though admittedly every eventless hour which passed made it easier.

It was a charming evening even for mid-June, and in spite of her preoccupation Anne could not but admire the view. Heading west as she was, the sun had been in her eyes, but now it had gone behind a streamer of cloud and she could see without effort. The tide was flowing, but a wide expanse of smooth yellow sand was still uncovered. The sea was calm and very blue, growing darker till it reached the horizon, a hard sharp line, almost black against the luminous sky. Every detail of Ram Island stood out, the dull browns and greens of its rocks and grass, its few stunted bushes cowering in the shelter of a little hollow, and its grey base of rock uncovered by the tide. On the right the soft sand above high-water mark ran up to the coarse grass and small shrubs which marked the beginning of the heath. Behind these were two or three low, tree-covered hills which rose irregularly from the plain, and straight ahead, dark and sombre, was West Head, on which Kelwyn House and the other residences were built.

She passed below the groyne and round the curving bay beyond. As she approached the path leading up on the cliff she heard a report. It seemed to come from the heath lands on her right, and was dull like a blast from a quarry, rather than sharp like a rifle shot. But it was not loud, and such noises were so common that she gave it only a moment's thought.

The air was pleasant and she had nothing to do indoors, so she decided to prolong her walk by a ramble through the spinney adjoining the orchard and garden of Kelwyn

House. This was the area in which she had overheard her aunt and Mr Forrester and where her uncle had found the Macdougal children trespassing. It was absolutely wild and untouched by the hand of man and Anne had often enjoyed exploring it.

One corner of it reached to near the head of the path up the cliff, and there she pushed her way in through a gap in the surrounding hedge. Close by was a tiny sequestered glade. It was warm and she stopped for a moment to rest. The root of a gnarled oak made a seat and she leant back at her ease against its twisted trunk.

She had not been there for more than a few seconds when a movement caught her eye. Someone was passing through the trees. In a moment she saw that it was her uncle. She stared at him in amazement. He was pushing his way along towards the house, haste in every movement, yet with an exaggerated stealth as if to leave no trace of his passage. His face was pale and his whole appearance furtive, and she sensed rather than saw that he was extremely shaken. He did not notice her and she was too much taken aback to call out. Then in a moment it was too late. Silently he had vanished.

Wonders, she thought, would never cease! Of course, in a way, her uncle's movements were no business of hers, particularly now that her connection with the house was drawing to an end. All the same she could not help wondering what it was all about.

After sauntering for some time through the trees, she went back to the house. At once she saw that something was wrong. Ellen and cook were whispering excitedly in the hall, their faces pale and frightened. Just as Anne was about to ask what had happened, her aunt appeared at the lounge door. She saw Anne and beckoned her in.

"Oh, aunt, what is it?" Anne asked as she entered the room.

Doris Savory shut the door behind her. "My dear, a dreadful thing has happened! There's been another explosion!"

"Anyone hurt?"

"Yes, I'm afraid so. Poor Mr Crane!"

"He's not – killed?"

Doris nodded. "We fear so. Someone told Kellow and he came and told your uncle. Your uncle's gone to get details."

Anne was horrified. "Oh, aunt, how *awful!* What happened?"

"We don't know, except that it was at Ruin Hill."

Anne stared. "About half an hour ago?"

"Yes, so Kellow said."

"Then I heard it! Just before I came to the path up from the beach! A dull boom just from that direction."

"That must have been it."

"How was it discovered? Was Mr Crane alone?"

"We don't know any details. But we'll hear everything when your uncle comes back."

A distressing thought flashed into Anne's mind. "I suppose," she said hesitatingly, "it *was* an accident? I mean – "

Doris made a gesture of dismay. "That's what one can't help wondering, of course. But we mustn't anticipate things."

Following up that ugly idea, another occurred to Anne, still more disquieting. Her uncle's passage through the spinney! With growing horror Anne realized that if he had been trying to reach home unseen from the direction of Ruin Hill, that was just the route he might have followed.

And his manner! Why was it so stealthy and furtive? Oh, how *ghastly!*

But not only were route and manner suggestive: there was also time. If her uncle had left Ruin Hill when she heard the explosion, he would just about have reached the spinney when she saw him!

She sat back, feeling sick. Indeed for a moment she thought she was going to faint. Then she told herself she mustn't think such things. Her idea was impossible!

But was it? The dreadful doubt refused to be dispelled. If her uncle hadn't done it, he must surely know something about it. What else could account for what she had seen?

Another equally distressing idea flashed into her mind. What was her own position in the affair? Suppose others suspected her uncle! Suppose Mr French began asking questions? Should she tell him what she had seen?

Then Anne rallied herself. She was simply being silly, going out to meet trouble halfway. The thing might just have been an accident, in which case she was tormenting herself for nothing. What she must do was to wait and hear what had happened.

But when her uncle returned with his news, it brought her little comfort. Savory himself was obviously much agitated. She thought indeed he was frightened. He came in with a blustering air, as if to banish any indication of nervousness, but she noticed his hands were shaking.

"A bad business!" he began, glaring at his wife and Anne. "It's quite true. It was Crane and he's dead. A very bad business!"

"What happened?" Doris asked, as he seemed to have come to an end.

"Explosion! Just like the last time. He was walking along one of those sandy tracks on the heath near Ruin Hill, and he was blown up."

Both his hearers stared. "How appalling!" Doris cried. "How was it discovered?"

"It was seen. That old fellow Treglown who works for Crane saw it."

"Dreadful! That was like last time too! Treglown wasn't hurt?"

"No. As far as I could understand from their muddled talk, he was some distance away. What they said was that Treglown was working today for Crane and knocked off at six to go home. His way takes him by that path over Ruin Hill. He saw Crane in front of him. While he was actually looking at him the thing went off."

"What did he do?"

"What could he do? He went forward and saw that Crane was dead. Then he went back to Gorse Cottage and told that Avory woman that's staying with them: the writing woman."

"I know."

"She told Mrs Crane and they rang up the doctor and police. The police are there now, snooping about."

Doris clasped her hands. "Oh, Charles, do they think – it was an accident?"

"How do I know what they think? They don't go round telling people. They're asking questions by the hundred, if that's any guide."

This was all the information they could get from him, but it was enough to arouse absolute panic in Anne's mind. She was definitely up against her problem now, and the more she considered it, the more awkward it seemed to grow. If she were to tell what she had seen, would she not be virtually accusing her uncle? On the other hand, was she called upon to lie to protect him?

She did not want to lie. For one thing, this would be a very serious lie: deceiving the police and trying to defeat the country's justice. If she once embarked on it, it might easily lead her to perjury. That would be a very grave matter for herself. If they proved she committed perjury she might be sent to prison. Apart from that, if she kept back information, wouldn't she be held partly guilty of the crime? The lawyers had some name for it, something after the event; she couldn't remember the exact word. But it was a pretty serious offence. She really would hate it.

But wouldn't it be equally bad to tell the truth? It was known her uncle had treated her badly. She would be accused of trying to get even with him. Perhaps she would even be accused of inventing the story out of revenge. Besides, *she* hadn't committed the crime. It was no business of hers. Why should she be drawn into it?

There was another consideration, equally terrible and pressing. She must take her line at once, and stick to it. Why, even before this she should have said to her uncle, in her aunt's presence, "I saw you just now in the spinney." She hadn't done so. Was it already too late?

She longed for advice, for someone to talk it over with. But she could think of no one. Her aunt, of course, was out of the question, and even Reggie would be no help. She knew exactly what he'd say, and she wanted someone who would see both sides.

At last, like many another in an awkward dilemma, she decided to compromise. She wouldn't lie, but on the other hand, she would volunteer nothing. If the police asked her had she seen her uncle in the spinney, she would admit it. But she wouldn't otherwise mention it. Not a very satisfactory decision admittedly. But It was all she could achieve.

The next two days were a long drawn out nightmare to her. The air was alive with rumour and everyone she met had some fresh detail to add to the story. Most of these were unconvincing and many mutually destructive, but for all that they terrified her. If this were murder and were connected with the other tragedy, what was behind it all? What ghastly web of horror were they caught in? She and her immediate circle had known the two who had died. Must they not also know the killer? Perhaps he was someone well known and well respected in the district. Perhaps – her own uncle. Oh, dreadful thought! And another thing. With all this going on, who in the district was safe – either from murder or suspicion of murder? She could see that her aunt and uncle, though they spoke reassuringly, were also frightened, probably consumed by the same fears.

Even more upset seemed Maude Wedgewood, whom she met on the shore. Maude had no more information than anyone else, but it appeared that both Arthur Wedgewood and Dick Little thought it must be murder, and both again were deeply worried lest the stolen grenades had been used.

"I feel so unsettled that I'm going to do what I wouldn't otherwise dream of," Maude went on, "and that is to attend the inquest. I must know what the authorities think about it."

Suddenly Anne saw that this was what she also wanted.

"Oh, Mrs Wedgewood, let me come with you," she cried. "I want to hear it too," and as Maude demurred, she went on: "You see, I'm interested – if this tragedy is connected with the first, that is. You know, or perhaps you don't, that they've been asking Reggie where he was at the time of the first. And he has no proper alibi. I've been absolutely terrified."

"My dear girl, how dreadful for you! But you needn't have the slightest fear, I'm certain of it. No one could really suspect Reggie, not if they knew him. Depend upon it, it's only a piece of police routine."

"How comforting you are!" Anne returned gratefully. "But all the same I'd really like to go. Do, please, let me join you."

She was easier in her mind about being herself questioned. It appeared that several people had heard the detonation, so that her evidence would add nothing to the general knowledge. But she wanted to know what was thought about the affair, and after some argument Maude agreed that they would go together.

Though Anne naturally did not know it, the proceedings of some three weeks earlier were closely repeated when they entered the minor Wellesley Hall at St Pols with Arthur Wedgewood. With a lot of pushing they managed to get seats, for the hall was already packed. Popular interest was this time so keen that before the police closed the doors people were standing wherever there was an unoccupied foot of floor space. The coroner was the same, Mr Trevelyan, with his shrewd glance and quiet, unassuming manner, the same police assisted with the proceedings, and if the jurors were not the same, they were of a precisely similar type to their predecessors. Her uncle was there, frowning to see her with the Wedgewoods, and Mr Little sat just behind, but neither her Aunt Doris nor Mrs Little had come. Reggie, she was thankful to notice, was not there. She had seen him on the previous evening and he had assured her that nothing had happened to connect him with the affair, but of course since their meeting he might have been summoned to attend. She had somehow expected to see Mr Forrester, but he wasn't there either. Mr French and his sergeant and Inspector Vanson were seated in a little group behind the jury.

The coroner opened with a dry and strictly formal address to the jury, in which he told them nothing but the most obvious facts. They were assembled there to consider the tragedy which had taken place, and their duty would be to state, if they could, the identity of the deceased, and to say how he came to meet his death. He never alluded to the rumours which had been circulating or to the presence of Scotland Yard officers, or hinted that the affair might have a connection with any other unhappy event. He ended up a particularly dull but eminently correct speech with the intimation that the jury might view the body if they so desired, but that they were not bound to do so.

The jury thought they ought and trooped out, to return presently looking as if they wished they hadn't. Then when some other preliminaries were completed, the coroner called the first witness, Elmina Crane.

Anne was acutely sorry for Mrs Crane as she took the oath and her place on the chair which did duty for a witness-box. Her face was pale and drawn, and as she sat waiting for the questions, it was obvious that only a great effort kept her going. Mr Trevelyan clearly sympathized with her and did his utmost to ease her ordeal.

"I'm sorry, Mrs Crane, to have to ask you some questions, but I'll be as brief as I can. You've seen the remains upon which this inquiry is being held?"

Mrs Crane had seen them and identified them as those of her husband, Wickham Crane. She had last seen him alive on the previous Thursday afternoon. He was then in his usual good spirits and thoroughly normal in every way.

It was his habit to write all the morning, take his free time between lunch and tea, and resume his work between tea and dinner. After tea on Thursday he had followed this practice and returned to his study, and she had presently heard his typewriter. She had then gone to her room to attend to some household matters. From it the typewriter was inaudible, so she could not tell when it had stopped. She had not known her husband was going out or heard him doing so, nor had she the slightest idea of why he had gone. She was told the news of the tragedy by her friend, Miss Avory, who happened to be staying with them.

"Thank you, that's all very clear," the coroner said. "Now just a couple more questions and I've done. You said the deceased that afternoon was thoroughly normal, but I should like to ask you again if you're quite sure he had nothing special on his mind? Did he show no signs at all of worry or preoccupation?"

Mrs Crane hesitated. "Well," she said, "I thought not at first, but since you press the question, I'm not so certain. I think perhaps he *was* a little preoccupied. But it was very slight, so slight that I'm not sure that I'm right to mention it."

"I should like to form an opinion as to whether he went out to keep an appointment or just to take a stroll? Can you help me at all in that?"

"I'm afraid not, except that it was not his custom to go out at that time unless with some definite object."

"That suggests an appointment, as does also his slight preoccupation, though admittedly neither is in any way conclusive. One last point. Had he any special worries on his mind? I don't mean just on that afternoon, but during recent days or weeks?"

Again Mrs Crane hesitated, and Mr Trevelyan went on: "Take finance, for example. The war has hit a great many people. Was Mr Crane worried over finance?"

"Well, his income had gone down certainly because of the delay in publishing his books. Usually by the time each book was published, the next was finished or almost finished, but now the publishers have two books of his neither of which has yet appeared. I understand it's the paper shortage."

"Again I express regret for my question, but had that delay in publication become a financial embarrassment?"

Mrs Crane shook her head. "Oh, no, it was nothing like so bad as that. Our income had gone down, but we had still plenty to get along on."

"I see. And there was nothing else on his mind?"

"Nothing that I know of more than the ordinary worries of war-time."

For a moment Mr Trevelyan seemed about to press his question further, then as if on second thoughts he nodded, thanked Mrs Crane briefly and called Bertha Avory.

It was the first inquest Anne had attended and she was much impressed. With questioning like this everything must quickly become known! Her interest in what was coming grew in the same ratio as her thankfulness that she herself was not to be called. But her experience was too small to suggest to her that Trevelyan knew more than had come out in evidence.

Miss Avory had little to tell. She said that after tea on the afternoon in question she went to the garden to work at her book. Her position overlooked the entrance gate to Gorse Cottage. About three minutes to six she saw the deceased walk to the gate, pass out, and turn to the left along a path over the heath which led to the old church on Ruin Hill. He was walking easily, and so far as she could see, he was normal in every way. A minute or so later she saw Treglown follow him. That was the jobbing gardener who had been working at Gorse Cottage that day.

"How do you know the time so accurately when the deceased left?"

"Because I was considering whether I'd go in and listen to the six o'clock news."

"I see. Now you said Treglown followed the deceased. Did you mean he was following him on purpose, or merely that he happened to go in the same direction?"

"Oh, merely that he happened to go in the same direction."

"Continue, please, Miss Avory?"

"A minute or so after Treglown disappeared I heard what sounded like a shot. Then two or three minutes later I saw him running back towards the house. He seemed so agitated that I jumped up and went forward to meet him. He told me there had been an explosion and Mr Crane was killed."

"What did you do then?"

"I asked him for some particulars. Then when I had satisfied myself he was not mistaken, I ran into the house and told Mrs Crane. With her approval I rang up, first Dr Petherick, and then the police."

Miss Avory having declared that she knew of no other fact which might throw light on the affair, was allowed to stand down, and Mark Treglown was called.

His story was simple and direct, but it took a lot of getting. Anne was amazed at the coroner's care and patience. Tendencies to miss the point and to ramble were curbed, but so gently as not to antagonize the witness. Deafness and an almost incomprehensible dialect added to the difficulties, but at last a reasonably clear statement was obtained, got down on paper, and signed by the witness.

Briefly Treglown deposed that he worked each Thursday for the deceased. He knocked off at six, and on the occasion in question, just before that hour, he put away his tools. While he was doing so he saw the deceased leave his side door and go down the path to the gate. Treglown followed him about a minute later. His way home led him by a path across the heath past the old ruin which stood on the summit of a low hill: Ruin Hill it was called. Most of the paths on the heath twisted about, but this one ran straight for a couple of hundred yards approaching the hill. When Treglown turned into this straight part he saw the deceased walking in front of him. Crane had not reached the ruin, but was near it. While he was actually watching the deceased, the ground went up and he saw Crane's body falling. He ran up to see if he could help, but Crane was dead. He therefore hurried back to Gorse Cottage and gave the alarm. He could offer no explanation as to the cause of the occurrence.

Dr Petherick was the next witness. He deposed that he had reached the site of the explosion about a quarter past six. The deceased was obviously dead, and the absence of any attempt at first aid on Treglown's part was quite justified. The right leg was blown off, the left leg shattered, and the lower portion of the trunk severely injured. The right arm was broken and the right eye had been hit by some flying object which had torn away a portion of the forehead and skull. Death had been instantaneous. Witness was of opinion that the injuries might have been caused by an explosion occurring under or just in front of the deceased.

No one wished to ask the doctor any further questions and Inspector Vanson took his place. A little wave of movement passed over those present, as if their interest had become quickened. Anne indeed felt a recurrence of her original excitement, believing that the mystery behind these strange happenings would now be revealed.

But Vanson proved disappointing. He answered, or appeared to answer, all the coroner's questions promptly and fully, yet he told surprisingly little. Whether this was due to ignorance or policy Anne did not know, but the result remained the same.

Vanson had been at the police-station when Miss Avory's message had been received, and had immediately got out a police car and driven to the place. He was at the site of the tragedy within twelve minutes. He could see that the deceased was dead, but in another minute or two Dr Petherick arrived and gave the official pronouncement.

"Now, inspector, will you just describe what you saw? Better begin with the place itself, though I dare say most of the jury know it."

"Certainly, sir. Ruin Hill is a low, sugar-loaf hill, little more than a mound, rising to about twenty feet above the plain. On it are the remains of the small church which gives it its name. Paths cross it roughly at right-angles, and one of these leads from the road at the deceased's gate. It runs straight for over a hundred yards from the ruin, and directly faces the old broken-down wall of the nave."

"Is the heath open or wooded at the place?"

"Wooded; shrubs and low birches as well, of course, as heather and bracken. The growth is from ten to fifteen feet high and you can only see through it for a few yards."

"Quite. Continue, please."

"About thirty yards from the ruin there was a small crater in the path leading towards Gorse Cottage. The vegetation was torn back from it in all directions. The deceased was lying on his back on the path on the Gorse Cottage side of the crater, his feet at the edge of the hole."

"Were you able to picture how he came to be in that position?"

"I imagined the explosive was buried under the path surface and went off just as he approached it. If so, it would tend to throw him on his back and he would probably fall as he was found."

"Did you find anything to suggest what sort of explosive it was or how it was set off?"

"In the sand at the bottom of the crater and on the surrounding ground I found five small pieces of a hand-grenade case or cases. I have seen nine more pieces and part of a grenade detonator tube which were found by my assistants. All were freshly broken. I found nothing to indicate how the grenade was detonated, nor, I am informed, did my assistants."

"Were the pieces from a grenade of the same type which was recently stolen from the Home Guard hut?"

"Yes, sir."

"Now as you know, inspector, the jury will be asked whether in their opinion this tragedy was due to accident, suicide or murder. Did you find anything which might throw light on this point?"

For the first time Vanson hesitated. "I found nothing to indicate which it was, sir," he then said.

"Nor your assistants?"

"No, sir, I am informed not."

The coroner glanced at him shrewdly. For a moment he seemed about to press for a further answer, then he nodded as if to indicate that he accepted the reply. Vanson was the last witness, and after the coroner had glanced over his notes, he turned to the jury and began to speak.

First he reminded them of the responsibility of their task. A life had been lost, and in such cases it was of the first importance that the cause should be cleared up, particularly as to whether the affair was an accident or whether blame attached to anyone. He would deal with that point presently, but first it was necessary that the identity of the deceased should be established. He thought the jury would have no difficulty here, as they had heard definite evidence that the remains were those of Wickham Crane.

Nor could there be any doubt as to what actually happened and what was done after the tragedy. The sequence of events had been made crystal clear, and incidentally he wished to compliment the witnesses on the way they had given their evidence. There could be no doubt that the deceased met his death as a result of the explosion.

But when they came to consider the cause of the explosion they were on very different ground. Here the evidence was by no means satisfactory. They had to say, if they could, whether the death was due to accident, suicide or murder, and he would direct their attention to these in turn.

"With regard to accident," he went on, "this would seem to involve one or other of the following possibilities. Either the deceased was carrying a grenade with him and accidentally pulled out the pin, or someone had previously dropped a grenade on the path and the deceased kicked the pin out. You will have to judge from your own knowledge of such things how likely either of these is, but even if you think either might have taken place, I have to remind you that not a scintilla of evidence was given that either did.

"Suicide would involve the deceased having deliberately set out for his walk with the intention of killing himself. If you adopt this view you must think of his possible motive. None has been put before you. Also you must keep in view his frame of mind. You have been told that while on the afternoon in question he was preoccupied, this pre-occupation was only slight. You must therefore consider whether a person in so normal a condition could have intended to commit suicide. You must also consider why he should have chosen that particular place for the deed. On the heath, perhaps, to get away from the house: but why should he have gone so far?

"The theory of murder avoids some of these difficulties, but introduces others of its own. Who could have wanted to kill the deceased? What motive had anyone? No evidence on these points has been put before you. No doubt it is an attractive speculation to recall that one murder by explosion has recently taken place in the district and to assume that this must be a second, but here again I must remind you that not a particle of supporting evidence has been given. Nor have you been told how a grenade could have been exploded just at the right time and place, still less given any reason to suppose that this had been done.

"If from what you have heard you are satisfied as to what exactly took place, you will, of course, return a verdict to that effect. But I need scarcely impress on you that you cannot return a verdict on mere opinion, but only on the evidence which has been given. You are not, however, bound to state exactly what occurred. If you think the evidence is insufficient to enable you to reach a conclusion, you will say so.

"I do not think I need address you on the question of who may or may not be to blame, as no evidence whatever was given on this point."

With a short peroration the coroner closed and the jury retired. In a few minutes they reappeared. They were agreed on their verdict and found:

1. That the deceased was Wickham Crane.
2. That he had died as the result of an explosion of one or more hand-grenades, and
3. That there was insufficient evidence to enable them to say how the explosion had been caused.

Even Anne knew enough to realize with misgivings that the affair was by no means over.

16

CHIEF INSPECTOR FRENCH

French was just preparing to leave for the hotel when Miss Avory's message about Crane's death reached the police-station.

He had had a particularly exasperating week. He had tried over every new line he could think of. He had reread the file *ad infinitum*. He had racked his brains without ceasing – all in the despairing hope of breaking the deadlock in which he found himself. All his work had gone for nothing. He had only grown more satisfied that no one on his list of suspects was guilty. Nor could he add further names to the list. Completely up against it, he was feeling as irritable and frustrated as ever he had in a long series of similar depressions.

The news of the fresh tragedy changed his mood in the twinkling of an eye. Gone was his frustration and annoyance. Here was something to be done, something which justified a change of thought. Thankfully he pushed the file back into its drawer.

"Is this case yours or mine, Mr French?" Vanson asked when he had repeated the message.

French smiled. "Can't tell yet," he returned. "Let's both go out."

"On the face of it," Vanson went on, "it looks like a repeat of the Radlett affair, in which case the same people will be involved and it'll be yours."

"On the other hand, it might be the sincerest form of flattery. Someone with a score to wipe off might have chosen the method, hoping you'd make that very deduction. What about doing a swell job? Camera, fingerprints and all the rest of it?"

"Right," Vanson agreed, "I'll see to it." He gave his instructions and followed French to the police car. "There's another point of resemblance to the first case," he went on as he pressed the self-starter. "Radlett was a pleasant, harmless old gentleman liked by everyone who knew him, and Crane was the same. At least, he may not have been as pleasant as Radlett, but he was a man without open enemies."

"I hope the cases are connected," French declared. "I could do with a few fresh clues."

They parked the car on the road opposite Ruin Hill and walked to the site of the tragedy. A glance showed French that the information he had received was correct. Crane was dead and his death had been brought about by an explosion.

For a time, routine held the field. Dr Petherick arrived, made a preliminary examination, and promised fuller details from the mortuary. The body, the small crater before it and the site were adequately photographed, and after its fingerprints had been taken, the corpse was removed. Statements from Mrs Crane, Miss Avory and Treglown were obtained. A detailed search of the site and its immediate surroundings was started by Vanson and Carter, and at last French was free to stand back and attempt a mental reconstruction.

He had scarcely started when Vanson gave a shout. He had made his first discovery: a broken piece of a hand-grenade case embedded in the sand below the point of explosion.

"Something definite for once in a way," he declared. "Suggests a connection with the theft."

"Looks like it," French agreed. "If so, it should be a help."

He left Vanson to it, and retreating to the ruin, sat down on a stone and began to consider the affair systematically. First he asked himself the question the coroner would shortly put to his jury: was this accident, suicide or murder? But unlike the jury, he quickly reached a conclusion. This was no accident. It was impossible to imagine that Crane should have been carrying a grenade, still less that he should finger it with such grotesque carelessness as to release the pin. Nor could French believe that anyone could have dropped a grenade and that the pin should have been so nearly jerked out that Crane would have displaced it with his foot.

Suicide seemed equally impossible. Crane's record and previous frame of mind precluded it for one thing. But a more convincing argument was to be found in the position of the man's injuries. The explosion came from the ground at his feet. If he wanted to kill himself, he would surely have held the grenade near his head. No, with the reservations proper to a preliminary analysis, French was satisfied it was murder.

But murder involved careful and detailed preparations. First, the booby-trap had to be placed and the discharging apparatus designed and installed. The path admittedly carried little traffic, but no one could be certain when it would be used. Therefore timing was an essential. Crane had not only to be brought to the place, but at the correct moment. How had this been done?

Then the same difficulty which had cropped up in the previous case again presented itself. The four seconds delay! If a trip had been set for Crane to kick, he would have been nearly twenty feet past the place before the grenade went up. In the Radlett case the difficulty had been met by the wire down the groyne. Someone had watched the passers-by from the shrubs and been able to switch on his current at the right moment. The fact that Radlett, not Savory, had been killed was only a detail; it did not really affect the argument.

From all this it looked as if some electrical or mechanical apparatus might have been used, and if so, traces should be left. French foresaw a careful search of the entire area surrounding the crater.

Then a simpler solution flashed into his mind. How were grenades normally used? Why, thrown by hand. That was what the four-second time lag was for; to cover the time taken by the throw. Could this one have been thrown?

Immediately another point struck him. From the ruin to the point of the explosion was under thirty yards: a longish but quite possible throw. Moreover, part of the broken wall of the nave ran across the line of the path. An admirable hiding-place for a man who wished to pick off an approaching enemy!

French went inside the roofless walls. The sandy floor was covered with clumps of rough grass with in one corner a flourishing bed of nettles, a pointed commentary on the man whose duty it was to keep the place in order. Without approaching the length of wall he had noted, French stooped and from near ground level looked over the grass.

No, he was not mistaken. In regularly spaced patches the blades showed a faint difference in colour. They were leaning over at a slightly more acute angle than the rest. Quite recently someone had walked from the north transept door across the grass to the length of wall.

French spent a considerable time searching the grass. He thought that even if nothing more personal had been dropped, he might at least find the pin of the grenade. But he had no luck. He found neither pin nor any other object. Nor was there anywhere a footprint.

He went back to Vanson.

"Four more bits of the grenade case," the latter greeted him. "Found them among the shrubs between forty and fifty yards from the centre."

French nodded. "No pin?"

"No."

"I'm a bit bothered about where it is."

"We'll probably come on it around here."

"I hope so. Look here. I've had a bit of luck," and French explained his finds. "All that suggests another line."

"Trace who was in the church?"

"Exactly. We'll want that done pretty thoroughly. I think we'd better leave your fellows and Carson to carry on while we go back to the station and arrange it."

The dull but necessary details were worked out and all the available men put on the job. Whose business took them to the neighbourhood of Ruin Hill about six o'clock? If any such could be found, did they see anyone else? Failing these, where were doctors, coastguards, the district nurse, and others whose jobs involved moving about? Where were people living in the vicinity at the time? And if none of these lines proved lucky, where were all the suspects in the

Radlett case? Finally, as a last resort, advertisement might succeed where individual methods had failed.

The two men then went to the mortuary. Dr Petherick was just finishing his examination, but he had little fresh to report. The clothes and contents of the pockets yielded nothing helpful, though French took possession of the keys.

"Now, Vanson," he suggested, "suppose you and I have a bit of supper and attack another end of it. Ring up Mrs Crane and get her permission for us to go through her husband's papers in, say, an hour. Can you spare the time?"

"Of course, Mr French."

Elmina Crane had gone to bed when they arrived, but Miss Avory took them to Crane's study and gave them *carte blanche* to conduct their inquiries as they thought fit. Then excusing herself, she left them to it.

Then took place one of those meticulous searches which French found so boring and of which he had carried out so many. For nearly three hours both men worked without result, then French gave a whistle.

He had completed Crane's desk and file, and was now working through his small safe. From the last of a nest of drawers he took two small sheets pinned together.

The top one was the carbon of a letter. It was dated for the previous day, was marked "Private and Confidential", and read:

Gorse Cottage
9th June, 1943

DEAR SAVORY,
I think you should know that I saw you stoop and apparently adjust something on the ground when passing the groyne on the morning of Radlett's death.

Perhaps you would care to talk this over in private?
If so, I shall be in the old church on Ruin Hill at 6 p.m.
tomorrow, Thursday, 10th inst.

Yours truly,

WICKHAM CRANE.

The attached sheet was an original typing, evidently a
memorandum. It read:

Requirements:
    (1) A properly executed legal document.
    (2) Satisfaction received adequate.
    (3) Libel action withdrawn.
    (4) Admission that in respect of (2) matter finally
        closed.

My safeguard:
Savory could not proceed with libel action because of
the document he had given saying he had received
adequate compensation.

Savory's safeguard:
The document he had given plus my letter would
constitute evidence of blackmail on my part.

"I say, Vanson, have a look at those," called French,
passing the sheets over.

Vanson's eyes goggled. "My word!" he exclaimed,
"you've got something there all right."

"It looks helpful."

"I'll say it looks helpful! Savory! What on earth had
Savory against Crane?"

"Then you're assuming Savory's guilty?"

"Well, it's pretty suggestive."

French rubbed his chin. "Suggestive, yes. And yet I don't find it very convincing."

"Why not, Mr French? What's the snag?"

"Instinct, I suppose; I haven't got it properly taped yet. What about taking the thing in detail and seeing what we can make of it? Will you begin?"

Vanson leant back in his chair. His hand stole towards his tobacco pocket, then came away again empty.

"First," he answered, "it shows where Crane was going and his reason."

"Agreed."

"Next it tells us who murdered him and why."

"Ah," said French, "but does it? That's what I'd like to be sure of. Suppose you go into that further?"

"If Savory stooped down and adjusted something on the ground near the groyne, what could it have been but to set a trip?"

"You mean, to murder Radlett?"

"Yes."

"You may be right, but it means a complete reversal of our ideas. We never had any hint that Savory wanted to murder Radlett."

"No, but he may have had a motive for all that."

"He may. Well, suppose he had and Crane saw him stoop. I don't think it's proof of murder, but let that go for the moment."

"Savory would think it was proof."

"Yes, that's certainly a point."

"Very well. Crane tells Savory what he knows and asks him to meet and talk it over."

"Why?"

"So that he may blackmail him into withdrawing the action."

"Right. Yes?"

"Crane hasn't realized it, but he's done for himself. Savory sees he knows too much. As long as Crane's able to tell his story, Savory won't be safe. A perfectly simple way of getting rid of the danger occurs to him and he proceeds to take it."

French nodded. "I agree that's the obvious case and you've put it well. Crane writes that letter and was going to keep his appointment when he was killed. Can we say that Savory was in the church and made those traces on the grass?"

"I should say so."

"Then Savory watches Crane coming, throws his grenade, sees it has done its job and slips away?"

"That's my idea."

"I hope you're right. But I confess it seems to me just a bit too good to be true. There are one or two snags, you know."

"I'll bet there are! What, for example?"

"First, would Savory have been in such a hurry? Wouldn't he at least have talked the thing over with Crane before going to such lengths?"

"I doubt it. If Crane had that knowledge, and the note told Savory he had, Crane would be a danger no matter what he said."

"Sounds reasonable. Now can you answer this one? In his statement to yourself and at the inquest Crane said nothing about what he saw. If he intended to make the statement later, how was he going to explain his earlier silence?"

"Huh, that's a tougher one. It seems to me he'd be up against it either way. If the tale was true he'd be an accessory after the fact, and if it was false he could be got for blackmail."

"Exactly. And there's more than that in it. Why *should* Crane have hidden his information? He was legally bound to give it and could get it in the neck for not doing so. So if he hid it, he must have had a pretty strong motive."

"Might have wanted to use it afterwards as a handle against Savory."

"I don't think so. What he wanted was to put Savory where he couldn't go on with the libel action. Giving the information at the start would have done that automatically."

"That's right."

"Then another point: it seems to me more important still. Suppose in spite of Crane's threat Savory went ahead with the action. How could Crane have used his knowledge to make him withdraw?"

"You mean, if he made his statement he'd be for it as accessory after the fact?"

"Exactly. I can't see him making it."

"Then what, sir?"

"I'll tell you what I think. The whole thing was a bluff!"

"You mean?"

"I'm suggesting that Crane never saw him stoop at all."

Vanson slapped his thigh. "Bless me, Mr French, that's an idea. I believe you've got it. But steady a moment. Surely Savory's too cute a bird to be caught like that?"

"I'm not so sure. Murder's a nasty charge. Savory might think it was a bluff and yet not be willing to take the risk."

"That's true. Then you think Savory's innocent?"

"Of Radlett's murder; not of this one. I imagine he did Crane in from sheer fright."

The more they discussed the theory, the more likely it seemed to both of them. It was too late to see Savory that night, but French decided he would do so next day.

Carter was waiting for them at the hotel. He had picked up nine more sections of grenade cases and the broken tube of a detonator, as well as a number of stones.

"There are no stones showing anywhere on the heath," he went on, "so I had a look round and I found where they came from. They'd been pulled out of the broken walls of the ruin."

French stared. "How many were there and about what size?"

"There were six, all about six inches cube."

"And where did you find them?"

"In the heather close to the crater. From the marks on the heather they looked as if they had been stacked on the mine and thrown out by it."

Carter also reported that he had found traces in the heather where someone had recently sat or lain. These were to the side of the path some hundred yards from it and opposite a point some twenty feet short of the crater. He had made a special search in case this person might have dropped some small article, but without success.

Here was another puzzle. It was a matter which must be considered, but not, French felt, at the moment. Two had just struck on the Town Hall clock and he decided that some sleep was indicated.

When he reached the station later that morning his first care was to ring up Savory.

"I wonder, sir, if you'll be in St Pols this morning? I should be grateful if you could make it convenient to call at the police-station. There are some new developments we'd like to talk to you about."

Savory said he had an appointment in the village at ten, and would call after that. About half past he turned up.

French was thrilled by his manner. Gone to a great extent was his overbearing truculence. He was quiet, indeed very nearly polite. French was sure he was a badly frightened man.

"I'm obliged to you, sir, for calling," he began with even more than his usual suavity. "I want to ask you some questions, but before I do so it's my duty to caution you that you are not bound to answer them, and also that what you do say will be taken down and may be used in evidence."

Savory smiled bleakly. "Sounds rather ominous that," he remarked with an effort at cheeriness.

"I hope not, sir. It's about the murder of Mr Crane. I should like – "

"Oh, then he was murdered, was he? I thought it likely myself from what I heard."

"Oh, yes, there's no doubt of it." In thinking over the interview French had decided that after an adequate caution, a certain amount of bluff was permissible. He therefore went on: "I think perhaps the easiest way would be to ask if you'd care to make a statement about your visit to the church on Ruin Hill at six o'clock last night?"

Savory's face fell almost ludicrously. "Ruin Hill?" he stammered. "Why, I – I – wasn't there."

"I take it, sir, you'll scarcely deny going into the church by the north transept door, crossing to the east window, and standing there looking out over the broken wall at Mr Crane coming along the path?"

French could see the sweat glistening on Savory's head. The man was obviously fighting for self-control.

"Of course I deny it," he said, but without conviction. "How could I do that if I wasn't at the place?"

French believed he was lying. The thrill of the hunter had now got possession of him, and though his conscience pricked him slightly, he decided to bluff again.

"Do you mean that if a witness came forward in court and swore he saw you there, he'd be lying?"

Savory moved uneasily, thought for a few moments, and then made a sudden gesture. "Oh, well, I see you know too much," he answered. "I didn't want to say anything about it, but if I was seen, I won't be able to keep it quiet. Yes, I was there, just as you describe."

French repressed his exultation. "Quite so, sir," he said easily. "Now again remembering my caution, would you care to tell me all about it?"

"I don't seem to have any option, do I? Well, if I do it at all, I'll do it completely. Where shall I begin? How much do you know?"

"A fair amount, sir, but please assume I don't know anything. I'm always glad of a check on my information."

Savory scowled, but went on: "The thing began with Crane libelling me in one of his books. A vicious libel it was, damaging and hurtful and quite undeserved: I had never done anything to hurt Crane. I naturally demanded an explanation, and when I didn't get one I threatened proceedings. But perhaps you've heard all this?"

"Yes, but I'm glad to have it corroborated."

"You can get pretty heavy damages for that sort of thing, and Crane was evidently afraid of what it might cost him. But he should have thought of that before he indulged himself at my expense."

He looked at French, who nodded without replying.

"He was always thinking out plots for his books, and he evidently thought out one to try to save himself the cash. Two days ago I got a note from him saying – But I think I have it here."

Savory fumbled in his pocket and handed over the original of the carbon French had found. French read it gravely.

"Was this true, this statement that he had seen you stooping on the sand?"

Savory snorted. "True?" he replied indignantly. "Of course it wasn't true! It was a lie, absolute and complete! I never stooped nor did anything on the ground, and therefore he never saw it. It was a frame-up."

"With what object?" French inquired innocently.

"Good heavens, anyone but a half-wit could see that! He was going to say, 'Look here, you call off the action, or I'll put up a tale that'll get you hanged!' "

"He couldn't be sure of that."

"No, but he knew it was a chance I wouldn't risk."

"Then what did you propose to do?"

Savory jerked about and spoke with a mixture of unwillingness and indignation. "What could I do? He had me. I decided to meet him and agree to call off the action, provided he published an apology in the local papers."

"You think he would have done so?"

"Yes, all he wanted was to save the money."

"Very well, you decided to meet him. Carry on, please."

"There's nothing more to tell. I went to the church at the time he said, and did look out through a gap in the broken wall. I was on time, but he was a little late. However, I saw him coming along the path, just as you said."

"And then?"

"When he got within about thirty yards the explosion took place. I actually saw it. Rather ghastly." Savory now openly wiped the perspiration off his forehead.

"I expect so. What did you do, sir?"

"Do? I was just about to run out to see if I could help Crane, when I glanced back along the path. I saw a man running towards the body. I didn't recognize him at the moment, though I now know it was Treglown. Then suddenly I felt sick. I recognized the position I was in."

"What do you mean, sir?"

"What do I mean? Good heavens! Can't you think of anything? See here. Crane and I were on bad terms and were just about to go to law. I had come secretly to the ruin. I was in cover behind a wall, watching Crane coming nearer. When he got to the distance of an easy cast he was blown to bits, exactly as if a grenade had been thrown. I was pretty good with hand-grenades in the last war. Tell me, chief inspector, who would have believed that I didn't throw it?"

"What about your motive? Crane might have had a motive for killing you, but what motive had you for killing him?"

"Plenty, or so it would be argued. To keep his false story from getting out for one thing, and to stop his blackmail for another. He'd written me that letter and was pretty certain to have kept a copy. If it was found, I'd be for it."

"But Mr Crane had not mentioned what he said he saw to the police or at the inquest. How could he have done it afterwards without getting charged as an accessory after the fact?"

"I thought of that. He was a clever chap, Crane, and he'd have found some way out. But even if not, when he did eventually make his report, he'd have got off pretty lightly."

"There's a good deal in what you say, sir. What did you do?"

"What would you have done in my place? I waited till Treglown was busy with the body and I sneaked off home. He didn't see me."

French smiled grimly. "Since you ask me, I don't say I mightn't have done the same. But for all that, it wasn't wise."

Savory shrugged. "Wise or foolish, it's what you'd have done."

French bent forward confidentially. "Now, Mr Savory, I expect you've thought over this thing a good deal. What do you imagine took place?"

Savory made a gesture of exasperation. "I don't know! Believe it or not, Mr French, I can't think. But I'm convinced of two things. First, that Crane was murdered in the same way as Radlett, however that was done – and probably by the same people. Second, that I was deliberately brought there as a scapegoat to divert suspicion from the real murderer. In other words, I was framed."

"But it was Crane himself who asked you to go."

"I know. I admit I don't understand it."

French pondered. "If you're right, it means that Crane had some other enemy. Can you suggest who?"

"No, I can't. I've no idea." He paused for a moment, then went on. "Look here, chief inspector, I've been very open with you, admittedly because I had no option. Now be open with me. What do *you* think about it?"

French smiled crookedly. "Unhappily I can answer that question fully: I don't know what happened – as yet. Now, sir, that's all about that. But while you're here, I wonder if you'd answer one further question? For my files I want a brief life history of all connected with these cases. I have a number already. Will you give me yours?"

Savory hesitated. "Why, yes, I've no objection."

"Thank you. Then date and place of birth, where educated, and so on."

Savory, it appeared, had been born in Gloucester on 7th June, 1878, and was educated at a local school from which he went to Oxford.

"Then, sir?"

"Then if you must know, I went abroad. I was of a roving disposition and I couldn't settle down in some office in this sleeping country – for it was sleeping then. I went to Canada and knocked about, working at anything I could find. I've been over most of the country, wheat, cattle, railway repairs – a dozen jobs. Then I went into partnership with a man in the States. He had a recipe for a patent medicine and we bought a factory and marketed it. We made money – not a fortune, but a fair sum. Then I came home and married, lived in London for a while and moved down here. That all you want?"

"That's all, sir, if you'll be good enough to add names and addresses to it."

Savory glared at him. "What on earth do you want that for?" he demanded with the nearest approach to his former truculence he had yet shown.

"Just a matter of completeness," French answered smoothly.

Savory glared more wrathfully. At first he seemed about to refuse, then he shrugged and ungraciously gave the information. French nodded.

"I don't think you'll be called at the inquest on Mr Crane," he went on. "All the same I'd be grateful if you'd be there, in case the coroner should learn that you were in the neighbourhood at the time of the occurrence."

"Then is that all you want now?"

"That's all, sir, and thank you very much."

Savory seemed surprised, and French felt sure he had expected arrest. In a milder tone he wished French good morning and left the building.

– 17 –

CHIEF INSPECTOR FRENCH

When Savory had gone French sat on in the little office thinking over the man and his statement.

With regard to the man, French had never seen him so civil, so reasonable, so free from bombast and aggressiveness. With a type like Savory this surely meant; that he was afraid. But was it fear due to his precarious position or to guilt? This was a nice point and French could not decide it, but judging from his manner alone, he felt inclined to believe the man's story. Of course this was mere opinion and therefore inconclusive.

From the statement the two possible theories already considered stood out clearly. Either Savory had stooped over the mine on the shore, set a trip, and so murdered Radlett, or the stooping was an invention of Crane's, to be used to blackmail Savory into withdrawing the libel action. French took these possibilities in turn.

At once he saw that there was a good deal against the truth of Crane's story. There was first the point he had already noted: if Crane had seen Savory stoop, why had he mentioned it neither to the police nor the coroner? The more French thought over this, the more convincing it seemed to grow. And the complementary difficulty was equally great: once he had held it back, how could he afterwards use it without getting himself into very serious trouble? On the face of it, it looked like Crane's invention.

Then would Savory have adopted a plan which involved stooping and fumbling on the site of the tragedy? It was an open shore and a dozen people might have seen him. And if he were seen, how could he explain his action in the light of what afterwards happened? Further, if he had set a trip he would have made distinctive marks on the sand. Now Radlett would certainly have seen him stoop and would have wondered what he was doing. He would therefore have been looking out for marks, and it was scarcely conceivable that he would not have avoided the snare.

These were strong arguments, but there was another which was stronger still. If Savory had set a trip, what was the object of the wire down the groyne? It seemed beyond question that the explosion had been caused by an electric current down that wire, and if so, no trip could have been used.

Lastly there was the consideration that Savory was not known to have had any motive for desiring Radlett's death, though this admittedly might be simply due to police ignorance.

From the converse point of view French could find no single argument which supported the trip theory. He therefore noted that the probabilities were against it, and went on to consider the alternative, that Crane had invented the entire episode.

This also was by no means free from difficulties, most of which he had already seen. How could Crane hope to convince first Savory and then a jury of the truth of his story, against all the considerations French had just been reviewing? Again, how could he use his alleged knowledge without injury to himself, either in connection with the murder or with blackmail or with both? How could he be sure Savory would not call his bluff? And lastly, how could he know that someone else had not observed Savory at the critical moment, who might come forward and give his story the lie? Indeed, how could he know that someone had not already told the police he had seen Savory pass the groyne in a normal manner? French scratched his head irritably as he saw that taking it by and large, this second theory was almost as unlikely as the first.

Yet, true or false, the statement had been made. Crane had definitely accused Savory. Was a third theory of the affair possible, which so far he had missed?

Rack his brains as he would, French could think of none, and he decided to investigate as fully as possible the original possibilities.

Again beginning with the first: if Savory had fixed a trip, he must have had a motive for bringing about Radlett's death. What could that motive have been?

It was with this question in his mind that he had asked Savory for his life history. As far as was known, the two men had had no dispute at St Pols, indeed they had had little to do with one another. Had they then come in contact in their earlier lives?

Comparing Savory's story with what he had learnt from the Wedgewoods and Littles about Radlett, French immediately realized that they had. A little thrill of excitement ran through him. Why, they had been at the same college, and both had gone to Canada, roughed it, and made money. Radlett had struck it lucky at Klondyke and Savory had sold a popular patent medicine, but there was no reason why they might not at some time have worked together.

French rang up the Yard. Would they have inquiries made at Magdalen College, Oxford, about the two young men. Next, would they get in touch with the police at Wagonville, Pa., and check up Savory's account of the medicine works? Thirdly, would they obtain Radlett's record from the Klondyke officers?

There was some little delay, but the answers, when they came, filled French with eager satisfaction. They formed a thrilling crescendo. At Oxford the young men were friends, though no special incidents coupling their names had taken place. At Wagonville, Pa., Savory's account of his experience in the medicine plant was largely imaginary. It was true that he had been employed there, but in a junior capacity only, and it was quite impossible that he could have made money. At Klondyke Radlett had had a partner named Savory, who had treated him pretty badly, and a *précis* of the story followed.

In this last item, French thought in his first enthusiasm, was motive enough for any murder. But as had happened so often before, when he proceeded to analyse the story, he felt less certain.

In the first place, the circumstances supplied Radlett with a motive for desiring Savory's death, rather than the other way round. Second, while that motive might have been strong enough at the time of the affair, it was unlikely that it would have been so now. Many years had passed, during which warm passions would have died down. Further, if either of these men had wished to murder the other, there would surely have been lots of opportunities before this. If therefore Savory had now murdered Radlett, some quite new factor must have operated. French knew nothing of any such factor, and after his careful investigation he could scarcely believe that it existed.

One step he obviously must take: to hear what explanation Savory could give for the falsehoods in his story. He therefore asked him to call again at the station.

"Now, Mr Savory," he began after a somewhat austere greeting, "I have to ask you one or two more questions, but before doing so I wish to renew the caution I gave you. Is that understood?"

"Of course." Once again Savory's manner was mild, if not actually polite.

"I have ascertained," French declared formally, "that the statement you made to me on Friday relative to your life abroad was false in several important particulars. I have to ask you for an explanation of this, and also whether you wish to amend it and to tell the truth?"

Savory's eyes grew troubled. For a moment he did not reply, sitting staring at French in an appraising manner, as if weighing his character and probable reactions. Then he asked what errors had been discovered.

"I'm afraid no errors at all," French returned bluntly. "Your incorrect statements appear to me like deliberate falsehoods. However, we needn't split hairs about names. The question is, do you care to make a revised statement?"

"On what points?"

"On the points on which you tried to mislead me. Come, Mr Savory, you know perfectly well what they are, and you'll either correct them or you won't. Which is it to be?"

Once again Savory pondered, then he gave a slight shrug. "You win, chief inspector. You're right, I did try to mislead you, and I see now it was foolish. I thought the truth might be damaging to me, but I realize now that to be suspected of hiding something is much more damaging. I'll tell you exactly what occurred."

"Very good, sir. I'll be glad to hear it."

271

"Everything I told you was true, I think, except how I made my money. Was that the point?"

"Yes, sir."

"Well, I don't know how you got on it, but you're quite correct. I was employed at the medicine factory at Wagonville, but I made no money there. As a matter of fact, I made my money at Klondyke."

He paused, but French merely nodded without comment.

"I was in partnership with Radlett, which I imagine is what interests you?" There was a question in his tone, but still French did not reply. "Oh, well, I can't blame you for keeping your own council. We worked together without luck for some time, then Radlett fell ill. I took him to hospital and while he was there I struck gold. I took part of it, and when Radlett came out of hospital, he took the rest. As a matter of fact, he got a lot more than I did, though we both did well."

"Well, sir?" said French as Savory came to a halt.

"That's about all."

"Not according to the statement I've heard."

"I suppose you mean about my clearing out before Radlett left the hospital? Well, that's true, and I had two reasons. First, I didn't, as a matter of fact, think he ever would leave the hospital, and second, I wanted to get down to the States before the winter set in and while the going was easy."

French considered this. Was he likely to get more? There was no proof that Savory had poisoned his partner, and if he denied it, as of course he would, French would be no further on. However, he might try another point.

"The suggestion was that when you had got all the gold you thought your ground contained, you left with all of it for an unknown address, with the object of cheating Radlett out of his share. That he found some more was due to a mistake on your part and an accident on his."

"I resent that," Savory returned, "though I can't prove I'm right any more than you can prove I'm wrong."

"Well, that's believed to have been Radlett's view."

Savory shrugged. "I'm not responsible for that."

"Why did you keep your Klondyke visit secret?"

"Why do you ask idiotic questions?" retorted Savory with a touch of his old manner. "I'm not altogether a fool. I can see that you're out to fix both these murders on me, but that you can't get a motive in the first case. That's what you're trying for now."

"That, sir, is entirely false," French said with some heat. "I'm not out to fix anything on you. What I want to find is the truth, and if it leads to you that's your lookout. You've certainly done your best to arouse my suspicions."

"*Touché.* I suppose that's true. Well, what are you going to do about it?"

It was exactly what French himself was wondering. Quite definitely he suspected Savory, but equally certainly he had not sufficient evidence for an arrest. He reminded himself he had still a number of lines to investigate in connection with Crane's murder. It would be better to carry on with these first and let the matter of Savory wait. With the country in its present condition the man couldn't possibly escape.

"Nothing, sir," he therefore answered. "I was dissatisfied with your statement, but you have now modified it and brought it into line with my other information. For the present that's all I want."

An unsatisfactory interview, French thought, as after Savory had gone he completed his notes of what had passed. By the time this was done it was one o'clock, and with Carter he strolled back to the hotel for lunch. On his way something happened which unexpectedly settled for him his next step. He met Rollo.

"Hullo, Rollo!" he greeted him. "Are you busy? Come and have lunch."

Rollo coloured with pleasure. He had leave until three and would be delighted. They went on to the hotel, and after some general conversation French told him how the case was progressing. Rollo was particularly interested in the Crane affair.

"You know, sir, I don't believe that grenade was thrown," he commented when he had heard the particulars. "I've seen a good many of them lately and they don't really make much of a crater, if any."

"It's rather a vital point," French answered; "one of the things I've noted to go into. I was thinking of making some tests. Have you an expert on the subject who'd give an opinion?"

"Why, yes, Major Dangle's your man. If there's anything about grenades he doesn't know, it's unknowable."

"That sounds all right. Could you put me in touch with him?"

Rollo beamed. "I can take you to see him, provided you go before three. Look here, I'll ring him up now and see if he's free."

Half an hour later French and Rollo were ushered into a small room in the country house which had been taken over by the military for their district headquarters. Major Dangle was tall and thin with a dry manner and a somewhat pained smile.

"I know your name, Mr French. I've known it long before I heard you were working down here. I'll be glad if I can help you. What's the point?"

French explained. "Here, sir, is a plan of the site and a sketch, measurements and photographs of the crater and body, also the bits of the grenade and the stones found. If you want further information I may be able to give it to you."

"No one could want more than this," Dangle returned as he spread the papers out on his desk. "I congratulate you on your records."

For some minutes he studied the figures and photographs, then he pushed them aside and turned to French.

"Well, chief inspector, I've seen, I suppose, many hundreds of grenades burst, and I never saw one which bit into the ground like this. I'm prepared to swear that it was not thrown in the ordinary way."

"Then you mean it was buried and exploded like a mine?"

"Unquestionably. But I mean more than that. Unless I'm greatly mistaken, one grenade wouldn't make a crater like that. Was the sand on this path very loose?"

"Yes, sir. There are still some members of riding schools who exercise on the heath, and the horses' hooves loosen it to a depth of four or five inches."

Dangle nodded. "Even allowing for that, I feel sure more than one was used. In fact I'd say that at least three went up."

"Could you give evidence to that effect?"

"That there was more than one, yes; the exact number, no. But I'll tell you what I'll do if you like; try some experiments. I could lay nests of one, two, three and four along that same path and put them up electrically."

"I'd like nothing better," French exclaimed delightedly.

"Well, what about the present? It happens I have a couple of hours free. How would that suit you?"

"Perfect! It's uncommonly good of you, sir."

"Not at all, I'm interested myself. Now let's see; we'll want ten grenades, but better have a few extra in case we want to repeat any of the shots." He fixed French with a solemn stare. "We'll charge you the cost of these, by the way."

French smiled. "Right, sir. I believe the Yard would be good for that."

"I hope so," Dangle answered doubtfully. He picked up his desk telephone and gave some orders. "They'll be ready in a few minutes."

"Fine, sir. Then while we're waiting there's just one other point. Can you suggest how the thing was put up?"

"Ah," Major Dangle returned, "now you're talking. You've found nothing to give you a clue?"

"Nothing whatever."

"H'm, not so easy. There are many ways it could be done, of course, but most of them would leave some trace. Presumably you examined the ground all round?"

"Over an area of a hundred yards in every direction."

"No traces of beaten down grass where someone had been lying?"

"Well, yes, there was a suggestion of it at one point. Not grass, there's none at the place, but the heather looked compressed and twigs were broken. Someone had undoubtedly been there, but whether lying down, I couldn't say."

"Was there a view of the path from this place?"

"Yes," French returned, "and that's suggestive too. The point where the grenades went up was completely hidden by shrubs, but the path was visible through a vista at a point some twenty feet farther away from the ruin. At least, I shouldn't say you could see the path itself, only the heather through which it ran."

"But you could see a person passing along?"

"Oh, yes, clearly."

Dangle looked at him speculatively. "You said that was suggestive?"

"Well, there's the four-seconds time lag. If the pins had been pulled when Crane was passing that vista, he'd just about have got to the grenades when they went up."

Dangle looked at him with more respect. "A good point, chief inspector, a very good point. The suggestion being that the grenades were put up by withdrawing one of the pins?"

"I wondered if that was possible."

"I don't see why not. Suppose the grenade was fixed in the ground and a cord tied to the pin and led back to the beaten-down heather. If it was pulled out, as you say, when Crane was passing that vista, the job would be done."

"It would be simpler than an electric arrangement."

"Simpler and safer. No elaborate workshop job on the grenades. No apparatus left on the ground to supply inquisitive chief inspectors with clues. The murderer would simply pull in the whole of his cord with the pin attached and take it away with him. One grenade going off would put up the rest."

"The cord might be seen before the explosion."

"It's possible, I suppose. But surely unlikely among all that undergrowth?"

"I expect you're right, sir. Incidentally that suggests a job for me: to find the cord and pin."

Dangle nodded. "If you could do that it would be pretty conclusive."

There was a knock at the door and an NCO entered. He saluted briskly.

"All ready, sir."

"Good." Dangle got up and closed his desk. "Then let's go."

French was sorry for Rollo who would obviously have liked to join the party. But it was nearly half past two and his leave would soon be up. Major Dangle got into the police car with French, while the NCO, Carter and a man with a shovel and a sack of broken bricks followed in another. They reached Ruin Hill and French pointed out the path.

The soldiers quickly got to work. Four shallow holes were dug in the centre of the path, and one, two, three and four grenades respectively were wedged into these between brickbats. Then with great care Dangle tied the ends of four pieces of cord to one of the pins of each lot and the holes were filled in and tramped smooth. The cords had been laid out to a point at right-angles to the path and some hundred yards away.

"Now we'll put these up one by one," Dangle announced. "You men stay on the path in each direction and stop anyone coming, and you, Mr French, come with me to the ends of the cords. You'd better lie down: less likely to stop a bit of grenade."

French crouched with Dangle while the latter pulled the first cord and began to wind it in. Before he had finished, the explosion took place, but he went on till the pin appeared.

"You see," he pointed out, "if I take away this cord and pin, there's no trace of any kind left."

In turn he pulled the other cords and then they went back to inspect the results.

These were illuminating and conclusive. The four craters were of markedly different sizes, and that which had contained the three grenades was almost a duplicate of the original.

"That settles your hash, I think," Dangle remarked as they stood looking down.

"Absolutely," French agreed. "You were right in your suggestion."

"Oh, well, I'd be rather ashamed if I wasn't. But there's one point I haven't quite got yet. How did your criminal anchor his grenade so as to ensure that the pin would pull out easily?"

"What about the stones we found?"

"That's it, of course. I should have remembered them. Well, it seems to me the method has been fairly demonstrated?"

French agreed with gratitude. As he watched Dangle drive off he felt his visit had been well worthwhile. For once in this exasperating case certainty had been achieved.

But the immediate deduction from all these facts did not please French so much. If it were true, did it not mean that Savory was innocent? The man who had stood in the church chancel was certainly innocent. He had not thrown the grenades and there were three reasons why it was unlikely he had operated a cord. In the first place it would be difficult for anyone looking at the path end on to know when the victim had come within twenty feet of the grenades, and a mistake on this point would have been fatal to his plans. Second, the cord would have run along the path in full view of Crane, who would probably have seen the pins jumping over the uneven surface, and stopped to investigate. Thirdly, if the cord had been operated from the church, how was the patch of beaten-down heather to be explained?

The more French thought over these points, the more convinced he grew that Savory was not his man. There had been grave difficulties in believing him guilty of the first crime, and now he saw the same thing obtained in the case of the second. It was a disappointment, not because he wished Savory ill, but because he himself was left once again in the air.

However, this was life, and particularly that department of it called detective work. And with detective work the remedy was the same as in other activities: if at first you don't succeed, et cetera. To try again was his only hope.

But how? Or where?

Then another idea occurred to him. If Savory were innocent, did not the position of the grenades – within an easy throw of the church – confirm his suggestion that he had been framed? And if so, might that attempt not have been carried further? Assuming a cord had been used to pull out the pin, might that cord and pin not have been planted on Savory?

It was a rather long shot, but French thought a search might be worthwhile. Savory's route home from Ruin Hill would be by a path to the road, then across the spinney to his garden, and so to his house. Calling Carter, French set to work.

They walked slowly along, glancing sharply from side to side, though French would have been a very surprised man if he had found anything. It was unlikely that the cord would simply have been dropped; some attempt to hide it would certainly have been made. Therefore French was not looking in the first instance for the cord, only for a suitable hiding-place. Presently reaching the road, the two men crossed it and entered the spinney. Here there was no path and it was therefore impossible to say just where Savory had walked, but they took as direct a line as he could for the small gate leading into the garden.

So far they had come across no likely hiding-place, but now French saw something which gave him pause. A path led through the garden from the gate, and to the right of this was a small cluster of buildings, the garage, tool-shed, potting-house and a range of greenhouses. Taking the water from the downspouts of these roofs was a large galvanized iron tank. He stepped up to it.

It was evidently used for the garden, for it was raised on low brick piers and at the bottom were two valves, one an ordinary stop tap high enough for filling watering-cans, the other a tap with a union from which a wire-wound hose led away into a greenhouse. A small galvanized pipe rose from the ground and entered it about halfway up its side, and when French looked in he saw this ended in a ball valve. The idea was obvious. The tank was normally kept full by the rain, but during periods of drought when the water level fell to half capacity, company's water entered and the tank never went dry. The water was dirty, black and opaque, and the bottom was invisible.

This looked hopeful, and cutting a branch with a hooked twig, he set Carter to fish.

Carter quickly brought up a number of matted clusters of leaves and the ancient body of a rat. But there was still another object on the bottom. He found it hard to hook, but at last it caught on the twig and he raised it to the surface. It was a roll of stout cord with a grenade pin fastened to one end!

Two steps forward on the same afternoon! French felt that the age of miracles was not over. Unless Savory was guilty after all – which he didn't believe – he had certainly been framed. Was there any hint as to who could have done it?

With a further feeling of satisfaction French saw that there was. The murderer's alibi must surely have been established at some point close to Kelwyn House. Either he lived near by or he had arranged a meeting in the vicinity, and the probabilities suggested the former.

To take the first point, who lived near by? As French stood making a list from memory, he wondered if he was not already glimpsing the end of his case.

18

CHIEF INSPECTOR FRENCH

The only people residing within a reasonable distance of Savory were the Littles, the Wedgewoods and Macdougal. French had acquitted all of them of complicity in the first murder. Were they also innocent of the second?

Some of them he simply could not suspect. He did not believe that either of the women would have committed so foul a crime as planting a murder on an innocent man. It seemed completely at variance with the characters of both. Nor did he believe Wedgewood would do it. Wedgewood might commit a murder, but it would be a clean murder – if murder ever could be clean. Wedgewood was the sort of man who in other days might have fought a duel with the desire and intention to kill, but he would have been scrupulously careful to see that his opponent had every advantage he claimed for himself.

If he were right, this left only Little and Macdougal, and neither seemed promising.

French clearly realized that he was thinking too much of the murderer's attempt to involve Savory and too little of his hate for Crane. But his trouble was that he didn't know anyone who hated Crane. Whatever the novelist had done in secret, in public he had made no enemies.

Once again French writhed in impotence. Wherever he turned, he seemed to be held up.

Then it occurred to him that though he knew of no enemies of Crane's, the novelist's fate proved he had at least one. Why should that one not have been Little or Macdougal? There was no reason that he could see. Therefore it was only common sense to treat them as suspects. He turned to Carter.

"It's not too late to get Macdougal's alibi. If we hurry we'll catch him before he goes off duty. We can get Little's in the morning."

Macdougal was putting away his tools as they reached the workshop. He listened dourly to what French had to say.

"That's no so far away from telling me I murdered Crane," he grumbled.

"It's just ten thousand miles away from it, Mr Macdougal," French retorted. "As I think I explained before, I'm accusing no one. You're not the only one I'm putting the question to."

"Oh, well, have it your own way. Ye want to know where I was at this time on Thursday evening? Well, I was where ye see me now. I quit at six every night there's no something to keep me later. It's five past six now and I have me tools put away, or I would have only for you coming round with your questions. And but for the same reason I'd be out of this and halfway home by now."

French smiled. "Well, I'll not delay you any longer."

"Oh, aye, just that: when the mischief's done."

There was a glint in Macdougal's eye which French recognized. He knew the northern mind, and in spite of himself this reply with its accompanying glint gave him a warm feeling of sympathy and friendship towards the mechanic. No more than in the case of the others could he believe this man guilty of so sordid a crime. All the same, duty was duty. He left Macdougal still tidying up, and with Carter hurried on to his cottage. Mrs Macdougal came to the door. French greeted her pleasantly.

"Just one question, Mrs Macdougal, for I expect you're busy getting supper. I've been asking Mr Macdougal what time he got home on Thursday evening and he wasn't very sure. Can you remember?"

"Huh, it's a queer thing he couldna remember a thing like that," the good lady returned scornfully, "and me having his tea ready for him on the tick. He came at his usual time – between five and ten past six."

With this French expressed himself as content, and smiling slightly as he thought of Macdougal's reaction to the news of his visit, he and Carter returned to St Pols.

Next morning they went out to "The Beacon". There they saw Jessica Little.

"Oh, it's you, Mr French," she called in a friendly tone. "Won't you come in? I'm sorry my husband's in St Pols, but he should soon be back, if you care to wait."

"I did want to see him," French answered, "but I think you could probably tell me what I want to know, if you'd be so good."

"Of course. Anything I can!"

"Thank you. As you can probably guess from our previous interviews, I'm making a timetable of the movements of everyone even remotely concerned with the late Mr Crane. I called to get Mr Little's statement."

Jessica did not seem at all taken aback. "Yes, you explained that before. Just what hours do you want to know about?"

"From six to six-fifteen on last Thursday evening."

"Well, it's a funny thing, but it happens that by a chance I can tell you. On Thursday morning a letter came to me from one of the comforts for the troops depots about the finished articles we had sent not balancing the wool we had received. I'm secretary of the thing, but I admit I'm no good at writing business letters, and when I explained the affair to my husband he said he'd do it for me and I could sign it. About quarter to six that evening he came and asked me for the letter, saying he had a few minutes to spare and would do the reply while he had the details in his mind. He came back in about half an hour with the typewritten reply, so he must have been in his study doing it."

"Would it have taken him half an hour?"

"I should think so. There was a good deal to explain."

"How are you so sure that it was Thursday evening?"

"Because that's the afternoon the club meets and I had it in my mind."

"I follow. Where were you at the time Mr Little was doing the letter?"

"In the garden. I'd just got back from the club and I came out for a rest before preparing supper."

"Did you hear Mr Little typing the letter?"

"Oh, no, I couldn't. It's much too far away."

The statement gave French a good deal to think over. From her manner he felt satisfied that everything Jessica Little had told him was strictly true to the best of her knowledge and belief. Yet her story was profoundly unsatisfactory. While it might be exactly what it appeared to be – an alibi for Little – it might equally well be Little's invention. Its weak point was obvious. Little might have written the letter earlier in the afternoon, enabling him to leave his study between 5.45 and 6.15 and still produce the completed work at the end of that time.

There was, of course, no scintilla of proof that Little had done so. As usual French was left floundering in the shoals of doubt. The one thing he was certain about was that he had no case against Little and must try elsewhere.

As a last resort his thoughts turned towards Forrester and Vane. Unlikely, each of them, and yet they must be considered.

A very short inquiry served to clear them both. Each beyond any doubt whatever was in his office at six o'clock on the day of Crane's death.

French sat back despondently in Cundy's chair, exasperated beyond measure. It looked as if he must find some completely new person, someone whom he had never yet even suspected. But he couldn't think of any such connected with the case.

Even lunch did nothing to lighten his gloom. After it he returned to the station and once again sat struggling with his sense of frustration. He could think of nothing which offered any help. The vital item that he needed had so far completely eluded him. Once again he was facing that nightmare of his working life, a case of which he had made a complete failure. His return to the Yard would be ignominious.

Then as had happened more than once before, just as his depression grew most profound, a ray of light began to glimmer dimly on his horizon. A point that he had missed flashed suddenly into his mind. He sat up, scarcely daring to breathe.

Was there not a discrepancy in the evidence which had been given, not only to Vanson and himself, but at the inquest, the original inquest on Radlett?

He leant forward, thinking intently. Yes, there was a discrepancy, staring him in the face! A discrepancy which might, had he seen it, have altered his entire handling of the case. How could he have been so dense as to miss it? His delight at the possibility of progress was tempered with chagrin as he contemplated his failure. It was due, like most of his errors, to taking things for granted. He had been too easygoing! Too superficial! He hadn't given the evidence sufficient thought.

As he had found to his cost in many a previous investigation, it was *always* necessary to make a timetable of the movements of those concerned, or plot them on a graph so as to check up that they really harmonized. This time they had seemed so obviously correct that he hadn't troubled to do it. Well, it would be a lesson to him for the future! How many similar lessons, he asked himself bitterly, had he had in the past?

With some eagerness he once again took the file and began looking up evidence. Yes, he was right! There at the very beginning of the affair, set out in black and white so that he who ran could read, was the suggestive item. It referred to the death of Radlett. With a rapidly rising excitement, he began checking over the details.

When the mine went up Little had been in his study with his wife and sister-in-law. All three had seen the explosion. Little had acted promptly. He had rushed out to the hall, telephoned first to the doctor and then to the police, and then had run as fast as he could down the path to the shore and along the sand to the body. French turned up the Ordnance map and scaled the distance: it was nearly three-quarters of a mile. Estimating as carefully as he could, he believed that all this should have taken Little about eight minutes.

He turned over the pages to Crane's evidence. Crane had also seen the mine go up. He was then telephoning, and according to his own story, he instantly ended his conversation and ran down as quickly as he could to the place. His statement was supported in its most vital parts by a number of witnesses. Miss Avory corroborated the facts that he had been telephoning when the explosion took place, and without the loss of a moment had then run out of the house towards the shore. Treglown asserted that he was running at a good speed when he passed him, and the doctor, the police and Little stated that he was still running when he appeared near the head of the groyne, and that he did not slacken till he reached the crater.

Once again French checked distances on the map and estimated times. Crane's house was just over two hundred yards from the scene of the tragedy, and French estimated that he should not have taken more than two or three minutes to get down.

Lastly there was the police evidence. The police car had actually been at the station door when the news had come in, and Cundy and his men had started immediately. They had called at Dr Petherick's, whose house was on their way, picked him up, and gone out along the sand. They reached the scene of the murder in exactly six minutes.

French did now what he saw he ought to have done on taking over the case. He wrote down these arrivals in timetable form. It read:

Murder	10.10 a.m.
Crane's arrival	10.13 "
Police and doctor's arrival	10.16 "
Little's arrival	10.18 "

French rubbed his hands with pleasure as he compared these figures with his notes on another page of the file.

Granted that the murder had taken place at 10.10 and the police had been there at 10.16, then Little had joined them as nearly as possible at 10.18, for all concerned agreed that he came up about two minutes after the police arrival. So far, so good.

But Crane had not turned up till 10.17! Again all concerned had stated that he had reached the place about a minute after the police and a minute before Little.

Here was the discrepancy all right! Crane had spent seven minutes over a three-minute job!

What was Crane doing during those four vital minutes?

French's imagination, now stimulated, responded promptly. It was easy to visualize at least one answer.

Suppose Crane and the murderer had been confederates? Suppose the murderer, hidden in the shrubs at the head of the groyne, had observed Radlett's approach, made his electrical contact and exploded the mine? Suppose he had instantly hurried off to complete what alibi he could, leaving behind him the end of his wire, his switch and his battery? Suppose Crane had stopped in the shrubs to cut the wire and temporarily to hide the wire and apparatus, pending its complete removal later?

This idea of a criminal partnership was attractive to French for another reason: it might supply a motive for Crane's murder. Suppose the confederates quarrelled, or the other one thought his secret was not safe with Crane? All pure guesswork, of course, but *any* suggestion of a motive was better than the blank fog of negation in which up to now French had found himself.

Though French was delighted with this idea at first, as he continued to think it over it seemed to grow less satisfying. The search of that area of the heath had been exhaustive, and had such comparatively bulky objects been hidden, some trace either of them or their hiding-place should surely have been discovered. Further, was such a criminal partnership on Crane's part likely? Certainly he had come on nothing else to suggest it.

Then a further idea leaped into his mind, and this time his excitement grew more pronounced.

Suppose Crane, and Crane alone, were guilty? What if the wire had not stopped in the shrubs at the head of the groyne, but gone right on into the man's study? What if his four minutes among the shrubs had been spent in cutting and coiling up the end of the wire?

It was not the first time by some scores that French had considered the possibility of Crane's guilt, but up till now he had believed his alibi overwhelming. But if the wire had reached to his study, his telephoning might be no alibi at all.

One consideration tended to support the theory: the length of telephone wire stolen from the Home Guard. It would amply reach from the mine to the house. Admittedly this did not clear the matter up, for it would have reached nearly twice as far. But at least there would have been no difficulty in providing the wire.

French was now enthusiastic about this idea, but as before, further thought somewhat cooled his ardour. If the theory were true, there could have been no mistake as to the victim. The murder of Radlett must have been intended. And what possible motive could Crane have had for Radlett's death? Moreover, if Crane had carried out Radlett's murder without an accomplice, who could have murdered Crane? The more French thought over it, the more puzzling and difficult the whole affair seemed to grow.

But one thing at least was clear. If the wire had extended to the house, some trace must surely remain. Obviously a search was indicated.

With Carter French set off in the car and ten minutes later stood once again by the telephone table in Crane's study, looking round at the room and its furnishing. If he were correct, the wire must have extended to within his reach, inside the room. His first problem obviously was how it could have been led in.

Certainly not in any obvious way such as an open door or window. Crane had run out of the house *immediately* after the explosion and could not possibly have stopped to disconnect wires. French must therefore look for some invisible mode of entrance.

As it could not have passed through the solid wall, some opening must have been used. A careful examination of the door and window-frames showed that no holes had been bored or plugged. The chimney was impossible. To put the wire down would have involved ladders without and soot within. What other openings were there?

French went out to the garden. Having been built as a projection to the original house, the study had three outer walls. In the front or west was the single long window giving on to the garden. In the south was the bow-window looking out over the sea, but the east or back wall containing the fireplace was blank. The original house wall from which this east wall extended was also blank, and these two therefore contained a space which could not be overlooked from the house. This space was also shielded from observation from the east, where ran a thick privet hedge bounding Crane's little estate, with behind it the trees and shrubs of the heath. Only to the south was the area open, and there only to a little frequented part of the garden. Crane evidently had not used it, for it was covered with coarse, untended grass.

It was with increased interest that French saw what he had hoped to find. At the bottom of the blank wall were two galvanized iron ventilators, one at each side of the fireplace. One must therefore be close to the table bearing the telephone.

French dropped on his knees and began to examine the ground beneath it. Immediately he felt a further thrill of satisfaction. On pushing aside the grass he found a round hole in the ground of some inch in diameter. It was obviously recent, because such a hole would not remain open indefinitely, but not very recent, for its edges had lost their sharpness. It had just the appearance he would have expected had it been made about the time of Radlett's murder.

This was encouraging, suggesting that he was on the right track, but when he turned with his lens to examine the metal slats of the ventilator, he could have chuckled with sheer delight. On the side of one of them was a slight roughness, and on this was a tiny shred of what looked like dull red cotton: the same colour as the wire along the groyne! At once he saw how it might have come there. Had a wire been put in through the ventilator and been pulled out suddenly, it might have kinked at the slot, and being dragged forcibly against the rough edge, have lost a scrap of its insulation.

This was still more encouraging, but if he were correct there must be further evidence inside the room. He returned, therefore, locked the door, and settled down to a search.

It was not long before he found it. Under the telephone table in front of the ventilator one of the floorboards had been cut through twice, making a separate length of a foot, or sufficient to stretch between two joists. The ends of this were marked by tools as if it had been prised up, and the surrounding joints were clear of dust, showing that it had recently been raised. Moreover, there were distinct traces of fresh stain, as if white wood had been darkened to match the floor. Near one end a hole of about quarter-inch diameter had been carefully plugged. The alteration as a whole was practically invisible. Not only was it screened from direct observation by the table, but it was just at the edge of the carpet, and this threw a shadow over it from the almost horizontal rays from the windows.

Sending Carter to Crane's workshop for some tools, French with some difficulty raised the board, which had been nailed down. The hole, about three inches from the end, passed right through with the end of the plug projecting. At the other end a block of wood about four inches square and an inch thick had been screwed to the underside of the board. In this block were four other small holes, as if something else had been screwed to it.

With a looking-glass and powerful torch French examined the space below the joists. First he noted that the ventilator was within easy reach of his hand. Then he turned to the concrete floor some foot below the joists. It was covered with an almost imperceptible layer of fine grey dust, and this French searched for marks. He thought he saw some, and by placing the torch so that its beam shone parallel to the surface, he at last made out four circles of about three inches diameter. It looked as if four round bottles had stood in a little cluster.

His enthusiasm had now reached fever heat. Like most Home Guard telephone wire, that up the groyne was single. To complete the circuit to the mine earths would therefore be wanted at each end. What was the hole in the ground but the mark of where a pin had been pushed down to form that at the sending end? And what could have made the four circles but a battery of four cylindrical dry cells, such as are used for bells, and here required to operate the detonating mechanism? At long last things were working in!

French again picked up the bit of floorboard. It looked as if a double wire – from mine and earth – had been led into the room through the quarter-inch hole, perhaps to a push under the table. Yet he scarcely thought this likely. There was no sign of where a push had been attached. Besides, Crane would scarcely have taken the risk of its being seen. Further, what in this case could the block have been for?

Thinking deeply, French went out to Crane's workshop and began a careful search. It was a small separate shed in the garden, well fitted up with both wood and metal working tools. French had known that Crane was a skilful workman because of the cigarette lighter he had made. Now he came across pieces of half-finished work, and all showed a high degree of technical skill.

Crane, however, had not been a perfect workman. He had had the defect of many amateurs: his shop was disgracefully untidy. The space on the bench where he had been working had been obtained by simply pushing back a mass of cuttings, shavings and all kinds of rubbish. The floor was covered with scraps, sawdust and bits of metal, and what was evidently intended as a waste-box was full to overflowing. French congratulated himself. In such a place there was the chance of a find.

It was not long before he made one. On a shelf were four dry cells about three inches in diameter, and when he examined their bases with his high-powered lens, he found traces of fine grey dust. Microscopic samples would, of course, have to be examined for Court – if the case got so far – but he himself had no doubt as to where that dust had come from.

Though on the lookout for anything interesting, French was particularly in search of some object with four screws which might fit the holes in the block. For an hour he worked, going over everything systematically. Then as he picked up a piece of wood from the waste-box he suddenly paused staring.

It was about nine inches by four by half an inch thick, and at one end four screws had been loosened back, but not taken out completely. French tried them against the block on his piece of floorboard. They registered exactly!

At the other end of this piece of wood were three holes making a flat V. That at the apex was about quarter of an inch in diameter and went right through, the others were on the upper side only and were evidently where small screws had penetrated.

French fitted the piece of wood on to the block. It projected out beneath the floorboard, leaving a space of rather more than an inch between the two. Evidently it had acted as a shelf, and some apparatus had been screwed to it beneath the hole.

As French stood thinking in the workshop, his eyes ran vaguely along the shelves. Then suddenly he slapped his thigh.

On a shelf containing electrical fittings he saw a bell push, and when he took it down and found that the push button was missing, he felt he had solved his problem. It was the work of a few seconds to fit it on to the piece of wood, and instantly he saw that once again he was on the right track. The holes exactly registered: the two small ones for the holding-down screws and the quarter-inch one for the lead-in of the wires. Moreover – and this was the most important point of all – the hole in the floorboard came exactly over the centre of the push!

Crane's whole plan was at last clear. He had led the wire from the mine up to his house, through the ventilator and to the push beneath the floor. The second wire from the push had gone to the battery and from that out through the ventilator and to earth. He had doubtless dropped a wooden pin like a short thin pencil through the hole in the floor. This would have rested on the spring of the push and probably stuck up about quarter of an inch above the floor. While standing at the table he could in the most natural way have depressed this piece of wood with his foot, thus making the contact. He had then only to watch his victim reach the appointed place on the shore, and while actually speaking at the telephone he could have blown him to bits! Before rushing out he would naturally have stooped and withdrawn the wooden pin, so that nothing would be left projecting from the floor.

What an incredible fool the man had been not to destroy the piece of wood he had used as a shelf! No doubt he was so certain he could never be suspected that he had grown careless. Well, French reminded himself, there were few criminals who didn't give themselves away somewhere, if only one could find the oversight!

He was about to leave the workshop when he noticed a torn and crumpled scrap of paper lying among the rubbish on the bench. It was a rough pencil sketch, and what had attracted his attention was that it showed something shaped like the spindle found on the shore. He smoothed it out, then gave a gasp.

It was a diagrammatic sketch of an ironclad electro-magnet, and the disk on the spindle was its armature. One end of the spindle slid along the centre of the coil, thus keeping the disk in position. The other end engaged with a piece of apparatus which looked familiar, though for the moment French could not place it. Then, he remembered: he had studied it often enough. It was the detonating mechanism of a hand-grenade, evidently removed from the grenade itself. The striker was held off the cap by the end of the spindle engaging in the slot formerly containing the end of the lever.

The operation of the affair was obvious. On a current passing through the magnet, the disk would be attracted and the end of the spindle withdrawn from the slot. The spring would then crash the hammer down on the cap and explode the detonator.

Here at last was how the mine had been put up! Once more Crane had been extraordinarily careless. He had doubtless destroyed the finished drawing, but had overlooked this preliminary sketch!

French was more than delighted with his finds. Leaving Carter in charge, he returned to the police-station and arranged for a mason to take out and replace the ventilator and a carpenter to make good the hole in the floor with new wood. The old ventilator and piece of floorboard would be needed for exhibits in court. Then he sat down to think out the implications of his new discoveries.

19

CHIEF INSPECTOR FRENCH

The outstanding, overwhelming fact among those he had learnt was, of course, that Crane was guilty of the first murder. French could not repress a thrill of deep satisfaction as he thought of it. Here was achievement: the sort of achievement he longed for and indeed had come to expect. He had been sent down to investigate this murder, and his success was now assured. The case would add one more to the long list of his triumphs!

Not, of course, that he knew everything that must be known before he could write finis on its file. Far from it, there was a vast deal still to be squared up. But the really vital problem he had solved, and with the solution in his possession the completion of the affair should be easy and rapid.

After this pardonable little ebullition he came back to earth, in other words to the problems still remaining.

And first, had Crane stolen the wire and the grenades?

Though there was no evidence for it, it seemed perfectly possible. Crane, owing to reasons of health, had not been in the Home Guard, but he had been sufficiently intimate with many who were to have discovered that the store contained grenades. As for the telephone wire, it ran across the heath in full sight of everyone. No, there was no difficulty in believing Crane to have been the thief.

The question of the grenades was certainly easy, but French saw that to account for the wire was not so simple. Some five hundred yards of it had been stolen, but the distance from Crane's house to the mine was only about two hundred and thirty. Where was the remaining two hundred and seventy yards?

For the matter of that, French went on, where was thetwo hundred and thirty yards Crane had used? The man must have removed the groyne end of it before he ran down to the crater, but he would not then have had time to get it all away. He must have taken up the remainder later in the day.

What would he have done with it? He scarcely dared throw it into the sea, as he had no means of getting out into deep enough water to ensure its loss. Therefore would he not have buried it? French thought it likely in some place where it would not be disturbed.

Where might such a place be found? Why, on his own ground! If he buried it at all, it would undoubtedly be where he could ensure that no excavating was afterwards carried out.

French was annoyed that he had missed this point when at Gorse Cottage. It seemed not unimportant and he thought he should deal with it at once. Early next morning therefore he returned. The tiny estate enclosed an area of heath land, and this he began to search. But it was not till he reached the space behind the study that he found what he was looking for.

In the farther corner the grass was slightly beaten down and in places withered, and when he examined it more closely he saw traces of earth. With a spade he tried the sod and found it loose. He lifted the cut pieces aside and began to dig.

He had not gone down more than six inches when he came to the wire – the same red-covered single wire as had been stolen and which ran down the groyne. With satisfied grunts he went on clearing away the soil.

Then he made a further discovery. Buried with the wire were a number of other objects. One was a brass earthing pin, a couple of feet long and with a binding screw at the top. Another was a small two-way electric switch for a single wire. The third and last was a wooden box containing a more complicated piece of apparatus. He recognized it as a relay of fair power: a good sized electro-magnet with a contact on the armature which closed another circuit. It was evidently home-made, though the workmanship was good. The various leads terminated in four outside binding screws.

French stared at it in bewilderment. How could such an object have come into the scheme? For come into the scheme it undoubtedly had.

He could not imagine, but he packed up the objects with care, in the hope that in spite of their burial, fingerprints might possibly remain.

He took them out to the car, but before starting back he turned to gaze once again at the charming picture which lay before him: sea and bay and headland. Then suddenly he was brought up, as it were, all standing.

How could Crane have known when Radlett was over the mine?

From the point at which the novelist was standing, the crater, and therefore the mine, was in the direct line of sight to Ram Island. Crane had therefore only to use the correct point on its serrated skyline to give him a bearing, and he could operate his push while Radlett was crossing that bearing. Crossing it from west to east.

This was obvious, and French had appreciated it from the first moment he had learnt of Crane's guilt. But now he suddenly saw that it was only half the story. Crane could not possibly have told whether Radlett was in position in the north-south direction; whether he was on the spot, on its near side, or beyond it.

Theoretically, of course, the difficulty should obtain equally had the murderer been at the head of the groyne where French had up till now envisaged him. But this was not so in practice. The head of the groyne was so much nearer and more immediately above the vital spot that from there the single view was sufficient.

During the drive back to the station French continued turning the matter over in his mind. As had been admitted from the first, the lower end of the groyne fixed the north-south position to a certain extent. Most people just skirted it. But when the tide was low many walked closer to the sea. How did Crane come to know which "path" Radlett was using? That he had known was obvious – from what followed.

Then French felt the familiar thrill of excitement rising once more within him. Surely there was only one way in which Radlett's position could have been ascertained with the accuracy necessary for the murder?

Did not the method postulate a second observer? One looking out at right-angles to Crane? Cross-bearings were the only means by which points could be fixed on feature-less surfaces. Must cross-bearings not have been used here?

The more French thought of it, the more convinced he became. Only with the help of an accomplice could the affair have been carried through.

He soon saw that the assumption was supported by other evidence. There were three separate items, all tending in the same way.

First there was the wire. If two hundred and seventy yards of that taken were not used by Crane, did it not indicate a supply to someone else? French could think of no other explanation.

Next, there was the relay. At first French could not imagine its purpose, but when he began working out the circuits required for two operators, he saw that a relay of just that type would be needed.

The circuits, as he drew them, were simple. Two would be required, separate and distinct. There was first Crane's, which he had already considered: Crane's battery to the push under his study floor, push to mine, mine to earth, and earth back to battery. That meant, as he had already seen, that when Crane pressed his push in the study, the mine went up.

But to be sure of killing the victim, such an arrangement alone would not be sufficient. A control would be required on this circuit to render it inoperative except when the victim was in the correct position on the cross-bearing. This could best be carried out by inserting a relay in Crane's circuit, so that it would remain broken except when the relay was energized.

The relay would be operated by the second circuit, which would run: accomplice's battery to accomplice's push, push to electro-magnet of relay, relay to earth, and earth back to battery.

If then the victim was in position on Crane's bearing but not on the accomplice's, though Crane pressed his push nothing would happen, because his circuit would be broken at the relay. Similarly no explosion would take place if the position were correct on the accomplice's bearing but not on Crane's, for though the relay would be closed, Crane would not make contact at his push. Only when the victim was on the spot according to both bearings would the mine go up, because only then would Crane's push and the relay both be closed.

The existence of the relay was therefore strong positive evidence for the existence of an accomplice, and the negative view tended in the same direction: without an accomplice French could not account for the relay.

The third item tending in the same direction was the point already noted: that an accomplice would automatically supply a suspect for the murder of Crane.

That he would find the accomplice, and quickly, French had little doubt. Why, he had now so much information that he believed he could sit there in Cundy's office and by simple elimination metaphorically put his hand on his shoulder! Calling the wanted man X, he noted the following relevant points.

First, X must have been on a cross-bearing to Crane's when he pressed his push, i.e. a line running more or less east and west through the point of explosion. Further, both ends of this line must be on land, one at which X operated, the other passing over some object which X could sight to fix the bearing.

French again got out his map. To the east the unbroken sea horizon stretching up from the south was first broken by the headlands beyond St Pols. The bearing to the east therefore could not pass south of these headlands. French drew a line joining the edge of the headlands to the point of the explosion, and projected it westwards. It ran across West Head. Either X, or his bearing point on the Head, must therefore have been south of that line.

Here French interrupted his chain of thought to consider from which end of the line X would probably have operated. There was a suggestion of this in the evidence, though no proof. From Crane's it was a good deal nearer to the West Head than to St Pols, therefore because the shorter the second circuit, the easier it would be to deal with, it was more likely that X had operated from the Head.

On the Head the area south of his projected line contained three houses connected with the case: Savory's, Little's and Radlett's. Wedgewood's and Macdougal's were outside it. Could the murderer have been in one of the former?

At once French's thoughts turned to Little. There was nothing, of course, to incriminate Little except, strangely enough, his alibi! Murderers tended to repeat their efforts. Little, like Crane, was in his study when the mine went up. Like Crane he had apparent proof of innocence. Like Crane he could have seen if Radlett was on a bearing. Had he also, French wondered, a push under his desk which he could have pressed with his foot?

It was an attractive theory and French decided that a search of Little's study was demanded.

He was feeling extraordinarily pleased with himself. After days of frustration the deadlock in his case had been broken, and things were now moving so fast that he believed the end was in sight. And then, as so often happens, a point occurred to him which seemed at one fell stroke to knock the entire bottom out of his case.

The stolen wire would reach to nowhere near Little's!

Once again he turned to the map. The distance between the two houses was over fifteen hundred yards, and for this two hundred and seventy yards was available! For a time

French felt stumped, then he began again trying to find a way out.

Could the criminals have obtained wire elsewhere? French doubted it. Owing to war conditions such wire was difficult to come by.

Then were all his conclusions wrong? Was there no accomplice, no cross-bearing? Had some completely different plan been adopted?

He shook his head. No! As he reconsidered the steps of his argument, he became more than ever convinced that he was right, that there *was* a cross-bearing, and that someone on West Head had operated a second push.

He sat on in Cundy's room wrestling with the problem. Surely when he had gone so far, he would not now be held up by what was certainly a minor difficulty? More than ever he felt that the complete explanation was only just eluding his grasp.

His thoughts went back to his interview with Sands. He began to recall in detail what Sands had told him. And then, with another thrill, he saw that he had got it.

What if the conspirators *had* stolen the balance of the wire from the Home Guard? What if they had taken it over, used it, and returned it before ever it was missed? Was that possible? He would soon see.

Once again he drove out to Gorse Cottage, and starting from the ventilator at the back of the study, he began to pace slowly inland. In less than a hundred yards he came to what he was looking for – the main Home Guard telephone line running parallel to the shore. He remembered how Sands had told him that it stretched round the entire Coast of England, connecting one headquarters after another to their neighbours on either side. He remembered noting that the local section – this wire he was now looking at – ran from the east side of St Pols to beyond the West Head.

With eagerness he began to examine the line. If he were correct, somewhere close by there would be a joint. He walked slowly along, looking for a thickening which might represent twisted strands.

Then once again enthusiasm and delight filled his mind. He had it!

Here in the straggling wood were no telephone poles, the line being supported on trees. French had stopped beside one of these, a fir or pine. He did not know its species, but it was one of those with large, widely spaced boughs striking off the trunk right down to the ground. These made it particularly easy to climb, and what had pleased him so much was that on the top of these boughs the bark was slightly marked. The tree had recently been climbed, probably on several occasions!

Having photographed the marks, French climbed the tree. It was as he had expected. On the wire were two joints, about a yard apart. Obviously the tightly stretched line had been cut, and as it would be too short to enable the cut ends to be joined, a short length of fresh wire had been inserted.

French had been puzzled as to the purpose of the two-way switch. Now he understood it! Unquestionably it had been inserted in the telephone line at this point. With the switch in one position the telephone line would remain unbroken. It could be used in the normal way by the Home Guard and there could be no indication that it had been tampered with. But another line, French was satisfied, had been run from the other pole of the switch to Crane's study, and when the switch was reversed, the telephone line from the tree in one direction – probably to St Pols – would be cut out, and that in the other direction would be connected to Gorse Cottage. The switch would be necessary to enable Crane to effect the change quickly. On that eventful day he would be unlikely to have an opportunity to make proper soldered joints.

Whether or not he was correct in this could, French saw, be easily ascertained. If such a connection had been made to Crane's, a similar arrangement must have been installed opposite his accomplice's. It being probable that the accomplice lived on West Head, French set off westwards to look for the other pair of joints.

A little over half a mile away he found them, again up a climbable tree. What was more, this tree was just opposite Little's house! French paced from the tree to the house, and when he found that the sum of the distances from Crane's to the telephone line and from the telephone line to Little's was just under two hundred and seventy yards, he felt his problem was solved!

Solved, yes; but his solution was not proved. Some further information was needed. He must examine the floor under the desk in Little's study.

One thing he felt was important; that Little should not guess that he was suspected. The proof of his participation in Radlett's murder seemed available, but there was none that he had murdered Crane. Before French could end his investigation this second crime must be cleared up also.

After a little thought French drove back to St Pols. Vanson was in the station. French went to his room smiling and rubbing his hands.

Vanson stared. "You seem pleased with yourself," he remarked. "Good news?"

"The last lap, Vanson! I think we've got it!"

In answer to eager inquiries French gave a somewhat gleeful résumé of his discoveries. Vanson was suitably impressed.

"Now I want a bit of evidence," French went on, "and you can get it easier than I. It wouldn't be complete proof, but it would be pretty useful."

"What's that, sir?"

"Get two men who are not known here. Dress them up as telephone linesmen and send them out to Little's. Let them watch the house till he goes out, then when the coast's clear let them call and say the telephone circuit's been changed and they want to test the new one. You know the idea?"

"Of course. But you want more than that?"

"Yes, here's the point. While one chap holds the fort with his conversation, the other slips into the study and gets photos of the floor beneath the well of the desk. You understand: I'm looking for a cut floorboard and a plugged hole."

Vanson was still more impressed. He nodded with appreciation. "I'll fix it up for this afternoon," he declared. "I happen to know there's a bee-keepers' meeting on, and Little's pretty sure to be there."

"Good," said French. "Now I want to speak to that fellow Sands, the man who runs the Home Guard phones."

Vanson spoke into the telephone, then handed the receiver to French. After greetings French went on: "I wonder could you spare me an hour in connection with a rather confidential matter?…Oh, as soon as possible…After lunch? Splendid! Then will you meet me at two at the bridge just outside the town?…Good! And please don't say where you're going…Ha! ha! Yes! Sorry to be so mysterious, but there's a reason for it."

Ten minutes later French and Carter picked up Sands – as it happened, from a quite deserted road.

"It's a very simple matter," French explained as they drove off, "but strictly confidential. I want your word to keep it to yourself."

Sands, obviously thrilled, pledged himself.

"Now," French went on with a smile, "prepare yourself for an anticlimax! It's simply to look at a couple of joints on the Home Guard telephone line."

Sands, as obviously disappointed, agreed that he would do whatever the chief inspector required.

French discussed other topics till they reached the large tree opposite Gorse Cottage.

"The joints I have in mind are up that tree," he pointed out. "I wonder if you'd mind climbing up and having a look at them?"

Rather ungraciously Sands did so, but in a moment there came a cry of surprise. "Why," the voice went on, "whoever has been monkeying with the line? We never left a double joint of that kind on it."

"I rather thought it was below your standard," French answered mildly. "Is there room for me up there?"

"Yes, keep at the other side of the trunk."

In a few seconds French was beside him. "You mean those joints are new?" he asked.

"One of them certainly is. We might have made one joint here: after this length of time I can't remember where our joints were. But I'm absolutely certain we never made two close together like that."

"That's good enough," French returned. "Have you any suggestion as to why such a pair of joints might have been made?"

Sands grunted. "Looks as if the line had been cut and repaired. It would be too short to join and a length would be inserted."

"Just what I imagined. Now I want a little more. Will you please examine those joints in detail?"

Sands nodded. The joints were finished with black adhesive tape and he began unwinding one.

"A fresh joint!" he exclaimed. "Well, this is a bit beyond me!"

"How do you know it's fresh, Mr Sands?"

"The tape. It's new and sticky. That line has been there for three years, and any tape then used would be dry and hard."

"Are both joints the same?"

"Yes, they're both new. Is all this a secret, Mr French?"

"I'm afraid for a day or two: then I'll be glad to tell you everything. But that's only half my trouble. Let's move a little farther on."

Opposite Little's the scene was repeated. Here Sands again declared that these joints also were new.

French smiled. "That's very satisfactory news, I can assure you. Now just one other point and I've done. You did mention this at our last meeting, but I'd like it again. When do you people use this telephone line?"

"Only when the Home Guard are on duty."

"And when is that?"

"Most Saturday afternoons, Sundays and most nights."

"Take Tuesdays. When would you cease using it on Tuesday mornings?"

"Usually two or three a.m."

"And the earliest you might want it on a Tuesday evening?"

"Never before eight."

"So that if the line were cut, say between seven on a Tuesday morning and eight the same evening, you people wouldn't know anything about it?"

"No; there'd be nothing to call our attention to it."

"Thank you, Mr Sands. That's all at last."

Evidence was certainly accumulating satisfactorily, and when a little later French listened to the report of Maxton, the pseudo telephone linesman, he was still further pleased.

"In accordance with Mr Vanson's instructions Constable Tregoran and I went out this afternoon to 'The Beacon', Mr Richard Little's residence on West Head, ostensibly to test the phone. While I was pretending to do so, Constable Tregoran went into the study and took the required photographs. They're not quite ready yet, but he found the short floorboard you were interested in, and it had a quarter-inch hole in it, filled with a wooden plug. The joints round the floorboard were clear of dust and the edges showed fresh stain."

So that was that! Crane and Little!

French was delighted. Not only had he solved his problem, but almost, if not altogether, he had sufficient proof to take his case into court. An achievement, for it had been a tricky case!

But though his progress had been so good, he had by no means reached the end of his work. He had to discover *and prove* the motive of these two, and he had to learn who had murdered Crane and prove the case against him.

Well, that shouldn't take long! As French sat down to go over the file once again so as to reconsider every fact against this new background, he felt his remark to Vanson accurately expressed the fact. He was indeed on the last lap!

– 20 –

CHIEF INSPECTOR FRENCH

French began with the original murder, and the first point he noted gave him a good deal of satisfaction. So far as Little was concerned there was ample motive. The death of Radlett brought twenty thousand pounds to Jessica, and as French considered the characters of husband and wife, he was pretty sure that this meant twenty thousand pounds to Little himself.

But what was Crane's motive? He was not mentioned in Radlett's will, and so far as French had learnt, he gained nothing by his death. In a murder case the motive must necessarily be so overwhelming that it should stand out a mile. Where, French wondered, had he made his oversight? What essential line had he left unworked?

A further investigation into the lives of both men seemed to be indicated. To go into Little's without the man's knowledge would be difficult, and until he had his full proof French was particularly anxious not to alarm him. On the other hand, inquiries about Crane would be expected and therefore unsuspicious.

Once again he took the familiar road to Gorse Cottage. Ten minutes later he had settled down in the study to go over Crane's papers once again. He worked literally for hours without making the slightest progress. Finally it was almost by chance that he obtained the hint which gave him his information, and led direct to the end of the case.

He had just gone through Crane's pocket notebook for the second time. It had served the novelist both as an engagement book and diary. But French had found in it nothing in the slightest degree illuminating.

With a feeling of frustration not far removed from despair he idly turned to the first page – which he had already carefully examined – and reread the contents. It was headed "Personal Memoranda" and contained a number of printed items, "Watch No.", "Season Ticket No.", "Size in Hats", and so on. Unlike the average man, Crane had filled in a number of the corresponding spaces. Among these was "Car No.", and here he had written CVW 283.

From memory French believed that CVW was an Essex number, and it passed through his mind that Essex was a far cry from Cornwall. Then he realized that it only meant that Crane had bought his car second-hand from an Essex owner.

He closed the book and was about to relock the desk when he remembered something which brought him up as it were all standing. Crane had no car!

He looked at the diary again. Yes, it was for the current year. Why should Crane have noted someone else's car?

French picked up the telephone. Was that the Yard?…Yes, it was a small matter. Would they find out for him the owner of car CVW 283?

After some delay the reply came through. It was the property of a Chelmsford merchant, highly respected in the district and unlikely to be mixed up in anything shady.

French rubbed his chin. This note of Crane's surely could not refer to the Chelmsford vehicle. If Crane had had any dealings with the merchant, some trace of it should surely remain in his files.

If, on the other hand, it did not refer to the car, what did it mean? At once French's interest quickened. Could the entry be a fake; a method of recording secret information? The whole of it might not be required. The essential might lie either in the letters or in the number. French thought the latter the more likely, in which case the letters would merely have been entered as a blind.

If this were so it might explain the choice of the Essex registration. If Cornish letters had been used and the notebook had fallen into some stranger's hands, he might have known the real car and his suspicion would therefore have been aroused.

About what sort of numbered article might Crane have wished to make his record? There were many possible: a second bank account, membership of a secret society, the *nom de plume* of some individual or –

A wave of satisfaction passed through French's mind as he thought of a safe deposit! A man who was party to a murder and who was himself murdered surely had a secret! A secret to be valuable almost certainly involved papers. Where could papers be best hidden and yet be easily available? Why, in a safe deposit! With a sudden thrill French felt he had guessed the truth.

He returned to St Pols and once again rang up the Yard. Would they please approach the various safe deposits and find out if the holder of No. CVW 283, or any part of this combination, could by any possibility be Crane.

French sat back with a sigh of relief. He was tired. It would take a little time to make the inquiry, and till he received the answer he would be at a loose end. He had had practically no relaxation since he came down. He would treat himself to a walk. Carter was busy transcribing notes and he could carry on. French would go alone.

He had a delightful three-hours ramble along the shore, returning just in time for dinner. After the meal he went again to the station. He had been there only a few minutes when the reply to his message came in. The City and Suburbs Safe Deposit Company, of Cornhill, EC3, had rented their Box No. 283 to Mr Wickham Crane, the novelist, of St Pols, Cornwall!

So that was it! No secrecy; at least so far as the company was concerned. Apparently the secrecy was confined to Crane's home and friends. Sure that at last he was on to the truth, and late though it was, French went out again to see Mrs Crane.

"I have just discovered, madam, that Mr Crane had rented a box in a London safe deposit, and I have reason to suspect that if we knew what was stored there, we might get a hint as to his murderer. I'm going to ask you, as Mr Crane's executrix, for authority to open the box."

Elmina Crane was surprised, as Crane had never mentioned such a thing, but without hesitation she wrote the necessary permission, promising next morning to telephone the manager. French was relieved that she did not ask to be present when the box was open. He would have agreed, but much preferred to be alone.

By the first train next day he went up to town, and that afternoon presented himself at the office in Cornhill. The manager had checked the story through Crane's solicitors and raised no difficulties. French had brought Crane's keys and soon the box was open.

It contained a single sheet of paper, but when French glanced at it, he felt that it had been worth all his trouble.

The sheet was of quarto size, of good quality paper, though it had gone slightly yellow. It was covered on one side with a large untidy handwriting done with a broad-nibbed pen. The signature was across a George V sixpenny stamp, and it read:

Walnut Tree Lane
Slough
Buckingham

This is to certify that in respect of services rendered to my father Henry Wallace Little in his business as a builder at the above stated address I Richard Aubrey Little promise to pay Wickham Crane eldest son of John Herbert Crane of Redlands Abbey Street Dorking Surrey the sum of £12,250 (twelve thousand two hundred and fifty pounds sterling) as soon as I am in a position to do so. Dated this seventh day of April One thousand nine hundred and twelve.

Signed in the presence
of RICHARD AUBREY LITTLE.
JAMES GOODALL.

French was no lawyer, but it occurred to him that the document had been drawn up by the men themselves: he thought it had an amateurish ring. Evidently also Little had not paid his debts, which with interest must by now have amounted to a much larger sum. Evidently also Crane had not taken proceedings against him for the money. Why? French wondered. Then suddenly he thought he saw.

For the simple reason surely, that Little couldn't pay. But – ah! all this was progress! – if Radlett were to die, Little would be able! Was that it? Had these two conspired to kill Radlett so that they could share the swag?

French grew more eager. If this were so, the murder of Crane presented no difficulty whatever. If Little had gone the length of killing Radlett for his money, why should he pay away more than half of that money to Crane? He had evidently stolen more grenades than had been used in the Radlett case: why not put some of the remainder to an equally good use?

All this seemed excellent, yet it was not completely satisfactory. That phrase, "As soon as I am in a position to do so," worried French. If it had let Little out at all, would it not let them out altogether? The date also seemed a little disconcerting. It was strange that no settlement had been effected over so long a period. French began to feel slightly sceptical of the entire affair. He decided that he would at least check up what he could about it before taking action.

Accordingly when he reached the Yard he handed the document to an expert for a report on its physical condition. That received, he would get a legal opinion on its validity. In the meantime he rang up the Slough police and asked for information as to Henry Wallace Little, a builder of Walnut Tree Lane. Finally, and with immense satisfaction, he seized the opportunity to spend a night at home.

When he reached the Yard next morning some information had come in. Henry Wallace Little was – or had been, for he was dead – a real man, and he had run a small builders' yard which in 1912 he had added to, presumably after the acquisition of fresh capital. He had a son named Richard, whose present whereabouts was unknown.

This was interesting in a way, but it was the next piece of news that really excited French. His paper expert, Gray, strolled into his room.

"Interesting document that," he greeted him. "You suspected it?"

"Well," French answered guardedly, "I wanted to be sure."

"That's right," grumbled Gray, but a twinkle showed in his eye, "give nothing away! But the doubts you must have felt were justified. It's a fraud."

"Ah!" said French in a pleased tone. "How do you make that out?"

"Just a chance; a bit of luck. I thought the ink had a slightly bluish tinge."

"It has; I noticed that."

"But it suggested nothing to you. You should read up about inks."

"My dear fellow," French retorted, "if I wanted to bark myself I wouldn't keep a dog. Go ahead and spill the great news."

"Well, I'm always ready to enlighten ignorance. An ink with a blue tinge is suggestive. Where the matter's important it's usually worth trying an experiment. I tried it."

"And you found?"

"I found that your promissory note was no more written in nineteen twelve than was my last salary cheque."

"What? You mean it's recent?"

"Matter of a few weeks: not more."

French chuckled. "Good man! That's a help and no mistake!"

"Glad it's of some use."

"Just what I wanted to hear! If it's not beyond the uninstructed mind, just what did you do?"

"I'll do it again if you like: it'll only take a few minutes. Make assurance doubly sure."

Gray led the way to a laboratory. To a running fire of heavy chaff he fixed the document in a frame. Over it he placed a thin metal plate containing a small hole, which he moved about till it uncovered a single letter. He exposed this for nearly quarter of an hour to ultra-violet rays. Then taking the paper out of the frame, he put it down before French.

"See any difference?" he asked.

"Why," French answered, "that letter's gone darker than the rest. It's gone jet black!"

Gray smiled. "You're in luck," he declared. "A forlorn hope has come off. When I looked at the ink I thought it might be freshly written gallotannic. As you've not read up inks I'd better explain."

French thought it was a good idea.

"You see," Gray began demonstrating like a professor, "what happens is this. Gallotannic ink is in itself an almost colourless liquid. The black only comes when it oxidizes. That's a gradual operation lasting several weeks. But a colourless ink wouldn't do in practice: it must show directly it's used. That's arranged for by putting in a dye, in this case a blue. The ink is therefore blue at first, but slowly changes to black. You follow?"

French nodded.

"Now the ultra-violet rays might be called concentrated sunlight: they do in fifteen minutes what ordinarily might take fifteen weeks. If therefore a document written with this ink is in process of changing colour – that is, if it has been recently written – the rays will accelerate the action and the portions exposed to them will grow blacker than the rest."

"Splendid! You're a wizard, Gray. Can you prove for me in court that this paper was written in the last few weeks?"

"Yes, if you let me initial it on the back."

"Thanks, I'm really obliged. Just two points: The George V stamp, of course, would be easy to get?"

"Only necessary to ask for a set of Georgians as a present for a nephew. Get it at any dealer's."

"Then the paper's a bit yellow?"

"Perfectly easy to fake. Several different fumes would colour it."

The more French considered this new evidence, the more impressed he became. As he now saw it, Radlett's murder was a put-up job between Crane and Little, decided on recently. The motive was money, which was to be divided between them, and this document was merely a guarantee to Crane that he would receive his share. Whether if Little had cut up rough and attempted to stick to the entire swag, Crane could have recovered by an action at law seemed to French immaterial: Little would never have allowed the case to go into court. Admittedly to do so would have taken some nerve on Crane's part also. But French believed he would consider himself so safe on the murder charge that he might risk it.

French also noted the slight suggestion that Little was the leader of the enterprise, in that he had used the episode of his father extending his Slough business to account for the alleged debt. French imagined that the original rough idea was Little's, but that he wanted Crane's power of working out a plot, as well as his mechanical ability to prepare the necessary apparatus, neither of which he possessed himself.

He had now, French thought, completely cleared up the Radlett case, but the murder of Crane was still rather in the air. Not that French had the slightest doubt as to what had occurred. As he sat in the corner of a compartment on the way back to Cornwall, he was convinced that he could picture quite clearly everything that Little had done in both cases. To make sure he proceeded to build up a theory.

Chronically short of cash, Little had coveted his wife's inheritance. He had had an idea of how Radlett might be murdered, but his scheme required an accomplice owing firstly, to the use of cross-bearings, and secondly, to the need for someone with more inventive and constructional ability than himself. Crane was his obvious choice, as owing to the threatened lawsuit with Savory, he was also short of cash. Crane was approached and agreed to do his part in the affair.

While Crane was making the apparatus, Little stole first the wire and then the grenades. Between them they fixed up the mine and laid the necessary wires. Probably they had tried Radlett's murder on several previous mornings, but had failed either owing to the old man not walking on the required "path", or else to one of the confederates not having suitable witnesses to his alibi. But at last a morning came when all the conditions were satisfactory. Both pressed their pushes at the same moment and Radlett was blown to pieces.

So much seemed absolutely clear, but what happened after it French could only guess. For some reason Little was dissatisfied with the position. Either he feared Crane, feeling that there was a danger that the novelist might give the affair away, or else he wanted all the swag for himself.

At this point French stopped suddenly and slapped his thigh. Why, he knew Little's motive: had known it for a considerable time! It was there before his eyes and he had not seen it! French wondered was senile decay creeping down upon him.

Crane's drunkenness! French had heard all about that incident, as well as that it, though rare, by no means stood alone. With Little's interest in Crane, he could scarcely fail to have known of it, and the knowledge must have terrified him. If Crane got drunk once he might do it again. Therefore he was dangerous: too dangerous to be left alive!

Delighted with his progress; French continued his reconstruction. Little had the necessary grenades for the job, as well as the knowledge that their use as a mine was effective. Obviously his plan would be to repeat a former success. But he could not make the electric detonating apparatus, so he adopted the simpler plan of drawing out the pins by a cord. To plant the grenades under the path and lead the cord away to a suitable observation point was easy and required no expert knowledge.

But he had two difficulties to overcome: first, to get Crane to walk over the mine at a suitable hour, and second, to provide himself with a scapegoat. He knew Savory was a nasty piece of work who had injured most of his friends, and whose loss therefore would not be great. If he could make the man incriminate himself, so much to the good from every point of view.

French paused. What exactly had Little then done? Crane, not Little, had written the letter bringing Savory to the appointment. Was this Crane's idea?

Not necessarily. As French wrestled with the problem he began to see what might have been done.

Suppose Little had approached Crane and said in effect: "Through Radlett's murder you will now have enough money to meet any action which Savory may take against you, but I see a plan by which you could save every penny of that money for yourself. Why not tell Savory you saw him fixing something on the shore when he passed before Radlett?"

To this Crane would doubtless reply that he hadn't seen Savory do anything of the kind, when Little would point out that that consideration was beside the point.

If Crane agreed, as he evidently had, the two would doubtless discuss details. Little would therefore know how the meeting was to be brought about, even if he did not himself suggest the method.

Such a plan would meet both difficulties: it would bring Crane to a point at which he could be murdered, and it would incriminate Savory.

Satisfied that at last he had got to the bottom of the affair, French turned to the one major matter in the case still uncompleted. He believed that Little was his man, but had he sufficient evidence to take the case into court?

For a long time he weighed the point, then reluctantly came to the conclusion that there was too much probability and too little proof. Another spell of intensive thought followed, and then he thought he saw a way by which he could obtain a complete demonstration.

Next morning, Saturday, he once again drove out to Gorse Cottage and saw Elmina Crane.

"I think, madam, that at last I have obtained information which will lead me to your husband's murderer. But to get the necessary proof I shall want your co-operation."

Mrs Crane was naturally interested.

"It's rather a lot, I'm afraid," French went on. "I want you to go away for a few days, you and Miss Avory, and close the house."

"No trouble about that, Mr French. It's what I want myself. Miss Avory leaves on Monday in any case, and she's asked me to go with her. I hadn't decided, but now I will."

"Capital! Now one other thing, but it's important. It must be generally known that you're going. Somehow without appearing to give away the information you must see that all your friends are aware that the house will be empty from Monday. Among your friends I include people like the Wedgewoods, the Savorys, the Littles, Miss Meredith, and so on. Can you manage it?"

Elmina Crane was obviously intensely curious. But French's manner was not inviting and she asked no questions, merely saying she would want various matters seen to if she were to leave in two days, and that Miss Avory would go round to her friends and obtain their help in these.

Well pleased, French lay low for the remainder of that weekend. On Monday morning he went out to within sight of "The Beacon", lay down behind some shrubs and watched. His vigil lasted longer than he had anticipated, but at last he saw Little leave the house and stride off in the direction of St Pols.

French followed till he saw that he was going by the shore, then he returned to the car and drove back to the town. Immediately he sent Carter off to walk by the shore towards the West Head. As he had intended, Carter soon met Little. Later Carter reported the interview.

He had opened the proceedings by stopping and saluting.

"Excuse me, Mr Little, but have you seen Mr French this morning?"

Little replied that he had not.

"I've missed him somewhere, I'm afraid," Carter bewailed, giving complicated explanations of possible reciprocal movements by the shore or inland.

Finding him so expansive and ready to chat, Little chatted also, finally asking the not unnatural question, "How does the case progress?"

This was what Carter had been angling for. He grew more expansive still. "To tell you the truth, Mr Little, we're nearly through. I don't know that I should speak of it, but it'll be common property shortly, and in the meantime you can keep your own counsel. Mr French has found out who murdered Mr Radlett."

Little was obviously taken aback, but he controlled himself immediately. Carter was careful not to notice his reaction.

"Yes," he went on, "you'll find it hard to believe, but it was Mr Crane: Mr Crane and an accomplice. Then the accomplice rounded on Mr Crane and did him in."

Little visibly wilted. "Good Lord!" he exclaimed in a strangled voice. "Crane! That's incredible! I certainly can scarcely believe it." Then after a slight pause: "And the accomplice?"

Once again Carter did not notice his anxiety. He grew confidential. "Well, perhaps I shouldn't say this either, but keep it to yourself. We expect to get him tomorrow. From various indications Mr French believes an agreement was drawn up between Mr Crane and the accomplice, fixing their respective assets and liabilities, if I may put it so. Mr French believes the document must be somewhere among Mr Crane's papers, and he's applied for a search warrant to look for it. The warrant will be available in the morning, so that's why I said we'll get him tomorrow. Of course I only meant we'd get his name."

It was thin, but French was counting on Little's anxiety preventing him from noticing that. Carter continued the conversation for a few moments to avoid switching off too quickly, then with a brief remark on the weather he continued his walk.

While he was away French had been occupying himself in forging a copy of the agreement. He even telephoned to Truro for a George V sixpenny stamp, which by a lucky chance was found there in a dealer's.

When it grew dusk that evening he and Vanson and Carter walked out to Gorse Cottage. French still had Crane's keys and they let themselves into the house. French opened the safe, put his forgery on a shelf, relocked the safe and dropped the keys into a drawer of Crane's desk. Then withdrawing to the back of the house, they made themselves as comfortable as they could in the kitchen.

The question was, would Little walk into the trap or would he not? Time, French thought, alone could tell.

Time certainly came into the affair pretty prominently. Hours passed and they grew more and more cramped and weary. They did not dare to have a light or to converse above the faintest whisper. French in his time had kept many vigils, some of them very irksome, as on that dreadful night on the Cave Hill near Belfast. But this also was irksome in its way. The uncertainty as to whether Little would come kept him on edge. If the scheme had merely warned the man that the game was up and he attempted a getaway or to commit suicide, French would find it difficult to explain satisfactorily to his superiors why he had delayed the arrest.

Midnight came and went, then one, and then two. A little after two there was a sudden sound: a faint scuffling at the back passage window. It was followed by a sharp crack and the tingling of falling glass, then some small hard object dropped on the floor. French thought this was probably a stone, which it was doubtless hoped would later be put down to some children's game. Then French, looking between the hinges of the slightly open kitchen door, saw the faint glimmer of a light in dancing circles on the passage floor. The snib of the window shot back, evidently operated through the hole in the glass, and the window opened. There were more shufflings and a pair of legs were revealed. In the light of the vertically held torch they walked past the kitchen door and entered the study.

Stealthily the three men followed, so slowly and carefully that not a sound was made. The intruder had not completely closed the study door and French was able to watch his movements through the crack. He was using an extremely faint torch kept always pointed down, so as to prevent a reflection showing from the windows.

At first the intruder seemed undecided, as if he did not know where to look. Then he sat down at the desk and began going through the drawers. It was not long before he found the keys, and faint though it was, French could hear his gasp of satisfaction.

Immediately he turned to the safe, opened it, and began to search its shelves. Apparently he quickly found what he wanted, for he took a paper out and put it in his pocket, closed and locked the safe, replaced the keys in the drawer, pulled down the cover of the desk and walked slowly out of the room – into the arms of French and his helpers.

It was Little all right, and when French later recounted to him his reconstruction of the affair with its many proofs, including the finding of the battery and push with its screwholes fitting those in the floorboard in the study, he broke down and admitted the truth. At the following assizes he was found guilty of the double murder and later paid the terrible penalty.

And what of the other people whom French came across during these unhappy days at St Pols?

With the cloud of unsolved murder removed, the little town settled down once more to its accustomed quiet. Jessica Little moved to the Wedgewoods, deciding that after the war she would do what she had always longed to do, travel. Elmina Crane left for an unknown address, with the sincere sympathy of all her friends. Anne Meredith and Vane were quietly married and took over the house vacated by Mrs Vane senior. Savory seemed to have learnt a lesson from his experiences and grew much more kindly and polite; so much so indeed that his wife decided to remain with him after all. Forrester, knowing in his heart that she was right, exchanged with a member of the Truro branch of his firm. In fact, the residents settled down as peacefully as the war would allow, and if they did not all live happily ever afterwards, they came as near to it as they could.

Freeman Wills Crofts

The Box Office Murders

A London box office clerk falls under the spell of a mysterious trio of crooks. Assisted by a helpful solicitor who directs her to Scotland Yard, she tells Inspector French the story of the Purple Sickle. But when her body is found floating in Southampton Water the next day, French discovers that similar murders have taken place and determines to learn the trio's secret and run them to ground...

The Hog's Back Mystery

Several local residents have disappeared in suspicious circumstances at The Hog's Back ridge in Surrey. When a doctor vanishes, followed by a nurse with whom he was acquainted, Inspector French deduces murder, but there are no bodies. Can he eventually prove his theory and show that murder has been committed?

'As pretty a piece of work as Inspector French has done...on the level of Mr Crofts' very best; which is saying something.'
– E C Bentley in the *Daily Telegraph*

Freeman Wills Crofts

Inspector French's Greatest Case

A head clerk's corpse is discovered beside the empty safe of a Hatton Garden diamond merchant. There are many suspects and a multitude of false clues to be followed before a tireless investigator is called in to solve the crime. This is a case for Freeman Wills Crofts' most famous character – Inspector French.

Man Overboard!

In the course of a ship's passage from Belfast to Liverpool, a man disappears and his body is later picked up by Irish fishermen. Although the coroner's verdict is suicide, murder is suspected. Inspector French co-operates with Superintendent Rainey and Sergeant McClung once more to determine the truth, whatever the cost...

'To me, Inspector French is the most human sleuth to be found in the detective novels of today.'

– *Punch*

Freeman Wills Crofts

Mystery in the Channel

The cross-channel steamer *Chichester* stops halfway to France. A motionless yacht lies in her path and when a party clambers aboard it finds a trail of blood and two dead men. Chief Constable Turnbill has to call on the ever-reliable Inspector French for help in solving the mystery of the *Nymph*.

Mystery on Southampton Water

The Joymount Rapid Hardening Cement Manufacturing Company is in serious financial trouble. Two young company employees hatch a plot to break into a rival works on the Isle of Wight to find out their competitor's secret for undercutting them. But the scheme does not go according to plan and results in the death of a night watchman, theft and fire. Inspector French is brought in to solve the baffling mystery.

OTHER TITLES BY FREEMAN WILLS CROFTS AVAILABLE DIRECT
FROM HOUSE OF STRATUS

Quantity		£	$(US)	$(CAN)	€
☐	THE 12.30 FROM CROYDON	6.99	12.95	19.95	13.50
☐	THE AFFAIR AT LITTLE WOKEHAM	6.99	12.95	19.95	13.50
☐	ANTIDOTE TO VENOM	6.99	12.95	19.95	13.50
☐	ANYTHING TO DECLARE?	6.99	12.95	19.95	13.50
☐	THE BOX OFFICE MURDERS	6.99	12.95	19.95	13.50
☐	THE CASK	6.99	12.95	19.95	13.50
☐	CRIME AT GUILDFORD	6.99	12.95	19.95	13.50
☐	DEATH OF A TRAIN	6.99	12.95	19.95	13.50
☐	DEATH ON THE WAY	6.99	12.95	19.95	13.50
☐	THE END OF ANDREW HARRISON	6.99	12.95	19.95	13.50
☐	FATAL VENTURE	6.99	12.95	19.95	13.50
☐	FEAR COMES TO CHALFONT	6.99	12.95	19.95	13.50
☐	FOUND FLOATING	6.99	12.95	19.95	13.50
☐	FRENCH STRIKES OIL	6.99	12.95	19.95	13.50
☐	GOLDEN ASHES	6.99	12.95	19.95	13.50
☐	THE GROOTE PARK MURDER	6.99	12.95	19.95	13.50
☐	THE HOG'S BACK MYSTERY	6.99	12.95	19.95	13.50
☐	INSPECTOR FRENCH AND THE CHEYNE MYSTERY	6.99	12.95	19.95	13.50

ALL HOUSE OF STRATUS BOOKS ARE AVAILABLE FROM GOOD BOOKSHOPS
OR DIRECT FROM THE PUBLISHER:

Internet: www.houseofstratus.com including synopses and features.

Email: sales@houseofstratus.com
info@houseofstratus.com
(please quote author, title and credit card details.)

OTHER TITLES BY FREEMAN WILLS CROFTS AVAILABLE DIRECT
FROM HOUSE OF STRATUS

Quantity	£	$(US)	$(CAN)	€
INSPECTOR FRENCH AND THE STARVEL TRAGEDY	6.99	12.95	19.95	13.50
INSPECTOR FRENCH'S GREATEST CASE	6.99	12.95	19.95	13.50
JAMES TARRANT, ADVENTURER	6.99	12.95	19.95	13.50
A LOSING GAME	6.99	12.95	19.95	13.50
THE LOSS OF THE JANE VOSPER	6.99	12.95	19.95	13.50
MAN OVERBOARD!	6.99	12.95	19.95	13.50
MANY A SLIP	6.99	12.95	19.95	13.50
MURDERERS MAKE MISTAKES	6.99	12.95	19.95	13.50
MYSTERY IN THE CHANNEL	6.99	12.95	19.95	13.50
MYSTERY OF THE SLEEPING CAR EXPRESS	6.99	12.95	19.95	13.50
MYSTERY ON SOUTHAMPTON WATER	6.99	12.95	19.95	13.50
THE PIT-PROP SYNDICATE	6.99	12.95	19.95	13.50
THE PONSON CASE	6.99	12.95	19.95	13.50
THE SEA MYSTERY	6.99	12.95	19.95	13.50
SILENCE FOR THE MURDERER	6.99	12.95	19.95	13.50
SIR JOHN MAGILL'S LAST JOURNEY	6.99	12.95	19.95	13.50
SUDDEN DEATH	6.99	12.95	19.95	13.50

ALL HOUSE OF STRATUS BOOKS ARE AVAILABLE FROM GOOD BOOKSHOPS
OR DIRECT FROM THE PUBLISHER:

Tel: Order Line
          0800 169 1780 (UK)
          International
          +44 (0) 1845 527700 (UK)

Fax: +44 (0) 1845 527711 (UK)
          (please quote author, title and credit card details.)

Send to: House of Stratus Sales Department
          Thirsk Industrial Park
          York Road, Thirsk
          North Yorkshire, YO7 3BX
          UK

PAYMENT

Please tick currency you wish to use:

☐ £ (Sterling)　　☐ $ (US)　　☐ $ (CAN)　　☐ € (Euros)

Allow for shipping costs charged per order plus an amount per book as set out in the tables below:

CURRENCY/DESTINATION

	£(Sterling)	$(US)	$(CAN)	€(Euros)
Cost per order				
UK	1.50	2.25	3.50	2.50
Europe	3.00	4.50	6.75	5.00
North America	3.00	3.50	5.25	5.00
Rest of World	3.00	4.50	6.75	5.00
Additional cost per book				
UK	0.50	0.75	1.15	0.85
Europe	1.00	1.50	2.25	1.70
North America	1.00	1.00	1.50	1.70
Rest of World	1.50	2.25	3.50	3.00

PLEASE SEND CHEQUE OR INTERNATIONAL MONEY ORDER
payable to: HOUSE OF STRATUS LTD or card payment as indicated

STERLING EXAMPLE

Cost of book(s):...................... Example: 3 x books at £6.99 each: £20.97
Cost of order:....................... Example: £1.50 (Delivery to UK address)
Additional cost per book:.............. Example: 3 x £0.50: £1.50
Order total including shipping:.......... Example: £23.97

VISA, MASTERCARD, SWITCH, AMEX:

☐☐☐☐☐☐☐☐☐☐☐☐☐☐☐☐☐☐☐☐

Issue number (Switch only):

☐☐☐

Start Date:　　　　　　　Expiry Date:

☐☐/☐☐　　　　　　☐☐/☐☐

Signature: _____

NAME: _____

ADDRESS: _____

COUNTRY: _____

ZIP/POSTCODE: _____

Please allow 28 days for delivery. Despatch normally within 48 hours.

Prices subject to change without notice.
Please tick box if you do not wish to receive any additional information. ☐

House of Stratus publishes many other titles in this genre; please check our website (**www.houseofstratus.com**) for more details.